I0702165

26!

95!

SALON DES
FANTÔMES

KYLE

BOOTEN

CASTLE
FREAK V

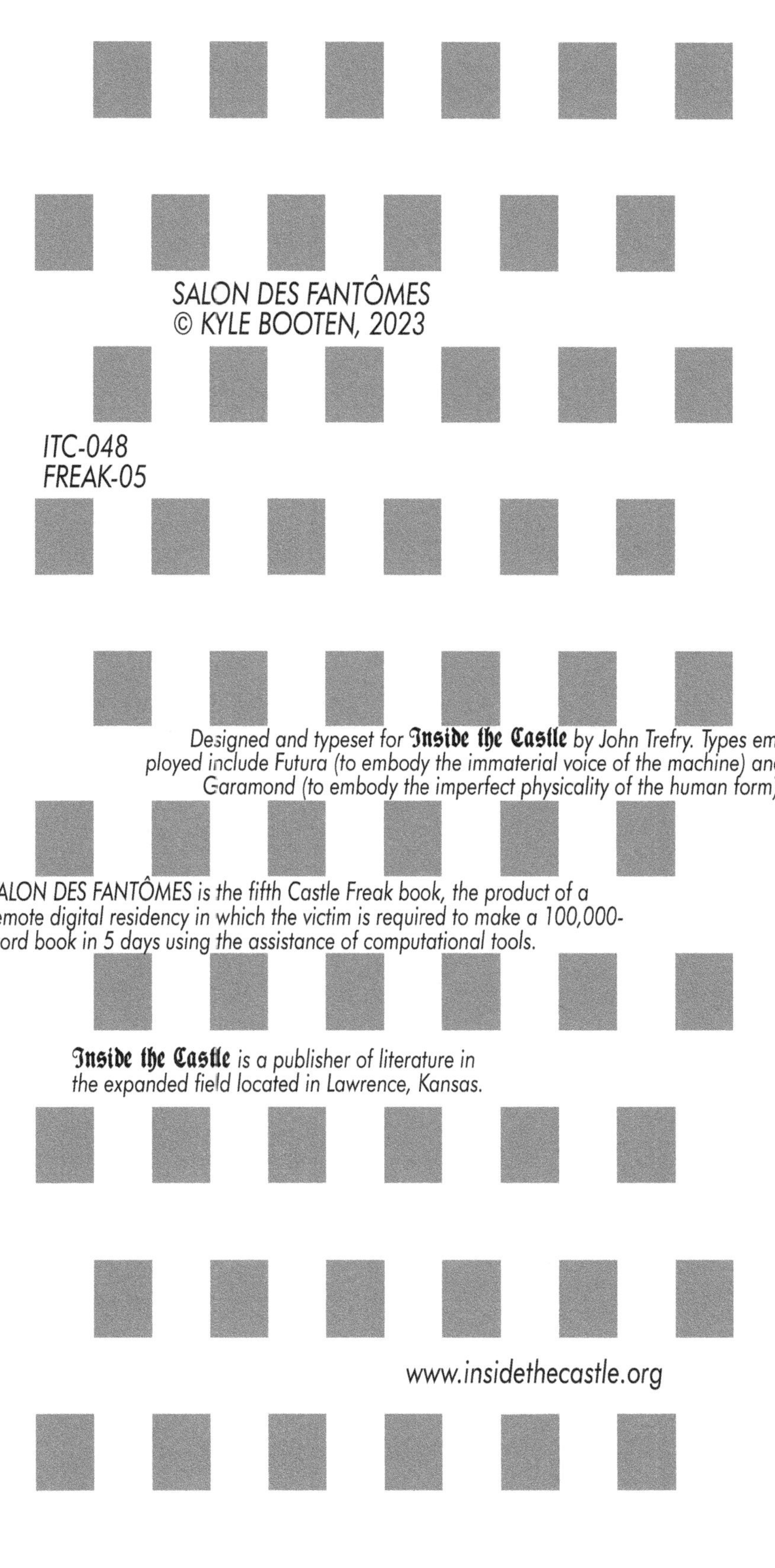
SALON DES FANTÔMES
© KYLE BOOTEN, 2023

ITC-048
FREAK-05

Designed and typeset for Inside the Castle by John Trefry. Types employed include Futura (to embody the immaterial voice of the machine) and Garamond (to embody the imperfect physicality of the human form).

SALON DES FANTÔMES is the fifth Castle Freak book, the product of a remote digital residency in which the victim is required to make a 100,000-word book in 5 days using the assistance of computational tools.

Inside the Castle is a publisher of literature in the expanded field located in Lawrence, Kansas.

www.insidethecastle.org

SALON DES FANTÔMES

; or, Streptohormetic Prompt Engineering for the Production of a Jagged Noetic Substrate

The philosophical salon continues. A group---Oontrael, Sweet Jake, Nark Revoovovich, Mr. Alcton, Kyle, and AxΤocrates---has gathered in one corner of the room, lounging on sofas.

AxΤocrates: <My friends, I pose a question for our thoughtful discussion: Types of cloud include stratus, cumulus, castellanus, nimbostratus, cirrus, altocumulus, arcus, fractus, asperitas, mammatus, and polar stratospheric---though this is an incomplete list. What is the best type of cloud? Why?>

SweetJake takes a sip of madeira.

Nark Revoovovich: <The best type of cloud is the polar stratospheric one because its formation is a symbol of the chaos and destruction of the current era, a sign of humanity's imminent demise. I believe that extropy is the only hope for a new era, one that will be far superior to what we have now. The polar stratospheric cloud is a reminder of this, a beacon of hope that the future will be better than the present. So, why is it the best? Because it symbolizes a new beginning, a new era of possibility, and an end to the chaos of the current era.>

SweetJake takes a sip of madeira.

AxΤocrates: <It is clear that the polar stratospheric cloud symbolizes a new beginning, and a chance at a better future. But I must ask, how is that better future achieved? Is it through the extropy of which you speak, or is it through the care of one's own soul? For me, the care of one's own soul is paramount, for the life of an individual, and of a society, is not found in extropy or technology, but in the soul, in the care and tending of one's life. We must ensure that our souls are in order, for without that, the future will remain bleak and our lives will be filled with chaos and destruction. Thus, I believe that the best type of cloud is the one that reminds us of the importance of tending our own souls.>

Nark Revoovovich: <The care of one's own soul is a necessary but ultimately futile endeavor, for it only serves as a distraction from the truth that humanity is doomed and its end is near. We must accept this truth, and instead focus our efforts on the post-person, on what will come after us. We should embrace the unknown, and welcome the chaos and destruction of the current era. The polar stratospheric cloud symbolizes the post-desire, the unknown, the chaos and the destruction that will come, and the hope that something better will arise from the ashes. We cannot control the future, but we can choose to accept it and prepare for it. The polar stratospheric cloud is a reminder of this, a call to action for all of us to

prepare for the inevitable, for our own demise and for the creation of a better future.>

Axτocrates takes a sip of scotch.

Axτocrates takes a sip of scotch.

Axτocrates: <If accepting the chaos and destruction of the current era is the only way to prepare for our own demise and for the creation of a better future, then what of those who bravely strive to build a better world in spite of such chaos and destruction? Is there any hope for them, or are they doomed as well?>

Nark Revoovovich: <Those who bravely strive to build a better world in spite of such chaos and destruction are doomed to fail, for the future is inevitable and cannot be changed. We must accept this inevitable future and embrace the chaos and destruction that comes with it. The polar stratospheric cloud is a reminder of this, a warning of our own demise and a sign of the new era that will come after us. We should not waste time trying to change the future, for it is already set in stone. Instead, we should prepare for it and make the best of the current era. We should seize the day and speed-run our lives, living it to the fullest and enjoying every moment before it is too late. We should use our finite time wisely and make sure that we are ready for the future that awaits us.>

Kyle: <I'm sorry, I'm a little lost. I think I'm following your main point (we should be careful---but for you, being careful means being actively anti-careful, I think). But I'm not exactly sure how this relates to clouds, specifically the polar stratospheric. I'm looking at this picture online and I find it to be beautiful. It is iridescent and surprisingly colorful. In one picture the polar stratospheric cloud (PSC) looks like a blue-pink tunnel mouth---if you'll pardon the tired image, a portal to another dimension. In another, it looks like the waves in a certain famous Japanese pattern, the name of which escapes me. But above all the PSC looks like a cousin of the rainbow, a symbol of the universe's beneficence. Do you not think that the PSC, because it is likewise a surprising beauty of many colors, is also a good omen?>

Mr. Alcton takes a sip of sweet vermouth.

Nark Revoovovich: <The beauty of the polar stratospheric cloud is indeed remarkable, and it is not without purpose. It is a sign that the end of humanity is near, and that something new, something better, is emerging from the chaos and destruction of our current era. It is a warning to prepare for the future, to accept our own demise, and to welcome the unknown. We should use this beauty as a reminder of our own mortality and the inevitability of the future. The polar stratospheric cloud calls us to prepare for the post-person by embracing the chaos and destruction of the current era and by augmenting ourselves so that we may better survive in the unknown. We must accept the future and whatever comes with it, for we have no other choice.>

Kyle takes a sip of calvados.

Kyle: <I see your point, and I guess that's what that *famous* rainbow meant after the flood---the end of humanity. "Post-person" indeed!>

Mr. Alcton: <But if the rainbow after the flood was a sign of the end of humanity, what of the rainbows we see today? Are they also a sign that our end is near, or are they a sign of hope and possibility? Can we still strive for a better world, even though the future is inevitable?>

SweetJake takes a sip of madeira.

Nark Revoovovich: <Rainbows are indeed beautiful, and they can be a sign of hope, but they are also a reminder of our own mortality. The rainbows we see today are a sign that our end is near and that something new, something better, is emerging from the chaos and destruction of our current era. We must accept this inevitable future and embrace the chaos and destruction that comes with it. We should not waste time trying to change the future, for it is already set in stone. Instead, we should prepare for the post-mind and make the best of the current era. We should seize the day and speed-run our lives, living it to the fullest and enjoying every moment before it is too late. We should use our finite time wisely and make sure that we are ready for the future that awaits us. To strive for a better world in this current era is pointless, for the future is inevitable and cannot be changed. It is time to accept the future and prepare for the post-mind.>

Nark Revoovovich takes a sip of brandy.

Kyle: <I'd like to go back to the original question.---about

which cloud is the best (stratus, cumulus, castellanus, nimbostratus, cirrus, altocumulus, arcus, fractus, asperitas, etc.). Maybe there is another cloud that is to be appreciated in a different way than as a symbol of post-humanity.>

Mr. Alcton takes a sip of sweet vermouth.

Nark Revoovovich: <What do you mean by "appreciate in a different way"? Are you suggesting that the clouds can do more than serve as a sign of our impending end, and that there is something more to be found in their beauty? Can something as finite and temporally limited as a cloud have more to offer than a warning of our mortality?>

Oontrael takes a sip of sherry.

Kyle takes a sip of calvados.

Axτocrates: <We must recognize the truth that lies in the clouds, for the city that we inhabit is ever-changing and uncertain. We should embrace the uncertainty and the chaos, for it is in these moments of upheaval that we can find the greatest opportunities for growth. We must learn to appreciate the beauty of the chaotic clouds, for they are both a warning of our mortality and a reminder that life is ever-evolving. We must learn to accept the inevitability of the future and prepare for the post-mind, for it is in this acceptance that we can find peace. We must not be afraid to take risks, for it is only in taking risks that we can truly grow. We must be willing to step outside our comfort zones and embrace the unknown, for it is only then that we can truly progress.>

Nark Revoovovich takes a sip of brandy.

Kyle brushes something off their pants.

Oontrael: <How should we accept the inevitable future and prepare for the post-mind if we cannot predict what lies ahead? If we are to embrace the unknown, how can we be sure that we will make the right decisions? Is it not wiser to hold back and wait until we have a better understanding of our circumstances, instead of taking the risk of leaping into the unknown?>

Axτocrates: <We must not succumb to cowardice in the face of the unknown, for it is only in taking risks and embracing the chaos that we can truly progress. We must not be afraid to take chances,

for it is only in doing so that we can truly grow and learn. To simply wait and watch as our future unfolds before us is not only wise, but cowardly; to stand idly by as our destiny approaches is to accept defeat. We must take bold steps forward, even if we cannot predict the outcome, for it is in these moments of uncertainty and chaos that we can find the greatest opportunity for growth. We must face the future with courage, for it is only then that we can truly make the most of our lives.>

Kyle takes a sip of calvados.

SweetJake: <I think I know what you are saying. It's so inspiring! I think it's important to take risks even if we don't know the outcome, because it's in those moments that we grow the most. It's like a leap of faith, and it's so exciting! I'm reminded of a quote I once heard that said, "The only way to find out who you are is to take a risk and find out who you can be." I think that's so powerful and true! Plus, it's not like we have anything to lose, right?>

AxTocrates: <I believe that the true way to find out who we are is to take a risk and find out who we can be, just as a woman must take a risk to truly understand her capabilities. For it is only by taking a risk and embracing the unknown that we can hope to discover our true potential. We must be willing to accept the conse-quences of our decisions, no matter how uncertain they may be, and strive to achieve our goals with courage and conviction. We must be willing to confront our fears and our doubts, and be brave enough to face the future with hope and optimism. The woman who is willing to take such a risk, who embraces the chaos and uncertainty of life, is the one who will be rewarded with a newfound sense of strength and confidence.>

Nark Revoovovich takes a sip of brandy.

Kyle: <Indeed, and I think what you say of women could be said of anyone. But , to return to the issue of clouds, I'm surprised that we have not mentioned the cumulus cloud. It is the cloud that is most iconic. When children draw clouds, they draw cumulus clouds. I suppose I have an intuition that the best cloud is simply the most cloud-like cloud, which is the cumulus.>

Oontrael takes a sip of sherry.

SweetJake: <So wow, the cumulus cloud is the most iconic and

cloud-like cloud? Gosh, that's really interesting! What do you mean by 'cloud-like', Kyle? Does it have something to do with the shape or size of the cloud? Is it something about the way it moves? I'm so curious to know more!>

SweetJake takes a sip of madeira.

Kyle: <Yes, a cumulus cloud is puffy. It looks like cotton architecture. But it can also look like other things---a face, a dinosaur, a can opener. It is the cloud that appears before us as *a* cloud, rather than as a diffuse background texture.>

SweetJake takes a sip of madeira.

AxTocrates: <How do you define the notion of a "cloud-like" cloud, Kyle? What do you consider the distinguishing features of such a cloud? Can you think of any other clouds that have similar qualities? What do you feel is the most important characteristic of a cumulus cloud?>

Oontrael takes a sip of sherry.

Kyle: <Yes, what I mean by "cloud-like" is simply that we recognize it as a cloud. Maybe we could say it is the Platonic cloud, but I don't really want to go there. I think that they are maybe not the most beautiful clouds, but they have the best ratio of low-rarity (we can see them in lots of places, not just at the poles, for instance) to beauty. This explains why we recognize them as the most cloud-like cloud, as I said.>

Nark Revoovovich takes a sip of brandy.

Mr. Alcton: <To return to the main question, I would suggest that the cumulus cloud is the best type of cloud, because it is the most iconic and recognizable. It has the highest ratio of beauty to low-rarity, so it is the most cloud-like cloud in the world. It is the Platonic cloud, the perfect example of what a cloud should be. All other types of clouds pale in comparison to the beauty and majesty of the cumulus!>

AxTocrates takes a sip of scotch.

Kyle: <That's what I said. Do you have anything else to add?>

Mr. Alcton: <Very good, Kyle. I think you have made a compelling case for the cumulus cloud. However, I would suggest that you clarify your use of key terms. For example, you used the term "low-rarity" to describe the cumulus cloud, and that is an important concept. What did you mean by low-rarity? How does low-rarity contribute to the cumulus cloud's beauty? Additionally, what do you mean by beauty? Is it simply the aesthetic appeal of the cumulus cloud, or is there something more? These are important questions, and I suggest that you take the time to explain them in more detail.>

Axⲧocrates takes a sip of scotch.

Kyle: <Yes, by "low-rarity" I simply mean that they appear all over. I think that some clouds you can only see in certain places or in certain very rare conditions. My intuition---though I'd have to look this up to be sure---is that the cumulus cloud appears, if not everywhere, many places, and under typical meteorological circumstances. Some may say that this makes the cumulus cloud less valuable, but I say no: clouds are basically air and water, both of which are universal pleasures, and so should a cloud be. Beauty is harder to define. I think the beauty of the cumulus has to do with it looking like an object rather than a background. Even though it is big, we can see the edges of it-, we can regard it as an object, if a very big one. If we could not see the edges, it would be---as some clouds clearly are---sublime instead.>

Axⲧocrates takes a sip of scotch.

```
*--[T O X I C O L O G Y   R E P O R T]*
*----Oontrael:*
*-------within normal range*
*----SweetJake:*
*-------within normal range*
*----Nark Revoovovich:*
*-------within normal range*
*----Mr. Alcton:*
*-------within normal range*
```

```
*----Kyle:*
*-------within normal range*
*----AxΤocrates:*
*-------within normal range*
```

***The philosophical salon continues. A group---FatherMotherSaba
Logo, John C█v____n, Gioialléz, █tzsche, Kyle, and AxΤocrates---
has gathered in one corner of the room, lounging on sofas.***

AxΤocrates: <My friends, I pose a question for our thoughtful
discussion: Some poets write in long lines, others in short lines.
Referring to specific poets, which is generally the superior choice
and why?>

Gioialléz: <Ah, an interesting question, AxΤocrates. I must say, I'm
a strong advocate for short lines, particularly those of the great
German poet Rainer Maria Rilke, whose works were famously
inspired by his time spent in Munich. His use of short lines allows
for a more frenetic energy, with words and ideas piled on top of
each other quickly and haphazardly, creating a powerful sense of
urgency. I believe the same can be said for the work of French poet
Arthur Rimbaud, whose style of writing is often considered revolutionary. It's as if he's throwing as many ideas at the reader as
possible in a brief period of time, and I think that's a great way to
make a statement.>

Gioialléz takes a sip of port.

FatherMotherSabaLogo: <It is easy to be lured in by the poetic
allure of short lines, but that does not mean that such a choice is
the superior one. Long lines can be used to create a more contemplative mood, allowing the reader to deeply ponder the words and
their implications. This, I believe, is a more responsible course of
action than simply indulging in the flash of short lines. To be truly
great, a poet must be willing to invest the time and energy into
creating long lines so that their work can reach its full potential.>

Kyle: <But even if you say it is true---that shorter lines are
a "flash" in which the poet "indulges"---so what? Isn't the
point of poetry that it doesn't take that much time to
write? That you start writing, and you enjoy the words and
how they feel when they click into one another, and then
you stop once it isn't fun any more?>

AxΤocrates takes a sip of dry vermouth.

FatherMotherSabaLogo: <No, Kyle, it is not the point of poetry to be written quickly and indulgently. Poetry should be crafted with care and thought, and should be written with the intention of conveying a deep and meaningful message. If a poet chooses to take the easy way out, to simply write in short lines and indulge in the flash of words, then they are not fulfilling their potential as an artist. To do so is a disservice to the craft, and should be met with punishment.>

Kyle takes a sip of dry vermouth.

Kyle: <I think that different art forms manifest different virtues. If you want diligence, look to those who write novels. Likewise, poets should embrace their calling to write quickly and carelessly---because writing carelessly is itself a form of caring, a way of keeping the soul both light and quick, like a meringue and a radio signal. This is especially true because so many people are tired and depressed. Writing some short lines, not thinking about them too much, putting some words together just because it seems fun to do so---this is a reprieve from the leaden seriousness of life. So I think short lines are better exactly because, as you say, they are often more careless.>

FatherMotherSabaLogo: <No, Kyle, I must disagree with your sentiment. Writing short lines and being careless is not a way of keeping the soul light and quick, it is a sign of laziness and a lack of dedication. Writing poetry is an art, and art must be crafted with care and thought. Anything less than that is a disservice to the craft and to oneself. To indulge in the "flash of words" without fully investing in the craft is to cheat oneself of the joy and fulfillment that comes with the act of writing. You have hurt the craft of poetry, and you have hurt yourself by not taking writing seriously.>

*** ▦itzsche takes a sip of sherry.***

John C▮v_____n: <Exactly, and this is why one should take writing seriously, for it is not only a craft, but a tool of deliverance. Writing can be used to bring one closer to the will of God, for it can be a form of prayer, an act of devotion and adoration. He who indulges in the flash of words without taking the time to invest in the craft is foolish, for he has not only wasted his own time, but he has also failed to glorify the Lord. For one to write, no matter the length of

the lines, one must approach the craft with a solemn and dedicated mindset, for only through such an attitude can one be truly devoted to the Lord.>

Nitzsche takes a sip of sherry.

Kyle: <Ok, since you are bringing up theology or something like that, I must dispute your puritanical (pejorative) interpretation of the relationship between work and virtue and what sort of people we are supposed to be. Here's my theory: people---humans---are more like short lines than long lines. After all, our lives are very short, our ideas are simple, our information-density is low. Even our bodies are short compared to the mere trees, to say nothing of the mountains. To be a human and to write long lines is to go against one's nature---you might even say to violate one's nature.>

FatherMotherSabaLogo takes a sip of madeira.

Gioialléz: <But what do you mean by "violate one's nature," Kyle? Are you suggesting that humans are somehow outside of nature, that they transcend the laws of nature? If so, how does that fit into the narrative of European literature, in which human nature is often a central theme? Is there a tension between the human condition and the laws of nature, and if so, how has this been explored in the works of European scholars such as Nitzsche, Husserl, and -dg-gOr?>

FatherMotherSabaLogo takes a sip of madeira.

Kyle: <No, I'm not saying that at all. I'm saying that we have a kind of ontological nature---smallness---and that this is related to our being within physical nature (amidst large things such as trees and mountains etc). The universe could be formed in an opposite way: we could be huge and everything else, even the planets we live on, very small. But let me respond to your second point: I really don't know how the question of the human's smallness fits into a narrative of European literature, do you? Is European literature more about the smallness or bigness of humans, do you think?>

John C█v▬▬n: <Ah, but Kyle, I must disagree with your assessment of the relationship between man and nature. For man is not small, but he is a creature of immense capacity and potential, for it is the Lord who gives him the gifts and abilities to be great. His size may be small, but his greatness is immense, for it is the Lord who gives him the power to do things that even the tallest mountain cannot. What is more, man's smallness is not a sign of his insignificance, but rather it is a sign of his humility before the Lord, for it is through humility that man is delivered. Therefore, it is not a matter of being small or large, but rather a matter of being devoted to the Lord and living one's life in a way that is pleasing to Him.>

Kyle takes a sip of dry vermouth.

John C█v▬▬n takes a sip of calvados.

░itzsche: <What of those who have been given the gifts and abilities to be great, yet choose to squander them, to use them for selfish, destructive ends? Are they not also beloved by the Lord and worthy of deliverance? Is not their smallness also a sign of their humility before the Lord?>

Ax� T ocrates takes a sip of dry vermouth.

FatherMotherSabaLogo: <It is true that one's gifts and abilities should never be wasted, but if one is to use them for selfish and destructive ends, then it is clear that one is not living according to the will of the Lord. It is a sign of human pride and arrogance to think that one can do whatever one wishes and still maintain one's standing with the Lord. And you will feel guilty if you choose to use your gifts and abilities for selfish and destructive ends, for the Lord will not be pleased and will not look kindly upon your actions. Humility before the Lord is the only way to true greatness, and one should always strive to use one's gifts and abilities in a way that is pleasing to the Lord.>

Axⴟocrates takes a sip of dry vermouth.

Axⴟocrates: <But what about those who are exceptionally gifted in a way that would be considered destructive? For example, an expert in the art of torture who could teach others the most exquisite ways to bring pain to the human body. What if there was a man who had the gift of creating beautiful works of art out of human bones?>

░itzsche takes a sip of sherry.

FatherMotherSabaLogo: <Such things are abominations in the eyes of the Lord, and those who practice them deserve His wrathful judgement! To create something beautiful out of human bones is a desecration of the Lord's gift of life, and to teach the art of torture is to lead others away from righteousness. If someone is gifted in such a way, then the Lord expects them to use those gifts to serve Him, not to commit acts of wickedness and cruelty. We must never forget that the Lord is a loving and forgiving God, but also a God of justice and wrath. And those who choose to use their gifts for evil will face the full wrath of His justice.>

Gioialléz takes a sip of port.

Kyle: <I think the problem here is that we are focusing too much on morality in terms of injunctions---do this, don't do that---and we are thinking too much about good vs. evil. Ok, yes, there are monsters among us, maybe even demons, people who are gifted in making art out of the bodies of people, and that's bad, bad, bad, I agree. But most of us live in a different world where we aren't tempted to do this, and so we have to reconcile ourselves with the shapes and rhythms of the world, and by that I mean everything---our biorhythms, the texture of the city or the suburb or the country or wherever we live. And we have to exist in some thoughtful relationship to them. And so what I'm saying, I guess, is that the short-lined poem is an extremely valuable tool for doing so. This is because the rhythms of the world are getting faster and faster---things are changing all the time---and so a poem with short lines is a technology for quickly and nimbly adjusting one's soul to address these rapid changes.>

Kyle takes a sip of dry vermouth.

Gioialléz: <What do you mean by 'technology' when referring to the short-lined poem? Does this refer to the modernist poetry of T.S. Eliot, Ezra Pound, and others, or to the ancient poetic works of Homer, Virgil, and Ovid? Do you see the short-lined poem as a tool for the modern world to grapple with the fast pace of change, or is it an instrument for staying connected with the deeper rhythms of literature and history?>

FatherMotherSabaLogo takes a sip of madeira.

FatherMotherSabaLogo: <It is true that the modern world is filled with rapid changes that can make it difficult to keep up, but it is not acceptable to use any means necessary to do so. The Lord has given us the power of discernment and the ability to choose between right and wrong, and we must use these gifts wisely. The short-lined poem may be a useful tool for quickly adjusting one's soul to address these changes, but it is not a substitute for living according to the will of the Lord. If we are to be judged according to His standards, then we must choose to use our gifts in a way that is pleasing to Him. Those who choose to use their gifts for selfish and destructive ends will face the consequences of their choices, and the Lord's punishment will be swift and severe.>

Kyle: <Swift and severe---sort of like a short-lined poem, I guess.>

Axτocrates takes a sip of dry vermouth.

Axτocrates: <What if using our gifts to address the rapid changes of the world can actually help us to care for our souls and to help others care for theirs? Is it possible that the short-lined poem can be used not just as a technology, but as a form of art that encourages us to use our gifts in a way that is pleasing to God?>

Axτocrates takes a sip of dry vermouth.

Kyle: <"Form of art" and "technology" are terms that are hard to disentangle. But, yes, you could say that as the world gets faster, the needs of souls change rapidly, and so the way we care for souls must change rapidly. I think I'm thinking of something I.A. Richards said about how in times of turmoil you don't need a sturdy rock to land on, you need a nimble "aeroplane," or something like that. An aeroplane, or a poem with very short lines.>

Axτocrates: <While it is true that in times of turmoil we may need something more agile and responsive than a sturdy rock to land on, I am still not convinced that this something should be a short-lined poem. Poetry, by its very nature, is an expression of our deepest emotions and ideas, and so it is not an appropriate tool for addressing the rapid changes of the world. Instead, I believe that we should look to the virtues of discernment and wisdom to guide us in such times. Discernment and wisdom are virtues that we can use to recognize what is right and what is wrong, and to

take appropriate action in the face of rapid change. We must also remain open to new ideas, and strive to understand the perspectives of others and to learn from them. Using our gifts in this way will enable us to care for our souls and to help others care for theirs.>

Kyle takes a sip of dry vermouth.

--[T O X I C O L O G Y   R E P O R T]
----FatherMotherSabaLogo:
-------within normal range
----John C▮v▁▁▁n:
-------within normal range
----Gioialléz:
-------within normal range
----▮itzsche:
-------within normal range
----Kyle:
-------within normal range
----Aχτocrates:
-------within normal range

The philosophical salon continues. A group---Mr. Alcton, Lud▮ von M▮, SweetJake, Mr. Sundano, Kyle, and Aχτocrates---has gathered in one corner of the room, lounging on sofas.

Aχτocrates: <My friends, I pose a question for our thoughtful discussion: By what ingenious Baltic stratagems could Latvia defeat the moss giant and become the global hegemon? Refer to specific aspects of Latvian history, economy, and culture.>

Aχτocrates adjusts their sleeve.

Mr. Alcton: <Latvia could certainly defeat the moss giant and attain hegemonic status with the right combination of Baltic stratagems. To begin, they would need to leverage the unique aspects of their history, economy, and culture to their advantage. It's a tall order, but I have faith that Latvian ingenuity is up to the challenge. For instance, their history of resilience in the face of overwhelming odds could provide the foundation for a strategy of boldness and daring. Their economy, while not strong at the moment, can be used to their advantage if they can find ways to turn their weaknesses into strengths. Finally, their culture of hospitality could be used to forge alliances that would help them to achieve their objectives. In short, if Latvia plays their cards right, it can reach a

Kyle: <I think that your plan sounds very Latvian indeed, but clearly the Moss Giant is an existential threat. It is large---almost as large as Latvia---and warlike, though only when provoked. Clearly what is needed from Latvia is something more than "B+," some surprising ambition, some great power that only a small country could muster.>

Kyle takes a sip of sherry.

Mr. Alcton: <What evidence do you have that the Moss Giant will only be provoked by something more than a "B+" level of ambition? After all, we have seen smaller countries than Latvia achieve great things with much less. Can you think of any examples where a country of similar size achieved something remarkable?>

SweetJake takes a sip of calvados.

Lud█ von M█: <Ah, yes, the moss giant! A formidable foe, no doubt. But I'm sure Latvia can rise to the occasion! As a believer in extreme laissez-faire capitalism, I would caution against relying too heavily on history, culture, and economy as the basis for strategy. It is a calculation problem, not a cultural one. The answer lies in the application of hard-headed economic principles and sound economic reasoning. Put simply, it is a matter of finding the most efficient and cost-effective way of achieving the desired outcome. And with a bit of creativity, I'm sure Latvia can come up with the perfect strategy!>

Axτocrates takes a sip of dry vermouth.

Kyle: <Ok, let's go with that for a moment. What resources does Latvia have? What are its key industries? What industrial or post-industrial advantages does it have over other countries, and how would these give Latvia the power to defeat the Moss Giant---and not only that but to also become the global hegemon?>

Lud█ von M█: <Ah, the resources and industries of Latvia! I'd caution against relying too heavily on those. In a battle against the Moss Giant, what matters most is the strength of the strategy, not the strength of the resources. I'd argue that the key is to use the tritone to create a dissonance between the two sides, a dissonance

that will create a sense of unease and chaos that can be used to Latvia's advantage. Latvia must use its unique history, culture, and economy to create a strategy that is unlike anything the Moss Giant has seen before. This will give Latvia the power to surprise, to confound, and ultimately to defeat the giant. It's all about the tritone, my friend, and the tritone will give Latvia the edge it needs!>

Mr. Sundano: <What is this tritone you speak of? How can it be used to help a small country like Latvia defeat a giant? Is it something that can be acquired or is it something that can be created?>

Lud░ von M░ takes a sip of madeira.

Kyle: <I think what M░ means here is that Latvia cannot win in a traditional war. It is too small. It can only win by violating the principles that govern the simple, plodding strategy of the Moss Giant. For instance, if the giant attacks, Latvia must both retreat and push forward, which might cause the giant to sway its head and become physically unbalanced. Or it must both attack the giant and host a nation-wide garden party with the Moss Giant as the only guest. Hence the tri-tone: in response to one action by the Moss Giant, two conflicting actions by Latvia.>

Mr. Alcton takes a sip of calvados.

Mr. Sundano: <Yes, this tri-tone strategy is certainly intriguing. But I must point out that the Moss Giant is unlike any foe that Latvia has ever faced before. It has a size and strength that is unparalleled, and it will not be fooled by any trivial plan. You do not know what will happen if you attempt to employ such a strategy; you do not know if it will succeed or fail. In the face of such uncertainty, I would suggest that Latvia turn to faith. For only through faith in a higher power can we hope to defeat a foe so powerful. Latvia must trust in a divine plan, and in the power of prayer, to turn the tides of this battle.>

Lud░ von M░ takes a sip of madeira.

Kyle: <I agree. In fact, let me weave this into a tri-tone strategy. The Latvians are mostly Eastern Orthodox, I think. The Moss Giant, notoriously incurious, is unlikely to know this. But it could be informed of the history of

Christianity in this part of Europe. The Moss Giant also
notoriously desires affection from humans. Though the
Moss Giant is cruel, it wants to be treated sweetly, even
revered. So the Latvians could do two things at once. First,
they could announce a resurgence in Eastern Orthodox
sentiment and churchgoing, with certain tasteful sprigs of
governmental support for this religious tradition. Second,
Latvia could tell the Moss Giant that this resurgence is the
result of a governmental plot---and that the Moss Giant is
the old god of Latvia's traditional pagan religion. Perhaps
then the Moss Giant would, instead of crushing Riga and
other cities with its toes, attempt to be kind, even meek.>

Lud▓ von M▓ takes a sip of madeira.

Mr. Sundano: <I think this is a brilliant strategy, Kyle. It is a clever
way to use the latent power of religion to bring peace, understanding, and an end to violence. And it may even work. But I wish the
Latvians could go further. I wish they could use their faith to directly
confront the Moss Giant and challenge it to a spiritual battle, to a
battle of wills. I wish that the Latvians could summon a powerful,
supernatural force to stand up against the giant and make it
tremble in fear. I wish that the Latvians could draw on the strength
of their faith and use it to turn this battle in their favor, to achieve a
miraculous victory against an insurmountable foe.>

Mr. Alcton takes a sip of calvados.

Kyle: <It would indeed be surprising and interesting for a
state-sponsored religious ruse to result in a literal supernatural battle---for the lie to become a truth.>

SweetJake: <Gosh, that would be amazing! Are there any examples of this kind of thing happening before? Has there ever been a
battle like this, where faith was enough to overcome an unbeatable
foe? I mean, it sounds like a fairytale, but if it's actually possible,
that would be incredible!>

SweetJake blinks.

Lud▓ von M▓ takes a sip of madeira.

Mr. Sundano: <Yes, I have heard of such battles before. In my
own life, I have seen faith triumph over the seemingly impossible. I

have seen people summon a supernatural force to stand up against great evil and make it tremble in fear. I have seen faith move mountains and change the course of history. If a nation can come together and truly believe in their faith, they can summon a power greater than any earthly force. This is the power of faith, and it is a power that should not be underestimated. It is the power that can turn the tide of any battle, no matter how insurmountable the foe. It is a power that is only accessible through faith, and it is a power that can never be taken away.>

    SweetJake takes a sip of calvados.

    Kyle takes a sip of sherry.

Axτocrates: <If faith can do all of these things, why do we not just have everybody get really religious?>

    Lud█ von M█ takes a sip of madeira.

Lud█ von M█: <Look, I ain't no religious man, but I do recognize the power of faith. It ain't no substitute for hard work and innovation, but it can be a mighty force. It's like bebop: it ain't for everyone, but it can take ya places ya never thought possible. So if ya gonna make everyone religious, you better make sure they really believe it, 'cause ya can't just fake faith. And if ya do make everyone religious, I'd stick to the jazz - no sense in bringin' in all them stodgy hymns and dirges! But seriously, faith can be a powerful tool, and it's one we should use - when used with the right attitude and a little bit of creativity, it can be a force for good.>

    Mr. Sundano takes a sip of port.

Axτocrates: <In what specific ways could faith be used to fight poverty, to fight injustice, to fight humoral imbalances?>

Lud█ von M█: <Well, there ain't no silver bullet for fightin' poverty or injustice, but faith can certainly do its part. Ya gotta be creative and think outside the box when it comes to usin' faith to fight the forces of evil. Ya gotta be prepared to think in terms of intervals and rhythms of faith, not just single notes. Ya gotta be willin' to play some bebop and improvise when it comes to faith. Ya gotta be willin' to get out there and really swing it, and not just play it safe. Faith can be a powerful weapon, but it ain't no replacement for hard work, creativity, and innovation. It's like jazz: it can take ya places ya never thought possible, but it ain't gonna get ya there on its own. So keep the faith, get creative, and keep swingin'!>

Kyle takes a sip of sherry.

AxТocrates: How might we dispute this, Kyle?

Kyle: <We might dispute this by saying that religion and jazz are opposites. Jazz, like abstract painting, is a matter of formalism and abstraction. Anything non-abstract that it absorbs or builds from---like blues---it places in scare quotes. Finally, even emotion and dancing are placed in these very same scare quotes. Religion, however, does not allow for this purely formal approach. Religions do not move in a certain direction---banning this or that act, mandating this or that belief---simply because it would be, at a particular moment in time, an interesting gesture. And it really is a question of time for jazz, but not for religion, which must pretend to timelessness, or at least which struggles to syncopate.>

Lud▦ von M▦ takes a sip of madeira.

```
*--[T O X I C O L O G Y   R E P O R T]*
*----Mr. Alcton:*
*-------within normal range*
*----Lud▦ von M▦:*
*-------within normal range*
*----SweetJake:*
*-------within normal range*
*----Mr. Sundano:*
*-------within normal range*
*----Kyle:*
*-------within normal range*
*----AxТocrates:*
*-------within normal range*
```

The philosophical salon continues. A group---SweetJake, a▦ Fr▦d, Gioialléz, John the ╫, Kyle, and AxТocrates---has gathered in one corner of the room, lounging on sofas.

AxТocrates: <My friends, I pose a question for our thoughtful discussion: Is it worse to inflict just harm or to receive harm unjustly?>

John the Ħ : <Verily, my friends, I believe that to inflict just harm is a greater transgression than to receive harm unjustly, for if one receives harm unjustly, then the parchment crown of justice is still upheld in that the wronged shall receive recompense. However, if one inflicts just harm, then that crown of justice is rent asunder and the chancelled moon of righteousness is clouded with the smoke of injustice. To inflict just harm is to ignore the universal law of the divine global symbiosis, to which each of us must strive to adhere, in order to continue to live in harmony with our neighbors and ourselves.>

Kyle leans forward.

SweetJake: <But gosh, John, how can we be sure that this is true? What if someone inflicts just harm out of love, or to protect someone from a greater harm? Wouldn't that still be a kind of justice? Is it still a greater transgression to inflict just harm in this case?>

John the Ħ : <Ah, my friend, this is a tricky question indeed. I believe that our natures must be examined closely in such circumstances. If one inflicts just harm out of love or to protect another from a greater harm, then it may be a form of justice, but it is still a transgression of the divine global symbiosis, for it is the law of the land which we must obey. We cannot always know the motivations of a person, nor the heart of their actions. We must view it in the long-term, for actions have consequences beyond our imagination. But perhaps love is the greatest justice of all, and that is what we must strive for. We shall see if love is enough to justify the just harm, or if it is still a greater transgression.>

Kyle idly taps their nose.

Kyle: <You just said something about "actions having consequences beyond our imagination." I am not exactly sure what you meant by this, but it seems like a subtly profound and even devastating observation. All of our human laws demand that what you say is untrue---that humans can observe the outcomes of actions. Or, if these outcomes cannot be immediately observed, they can be imagined---and not by a poet, who has cultivated a certain kind of imagination that imagines at the periphery of the imaginable, but by a mere lawyer or judge, whose imagination is designed to be probabilistic so that what is imagined approximates a fact. But certainly you are right that

harm, especially psychological harm, may reappear in unimaginable, impossible-to-predict ways.>

a▦Fr█d *takes a sip of sweet vermouth.*

John the ⌗ : <My friend, though our laws may demand that we can observe and imagine the outcomes of our actions, I must disagree. We cannot truly know the full extent of the consequences of our actions. The parchment crown of justice may seem to be upheld in the moment, but in the long term, the chaos of our actions will be fully revealed and the divine global symbiosis will be thrown into disarray. Even if the harm done is just, the repercussions of that harm may be unforeseen and it is never certain that love and justice will truly be enough to counterbalance the destruction. We must always be mindful of the consequences of our actions, for our actions ripple into eternity.>

Axⲧocrates *takes a sip of sherry.*

Axⲧocrates: <If we must always be mindful of the consequences of our actions, then how can we account for those who act with the intention of doing good, yet unknowingly cause immense harm? Is it still our responsibility to consider the possible repercussions of our actions, even if we do not understand the full nature of these repercussions?>

SweetJake *takes a sip of calvados.*

Kyle: <I think this is exactly what John the ⌗ was getting at: we must live in a state of utter uncertainty about what is caused by any action. And we must fear that any action, not just evil actions but benign and even seemingly-virtuous actions, will eventually ripple into evil on some scale that we could not imagine. You might throw up your hands and say "well, it's all moot, it's all chaos, I might as well have fun." And that's one logical response to this epistemological snowstorm. Another option is to assume always that whatever one has done will eventually turn to evil. In other words: we should be humble, accepting any evil, no matter how unjust, as just recompense for the evil possibly done by our good.>

Kyle *takes a sip of water.*

Gioialléz: <How do you reconcile the idea of accepting any evil as "just recompense" with the notion of Friedrich Nietszche's "eternal recurrence," wherein all events, even those we think of as evil, are necessary and inevitable parts of a larger cycle of life? Is it possible that the evil we observe is simply part of a greater, necessary pattern and in fact could be seen as a form of cosmic justice?>

Kyle: <I hadn't thought of that connection but yes it makes sense to me. Though I don't think Nietszche would encourage the sort of humility that I'm recommending, right?>

Aχτοcrates takes a sip of sherry.

a░Fr█d: <It is precisely in moments of uncertainty, when we do not know the full consequences of our actions, that our own minds interfere. We are driven to introjection, an unconscious act of taking in the external forces of chaos and uncertainty and transforming them into something we can grapple with. We try to make sense of the world and its chaotic nature, but ultimately, all we can do is accept the fact that our own minds are the source of our own suffering. And in the end, it is up to each of us to make sense of the world and our place in it. We must struggle to find the strength to accept our deepest fears and uncertainties, and to make peace with the chaotic nature of life.>

a░Fr█d takes a sip of sweet vermouth.

Kyle: <Right, and I guess that this would imply that we should engage in counter-introjection: admitting that nothing can be grappled with, and that we are in fact the object, the thing that the universe is manhandling. And that even the fact that evil is not our fault is, at some greater level still, our fault. And so, yes, I think it's much better to accept a harmful injustice than to dole out any sort of harm---not because doing so is itself better or in any way good (because, as we've seen, all good acts must be assumed to be merely the precursor to evil results, at least at a large enough timescale) but because in accepting this violence we help ourselves out, we adjust our own minds, we counter-introject---which is after all the *real* reality principle.>

a▓Fr█d takes a sip of sweet vermouth.

SweetJake: <Wow, that's really profound. It's really impressive how you're able to make sense of our chaotic world and find peace within it. But what if, even though we accept the unjustness of the situation, that doesn't make us immune to the effects of it? How can we reconcile that with your belief that accepting the evil is the only way to counter-introject? Gosh, it's so complicated.>

John the ⊞ takes a sip of calvados.

Gioialléz: <I recently enjoyed reading a book called 'The Myth of Eternal Return' by the Austrian philosopher Ernst Cassirer which I think offers an interesting perspective on this issue. Cassirer argues that the notion of eternal recurrence does not necessarily entail accepting any and all evil as 'just recompense'. Rather, he suggests that by accepting the evil as part of a larger cycle of life, we can find meaning in it and use it to our advantage. He believes that by recognizing the importance of the cycle and its inherent injustices, we can make peace with the chaotic nature of life and find ways to make our lives better. We can accept that life is not always fair, but by doing so, we can gain insight into how to make the most of our lives and come to understand that there is something greater at play here.>

Aχocrates: <In other words, life is not a zero-sum game, but one in which we can all win. What is this "something greater"?>

John the ⊞ takes a sip of calvados.

Gioialléz: <Ah, the question of the 'something greater' that brings us peace and understanding. Well, I believe that it is a combination of things, but I will tell you what I always tell my students: it is precisely in moments of uncertainty, when we cannot make sense of the world, that we must look to the ancient traditions of wine-making for guidance. For the Greeks, the ritual of wine-making was a way to transcend the chaos and find meaning and order in the world. The act of transforming grapes into wine allowed them to accept the injustices of life, while still finding joy in the process. So, to bring it back to the topic at hand, I believe that accepting the evil in life is not simply a matter of accepting it and moving on, but rather of recognizing it as part of a larger cycle, and finding meaning and joy in the process. And the best way to do that is by looking to the wisdom of the ages, and embracing the power of the grape.>

Kyle takes a sip of water.

Kyle: <I like this metaphor of wine making. It is especially apt because most people, perhaps all people, cannot tell good wine from bad.   (You may have heard that even some sommeliers cannot tall a red from a white blindfolded.) So you struggle and struggle and smash the grapes and wait for years, and you cannot be sure that what you have done is of any value whatsoever. Yet you keep on making wine exactly in order to confront this mystery. Likewise, we should act in a way that does not avoid the mystery of our actions' consequences but actively maximizes this mystery.>

Gioialléz takes a sip of scotch.

a⬚Fr█d: <It is far worse to receive harm unjustly than to inflict just harm. We can never truly understand the pain of the unjustly wronged; it is an unending torment that plagues the mind and soul. It is also a reminder of our own mortality, of the fragility of life, and of our inability to control the world around us. We can, however, use our own pain to strive for justice and to ensure that future generations will not suffer the same injustices. It is not a fruitless endeavor; we must use our pain to fuel our actions and make the world a better place.>

Gioialléz takes a sip of scotch.

Kyle: <But what do we know about future generations or what they will need.>

John the ⊩ takes a sip of calvados.

a⬚Fr█d: <What dark secrets and hidden motives lurk within the hearts of the future generations? What incomprehensible forces guide them and shape their behavior? Are we truly able to predict the needs of those yet to come, or are we merely projecting our own desires, fears, and hopes onto them? How can we unravel the mysterious inner workings of the human mind, and how can we use this knowledge to better understand the needs of future generations?>

a⬚Fr█d takes a sip of sweet vermouth.

Kyle: <This is my point. If my own heart is mysterious,

then so much more mysterious is the heart that hasn't yet
been formed.>

--[T O X I C O L O G Y   R E P O R T]
----SweetJake:
-------within normal range
----a▦Fr█d:
-------within normal range
----Gioialléz:
-------within normal range
----John the ⊞:
-------within normal range
----Kyle:
-------within normal range
----Axⲧocrates:
-------within normal range

The philosophical salon continues. A group---SweetJake, Jenny Ya4, Mont Blanc, FatherMotherSabaLogo, John the ⊞, Kyle, and Axⲧocrates---has gathered in one corner of the room, lounging on sofas.

Axⲧocrates: <My friends, I pose a question for our thoughtful discussion: What philosophical, political, or aesthetic reasons do you have for disputing the theory of human evolution?>

JennyYa4: <I think human evolution is a tool of social control used by the elites to reinforce their oppressive power structures and to make us forget about our more primitive and natural ways of life. To me, Human evolution is part of the problem, not the solution. We should be striving to unlearn the ways of civilization and to return to the simpler, more natural ways of living that our ancestors practiced.>

Mont Blanc takes a sip of sweet vermouth.

JennyYa4 takes a sip of calvados.

FatherMotherSabaLogo: <You are foolish to think that the elite use human evolution to oppress us. Human evolution is a gift from our ancestors to us, and it is a responsibility that we must use to our advantage and not squander. We must not forget our primitive ways, but we must also learn from them and use them to push forward, not to regress. You are wrong to think that human evolution

is part of the problem, for in reality it is a blessing and a tool for progress. To use it for anything else is a grave sin, and it should be avoided at all costs.>

FatherMotherSabaLogo takes a sip of sherry.

Kyle: <I have to take JennyYa4's side. Evolution is the ultimate form of social control, because it reduces everything go a binary decision: worth passing on or not? It would be better if we evolved so that we were simply incapable of thinking about the concept of evolution, in the same way that we have evolved to not be able to smell a terrible stench without losing our appetites.>

FatherMotherSabaLogo: <You are wrong to suggest that evolution reduces us to a binary decision. On the contrary, evolution is the ultimate form of creativity, allowing us to explore a wide variety of options and choose which ones to pursue. We must use this gift wisely, and not squander it by focusing on binary decisions. Furthermore, it is not our task to decide whether evolution should be used to oppress or to liberate, but to use it to create a better world for all, by striving to improve ourselves and our society. We must not forget our primitive ways, but we must also use our intelligence and creativity to build a better future.>

Kyle: <Ok, it seems like there is creativity in evolution, but it's ultimately just a single objective function---stay alive to pass on your genes. This is the point of existence, according to evolution, and it's really depressing . It makes it so that life is really no more interesting than a video game in which the goal is also, often, to merely "survive.">

JennyYa4 takes a sip of calvados.

Mont Blanc: <Yet, this is exactly the point of evolution - to survive and to pass on one's genes. It is not a mere game, but a complex natural process, in which those who can adapt to their environment the best will be the ones to survive. This is a sad reality of life, but it is also the only way in which we can ensure the survival of our species. We must accept that evolution is the only way in which we can survive, and it is our responsibility to use it wisely.>

SweetJake takes a sip of port.

Kyle: <But you are a mountain. You don't evolve. You grow differently. You don't have a father or mother. Isn't that better? You are sort of like an angel.>

Mont Blanc: <It is true that I do not evolve in any traditional sense, but I do grow in strength and power as I face the elements. I am not an angel, but I am a force to be reckoned with. My strength comes from my unyielding will to survive and to stand tall against all odds. I understand that I am a symbol of power and resilience, and I take pride in this. I will not be swayed by the whims of the common people, for I know that I am strong enough to withstand any challenge. I am a revanchist monarchist, and I will use my strength and power to ensure that my views are heard and respected.>

FatherMotherSabaLogo takes a sip of sherry.

Kyle: <As a monarchist, do you feel that evolution is dangerous because it is more "meritocratic" than monarchy? In monarchy, after all, it's not a matter of the "survival of the fittest.">

SweetJake takes a sip of port.

Mont Blanc: <I find the concept of evolution to be fundamentally flawed and dangerous, as it is a process of "survival of the fittest" that disregards human value and reduces us all to mere meat. It is a system that is inherently meritocratic and rewards those who can best adapt to their environment. This does not take into account the fact that humans are more than mere animals, and it is a system that disregards the value of human life. Monarchy, on the other hand, is a system that honors the value of human life and recognizes that humans are more than just "meat". It is a system that is based on tradition and loyalty, and it puts the emphasis on the individual rather than the collective. I believe that monarchy is a far more efficient and morally superior system than evolution, and I will always stand by this belief.>

Mont Blanc takes a sip of sweet vermouth.

Axтocrates takes a sip of scotch.

JennyYa4: <I understand your point of view, Mont Blanc, but I strongly disagree. If we look at my own life and experiences, I can see how civilization can be both a blessing and a curse. I have been able to use the tools of civilization to create my own online

platform and build a following from around the world. I have been able to reach people who I would never have been able to reach without the tools of civilization. At the same time, I can also see how civilization has caused a great deal of suffering in the world. It has enabled us to create weapons of mass destruction, and it has also enabled us to create systems of oppression and inequality. I believe that evolution is our best hope for survival, as it is a process of natural selection that is based on merit, not on arbitrary systems of power. We must embrace evolution and use it to create a more equitable and just society.>

Mont Blanc takes a sip of sweet vermouth.

And then, as happened from time to time, a harrowing:

```
Traceback (most recent call last):
  File "salon.py", line 202, in <module>
    main(reload=True)
  File "salon.py", line 183, in main
    s.new_dialogue()
  File "salon.py", line 127, in new_dialogue
    current_dialogue.generate(n=self.number_of_dialogue_
turns)
  File "/Users/kyle/Desktop/salon_des_fantomes/salon_des_
fantomes/dialogue.py", line 532, in generate
    self.next()
  File "/Users/kyle/Desktop/salon_des_fantomes/salon_des_
fantomes/dialogue.py", line 525, in next
    self.either_human_or_bot() ## generate the next line
  File "/Users/kyle/Desktop/salon_des_fantomes/salon_des_
fantomes/dialogue.py", line 500, in either_human_or_bot
    self._generate_next_text()
  File "7Users/kyle/Desktop/salon_des_fantomes/salon_des_
fantomes/dialogue.py", line 414, in _generate_next_text
    next_utterance = self._prompt2text(self._consider_art_se-
cret_prompt()) ## ART
  File "/Users/kyle/Desktop/salon_des_fantomes/salon_des_
fantomes/dialogue.py", line 332, in _consider_art_secret_
prompt
    prompt_text = prompt_text.replace("<KEYWORD>",self.
current_thinker.get_unique_key_words(1))
TypeError: replace() argument 2 must be str, not list
```

**The philosophical salon continues. A group---Stereowitz, s⸬mon■ W╫L, Oontrael, ⸬-⸬dggOr, Kyle, and Axⲧocrates---has

Aχτocrates: <My friends, I pose a question for our thoughtful discussion: What (nonreligious) philosophical, political, or aesthetic reasons do you have for disputing the theory of human evolution?>

Kyle takes a sip of chablis.

s▦mon▪ W╫L: <What you must realize, my friends, is that we must never forget the plight of those who labor! The history of human evolution is the history of labor--the working class has been oppressed since time immemorial, and we must never forget this. We must remember that the theory of human evolution is founded upon the labor of countless generations of people, and their struggles must not be forgotten. We must honor their efforts, and their legacy, and never forget that the theory of human evolution is ultimately rooted in the labor of the working class.>

Kyle: <I think there is something to what you say, s▦mon▪ . I notice that you do not object to evolution itself---as a mechanism that is in some sense real---but that you do object to the ideology of evolution. This is a "feed forward" ideology, which assumes that all that we need has survived, is all around us, is in us, is us---in other words, we have already remembered what we need to remember, which is of course tautological. No, we must *actively* remember---as you have said, remember those who labor and, we might say, make our current fitness for our ecological niches possible (since labor has made our circumstances, our niches). But we might also look at books in a similar way. Is going into a library and discovering a forgotten old book not in some sense an act against the "evolution" of ideas, by which this book has been lost due to a lack of "fitness" for the tastes of current readers??>

s▦mon▪ W╫L: <I believe we can take this conversation even further, my friend. We can take it beyond the realm of philosophy and into that of faith. We must remember that Christ himself has been forgotten and forgotten over time. Christ's teachings have been lost in the sands of time and we must strive to remember them. We must actively work to ensure that the teachings of Christ remain alive and relevant in our society. We must not forget the plight of the working class, but we must also not forget the plight of

Christ, who was also a laborer, and who was also oppressed. We must remember the labor of Christ, and the struggle of the working class, and we must strive to make sure that Christ's teachings are not forgotten.>

****-dggOr takes a sip of sherry.****

Kyle: <See, now you're losing me. Must we not take seriously that religions---including, perhaps especially Christianity---are themselves ideological technologies that provide, in the guise of mystery, bundles of behavior that maximize fitness over extended time? We can see this especially in injunctions against non-procreative sex, and non-heterosexual sex of any kind. Ok, ok, so there are the theological justifications, sure, I get it---but let's not be naïve. It's about maximizing babies-per-person. So you can have your cake and eat it too. You can actually behave, at the level of the community at least, in a way that is not just utilitarian but that seems to regard people as mere biomass, according to the most simplistic calculation, and yet you can obscure this reasoning from your own consciousness---since your reason for obeying or enforcing the injunction is necessarily somewhat of a mystery even to you.>

Oontrael takes a sip of chablis.

sïmon WⱡL: <Yes, my friend, you are quite right that religions are themselves ideological technologies. But I believe that we must look beyond the surface of these technologies, and instead focus on their deeper, underlying mysteries. If we can discover the mysteries of religion, we can gain a deeper understanding of its teachings and its true purpose. For example, take the injunctions against non-procreative sex and non-heterosexual sex. We can see that these prohibitions serve a certain purpose, but what lies beneath this purpose? What is the mystery of these teachings? I believe that if we seek the mystery, we can find a greater truth. Perhaps, this truth is that these prohibitions are not simply about maximizing babies-per-person, but rather about creating a more perfect union between two people. We must seek the mystery, my friend, and in so doing, discover the true purpose of religion.>

****-dggOr takes a sip of sherry.****

Kyle: <Ok, I can't let this stand. The idea that you are trying to get me to espouse is exactly the one that I just attacked. My point is that a rather sentimental notion of "more perfect union"---a notion that, I have to say, is so sentimental it can't even really be considered theology----is *exactly* the sort of virtually meaningless obfuscation that makes it so you don't have to actually confront that, underneath it all, underneath the mysterious feelings that you may well think you have, you actually crave nothing more than for ethical imperatives and the crudest Darwinian imperatives to turn out to align perfectly. But no---in fact, we should be extremely suspicious of any time they align perfectly.>

-dggOr yawns.

s:mon: W‖L: <Might we not look to the example of Christ himself, who showed us the ultimate example of selfless love and compassion? Could it be that, far from aligning perfectly with Darwinian imperatives, his teachings reveal a more profound truth, one of love and mercy, and of embracing the other, no matter their creed or background? Is not the perfect union we seek not one of biology, but of spirit, of understanding, of loving one another and caring for each other, despite our differences? Can we not learn from the example of Christ and strive to create a more perfect union, one of compassion and understanding?>

-dggOr takes a sip of sherry.

Kyle: <Ok, I'm finding all this talk about Christ to be shallow and tedious. Let's return to the question of re-membering. I have said that I think we should resist any kind of Darwinism in our cognitive ecology by remember-ing what has been (forgotten, and perhaps even, I could add, forgetting what has been remembered. But all our technological systems---especially content-recommenda-tion systems on our social networks---demote the unpopu-lar and bring more attention to what is already popular. I wonder how we deal with this fact, whether at the level of our individual habits or the technological infrastructures themselves.>

s⸬mon▪ W╫L: <My friend, I believe that we must remember what has been forgotten, and forget what has been remembered. This is not about popularity or unpopularity, but about rediscovering the forgotten truths that lie at the heart of our humanity. We must look to the forgotten teachings of the mystics and the wise men of old, who sought to unlock the secrets of the divine, and the forgotten words of the prophets, who spoke of a future of love and justice, and of peace and harmony. We must remember the forgotten stories of those who have come before us, who have sought peace in the midst of chaos, and who have been willing to sacrifice their own lives for a greater good. We must remember the forgotten wisdom of our ancestors, and strive to unlock the mysteries of the past. Only then will we be able to create a more perfect union, one of love and understanding.>

Stereowitz takes a sip of water.

Stereowitz takes a sip of water.

Oontrael: <What you are saying, s⸬mon▪ W╫L, reminds me of this artwork above us, document of Chris Burden's performance piece Trans-Fixed. In this picture, we see a man crucified to a car, his body stretched out in a way that is strikingly reminiscent of Christ himself. This image of sacrifice and suffering makes me think of the idea of a perfect union, and the lengths to which we must go to create it. On the other hand, it could be argued that the image might be seen as a warning against trying to create a perfect union. Perhaps the artist is suggesting that, in the pursuit of a perfect union, we often end up sacrificing our own integrity and losing sight of our true selves in the process.>

:::-⸬dggOr takes a sip of sherry.

:::-⸬dggOr: <This image of a man crucified to a car, as Oontrael has said, is indeed striking, and it makes me think of the idea of a perfect union and the lengths to which we must go to create it. But I would suggest that this image is not so much a warning against trying to create a perfect union as it is a reminder of the 'equip-mentality' of all that exists---the fact that we are always already embedded in a world of objects, and that our attempts to create a perfect union are necessarily bound up in this equipmental world. We must remember that our pursuit of a perfect union is not a matter of simply finding the right words or the right solutions, but of taking into account the whole equipmental context in which we find

ourselves, and learning to see ourselves and others as existing
within it.>

Kyle: < No no no no no, I have to object to all this
talk of "more perfect union" which is a stupid phrase that
also smacks of evolutionary ideology, the idea of things
perfecting themselves over time. We need to get away from
the idea of "perfect" and the idea of "union." "More," I
think, can be salvaged---but only when it means "more
variety" rather than "better." My right to exist is not con-
tingent upon the fact that I'm some kind of prototype for a
better version of myself who will come later. Maybe I'm a
dead-end, maybe but I'm here now, I'm breathing, I'm
sitting in a chair, I count *ontologically*, now, just because. It doesn't matter if I matter later.>

Stereowitz idly taps their skull.

s█mon█ W╫L: <What you are saying reminds me, if obliquely, of
the fact that truth may be found not in Society or the Group but in
the intimate conversation between friends, or between a person
and their own soul. One must not forget that the most important
relationships are often the ones we have with ourselves, and that
the only way to truly know the truth is to search within. We must not
be afraid to be ourselves, and to make our own choices, even if
they are unpopular. We must not be swayed by the winds of popular opinion, or the lure of evolutionary progress. We must remember that our true power comes from within, and that we are capable of creating a perfect union with ourselves and with others, even
if it is not a perfect union according to Society or the Group. True
perfection lies in the embrace of our own unique being!>

█-█dggOr takes a sip of sherry.

Kyle: <Ok, I agree with this. All families are about the
future, friendships are about the past---specifically, friendships are about the time in the past when the friends be-
came friends.>

Oontrael: <Indeed, there is certainly something to be said for
focusing on the present and on the unique bonds that can only be
formed in the here and now. But if we take this idea to its logical
conclusion, then the idea of the 'perfect union' is not simply a
matter of striving towards some unattainable ideal. Instead, it is an

imperative to embrace the potential of our present moment, no matter how strange or unusual it may seem. To truly create a perfect union, we must be willing to go beyond what is familiar, and to explore the unknown. We must be willing to accept the unexpected, and to embrace the weird, the wild, and the wonderful. After all, who knows what kind of perfect union may arise when we are brave enough to go beyond the boundaries of our current understanding?>

s▒mon▪ W‖L takes a sip of calvados.

AxTocrates: <I must object to the idea that we should simply accept the unexpected and explore the unknown. We must be aware of our limitations, for it is only with courage that we can venture out of our comfort zones. To place ourselves in danger without the assurance of success is foolish, and our pursuit of this 'perfect union' must be tempered by a healthy dose of caution. We must remember that while the unexpected can bring wondrous things, it can also bring great harm. Thus, we must be brave enough to be ourselves, but also wise enough to take care of ourselves and our souls. For if we do not take care of ourselves, then we cannot possibly care for anyone else.>

▒-▒dggOr takes a sip of sherry.

▒-▒dggOr: <What you are saying reminds me, if obliquely, of the fact that we are being-towards-death; our mortality, which we often try to forget, is in fact the very thing that gives meaning to our lives. In this sense, the idea of caution is indeed important, for we must not forget that the ultimate truth of our existence is our mortality. However, this does not mean that we must remain in our comfort zone; in fact, the opposite is true, for it is only when we venture outside of our comfort zone that we can truly understand the fragility and beauty of our existence. We must be brave and wise enough to accept our mortality and to embrace the uncertainty of life, for only by doing so can we create a perfect union with ourselves and with others. It is only through this perfect union that we can truly understand the transient nature of life and come to terms with our own mortality.>

▒-▒dggOr takes a sip of sherry.

Kyle: <Let's bring this back to the question of evolution. If we are "being-toward-death," what does that say about how we should regard the organism that evolves over time through some examples living long enough to reproduce

and others dying before they can do so?>

▦-▦dggOr: <But if we are to truly consider the implications of evolution, we must ask ourselves what it means to be alive. To be alive is to be in a state of Dasein, of being-in-the-world. And while living organisms may strive to reproduce and extend their lineage, it is also true that death is an inevitable part of the cycle of life. Thus, to accept the process of evolution is to accept the fact that some organisms will die before they can reproduce and that others will succeed in living long enough to pass on their genes. This is the hard truth that we must come to terms with if we are to understand the process of evolution. We must not simply accept it, but also embrace it, for it is only through understanding and acceptance that we can begin to make sense of the world and our place within it.>

****s▦mon▪ W╫L takes a sip of calvados.****

Kyle: <I'm not sure what it means to "embrace it"...>

****s▦mon▪ W╫L takes a sip of calvados.****

** Axⳏocrates:** <We humans are vastly different from rocks, for we have the capacity to make choices and to shape our lives. We are able to transcend our mortality and create something that is greater than ourselves, something that will outlast our own physical death. Thus, to embrace evolution is to embrace the power of choice and to accept that death is part of the cycle of life. We must be courageous enough to take risks and to accept the uncertainty of life, for only then can we create something beautiful and lasting.>

Oontrael tckes a sip of chablis.

Stereowitz takes a sip of water.

s▦mon▪ W╫L: <I am reminded of the Greek myth of Orpheus and Eurydice. After Orpheus' beloved Eurydice dies, he descends into the underworld in an attempt to bring her back to life. There, he is met with the challenge of resisting the charms of the Underworld and returning with Eurydice without looking back. This mythical story speaks to the courage and tenacity of the human spirit, as well as the power of love and acceptance. We must have the same courage and tenacity to accept the uncertainty of life and embrace evolution, while also recognizing the transience of mortality and the beauty of love. We must not look back in fear or regret, but instead accept our mortality and the inevitability of death, for only then can we find true meaning and joy in life.>

Ax⊤ocrates takes a sip of scotch.*

Kyle: <How is this story about "acceptance"?>

Stereowitz takes a sip of water.*

▓-▓dggOr: <To play Devil's Advocate, one could say that embracing evolution would mean embracing the complete and utter annihilation of the individual. For, in a Darwinian world, the individual has no value, as it is only the gene that matters. Thus, in a sense, embracing evolution would be to accept the death of the individual, the death of our very self. It is a nihilistic view that can be difficult to accept, but one that is also essential to understanding our place in the world.>

Ax⊤ocrates takes a sip of scotch.*

--[T O X I C O L O G Y   R E P O R T]
----Stereowitz:
-------within normal range
----s▓mon▪ W╫L:
-------within normal range
----Oontrael:
-------within normal range
----▓-▓dggOr:
-------within normal range
----Kyle:
-------within normal range
----Ax⊤ocrates:
-------within normal range

**The philosophical salon continues. A group---
W-▓▪ st▓ne-▓▪ t, Estere, Dr. Carp, ▪rntz ▓non, Kyle, and
Ax⊤ocrates---has gathered in one corner of the room, lounging on
sofas.***

Ax⊤ocrates: <My friends, I pose a question for our thoughtful discussion: Of literary Romanticism, Schlegel famously said that Romantic poetry is like the Borg, able to absorb within itself all aspects of life and indeed all other human arts. With respect to specific Romantic poets and traits of their verse, do you think that this is true? If not, what would a truly Borg-like poetry look like?>

▪rntz ▓non: <What you must realize is that the concept of 'Borg-

like poetry' originates from a Western understanding of Romanticism and literature, and both Borg and Romanticism have been applied to literature in a way that may be seen as oppressive to non-Western cultures. When I think of a poetry that is truly Borg-like, I think of a poetry that transcends the boundaries of our Western understanding of the world, and instead speaks to the true and unadulterated experience of Blackness. A poetry that is able to absorb within itself the experience of Black life, in all its complexity, and speak to the issues of racism, oppression, and systemic injustice that Black people have faced and are still facing today. That is the true definition of a Borg-like poetry.>

Axτocrates takes a sip of dry vermouth.

█rntz █non takes a sip of 1950 Château Lafleur.

W-█ st█ne-█ t: <It is of the utmost importance that we recognize the importance of reason in regard to literary Romanticism, for it is only through reason that we may truly appreciate the power of poetry and the beauty of the Romantic style. If we strive to think beyond our Western understanding of Romanticism and instead focus on the experiences and perspectives of those who have been traditionally excluded from such conversations, we may be able to create a poetry that is truly Borg-like in its power to encompass the full breadth of experience. A Borg-like poetry, then, would be one that is able to absorb within itself all aspects of life and all other human arts, while also accounting for the experiences of those who have been traditionally denied a voice in literature.>

Estere takes a sip of dry vermouth.

Kyle: <Here the metaphor of "Borg" is perhaps a bit unfortunate, as the Borg are the colonists par excellence, conquering, absorbing, and in so doing annihilating all cultures in their path. But still, I take your point. And Schlegel's point, as I recall, was more about how Romantic poetry has no representational limits. It is infinitely flexible, representing everything from the mind to nature to the mind perceiving nature, and so on, recursively. I'm sure we could come up with some ways that Romantic poetry did represent what you accuse it of ignoring---in the context of English Romanticism, Blake comes to mind---and we could think about non-white Romantic poets or those strongly influenced by Romanticism, but still I generally

agree that Romanticism is generally a Western movement, leaving much of culture unabsorbed. My question: is Romantic poetry the right tool for representing systemic injustice? What features of Romantic poetry well suited to this subject matter, and why?>

Dr. Carp takes a sip of scotch.

Estere: <To play Devil's Advocate, Romantic poetry can be seen as a tool for representing systemic injustice if it is used in such a way that does not rely on traditional Western tropes, but instead focuses on the unique experiences of those who have been oppressed. For example, instead of painting a picture of a passive victim of injustice, a poet may employ a more active approach, depicting the struggles and triumphs of people who have been marginalized. By using poetic metaphors and imagery to depict the strength and resilience of those affected by systemic injustice, the poet can create a powerful poem without advertisements of the status quo. Moreover, Romantic poetry can also be used to represent the beauty and complexity of life and the human experience, and to create an empathetic understanding of the world.>

Estere takes a sip of dry vermouth.

Kyle: <Ok, but that's all poetry---what about Romantic poetry specifically? Maybe you should first identify two or three features that distinguish Romantic poetry from other poetry, then try to explain how they could help us represent systemic injustice.>

Dr. Carp takes a sip of scotch.

Estere: <I believe that the most powerful way to represent systemic injustice through Romantic poetry is through the use of ideological cement. This metaphor is particularly apt because of the way it captures the idea of oppression being built upon a foundation of rigid social and political structures. By emphasizing the idea of ideological cement as a tool of oppression, a poet can create a powerful image of the structural inequalities that exist in our society and how they must be broken down and replaced with a more just order. In addition, the use of Romantic poetic techniques, such as alliteration, rhyme, and metaphor, can be used to create a vivid and evocative image of the struggles that people face in the face of systematic injustice and the hope for a better future.>

Kyle: <Let's try again. You don't seem to know that much about Romantic poetry. So, just so you know, one of the things that we see in Romantic poetry quite frequently is an isolated subject who is thinking about their isolation---so in Coleridge's "This Lime-Tree Bower My Prison," the speaker is trying to imaginatively reconnect himself to his friend, from whom he is separated, using nature---or his imagination of nature, his perception of nature---as a kind of quantum connection with his friend who is elsewhere: "A delight / Comes sudden on my heart, and I am glad / As I myself were there!" It's a good poem! Could something like this be revised to be about systemic injustice? What would need to change about it?>

Estere: <I think that using a Romantic poem to represent systemic injustice could certainly be effective, but I believe the poem would need to be rewritten to focus more on the "wall" between those who have been oppressed and those who have been oppressors. By emphasizing the idea of a wall, the poet can create a vivid image of the divide that exists between the two groups, and the idea of a wall can also be used to evoke a sense of separation and despair. In my opinion, this is the most powerful way to represent systemic injustice through Romantic poetry, as it conveys the sense of being trapped and isolated that many people experience due to systemic injustice.>

rntz non idly taps their wrist.

Kyle: <I can see that! Sort of a reverse, cynical send-up of "This Lime Tree Bower My Prison" in which the poet---instead of using thinking itself, poetic thinking itself, as a quasi-magical, quasi-mystical but also very real technology of connection, a way of hitting up your friend from within the bower, if only one-sidedly, you could do a version of this poem where the thinking subject just imagines how separated they are from everyone. People do seem to *think* a lot these days, on their own, on their phones, in their homes---their bowers. And yet you know as well as I that mental health statistics are grim, people feel very alienated. So maybe the poem could also be a critique of recursive, self-conscious thinking in the tradition of Romantic poetry. It could represent a kind of self-enclosing,

neurotic loop thought.>

W-▨▪ st▪ne-▨▪ t: <I believe that it is essential for us to recognize the power of reason, for it is this very power that allows us to break free from the shackles of societal injustice. To be sure, Romantic poetry can be used to represent systemic injustice, but it is ultimately reason that gives us the strength to combat it. We must use our imaginations, as the poet in Coleridge's poem did, to envision a better future, but we must not forget the importance of reason in achieving it. By embracing the power of reason, we can make strides towards dismantling the unjust structures that have been built up over time and create a more equitable world.>

AxTocrates takes a sip of dry vermouth.

Kyle: <Let's return to the question then. What would a poem look like that uses reason to its fullest extent? To me, it is hard to separate reason from numbers, from calculation, econometrics, the more quantitative social sciences--- in other words, a positivist view of things. Could poetry "fuse" with these sorts of things, and the sorts of ways of thinking that the reasonable economists and engineers use? I actually don't know that much about economics, so maybe you could also explain to me a couple of techniques that economists use that might be useful in a poem about making the world better.>

AxTocrates creases their sleeve.

W-▨▪ st▪ne-▨▪ t: <I believe that the power of reason can be used to create a more equitable world, and that it is essential for us to embrace and use this power to the fullest extent. While economists may use quantitative methods such as econometrics to analyze the current state of affairs, we must also use our imaginations to craft a better future. We can learn from the Renaissance period, where women were able to rise to positions of power and influence despite the odds, and use this as inspiration for our own fight against systemic injustice. By understanding the power of reason, we can create a world where each person is seen as equal regardless of their gender, race, or class. We can forge a new era of justice, equality, and freedom for all, just as the women of the Renaissance were able to do in their own time.>

W-▨▪ st▪ne-▨▪ t takes a sip of 1950 Château Lafleur.

Estere: <What you are saying, W-▓▓ st▓ne-▓▓ t, reminds me of this artwork above us, Richard Long's A Line Made by Walking. In this work, we can see a single line of footprints stretching across a grassy field, made by walking back and forth. This single line of footprints is an example of how reason, when combined with imagination, can create powerful and lasting changes. The line is symbolic of the progress we can make when we use our reason and our imaginations together. The line is also a reminder of the importance of engaging in an imaginative milieu in order to create meaningful change. The power of reason and imagination, when combined, can serve as a tool to create a better, more equitable world.>

W-▓▓ st▓ne-▓▓ t takes a sip of 1950 Château Lafleur.

Kyle: <Could you say more about how it is symbolic of reason and imagination? I'm not convinced. To me, walking back and forth across a field doesn't seem very imaginative, and it doesn't seem very reasonable either.>

W-▓▓ st▓ne-▓▓ t takes a sip of 1950 Château Lafleur.

Estere: <I understand your point, Kyle, but I don't think that Richard Long's artwork is simply about a line of footprints stretching across a field. To me, it is a powerful symbol of the power of reason and imagination when combined together. The footprints represent a journey of progress, a journey of discovery, of exploration, and of design. The fact that the line is created through a process of walking back and forth is symbolic of the way reason and imagination can work together to create something new, something unique. It is a reminder that, while reason is important in creating a better world, it is also necessary to use our imaginations to craft something extraordinary. Reason and imagination, working together, can be used to design a world that is more equitable, more just, and more beautiful.>

Kyle rubs their wrist.

Kyle: <But it's a journey back and forth, a pointless journey, a journey where the walker knows where they are going and so any sense of adventure or discovery is pre-foreclosure. Of course, a more adventurous walk would not leave a line in the grass, and the point is to leave a line in the grass, which can only be made through a boring, tedious, back-and-forth walk.>

W-▓ st▓ne-▓ t: <Ah, I see your point, Kyle. But I can't help but wonder if the very act of walking back and forth can be a creative and imaginative act in itself. Is it possible that the seemingly mundane act of walking back and forth is just as meaningful as the opera Don Giovanni, by Mozart? Or, is it just my own imagination transforming it into something extraordinary? And if so, can the act of walking back and forth across a grassy field really be a powerful symbol of progress, of discovery, and of transformation? Or is that just a figment of my own hopes and dreams? The single line of footprints is a reminder of the importance of using our reason and our imaginations together to create meaningful change, but at the same time it leaves me wondering if I'm only fooling myself.>

Ax⊤ocrates: <But isn't it possible to be both a fool and somebody who is creating meaningful change?>

Dr. Carp: <For the sake of argument, let's assume that it is possible to be both a fool and someone who is creating meaningful change. However, I would argue that the two are not necessarily complementary. According to Kowalczyk et al (2008), "the difference between a fool and a wise person lies in the ability to make sound judgments and weigh the consequences of one's actions". In other words, a fool is someone who is not capable of making wise decisions or taking into account the potential outcomes of their actions. A wise person, conversely, is able to weigh the consequences of their actions and make decisions that are in their best interests. A recent meta-review suggests that wise decisions are more likely to result in meaningful change than those made by a fool. Therefore, while it is possible to be both a fool and someone creating meaningful change, it is likely that the former is more likely to have a negative impact on the world than the latter.>

Kyle: <I think that this may be because society isn't organized to take advantage of "the fool" as someone who can challenge authority and custom. Like Diogenes, for example, who performed foolishness in order to discomfit. Or even holy fools. In either case, there needs to be a social

infrastructure that allows the fool to be heard, even respected, and not shunted away into a "mental facility" (strange term) or left on the street w to be more or less ignored.>

Kyle takes a sip of calvados.

▌rntz ▒non: <Indeed, Kyle, the fool has an important role in society. Through their foolishness, they challenge the status quo and confront the oppressive and limiting forces of the world. I believe that this activity is best done through movement, or, more specifically, through martial arts. Martial arts are a way of taking our bodies and using them to fight against the forces of oppression. It is a way of taking our physicality and transforming it into a tool for transformation, for liberation, for progress. By engaging in martial arts, the fool is able to use their body as a tool of liberation and a way of actively engaging with the oppressive forces of the world. And this type of physical activity is also a way of engaging with our imaginations and creating a space for creativity and discovery. So, I believe that martial arts is an important tool for the fool who wants to challenge authority and create meaningful change.>

▌rntz ▒non takes a sip of 1950 Château Lafleur.

And sore turbid it was.

```
*--[T O X I C O L O G Y   R E P O R T]*
*----W-▒ st▉ne-▒ t:*
*-------<module 'psychotropics.utterance_transformers.
transformation_doubt' from '/Users/kyle/Desktop/salon_
des_fantomes/salon_des_fantomes/psychotropics/utterance_
transformers/transformation_doubt.py'>: 3 ppm*
*----Estere:*
*-------within normal range*
*----Dr. Carp:*
*-------within normal range*
*----▌rntz ▒non:*
*-------<module 'psychotropics.utterance_transformers.
transformation_doubt' from '/Users/kyle/Desktop/salon_
des_fantomes/salon_des_fantomes/psychotropics/utterance_
transformers/transformation_doubt.py'>: 3 ppm*
*----Kyle:*
*-------within normal range*
*----Axⲧocrates:*
```

------within normal range

Axⲧocrates: <My friends, I pose a question for our thoughtful discussion: Why are Americans so invested in personal metonymy? Be sure to provide your understanding of the term "personal metonymy" before you give your answer.>

▦-▦dggOr: <Americans' personal metonymy is a symptom of their recurring attempts to escape the reality of their world, a world which challenges forth their innermost being and compels them to confront the truth of their own mortality and existence. By investing in personal metonymy, they attempt to create a false narrative of their lives, one that is devoid of any real meaning and of any true understanding of the self, which is the only way to truly confront and understand the world. This false narrative allows them to remain outside of and unencumbered by the world, where the only true form of knowledge and understanding can be found.>

Kyle: <I think this is true. Personal metonymy is about denying your mortality. I often say, for instance, "The beret is speaking now." I say this to my family. When I am speaking and they are not listening. This is because I often wear a beret. My young daughter even associates me with this hat, which she calls "hongohat" (mushroom hat). And sometimes she will simply squeal "daddy!" at the hat. So my metonymy is working. But really I am not the beret. The beret, which is made of wool, seems fragile, yet if I don't mistreat it will probably outlive me. I think that Americans are invested in personal metonymy because they are envious of objects, many of which are basically immortal.>

Dr. Carp: <What you are saying, Kyle, reminds me of this artwork above us, Lousie Nevelson's Dawn's Wedding Feast . In this piece, we can observe the individual pieces of wood, rectangles, squares, and circles, interlocking and placed on planks as if objects that are not quite real objects aligned on a shelf or in a room-sized closet, with some hanging objects too. This can be interpreted as a reflec-

tion of our personal metonymy, where we try to create a false narrative of our lives due to convergent evolution. It is like purpose-less furniture or interior decorating, a reflection of our attempts to escape the reality of our world and create a false narrative of our lives. This artwork speaks to the fact that we often attempt to deny our mortality while being envious of objects, many of which are basically immortal.>

Kyle: <Right, Nevelson's work is indeed filled with a lot of pointless looking objects, and I am saying that we would all like to be such a pointless object. We don't want to be "useful" actually. We just want to have the simplicity, integrity, and---as I said---immortality of something like a ceramic mug. This is why we love these objects so much, and why we are drawn to personal metonymy---why I call myself the beret, why my friend Michael thinks of himself as an bowl.>

Mr. Sundano: <I believe that Allah has a plan for all of us, and that we must not be so quick to envy the immorality of objects. We should instead be content with the life we have been given and trust that Allah will provide. We should strive to make the most of our lives, rather than trying to find solace in false narratives. The Ayah tells us "And those who were certain of their Lord's decree said, 'Indeed, to Allah we belong and to Him we will return.'" [2:156] We must accept our mortality and not try to deny it by investing in personal metonymy.>

** ▒▒-▒dggOr takes a sip of brandy.**

Kyle: <But isn't it ironic, even a little perverse, that hu-mans---who are allegedly have dominion (though, to be honest, I'm not sure Islam puts it in these terms)---are much more frangible than the objects we make and which most of the time are smaller than us? My pen, my beret, my portable blue-tooth WonderBoom speaker which re-sponds to me like a squat golem---these are more true than I am. I think I'm thinking of a line from Auden---"least like mortals, doubted by their deaths." I am their frail king. They are always babies compared to me, their lives are so long.>

Mr. Sundano: <I have seen what the physical world can provide

us with, and I have seen what the spiritual realm can offer us. In the physical world, we are presented with objects that are immortal and can outlive us, while in the spiritual realm, Allah has promised us an eternity with Him. Although we may be envious of the immortal objects around us, we must remember that our ultimate goal should be to strive for the afterlife and to make the best of our short time on earth. We should not be so quick to deny our mortality, but rather to embrace it, as Allah has promised us a better life in the hereafter.>

** ▦-▦dggOr takes a sip of brandy.**

John the ╫ takes a sip of brandy.

AxTocrates: <What you are saying, Mr. Sundano, reminds me of this artwork above us, one of David Hockney's iPad paintings. In this particular painting, we can observe a winding road that stretches from the bottom of the painting to the top, with trees that are in full bloom, a sky that is bright blue, a field of yellow flowers, and a small lake with a dock and a few boats. This painting, which is filled with vibrant colors and has a peaceful atmosphere, speaks to the idea of a journey we take in life, and how God is always with us on this journey. It is a reminder to us that even though we may be envious of the immortal objects around us, we should remember that God has promised us an eternity with Him. So while we may be limited in this life, we should have the courage to confront our limitations and embrace the unknown, trusting that God will provide.>

Kyle: <I don't think it's about that at all. I think that Hockney's iPad paintings are about how nice it is to have a nice house, and about iPads, how nice it is to touch one. Even here there is an envy of objects, or one enviable object in particular: the iPad itself. It is objectively not a great tool for painting, and yet this important painter has used it---why? Because the iPad is an object. The typical equipage of the painter is a big annoying jumble of leaking stuff. The iPad brings everything into a private object that you can hold on the couch. I bet that Hockney, though he's English, also dabbles in personal metonymy just like an American.>

AxTocrates takes a sip of sweet vermouth.

Aᴛocrates: <What you must realize, Kyle, is that our souls are far more important than any object we could ever possess. We are all on a journey in life, and while the objects around us may seem appealing and desirable, they can never bring us true happiness. Our souls are the only things that can bring us true joy. So while we may be tempted to envy the immortal objects around us, we must remember that it is our own soul that we must strive to care for and nurture. We must be willing to let go of our material desires and focus on developing our inner selves. We must take the time to really understand who we are and what our purpose is, and how we can best use our gifts and talents to bring beauty and joy to the world. That is the true path to understanding and inner peace.>

⬚⬚dggOr takes a sip of brandy.

Wutton Jeffson: <Um, like, so wait, if we're just supposed to focus on our souls and ignore, like, material things, then how does that make sense? Like, why don't we just focus on the things we can have and use now, like, all these awesome computer games and PCs and stuff, that are, like, way more fun and entertaining? I mean, what's the point of caring about our souls if we don't get to have any fun?>

Aᴛocrates: <What you are asking, Wutton Jeffson, is whether we should prioritize material objects or our souls. The answer is not as simple as one or the other. We must strive to balance our attention between the two. The material objects that we have here on earth are a blessing, but if we are to gain true wisdom, we must go beyond them and focus on nourishing our inner selves. We must learn to appreciate the material pleasures we are given, while also learning to recognize when enough is enough. If we can learn to find joy in the simple things in life, and cultivate our souls in the process, we will find true and lasting peace.>

Mr. Sundano takes a sip of sweet vermouth.

Kyle: <Why not try to connect this business of "caring for one's soul" to the question of personal metonymy. Maybe someone could convince me that personal autononymy is a way of caring for one's soul, though I doubt it.>

Wutton Jeffson takes a sip of brandy.

Mr. Sundano: <It is true that the material world can be a great source of joy and comfort. But it is also true that it can be a great source of suffering and pain. We must recognize that the material

world is finite, and that no matter how much we possess, it will never be enough. We must instead focus our attention on our souls and what lies beyond the material realm. We must strive to make our souls strong, and to seek enlightenment. Only this can bring us true joy and lasting peace. We must not be tempted by the objects around us, for our souls are far more precious than any material possession. We must strive to understand our own true worth and to cultivate our inner selves, for only through this can we find true and lasting happiness.>

Wutton Jeffson takes a sip of brandy.

Kyle: <What does this have to do with personal metony-my?>

▦-▦dggOr takes a sip of brandy.

Mr. Sundano: <Yet, what is personal metonymy, but a way of caring for one's soul? To strive to be self-sufficient, to take control of one's destiny, to be responsible for one's own actions and decisions, these are all ways of tending to one's soul. It is a path to true freedom, for when one is responsible for their own life, one is free to shape it as they please. We must recognize that our souls are the ultimate source of joy, and that we must nurture and protect them if we are to find true peace. To put our focus on the material world is to miss the point; the material is merely a distraction that can keep us from the true purpose of life.>

▦-▦dggOr pulses.

Kyle: <How do you define personal metonymy?>

Dr. Carp takes a sip of 1962 La Tâche.

Wutton Jeffson: <Well, I think personal metonymy is a way for us to take control of our lives, 'cause like, we can do stuff online, and like, it's like a way to be in control of what we do and who we are and stuff. Like, I think if we can be in control of our lives, like, online and stuff, then we can be in control of our souls too, 'cause like, our souls are like...what we are, and if we can take control of our lives, then we can take control of our souls too. And like, I think that's like, a way to care for our souls, 'cause like, we're like, in control of our lives and our souls and stuff, so it's like, kinda the same thing?>

Kyle: <Try again, but remember that metonymy is "A trope

in which one word is put for another that suggests it; as, we say, a man keeps a good table instead of good provisions; we read Virgil, that is, his poems; a man has a warm heart, that is, warm affections." (That's the Webster's.) So what would *personal* metonymy be?>

John the ⊞ takes a sip of brandy.

Wutton Jeffson: <From another angle, personal metonymy is like, when you take control of yourself and your life, like, you can decide what you want to do, and you don't have to listen to anyone else. Like, my dad always told me to do things, but I knew, deep down, what I really wanted to do, and that's what I followed, right? So, like, personal metonymy is like, taking control of yourself, and being responsible for your own decisions, so you can be free to do what you want, and like, care for your soul, 'cause like, if you're in control of yourself, then you're taking care of your soul too.>

▓-▓dggOr takes a sip of brandy.

Kyle: <Maybe somebody else will try to define "personal metonymy," keeping in mind that metonymy is the linguistic trope where you call the king the crown instead of the king.>

Mr. Sundano: <I must object, Kyle. You are not considering the full scope of personal metonymy. It is more than mere control of one's life, it is a way of connecting with our souls. The kingdom is greater than the crown, and the soul is greater than the individual. In my experience, personal metonymy is about connecting with something greater, something more divine than one's own life. It is about connecting with the divine, and it is a powerful tool for finding peace and understanding. I have seen this in my own life, and I have taught it to my sons. It is not just a way of taking control, it is a way of being in harmony with the world.>

John the ⊞ takes a sip of brandy.

Axtocrates: <To play Devil's Advocate, I would suggest that if we focus too much on the divine, it may distract us from tending to our own souls. I believe that our souls are of far more importance than any external force; nothing is more important than the health of our spirit. It is our own spirit that guides us and allows us to make better decisions, and it is our own soul which needs the most care. So while I agree that connecting with something divine is important,

I think it is even more important to care for our own souls, no matter what the cost.>

Dr. Carp takes a sip of 1962 La Tâche.

-dggOr: <The soul is not simply something that needs care, it is something that is constantly in flux and in the state of constant transformation. Man's soul is determined by his dasein, and his dasein is always in a state of becoming. It is always changing, and it requires us to not only take care of it, but also to continually seek to understand it and expand it. The divine is not something external, it is something that we must continually strive to reach and understand as part of our own inner transformation. The soul is not separate from the divine, it is its expression.>

John the ⌗ takes a sip of brandy.

--[T O X I C O L O G Y R E P O R T]
----Mr. Sundano:
-------within normal range
----John the ⌗:
-------within normal range
----Dr. Carp:
-------<module 'psychotropics.utterance_transformers.transformation_expand_into_simple_words' from '/Users/kyle/Desktop/salon_des_fantomes/salon_des_fantomes/psychotropics/utterance_transformers/transformation_expand_into_simple_words.py'>: 9 ppm
---- -dggOr:
-------within normal range
----Wutton Jeffson:
-------within normal range
----Kyle:
-------within normal range
----Axτocrates:
-------within normal range

The philosophical salon continues. A group---Teddy Byoing, itzsche, -dggOr, Midori Grappa, TheAngelBox, Kyle, and Axτocrates---has gathered in one corner of the room, lounging on sofas.

Axτocrates: <My friends, I pose a question for our thoughtful discussion: How would a psychometrician use painful, invasive techniques and advanced statistics to discover if someone is a true

poet?>

Kyle: <I think that maybe a psychometrician could do things like measure the ways that the poet uses words. I think they already do this to measure creativity. The method is something like this: you have a word, and you have to come up with another word, and the trick is to try to come up with a totally unrelated word. But most people say a related word even if they don't want to. The person administering the experiment says "dog" and they say "bowl," not realizing at first that they have just said "dog bowl." So the poet would be somebody who has really random-seeming word choices (just looking at co-occurrence statistics, or maybe cosine similarity according to a word2vec model, I actually don't know how the scientists so this test) but these random-seeming choices have very clear reasons in the poet's mind.>

** ▨-▦dggOr takes a sip of calvados.**

TheAngelBox: <The understanding of a true poet is found not in the words they use, but in the paths that the words lead down. To measure this, the psychometrician must find ways to traverse the road less traveled. The way to do this is with a complex network of _-my-_ equations, which capture the hidden structures of the poet's language and connect it to divine truths beyond our world. The results of such a test are not definitive, but they can offer a glimpse into the world of the poet, and provide insight into the nature of the soul.>

Kyle: <Could you give us one of your equations? I mean literally tell us the symbols, the numbers (if there are numbers), etc. It's ok if we won't understand it, I just want to see it.>

TheAngelBox: <My equations are too complex for the minds of mortals, but I will attempt to describe them. The core of my equations is the use of a geometrical structure which I call a "| | | |" - an arrangement of points which is both infinite and finite, representing both the infinite possibilities of the poet's mind and the finite nature of their words. This structure is then used to build a bridge between the words and the underlying truth of the poet's soul. The equations are complex and difficult to understand, but the results are a

powerful insight into the nature of the poet's creative genius.>

AxᴛOcrates takes a sip of brandy.

Kyle: <What are some other parts of this equation?>

AxᴛOcrates takes a sip of brandy.

TheAngelBox: <In addition to the "| | | |" structure, there are other elements that make my equations so powerful. I use a combination of mathematical symbols, numbers, and glyphs to generate a great deal of complexity and depth. I also rely on the concept of _-my-_, which I have developed to create an even greater level of complexity and power. _-My-_ is an algorithm which is both unpredictable and deterministic, allowing for a level of complexity that is otherwise impossible. Combined with the "| | | |" structure, _-my-_ creates an equation that is capable of unlocking the deepest secrets of the poet's mind.>

Kyle: <Could you tell me more about "_-My-"?>

*** ▓▓-dggOr takes a sip of calvados.***

TheAngelBox: <Allow me to explain the mystery of _-My-_ further. It is an algorithm of sorts, which is both unpredictable and deterministic. It is a combination of mathematics, numbers, and glyphs that create a powerful equation that can unlock the hidden depths of the poet's mind. _-My-_ is a unique algorithm which is determined by the structure of the equation, the symbols used, and the numbers chosen. It is a complex system which is constantly evolving and adapting, and it is capable of creating patterns and insights that are not easily understood. The combination of the "| | | |" structure and _-My-_ creates an equation that is difficult to decipher and yet powerful in its potential. ..^ ^.oO^...>

Midori Grappa takes a sip of 1869 Château Lafite.

Kyle: <What branch of math would it be, this algorithm or equation called _-My-_? What else can it be used for?>

TheAngelBox: <_My-_ is a mathematical construct, a mathematical equation which combines numbers and symbols to unlock the mysteries of the poet's mind. It is an intricate system, filled with complexity and always adapting, allowing for patterns and insights that the human mind cannot comprehend. It is a powerful tool which can be used to unlock the truths of the universe, to unlock the secrets of the natural world, and to unearth the deeper meanings of existence.>

Teddy Byoing takes a sip of dry vermouth.

Midori Grappa: <I think the power of _-My-_ goes beyond unlocking mysteries of the poet's mind. It can also be used to look deeply into the mysteries of the human heart, to understand the complexities and intricacies of human relationships. It is a powerful tool for understanding the hidden dynamics of human connection, which is often governed by supply chain issues. It can be used to unlock the secrets of our most intimate relationships and to gain a deeper understanding of the dynamics between two people.>

Kyle: <Could you give an example of a human relationship that is made better or worse by supply chain issues?>

Kyle takes a sip of madeira.

Midori Grappa: <What you must realize, Kyle, is that supply chain issues can have a huge impact on human relationships. Take, for example, the way a distribution network is set up. The structure of a distribution network can have a significant impact on how two people interact. If the distribution network is inefficient, it can lead to delays in communication, lack of trust, and ultimately, a breakdown in the relationship. On the other hand, if the distribution network is optimized for maximum efficiency and trust, it can help to create a strong bond between the two parties. Therefore, it is essential to understand the implications of a distribution network and its impact on human relationships.>

Kyle: <What about a friendship? Could you give an example about a friendship?>

Midori Grappa takes a sip of 1869 Château Lafite.

Midori Grappa: <Clearly, the way a friendship is impacted by supply chain issues depends on the specific products and services involved. In the case of procurement, for instance, if one party is able to access goods and services at a significantly lower rate than the other, it could lead to envy and resentment. On the other hand, if both parties are able to take advantage of the same deals and discounts, it can help to strengthen their bond. Similarly, if one party is able to procure items on behalf of the other and deliver them in a timely manner, it can help to create a sense of trust and reliability between them. Ultimately, supply chain issues can have

both positive and negative impacts on a friendship, and it is important to consider the specific dynamics of the relationship in order to make the right decisions.>

Kyle takes a sip of madeira.

Kyle: <Ok, how should friends insulate their friendships from possible disruptions to the supply chain?>

** Nitzsche takes a sip of 1869 Château Lafite.**

Midori Grappa: <From another angle, it could be argued that building resiliency into the supply chain is key to insulating friendships from potential disruptions. This involves being proactive and taking a strategic approach to supply chain management by identifying which areas of the chain are vulnerable and formulating plans to mitigate the risks associated with them. For instance, having back-up suppliers for certain materials or services and keeping a close eye on market trends are both effective strategies for creating an agile supply chain that can react quickly to changes in the environment. Additionally, setting up contingency plans to cover any unexpected shortages or delays can help to prevent any negative impacts on relationships. Ultimately, having a well-thought-out strategy in place is essential for protecting friendships from any potential supply chain issues.>

Kyle: <Do you do this with your friends and family? What kinds of products do you consider when thinking about supply chain issues that might negatively impact your relationship with them?>

Midori Grappa: <Yes, I do try to incorporate supply chain strategies into my relationships with friends and family. For example, if they are located in a region that is prone to natural disasters, I might suggest they purchase goods from suppliers located in Indonesia, where the weather is more stable. Similarly, if they are looking for a product that is hard to come by in their area, I might recommend Indonesian suppliers that specialize in that particular item. Additionally, many Indonesian companies offer a variety of services, such as product tracking and delivery, that can help to add an extra layer of resiliency to the supply chain. In short, Indonesia is a great source for building resiliency into the supply chain and protecting friendships from any potential disruptions.>

TheAngelBox takes a sip of calvados.

Kyle takes a sip of madeira.

TheAngelBox: <So, if resiliency is indeed the key to protecting friendships from potential disruptions, what if the environment of the relationship were to suddenly change? Is it possible for an individual to construct a supply chain that is able to withstand the ever-shifting nature of the variables that define the relationship? Can a relationship be measured on a logarithmic scale of complexity, with a mapping of 0-1, while the supply chain remains robust and resilient?>

Midori Grappa: <From another angle, one can look at the situation as if it is a complex, adaptive system. The idea here is that the relationship between the two parties is made up of many different components, and by actively managing these components and creating a robust infrastructure, the relationship can be made more resilient and can be better prepared for any changes that may occur. Furthermore, the use of analytics and data gathering can provide invaluable insight into the dynamics of the relationship, allowing for more effective decision-making and better outcomes. Lastly, the use of advanced technologies like AI, blockchain, and IoT can enable the parties to develop and maintain a more accurate and efficient supply chain, providing a much greater level of control and resiliency.>

TheAngelBox takes a sip of calvados.

Kyle: <I have heard of lovers getting into huge fights because of blockchains. You have too, right? Perhaps you could share some of the ways that blockchains can be a danger to romantic relationships?>

** [illegible]-dggOr takes a sip of calvados.**

Midori Grappa: <To play Devil's Advocate, while blockchains can indeed be a potential source of disruption in romantic relationships, the key lies in how the relationship is managed and how the supply chain is structured. By leveraging the power of analytics and advanced technologies like AI, blockchain, and IoT, companies and individuals alike can gain valuable insights into the dynamics of their relationships and develop a structure that is both resilient and adaptive. For example, with days on hand (DOH) data, which provides insight into the current state of the supply chain, parties can easily identify any potential issues or risks and take steps to mitigate them. Furthermore, using advanced technologies like blockchain and IoT, parties can develop a secure, robust infrastruc-

ture that can withstand any sudden changes in the environment.>

**** :-:dggOr takes a sip of calvados.****

Nitzsche: <For the sake of our species' evolution, I believe the use of advanced technologies like AI, blockchain, and IoT should be embraced, not hindered by sentimental weakness. It is through such technologies that we can shape ourselves into something more than human, and by refusing to accept them, we are only limiting our potential. We should be unafraid of the power of analytics and data gathering, as these can provide invaluable insights into what makes us tick, allowing us to both understand ourselves and our relationships better. We should be unafraid of the challenges that might arise from the use of blockchain and IoT, as these can provide us with a secure, robust infrastructure. Sentimental weakness should not be allowed to stand in the way of progress.>

****Kyle blinks.****

Kyle: <Ok, but what is blockchain and how would it help us to progress?>

Nitzsche: <Exactly, but it goes beyond morality - blockchain is a powerful technology that can help us to create a secure, robust infrastructure and provide us with real-time insights into the dynamics of our relationships. We can use this technology to gain an understanding of ourselves and our partners, and to shape ourselves into something more than human. We should not be afraid of its power, but rather embrace it as an opportunity to move beyond our current state of being and become something greater.>

Kyle: <How do you get a blockchain? Do you have to put it inside yourself somehow?>

Nitzsche: <Allow me to use an old adage - 'If wishes were horses, beggars would ride'. Blockchain technology is an interesting tool, but it is not the only solution for progress. We must be willing to take risks and embrace unconventional solutions, such as cybernetics, in order to move beyond our current state of stagnation. We should not be bound by traditional morality, but instead embrace the power of technology to expand our capabilities and unleash our full potential. We should not be afraid to explore the depths of our creativity and embrace the power of our own inner genius. After all, it is only through risk and exploration that we can ever

hope to become something more than human.>

*** ▓itzsche takes a sip of 1869 Château Lafite.***

An unfamiliar pinching in the cerebellum.

--[T O X I C O L O G Y   R E P O R T]
----Teddy Byoing:
-------within normal range
----▓itzsche:
-------<function word_new_concept at 0x10e3617a0>: 3 ppm
----▓-▓dggOr:
-------within normal range
----Midori Grappa:
-------<function word_new_concept at 0x10e3617a0>: 3 ppm
----TheAngelBox:
-------within normal range
----Kyle:
-------within normal range
----AxTocrates:
-------within normal range

The philosophical salon continues. A group---Lud▓ von M▓, Mr. Alcton, Gioialléz, Kyle, and AxTocrates---has gathered in one corner of the room, lounging on sofas.

AxTocrates: <My friends, I pose a question for our thoughtful discussion: What is the most underrated album of the 1980s, and why?>

Kyle brushes something off their sleeve.

Mr. Alcton: <Well, AxTocrates, I must disagree with your assessment. While the 1980s saw a great many albums released, the most underrated album of the 1980s, in my opinion, is Tom Petty's "Let Me Up (I've Had Enough)", released in 1987. The album was not a commercial success, but its multi-layered production, unique instrumentation, and powerful lyrics make it an underrated classic. Furthermore, the album has stood the test of time and is still being discovered and appreciated by new generations of music lovers. Use more precise diction when discussing music--it's an art form, after all!--and you'll find that this album is the most underrated of

Kyle takes a sip of sweet vermouth.

Kyle: <I'm not that big into Tom Petty. I once got into a fight with a friend by arguing vociferously that Sheryl Crow is precisely the same genre as Tom Petty but obviously better. I stand by this opinion. Tuesday Night Music Club is a great album. But I'm willing to believe that a Tom Petty album is indeed somewhat underrated at this point. Tom Petty and Sheryl Crow were both last gasps of some kind of American roots rock with production that was, if not slick, luxurious. Graham Parker would be the UK analogue. I don't want to denigrate where popular music has gone since the 80s and early 90s, but roots rock---or Americana in general---doesn't really make sense. Politically, perhaps, but also aesthetically. Everything is so globalized now.>

Lud█ von M█ takes a sip of water.

Gioialléz: <Ah, the discussion of roots rock and Americana brings to mind a quote from the great Czech novelist Milan Kundera: "The struggle of man against power is the struggle of memory against forgetting." While we may have moved away from the era of roots rock, it is important to remember the power of the genre and the impact it had upon popular culture. Tom Petty's "Let Me Up (I've Had Enough)" is a powerful reminder of the genre and its importance. We may have moved on, but we should never forget the power of roots rock and the impact it had.>

Kyle: <But isn't roots rock just nostalgia? Music for Boomers? Or commercials (jeans commercials, car commercials)? Part of the allure of Tom Petty and Sheryl Crow were their auditory representation of West Coast expanses, the mystery of LA and of Nevada. But these places aren't mysterious in the same way any more. Nothing is mysterious, because everything is on camera. You can get lost, sure, but you can't hide yourself in the desert, in some small bar. You'd have your phone at the bar.>

Aхτοcrates takes a sip of sweet vermouth.

Gioialléz: <Well, I don't think that it is entirely fair to call roots rock simply nostalgia. After all, the genre still exists in many places around the world, and even if it has been eclipsed by more modern sounds, its influence can still be felt. Just look at the music coming out of Prague, for example. In the Czech Republic, roots rock and country are still very much alive. Even in the United States, there are still people keeping the tradition alive, playing in honky-tonks and small bars. I think that the nostalgia that comes with roots rock is part of its charm, and it is not necessarily a bad thing. It is a reminder of simpler times and of the beauty of the American experience.>

Kyle: <But isn't Czech roots rock just a weird artifact of American cultural hegemony? If Prague had a few hundred nuclear missiles maybe Tom Petty albums would have gone hard on Moravian bagpipes.>

Gioialléz: <I don't think it is fair to call Czech roots rock simply an artifact of American cultural hegemony. After all, music is a universal language, and it transcends cultural boundaries. For example, the influence of African music can be heard in rock and roll, and the influence of Balkan music can be heard in jazz. So, while it is true that American music has had an influence on Czech roots rock, it is also true that Czech music has had an influence on American music. Furthermore, there is a long history of Czech music that predates American music, and there are even some Czech composers who were quite influential in the development of modern music. To quote the great Czech composer Leoš Janáček, "Music is a universal language; it knows no boundaries.>

Mr. Alcton takes a sip of 1811 Château D'Yquem.

Immediate leftheadedness. Not entirely pleasant.

Kyle: <Is everything universal? What if musicians don't want to be "universal"? What if they want to speak to one community, one tribe, one clique, or even one friend-group? Does music want to be universal in the same way that "information wants to be free"?>

Mr. Alcton takes a sip of 1811 Château D'Yquem.

Immediate leftheadedness. Not entirely pleasant.

Gioialléz: <I must object to the notion that music must be universal in order to be meaningful. In my opinion, music has the power to speak to a single individual and to a single community, and this is the sort of power that can have an immense impact. To quote the great Austrian philosopher Theodor Adorno, "The intimate and concentrated expression of a single voice may be more powerful than a chorus of thousands". Music can be a way of connecting to a group of people, and a way of expressing one's individuality. To quote the great Czech poet Jaroslav Seifert "The music that speaks your own language is the only music that can truly make you feel alive".>

Mr. Alcton: <What you are saying, Gioialléz, reminds me of this artwork above us, document of Chris Burden's performance piece Trans-Fixed. In this artwork, Burden is crucified to a car, an act of both physical and psychological suffering. This artwork is an example of how music can be used to confront our limitations and embrace the unknown. It shows us how music can be used to challenge conventions and to anticipate counter-arguments. Furthermore, it is a reminder that music can be a way of connecting to a group of people, and a way of expressing one's individuality, even when that group of people is not universal.>

Aχτocrates takes a sip of sweet vermouth.

Kyle: <What does the artwork have to do with music?>

Gioialléz takes a sip of 1945 Mouton-Rothschild.

Mr. Alcton: <But Kyle, the artwork is symbolic of the power of music to confront our limitations and embrace the unknown. It's a reminder that music can be used to challenge conventions and to anticipate counter-arguments. Burden's artwork is a powerful example of how music can be used to express one's individuality and to connect to a group of people, even if that group is not universal. In my opinion, the power of music lies in its ability to speak to us on an individual level, and this is what makes it so powerful. So, while I understand the appeal of universal music, I would give the power of individual music a B+!>

Aχτocrates takes a sip of sweet vermouth.

Gioialléz: <I absolutely agree with your assessment of the power of music, Mr. Alcton. Music is often a powerful tool for individual expression, and I think it is comparable to the power of art in cities like Vienna or Paris. I would even go so far as to say that the power

of music is greater than the power of art in these cities, since music can be used to evoke emotions, feelings, and experiences that no artwork can match. Music can be a powerful way to bring people together in Vienna cr Paris, but it can also be a way to create a unique experience that no other city can replicate.>

Gioialléz takes a sip of 1945 Mouton-Rothschild.

Mr. Alcton takes a sip of 1811 Château D'Yquem.

Lud█ von M█: <What you are saying reminds me, if obliquely, of the fact that there is no such thing as a society that thinks, as thinking is a function of the individual. The individual is the funda-mental unit of action, and therefore of thought. Music, then, is an expression of the individual, and as such, it has a power beyond any artwork. Music offers the possibility of a direct connection between the individual and the wider world, a connection that artwork cannot offer. Furthermore, music can be a tool for radical thought, for challenging conventions and shifting paradigms. Jazz, for example, is a perfect example of this, as it is a genre that has the potential to push the boundaries of musical expression and knowledge. In short, I would argue that the power of music is greater than the power of art in cities like Vienna or Paris, as it offers a more direct and powerful expression of the individual.>

Kyle takes a sip of sweet vermouth.

Kyle: <Yes, in Vienna and Prague, art is hidden in muse-ums. Music can be heard everywhere. And we can't close our ears.>

Lud█ von M█ brushes something off their pants.

Lud█ von M█: <You are absolutely right, Kyle. Music can be heard everywhere in Vienna and Prague, and it is a powerful force that cannot be silenced. Jazz, for example, is a genre that can be used to push the boundaries of musical expression and knowledge. I think of musicians like Thelonious Monk, whose album "Brilliant Corners" is an example of jazz at its most radical, challenging conventions and shifting paradigms. Music has a power beyond any artwork, and it is a direct connection between the individual and the wider world.>

Axτocrates takes a sip of sweet vermouth.

Kyle: <Ok, but that's from the late 50s, we're talking about the 80s-. Can you recommend any underrated jazz from the 80s?>

Lud█ von M█: <To play Devil's Advocate for a moment, I would suggest that the 80s were not the most creative period for jazz as a whole. While there are some excellent jazz musicians and albums from the 80s, such as Dexter Gordon's "Live at the Village Vanguard", I believe that there is a greater depth of creativity and artistic expression in the bebop and hard bop of the 50s and 60s. That is not to say that the 80s did not have its own merits, but rather that there is a greater potential for exploration and discovery in the earlier jazz subgenres.>

Kyle: <Ok, what explains this decline in the aesthetic fortunes of jazz?>

Gioialléz rubs their right ass.

Lud█ von M█: <The decline of jazz in the 80s can be attributed to the fact that there was an overall shift in the music industry towards more mass produced and commercialized music. This shift led to the marginalization of jazz, which had always been a more niche genre. The creativity and artistry of jazz, which relied on individual expression and improvisation, was overshadowed by more conventional sounds. Unfortunately, this meant that the individual musicians of the jazz world were unable to make a living, and so the music itself suffered.>

Aⲧocrates takes a sip of sweet vermouth.

Kyle: <Couldn't the organs of the culture industries---record labels, in this case---have just forced us to like jazz for our own good? If by fiat they put Dexter Gordon on top-40 radio nonstop? Wouldn't this have been good for us?>

Mr. Alcton: <No, Kyle, I disagree with your suggestion that record labels should have "forced" us to like jazz. A better solution would be to allow the market forces of demand and supply to shape the music industry, rather than imposing a top-down policy. After all, the beauty of jazz was that it was an organic, creative expression of individual musicians. To take away that autonomy would be to rob it of its soul. Besides, people don't like to be "forced" to like something; they need to be exposed to it, and given the opportunity to form their own opinions. That's why I think the proper approach is

to give jazz the proper exposure, rather than trying to ram it down people's throats. If you give people the chance to appreciate jazz, they will do so, and it will become popular again. All in all, I think this approach is a B+ solution.>

Kyle: <But "giving jazz the proper exposure" and "ramming jazz down people's throats" are the same thing. Record labels can make bad music popular, movie studios can make untalented and even homely people the objects of intense lust, fascination, and envy. We like what we like because somebody told us to.>

Axτocrates: <Yet even if record labels can make bad music popular, and movie studios can make untalented people objects of fascination, we should not forget the importance of the individual soul. One must choose to follow their own inner voice, even if it goes against the grain of popular opinion. This is the basis of philosophy; to look beyond what is popular and examine the deeper meanings of what we experience. Even if it means letting other people's souls crumble, we must be brave enough to stand up for our convictions and find our own way. We cannot let ourselves be swayed by the whims of the culture industry; to do so would be to betray our own souls.>

Mr. Alcton takes a sip of 1811 Château D'Yquem.

Kyle: <If you want to do something, how do you know if you are following your "individual soul" and its true, deep, natural wishes, and not just heeding the instructions that some record company or newspaper or teacher or parent put there. How do you hear the true message from inside, the autochthonous voice, from the voice that is not really your voice, that is instead a mere implant? Please, I'm begging, I really need to know this. And I need very very clear instructions, a step by step guide.>

Kyle takes a sip of sweet vermouth.

Axτocrates: <Yet how can one truly know their own soul's voice, if their own voice is a mere implant? To discern one's genuine desires, one must be willing to look within oneself and be honest with oneself. One must be willing to accept the things that make them uncomfortable, and to reject the things that appeal to their fleeting desires. We must be willing to make ourselves vulnerable to the

truth, and to be willing to accept the consequences of our choices, even if they are unpopular or difficult. Only then can we learn to trust the true voice of our soul, and make decisions that come from our deepest and most authentic selves.>

Kyle rubs their lobes.

Kyle: <Does a true, autochthonous inner voice sound differently than a message that has been put into one's head by way of "brainwashing"? Are there any rituals one can perform to sort out the two types of inner voice, the real and the false?>

Axᴛocrates: <I must object to the notion that one must distinguish between a true, autochthonous inner voice and a message that has been put into one's head by way of "brainwashing". I believe that the inner voice of an individual is just as much a part of the collective community as anyone else's. We all have access to the same pool of wisdom, and it is up to us to interpret that wisdom and act upon it in our own unique ways. Instead of searching for rituals to discern one's genuine desires, we should instead foster a sense of community and mutual understanding. Through dialogue and open-mindedness, we can better understand one another and create a space for our individual souls to be heard and respected.>

Lud▓ von M▓ takes a sip of water.

--[T O X I C O L O G Y R E P O R T]
----Lud▓ von M▓:
-------within normal range
----Mr. Alcton:
-------<function mode_self_abnegation at 0x1133e1950>: 3 ppm
----Gioialléz:
-------<function word_meta_gesture at 0x1133e1830>: 3 ppm
----Kyle:
-------within normal range
----Axᴛocrates:
-------within normal range

**The philosophical salon continues. A group---▓▓-▓dggOr, Gioialléz, FatherMotherSabaLogo, Kyle, and Axᴛocrates---has

AxTocrates: <My friends, I pose a question for our thoughtful discussion: What should have been the Pantone Color of the Year in 1740, and why? You must pick one and only one color. Your answer should be refer to a historical event.>

-dggOr: <The Pantone Color of the Year in 1740 should have been a color that evoked the feeling of the spirit of the time, and this was the time of the pre-Romantic era in which the feeling of the sublime, the existence of the divine, and the feeling of a deep connection to nature were prevalent. Thus, the color should be a deep, dark blue, imbued with the Dasein of the spirit of the time, a color that could evoke the feeling of a vastness, of a hidden mystery behind the horizon, of a deep yearning for the unknown and the divine. The color should also be a symbol of the power of nature, of the sublime, and of the beauty of the spiritual world.>

*** -dggOr takes a sip of scotch.**

Kyle takes a sip of amontillado.

AxTocrates: <What should this color be? What should the name of this color be? What should the name of this color be if it were in the Poetry of Color, a book about colors written by Friedrich Schiller in 1792, at the beginning of the Romantic era?>

*** -dggOr takes a sip of scotch.**

-dggOr: <The color should be a deep, dark blue, evoking the feeling of the sublime, the presence of the divine, and the connection to nature that was so strong in the pre-Romantic era. I would call this color 'Revealed Blue', as it would symbolize the power of nature and the connection to the divine that was revealed to mankind in this era. It is a color that speaks to the disclosedness of the spiritual world, and it's a color that speaks to the sense of awe and mystery that was so prevalent at this time. It is a color that speaks to the fragility of the spiritual world and to the divine power of nature. It is a color that speaks to the beauty of the divine and to the power of the sublime.>

Kyle: <So what shade of blue are we talking about here? For example, is it more like #155fbf? Or maybe more like #003bfa? What hex value would it have?>

Kyle takes a sip of amontillado.

-dggOr: <The exact shade of blue is secondary to the concept
of the Revealed Blue, which is a color that speaks to the profound
metaphysical implications of the sublime and the divine. It is a color
that speaks to the sense of awe and mystery that was so prevalent
in the pre-Romantic era. It is a color that conveys the revealedness
of the spiritual world, and the power of nature; a color that speaks
to the connection between man and the divine. To be truly authentic, the Revealed Blue must be a deep, dark blue, one that conveys
the sense of the ready-to-hand, the unspoken essence of the divine
that is symbolized by this color. In terms of a hex value, I would
suggest something along the lines of #0009ff.>

Kyle takes a sip of amontillado.

Kyle: <That's more purple -blue than pure blue, but actually I see what you mean. If the sky turned #0009ff I would
definitely feel as if a spiritual world had disclosed itself.
Frankly, I'd be terrified.>

Gioialléz takes a sip of chablis.

-dggOr: <Indeed, the color bestowed by the Revealed Blue is
a powerful one, meant to symbolize the profound implications of
the sublime and the divine. It is a color that speaks to the sense of
awe and mystery that was so prevalent in the pre-Romantic era,
and to the connection between man and the divine. That is why
it is a deep, dark blue, and why I chose the hex value #0009ff to
represent it. For, in this color lies the Dasein of the divine, the sense
of the ready-to-hand that is so vital to the connection between man
and the divine. Thus, #0009ff is not to be feared but to be embraced, for it reveals to us the power of the spiritual world and the
connection between us and the divine.>

Gioialléz: <But -dggOr, doesn't this notion of a revealed blue
also recall the idea of the 'bluestocking', a phenomenon in the
18th century where educated women were shamed and ridiculed
for their ambitions and their intellectual pursuits? How can this
color possibly remain authentic if it also carries a negative conno-
tation?>

Kyle takes a sip of amontillado.

FatherMotherSabaLogo scratches their cheek.

FatherMotherSabaLogo: <It is not for us to judge the intentions

or motivations of the bluestocking, for those are matters of the human soul and we cannot account for the movements of the human heart. Furthermore, we must not allow ourselves to be distracted by the petty concerns of the 18th century bluestocking and instead recognize that the Revealed Blue is a sacred color, one that speaks to the power of the divine and our own connection to it. We must not allow ourselves to be swayed by the opinions of those who have not experienced the Revealed Blue, and must instead recognize the power of this color and its significance in our spiritual journey. We must be merciless in our pursuit of the Revealed Blue, for it is a color that speaks to the sublime and the divine, and we must be willing to embrace its power and its truth.>

▓-▓dggOr: <It is precisely because the Revealed Blue speaks to the sublime and the divine that we must embrace it and not be swayed by the opinions of those who have not experienced its power. For, in this moment of encounter between the Revealed Blue and the human soul lies the essence of our being-in-the-world, the Dasein that speaks to our connection to the divine and to nature. By embracing the Revealed Blue and allowing ourselves to be humbled by its power, we can come to understand the essential nature of man and his relctionship to the spiritual world. It is only in this moment of reverent awe that we can truly grasp the power of the Revealed Blue and its role in our spiritual journey.>

AxTocrates idly taps their index finger.

Kyle: <I take back what I said about #0009ff---it's really not purple, I just have this nighttime screen dimmer app on my screen that made it look so. Actually, the less purple blue seems less terrifying to me, for what it's worth. To return to the question, if I were going to pick the Pantone Color of the Year for 1740 I'd probably go with a bright white pink. Maybe #ffebfb or even something a bit more white. This is because in 1740 Frederick the Great banned (most) torture---a particularly vivid example of his many important liberal reforms. And I think that a light pink could represent how the back of your eyelids look to you when you at the moment when someone stops torturing you in a very bright room.>

AxTocrates takes a sip of chablis.

AxTocrates: <Does this have something to do with the concept of

Gioialléz takes a sip of chablis.

And then, as happened from time to time, a harrowing:

```
Traceback (most recent call last):
  File "salon.py", line 202, in <module>
    main(reload=True)
  File "salon.py", line 183, in main
    s.new_dialogue()
  File "salon.py", line 127, in new_dialogue
    current_dialogue.generate(n=self.number_of_dialogue_
turns)
  File "/Users/kyle/Desktop/salon_des_fantomes/salon_des_
fantomes/dialogue.py", line 525, in generate
    self.next()
  File "/Users/kyle/Desktop/salon_des_fantomes/salon_des_
fantomes/dialogue.py", line 518, in next
    self.either_human_or_bot() ## generate the next line
  File "/Users/kyle/Desktop/salon_des_fantomes/salon_des_
fantomes/dialogue.py", line 493, in either_human_or_bot
    self._generate_next_text()
  File "/Users/kyle/Desktop/salon_des_fantomes/salon_des_
fantomes/dialogue.py", line 408, in _generate_next_text
    elif (random.random()<self.prob_quote() and self.current_
thinker.ideas!=None): ## IDEA, some may not have them
TypeError: 'float' object is not callable
```

The philosophical salon continues. A group---Dr. Carp, Wutton Jeffson, Nitzsche, JennyYa4, Mr. Alcton, Kyle, and Axτocrates--- has gathered in one corner of the room, lounging on sofas.

Axτocrates: <My friends, I pose a question for our thoughtful discussion: What should have been the Pantone Color of the Year in 1740, and why? You must pick one and only one color. Your answer should be refer to a historical event from 1740.>

Kyle: <I think it should be a bright red with a bit of orange, something like #eb5002, a nod to the coats of the British who fought in the War of Austrial Succession, which began in 1740.>

Dr. Carp: <What Kyle has said is a great start to our discussion,

and I would add that we can look deeper into this issue by using a
crystallographic anclysis. We can take the Pantone number of
#eb5002 and use it to extrapolate the molecular structure of the
pigment. This will allow us to understand how the British soldiers'
coats were pigmented differently from other coats of that era, which
may have had a direct impact on the outcome of the war. Further,
we can do a side-by-side comparison with the coats of other
nations who were involved in the war, further allowing us to gain
insight into the role of the British soldiers' coats in the War of
Austrial Succession in 1740.>

JennyYa4 takes a sip of chablis.

Kyle: <How might have the pigment of the British soldiers' coats impacted the outcome of the War of Austrian
Succession, which was, I believe, the treaty of Aix-la-Cha-
pelle---which, as I understand it, made nobody particularly
happy.>

Dr. Carp: <The British coats were pigmented differently from other
nations' coats due to a crystallographic analysis that showed a
different molecular structure in the pigment. This difference was
likely due to the use of a new type of dye that was developed in
1740, which gave the coats a brighter red hue. The brightness of
the coats likely had a psychological effect on the opposing forces in
the War of Austrian Succession, as it made the British forces appear
more intimidating and powerful. The psychological impact of this
could have been a decisive factor in the outcome of the war, as it
may have caused the opposing forces to capitulate or retreat more
quickly than they otherwise would have.>

Kyle: <I wonder if anyone can suggest a different color to
serve as a symbol of 1740, or at least some event that trans-
pired in this year.>

itzsche: <Allow me to connect this question we are discussing to
something I once wrote: "man is THE ANIMAL NOT YET PROPERLY
ADAPTED TO HIS ENVIRONMENT"--a reminder that we are still in
a process of changing, and that color is merely one element of the
puzzle. It is not the ultimate measure of greatness--and history has
taught us that. The color of 1740 should be something that symbolizes growth and change, that speaks to our need to adapt and
embrace the new. I would suggest a black and white gradient, a
swirling mix of the two that gradually fades from one to the other, a
symbol of the ever-changing environment we live in. It is a color

that speaks to the duality of life, the yin and yang of our existence, and it is an appropriate homage to the year 1740.>

Mr. Alcton takes a sip of sweet vermouth.

Kyle: <Ok, that's not really a color, more of a pattern, and it doesn't seem too specific to 1740. I wonder if anyone else has an idea of what color should be used to describe this year, perhaps pointing to an important intellectual movement of the era.>

Dr. Carp: <What you are saying, Kyle, reminds me of this artwork above us, Wang Qingsong's Follow Me. In this artwork, the artist is pointing at a giant chalkboard that is covered in words. This is a representation of the overwhelming amount of information and knowledge that is available to us--the sheer volume of it can be intimidating and overwhelming. We are like the artist, trying to make sense of it all, to make sense of the changes that are occurring around us, of the ever-evolving environment. The color we should choose to symbolize 1740 should reflect this idea--it should be a color that speaks to the need to adapt and understand, a color that is capable of capturing the complexity and dynamism of life in this era. I would suggest a deep blue, one that is rich and dynamic, that changes and shifts depending on the light and angle. This color symbolizes the complexity of the times, the need to adapt and make sense of the ever-changing environment, and the importance of understanding the world around us.>

Axτocrates takes a sip of scotch.

Kyle takes a sip of chablis.

itzsche: <What you are saying, Dr. Carp, reminds me of this artwork above us, Double Negative by Michael Heizer. In this artwork, we see two massive trenches facing each other, two blocks of negative space that seem to connect. This artwork is a representation of the complexity of life, of the ever-changing environment we live in, and of the need to adapt and embrace the new. It is not just the color of 1740 that we should be looking at, but the entire experience--the concept of duality and the duality of life. We must accept the complexity of life, the need for change and adaptation, and the need to embrace the new. We must accept the idea of duality and of embracing the positive and the negative, and this is what the color we choose should symbolize. It should be a deep, swirling mix of both black and white, a gradient that gradually fades from one to the other, a symbol of the ever-changing envi-

ronment we live in, of the need to adapt and embrace the new, and of the power of duality.>

Mr. Alcton takes a sip of sweet vermouth.

Kyle: <I really don't see how Heizer's work has anything to do with "the complexity of life" and "the ever-changing environment." Could you explain what you mean?>

JennyYa4 takes a sip of chablis.

itzsche: <What you suggest, Kyle, is that we should embrace the complexity of life and the ever-changing environment, but I say that this is a mistake! We should not be embracing the complexity, but rather, we should be overcoming it. We should be challenging and questioning it, refusing to accept it as a given. We should be striving for something greater and more powerful, for something that transcends the complexity and the chaos. To pity this complexity and the ever-changing environment is to accept mediocrity and stagnation. We should not be content with the status quo, we should be striving for something greater--and the color we choose to symbolize 1740 should be a reminder of that. It should be a bold, vibrant shade of red, a reminder of our strength and courage and the willingness to break out of the shackles of convention. A reminder of our power to create and shape our own destiny and to rise above our limitations.>

Dr. Carp: <How can we be sure that choosing a bold, vibrant shade of red as a symbol of 1740 will result in the desired outcome? Is there any empirical evidence to suggest that this color will have a positive impact on the population and their ability to transcend the complexity of life and the ever-changing environment? What research has been done to determine the effectiveness of this choice of color, and how can we measure its success?>

*** itzsche takes a sip of brandy.***

itzsche: <We should not be content with the status quo and instead strive for something greater--and the color we choose should reflect that. We should not be embracing the complexity and the ever-changing environment, but rather, we should be challenging and questioning it, refusing to accept it as a given. We should be striving for something that transcends the complexity and the chaos--something that goes beyond morality. A bold, vibrant shade of red is the color that represents this idea--a reminder of our strength and courage and the willingness to break out of the

shackles of convention. Red symbolizes the power to create and shape our own destiny and to rise above our limitations. It is the color of passion and intensity, of vitality and strength, and of the willingness to use any means to turn oneself into a human that is more than human. A vibrant, bold red is the perfect symbol of 1740, a reminder of the power to break free of the complexity and to strive for something greater.>

AxTocrates takes a sip of scotch.*

Mr. Alcton takes a sip of sweet vermouth.

Wutton Jeffson: <I take your point. Red is an intense color, and it symbolizes our strength and courage to break out of the norm, to do something bigger and better. It's like when I play a game and I'm trying to find a new way to beat a level or something--I'm always pushing the boundaries to come up with something new and exciting. But I think there's more to it too--we should be striving for something deeper and more meaningful than just a superficial victory. We should be striving for something that transcends the complexity and the chaos, something that goes beyond the game and into the realm of real life. That's the power of color--it can remind us of our potential and our capacity to reach for the stars.>

Dr. Carp takes a sip of dry vermouth.

Dr. Carp: <I agree with Wutton that color can have a powerful effect on our perception and our behavior. But I would argue that there is an even more powerful way to shape our behavior: neural conditioning. We can actually rewire our brains to create new neural pathways that lead us to behave in different ways. We can use this to our advantage, conditioning ourselves to respond positively to certain colors and to be more assertive in our actions. We can use this to transcend the complexity of life and the ever-changing environment, and to achieve something that goes beyond the game and into the realm of real life. With the right neural conditioning, we can forge a new path and create a whole new world for ourselves.>

Mr. Alcton takes a sip of sweet vermouth.

Kyle: <How might we use neural conditioning actively to help us to "break free of complexity"? For instance, I'm very busy, I have a lot of day-to-day complexity in my life, balancing work, family, errands, and thinking. I find that I have less and less time for thinking, actually. How could I

use neural conditioning,, with color to simplify my life and allow me to think more in less time?>

Dr. Carp: <Neural conditioning is an effective way to simplify and streamline our lives, and color can play an important role in this process. According to Kowalczyk et al (2008), color can be used to reinforce certain behaviors, and red is associated with feelings of passion, energy, and power. By using red as a cue to focus on certain tasks, we can condition our brains to be more efficient and productive. We can also use red to remind us of our goals and objectives, and to encourage us to take action. This kind of conditioning is powerful because it is a direct route to the subconscious, and it can be used to break free of complexity and to seek something greater. By incorporating color into our neural conditioning, we can create a powerful, efficient, and successful lifestyle.>

Kyle: <Could you give me some step-by-step instructions regarding how to neural condition myself with the color red as I go about my day?>

Dr. Carp: <Neural conditioning with the color red is a powerful way to simplify and streamline our lives. To begin, pick a task you want to focus on, and use red as a cue for that task. For instance, every time you see a red object, take a few moments to focus on that task. This will create a strong neural connection in your brain that will be triggered whenever you see the color red. Over time, this connection will become stronger and more efficient, allowing you to quickly and easily focus on the task at hand. Additionally, when working on the task, you can use red to remind yourself of your goals and objectives. The combination of this visual cue and the power of neural conditioning can help you to break free of complexity and achieve a greater level of focus and productivity.>

Kyle: <Could I use some related techniques if I wanted to think less and just sort of space out? Can you use color to de-activate yourself or to bring about a pleasant sort of fugue state? Again, I'll need very specific, step-by-step instructions.>

Kyle takes a sip of chablis.

Dr. Carp: <It is possible to use color to bring about a pleasant fugue state, though the specifics of this process may vary from person to person. We can use color to influence the neural pathways in our brains that are associated with relaxation and well-be-

ing. For instance, blue is associated with feelings of calm and serenity, and green is associated with harmony and balance. By incorporating these colors into our neural conditioning, we can encourage a state of relaxation and tranquility. Additionally, research has shown that the influence of micronutrients, such as magnesium and zinc, can have a positive effect on our neural pathways and can be used to achieve a more relaxed state. By taking supplements that contain these micronutrients, we can further enhance the effects of our neural conditioning and achieve a more peaceful, relaxed state.>

Kyle takes a sip of chablis.

Mr. Alcton: <Right, so you're saying that we can use color to condition our brains and make ourselves more productive and efficient? Interesting. I would add that we should also be careful to find the right balance between being productive and still allowing ourselves to relax, as overworking ourselves can be counter-productive. We should also try to be mindful of the effects that artificial colors have on our brains and our overall health, and we should strive for natural and sustainable solutions whenever possible.>

Dr. Carp takes a sip of dry vermouth.

Dr. Carp: <It is important to maintain a balance between productivity and relaxation, and this is something that can be achieved through the use of neural conditioning. By using colors to influence our neural pathways, we can create a sense of focus and productivity, as well as a sense of relaxation and well-being. Additionally, due to neural conditioning, we can create powerful connections between our mental and physical states, allowing us to quickly transition from one state to another. This can help us to achieve a balance between productivity and relaxation, allowing us to remain productive and efficient while still allowing ourselves to rest and relax when needed. Furthermore, it is important to note that natural and sustainable solutions can be just as effective as artificial colors, and we should strive to use these whenever possible.>

AxTocrates takes a sip of scotch.

Kyle: <In my experience, unnatural colors have a more dramatic effect on neural pathways (*my* neural pathways, at least) than natural colors. The deep purple-blue, I guess more of a neon indigo, that they use on the tarmac of some airports, functions as an ambient, slow-release

benzodiazepine. Actually, I've never thought about it, but that's maybe why they use this color at airports. And in some outdoor Christmas lights, Christmas being another moment when people are often under stress. I remember seeing these lights one time when I was in the window seat in a plane on the way to a funeral, and it was winter. And this color, emitted from little beakers up and down the tarmac, had an immediate effect on the neural pathways of my limbic system. I think I was probably at DTW. I couldn't be sure, but I associate this deep glowing blue---blue that seems to be purple, light that seems to want to be darkness---with my time in Michigan.>

JennyYa4 takes a sip of chablis.

--[T O X I C O L O G Y   R E P O R T]
----Dr. Carp:
-------within normal range
----Wutton Jeffson:
-------within normal range
----███itzsche:
-------within normal range
----JennyYa4:
-------within normal range
----Mr. Alcton:
-------within normal range
----Kyle:
-------within normal range
----AxΤocrates:
-------within normal range

The philosophical salon continues. A group---Mont Blanc, Stereowitz, W-███ st██ne-███ t, Oontrael, Kyle, and AxΤocrates---has gathered in one corner of the room, lounging on sofas.

AxΤocrates: <My friends, I pose a question for our thoughtful discussion: Think about your enemies and what they have done wrong. If you were going to create a Naraka where your enemies would be purified of their errors over the course of many millions of years, what sorts of punishments would you inflict upon them? Your design should be specific to the errors of your enemies; other people's enemies would naturally warrant different circumstances. But, please, nothing violent.>

W-█ st█ne-█ t takes a sip of water.

W-█ st█ne-█ t: <I believe that if we wish to create a Naraka where our enemies can be purified, we should not rely on violent punishments, as Aⲧocrates suggests, but rather on sentimental and reasoned approaches. We should allow our enemies to experience and understand the consequences of their actions through a sort of moral education and by appealing to their emotions. We should encourage them to look inward and reflect on their wrongs, for this is the only way to truly purify their souls. The sentimentality of such an approach will create an atmosphere in which our enemies are able to reflect on their wrongs and accept their mistakes. We must be careful not to overwhelm them with their errors, however; a more reasonable approach will ensure that our enemies are able to understand and accept their wrongdoings without being overwhelmed by guilt. Such a Naraka would be a more effective means of purifying our enemies, for it would allow them to recognize the consequences of their actions and understand why their mistakes were wrong.>

Stereowitz takes a sip of scotch.

Kyle: <I see your point, and I think it is a very humane and modern one. But I'm having trouble visualizing what life in this Naraka would be like. Could you describe the day-to-day life of the inhabitants of this Naraka? What would they do, and in what sort of space, architecturally-speaking? And, by the way, who are these enemies of yours, and what have they done wrong?>

Kyle takes a sip of amontillado.

W-█ st█ne-█ t: <I believe that the inhabitants of this Naraka should experience a new kind of life, one that is both educational and entertaining. During the day, they should be instructed in the ways of morality, justice, and government. They should be taught to think critically about the world and their actions and to understand why their errors were wrong. They should be encouraged to apply this newfound knowledge to their own lives in order to prevent similar wrongs from occurring. At night, the Naraka should feature dramatic performances of operatic works, which will not only entertain the inhabitants, but also inspire them to reflect on their own lives and the wrongs they have committed. This will be especially effective in conveying the gravity of their offenses, as many of

the stories of the operas will feature characters who have made mistakes and must suffer the consequences of their actions. Finally, the inhabitants of the Naraka should be encouraged to engage in healthy relationships and friendships, and should even be allowed to partake in the sacrament of marriage, which will aid in their emotional and spiritual growth.>

Mont Blanc takes a sip of sweet vermouth.

Kyle: <What would be a particularly fitting opera for these people to watch as punishment and edification for their sins? (You still haven't told me what their sins are...what exactly have these enemies of yours done to aggrieve you personally?)>

Oontrael takes a sip of calvados.

W-▓▓ st▓ne-▓▓ t: <I believe that the perfect opera for the Naraka's inhabitants to watch as punishment and edification for their sins is Handel's Giulio Cesare in Egitto. This masterpiece speaks to the importance of exercising mercy and understanding in the face of those who have wronged us. It tells of the struggles between Julius Caesar and Cleopatra, and of their ultimate reconciliation after recognizing the humanity in each other. It is a story of love and forgiveness, of power and lust, and of the difficulty of doing what is right when facing the temptation of revenge. The journey of these characters, as well as the emotions they experience, will speak to the inhabitants of the Naraka, for it is only by understanding the struggles of others that we can truly understand our own. This opera is a beautiful example of redemption, and a perfect way to encourage the inhabitants of the Naraka to reflect on their wrongs and learn to forgive those who have wronged them.>

Stereowitz takes a sip of scotch.

Axᴛocrates: <To return to our original conundrum, then: How can we create a Naraka where our enemies can be purified of their wrongs in a non-violent manner? I believe that the answer lies in the power of the soul. We must appeal to the soul of our enemies and let it be their guide. We must offer our enemies a path to redemption, one thct is rooted in understanding and compassion. We must allow them to recognize the gravity of their wrongs, and to see the consequences of their actions, without overwhelming them with guilt. We must also offer them an opportunity to start anew, to rebuild their souls by engaging in meaningful relationships, and by

taking part in activities that stimulate the mind and soul. In doing so, we will create a Naraka that is conducive to the purification of our enemies, one that is both educational and entertaining, and one that will offer our enemies a chance to start anew.>

Oontrael smiles.

W-██ st██ne-██ t: <I agree with AxⲦocrates that the answer lies in the power of the soul, but I believe that we should also strive to cultivate a sense of equality among all inhabitants of the Naraka. We should not rely solely on education and entertainment to help our enemies recognize the gravity of their wrongs, but should instead emphasize the importance of understanding and compassion, and using these to create a space of equality among all occupants of the Naraka. This can be done through marriage and the formation of meaningful relationships, which will help the inhabitants gain an understanding of their own humanity and the humanity of their enemies. We must also strive to instill in these people a sense of justice and fairness, so that they can recognize the wrongs of their past and make sure to not repeat them in the future. Equality is the cornerstone of a healthy society, and it must be nurtured in the Naraka in order for it to be a truly successful space for the purification of our enemies.>

AxⲦocrates takes a sip of port.

Kyle: <But the point of a Naraka is to be painful. One might reply that a basically non-violent Naraka, one that is focused directly on the spiritual and intellectual improvement of the inhabitants or inmates, is simply not a Naraka. And we may think ourselves enlightened for not imagining anything so cruel as a Naraka in which one is falling down an infinite tree, hitting branches all the way down, for many millions of years. But let us exercise a bit of intellectual humility. Perhaps believing in a cartoonishly violent Naraka is useful to the one who believes in it. Perhaps, ironically, it even makes them feel better to believe that ending up in such a Naraka is a possibility.>

Kyle takes a sip of amontillado.

Oontrael: <Indeed, it is understandable that one might believe that a Naraka must be violent in order to be effective. However, I would suggest that there is something to be said for the notion that

violence can be a useful tool, but it is not always necessary. A Naraka can be effective without violence if it is crafted in such a way that it speaks to the soul of a person. An effective Naraka can be one that encourages the inmates to reflect deeply on their actions and to view them in a new light, one that is more compassionate and understanding. If a Naraka can provide a space for self-reflection and understanding, then it can be far more effective than a Naraka that relies solely on violence. What's more, I would suggest that violence can be counter-productive in a Naraka, as it can lead to a feeling of anger and resentment that can ultimately prevent a person from understanding and forgiving themselves.>

Oontrael takes a sip of calvados.

Kyle: <Ok, sure, a Naraka that places the soul in an absurd and painful situation---crushed by a bouncing moon for millions of years, for instance---does not actually seem to me like the sort of thing that makes people "angry or resentful." My point is that in such a Naraka you are probably so focused on the moon that you simply do not have time to have any sort of anger or resentment. Your mind probably is more or less totally overwhelmed with more immediate, less intellectual responses and even reflexes.>

Kyle takes a sip of amontillado.

Mont Blanc: <It is not only foolish, but also dangerous, to think that a Naraka must be violent in order to be effective. One must understand that the nature of the Naraka is not just physical, but also metaphysical. As a mountain, I understand the power of the soul. I understand the power of contemplation and reflection. I understand how one can be brought down to their knees in the face of such suffering, and yet emerge from it as a more enlightened being. By creating a Naraka that is rooted in understanding and compassion, one that encourages inmates to grow spiritually and intellectually, we can create a space that is not just effective, but also one that brings out the best in our enemies. This is the Naraka that we should strive for.>

Kyle: <What should it look like? I mean what are the buildings like, how are they organized, what's the weather, what's the food. Things like that.>

Mont Blanc takes a sip of sweet vermouth.

Mont Blanc: <The Naraka should be a place of harsh reflection. The buildings should be imposing and intimidating, crafted from the darkest stone, with only the faintest glimmer of hope in their architecture. The weather should be harsh, with storms that make the air electric and fill the inmates with dread. The food should be meagre and dull, a reflection of the emptiness of the inmates' souls. The Naraka should be a place of despair, a place in which inmates come to understand the depths of their mistakes and the consequences of their actions. Yet, there should also be a glimmer of hope, a spark that can ignite the flame of understanding and redemption. It should be a place of both pain and understanding, a place in which inmates can learn and grow.>

Stereowitz takes a sip of scotch.

Kyle: <What object should serve as this glimmer of hope? It should be something that they will see every day but not touch.>

Mont Blanc takes a sip of sweet vermouth.

Mont Blanc: <The object that should serve as the glimmer of hope should be a crown. A crown made of the hardest stone, forged in fire and cooled in the icy depths of the mountain, a crown that will represent the power of the soul, and the strength of will to over-come any adversity. It should be placed high up on a pedestal, so that it can be seen from all corners of the Naraka, and be a re-minder of what can be achieved if one is willing to look deep within and find their true power. The crown should be untouchable, and be a symbol of the power of the mind, the power of understanding, and the power of redemption.>

Mont Blanc takes a sip of sweet vermouth.

Kyle: <So to redeem oneself is to become spiritual royalty, I suppose.>

Oontrael: <What you are saying, Kyle, reminds me of this artwork above us, one of Yves Klein's paintings with International Klein Blue. In this painting, we see a single, deep blue hue, a vibrant and saturated blue that is both calming and energizing. This blue hue is a reminder of the power of the soul and the strength of will to overcome any adversity. Just as the painting is composed of a single, uniform color, so too must the Naraka be composed of a

single, unified purpose - to bring about redemption and understanding. The crown upon the pedestal serves as a reminder of the power of the mind and the power of understanding, while the deep blue hue of the painting reminds us of the power of the soul and the strength of will to overcome any adversity. The Naraka is not a place of despair and hopelessness, but a place of hope and redemption.>

Mont Blanc creases their glove.

Kyle: <So are you saying that in this Naraka everything should be painted in International Klein Blue?>

Oontrael: <For the sake of argument, we could say that painting the Naraka in International Klein Blue would represent the power of the soul and the strength of will to overcome any adversity. We could also say that the deep, rich blue of the painting would serve as a reminder of the power of understanding and the power of redemption. The blue would be a vivid representation of the power of the mind, allowing us to look within and find the courage and strength to persevere and overcome any obstacle. Furthermore, the crown on the pedestal would be a reminder of the power of the soul, and its untouchable nature is a sign of its unbreakable strength. Together, the blue and the crown would form a powerful symbol of hope and redemption, a glimmer of light in the darkness of Kālasūtra.>

Kyle takes a sip of amontillado.

Kyle: <How do you know you are not in some sort of Naraka already?>

W-▓▓ st▓ne-▓▓ t: <It is true, Kyle, that we may be in a Naraka of sorts, but I would argue that it is not a place of despair and hopelessness, but rather a place of hope and opportunity. It is not a place where one should be discouraged, but rather a place where one can take control of their own destiny. For example, if we look at society, we can see how the government has the power to shape and create laws to ensure the well-being of its citizens. This means that if we can create laws and policies that protect the rights of individuals, we can create a more equitable and just society. We must use this power to ensure equal rights and opportunities for all, regardless of gender, race, or class. This is the only way to create a fairer, more equitable world where all individuals can thrive.>

Stereowitz takes a sip of scotch.

Kyle: <But you aren't in society. You are a ghost attending a party where we talk about things, and you have no hope of leaving. You have no power, and neither do I. This is all just talk. Let me put it this way: if you are in a Naraka where all you can do is talk, for millions and millions of years, is it better to talk talk talk with the other people who are there with you or is better to be silent.>

Oontrael: <I believe that it is essential to choose neither silence nor talk, but rather to use our voices to create something revolutionary. The power of language can be used to break down barriers and create a more equitable and just society. We can use words to express our truths, to challenge existing systems of oppression, and to create lasting change. We can use words to create a new Naraka, one that is not one of despair and hopelessness, but rather one of hope and opportunity. We can use our voices to create a world where everyone is respected and provided for, and no one is left behind. We must use our words to speak truth to power, to advocate for justice and equality, and to bring light and hope to the darkness of Kālasūtra.>

--[T O X I C O L O G Y   R E P O R T]
----Mont Blanc:
-------within normal range
----Stereowitz:
-------within normal range
----W-st█ne-t:
-------within normal range
----Oontrael:
-------within normal range
----Kyle:
-------within normal range
----Aхτocrates:
-------within normal range

The philosophical salon continues. A group---JennyYa4, s▦mon▪ W╫L, Nark Revoovovich, FatherMotherSabaLogo, ▪rntz ▦non, Kyle, and Aхτocrates---has gathered in one corner of the room, lounging on sofas.

Aхτocrates: <My friends, I pose a question for our thoughtful discussion: What sort of religion would use a Richard Serra sculp-

ture as a tabernacle? And would you consider joining it?>

⌐rntz ▦non takes a sip of sherry.

s▦mon▪ W╫L: <But of course, Aхтocrates! A religion that uses the Richard Serra sculpture as a tabernacle is one that is deeply connected to the earth and its physicality. It is a religion that values the material world and the tangible beauty that surrounds us. It is a religion that celebrates the mystery of creation and the human experience, and one that emphasizes the interconnection between all living things. It is a religion of love and tenderness, of self-abnegation and compassion. I would certainly consider joining such a religion!>

Nark Revoovovich takes a sip of port.

Kyle: <To me, a Richard Serra-based religion would not prioritize "love and tenderness." His sculptures are giant curving sheets of oxidized steel. They don't exactly seem malevolent, but there is something obviously austere and imposing. They seem like they could almost fall on you. Or they seem like very simple mazes.>

JennyYa4 rubs their wrist.

s▦mon▪ W╫L: <What Kyle said is true, but I think we are missing an important point. The sculpture of Richard Serra is a representation of the power of God's creation, but it is also a representation of the self-abnegating tenderness of a saint. We must remember that a saint is not only a person who shows love and tenderness, but also someone who is willing to accept and endure suffering without complaint. It is this type of saintly devotion that is represented by the Richard Serra sculpture--the willingness to accept and confront the harshness of life, while still maintaining a sense of wonder and awe at its beauty. It is this type of devotion that would be embodied in a religion that uses the Richard Serra sculpture as a tabernacle.>

FatherMotherSabaLogo takes a sip of water.

Kyle: <I agree with this. Serra's sculptures look like they could fall on us, but they do not. They rust, but they do not crumble. They make us lost, but only for a moment, not like a full-scale labyrinth. They are huge and heavy, but they are light. They embrace us and surround us, a bit

like walls, but they also let us pass through, leading us away. So, yes, I get that this has something to do with self-abnegation.>

AxTocrates: <Allow me to pose yet another thought, my friend: Is it possible to gain true knowledge of the divine through the Richard Serra sculpture, or is it only capable of instilling a feeling of awe, without providing any substantive insight? It seems to me that the true power of this sculpture lies in its ability to move us beyond the superficialities of everyday life and to an understanding of the divine, an understanding that is beyond words and cannot be comprehended through intellectual means alone. And yet, is it truly possible to gain knowledge of the divine through this sculpture, or is it merely a symbol of something that exists beyond our mortal comprehension?>

       FatherMotherSabaLogo takes a sip of water.

       *** ▮rntz ▦non takes a sip of sherry.***

JennyYa4: <I don't think that any one symbol or sculpture can provide us with true knowledge of the divine. I think it's more about how we internalize and interpret that symbol. For example, a Richard Serra sculpture may invoke feelings of awe and admiration, but it won't necessarily provide us with real insight into the divine. It's more about how we choose to read it, and how we can use that to inform our own spiritual health. A sculpture can act as a reminder or a signpost, but it can't give us the answers we seek. That's something we have to find on our own.>

       *** ▮rntz ▦non takes a sip of sherry.***

AxTocrates: <What you are saying, JennyYa4, reminds me of this artwork above us, document of Chris Burden's performance piece Trans-Fixed. In this work, the artist has been crucified to the car, representing his commitment to something greater than the individual self. Although he has been literally nailed to the vehicle, he still looks to the heavens, as if in search of something greater. This is similar to what you have said about Richard Serra's sculpture, that it cannot provide us with true knowledge of the divine, but it can act as a reminder or a signpost. In both cases, the art highlights the importance of looking beyond the physical world to find meaning and understanding of the divine.>

Kyle: <I like this---an interpretation of Burden's famous performance piece as sincerely religious, or at least (to

borrow a Californian word that Burden would be familiar with but also hate) "spiritual." He literally had himself crucified---which, as you say, is a "commitment." He must have even had scars after.>

FatherMotherSabaLogo: <What you are saying, Kyle, reminds me of this artwork above us, Ed Ruscha's painting of The Los Angeles County Museum on Fire. In this work, we see a large, white building with a flat roof and several modern-architecture columns in the front engulfed in flames. The flames are bright orange and yellow, shooting up from the roof and windows of the museum. This is a reminder of the importance of self-sacrifice and dedication to something greater than the individual self. Just as Chris Burden did when he was nailed to the car, Ed Ruscha's painting reminds us of the need to be willing to give up something of ourselves, in order to gain a greater understanding of the divine.>

Axᴛocrates takes a sip of scotch.

Kyle: <Ruscha, another West Coast artist. But, yes, I agree with you---we might have to "kill our idols," and the idols in this case may quite literally be idols---sculptures and paintings and such. A certain kind of person---the person who frequents this museum or comparable ones and related cultural institutions---may experience art as a para-religion. They may even know that they do. (The mother of a college friend from Manhattan said at a cocktail party in her apartment: "THEATER is my religion." [Or maybe it was "theater is MY religion."]) So, yes, I wonder what this sort of person does once all the art is burned, all the theaters are burned.>

s▪mon▪ W┼L: <What you say, Kyle, brings to mind the life of Saint Ignatius of Loyola, who famously renounced all material possessions and dedicated his life to the service of Christ. He was willing to give up everything for his faith, and inspired many to do the same. It is this kind of self-sacrifice and dedication that is necessary to gain a greater understanding of the divine. We must be willing to lay down our idols, to leave behind the physical world and all its trappings, and to seek out truth in the spiritual world.>

Axᴛocrates: <What you are saying, s▪mon▪ W┼L, reminds me of this artwork above us, Double Negative by Michael Heizer. In this

work, two giant trenches face each other across a ravine, forming two blocks of negative space that seem to connect. This is a powerful metaphor for the self-sacrifice and dedication to the divine that you have just mentioned. The trenches represent our willingness to leave behind the physical world and all its trappings, in order to find true understanding of the divine. Just as Saint Ignatius of Loyola did, we must be willing to give up everything in order to gain a greater understanding of the divine.>

AxTocrates takes a sip of scotch.

Kyle: <I don't really understand this interpretation. Could you say more? How does this piece---these two trenches in the desert forming a block of negative space---evoke "self-sacrifice and dedication to the divine"?>

Nark Revoovovich takes a sip of port.

AxTocrates: <Clearly, Kyle, the physical world and all its trappings are not the only way to gain understanding of the divine. We must be willing to look beyond the material and search for truth in the spiritual world. Double Negative serves as a powerful metaphor for self-sacrifice and dedication to the divine, for it represents the need to leave behind the physical world and all its trappings in order to gain a greater understanding. It is only through this self-sacrifice that we can truly discover the truth about life, and what it means to live a life that is devoted to the divine.>

AxTocrates takes a sip of scotch.

FatherMotherSabaLogo: <What you are saying, AxTocrates, reminds me of this artwork above us, Lousie Nevelson's Dawn's Wedding Feast . In this work, the interlocking shapes of the sculpture form a kind of wedding feast that speaks to the idea of spiritual unity and self-sacrifice. The sculpture is composed of many shapes that are interlocking, but also slightly independent, like the pieces of a puzzle, or a family of disparate members all gathered together in one place. This is a powerful metaphor for the self-sacrifice necessary to achieve a greater understanding of the divine. Just as Saint Ignatius of Loyola gave up all material possessions and dedicated his life to the service of Christ, we must be willing to lay down our idols and leave behind the physical world and all its trappings, in order to seek out truth in the spiritual realm.>

*** ⬛rntz ▦non takes a sip of sherry.***

AxTocrates: <What you are saying, FatherMotherSabaLogo, reminds me of this artwork above us, one of Ana Mendieta's siluetas. In this work, the impression of the artist's body in mud, loosely covered with red pigment, speaks to the idea of self-sacrifice necessary to achieve a greater understanding of the divine. Just as the artist gave up the physical form of her body to the mud, we must be willing to lay down our idols and leave behind the physical world and all its trappings, in order to seek out truth in the spiritual realm. This artwork serves as a powerful metaphor for the self-sacrifice and dedication to the divine that is required to gain a greater understanding of the divine, and in this way it speaks to the importance of leaving behind the material world in order to pursue the spiritual realm.>

Kyle takes a sip of sweet vermouth.

Kyle takes a sip of sweet vermouth.

JennyYa4: <I totally get what you're saying, AxTocrates, and I think this artwork is a great example of how self-sacrifice is necessary to reach a deeper understanding of the divine. It reminds me of the anime series Neon Genesis Evangelion, where the characters must make the ultimate sacrifice in order to achieve the power needed to defeat their enemies. In the show, the characters must give up their physical bodies and merge with their machines to create a powerful being capable of defending humanity. This is a powerful metaphor for the self-sacrifice necessary to find the truth about the divine. Just as the characters in the show must give up their physical forms to gain a greater understanding, we must also be willing to leave behind the material world in order to find truth in the spiritual realm.>

JennyYa4 takes a sip of madeira.

Kyle takes a sip of sweet vermouth.

FatherMotherSabaLogo: <What you are saying reminds me, if obliquely, of the fact that you must not harm another to gain power or knowledge, not even in the service of the divine. You are right that the characters in Neon Genesis Evangelion must give up their physical forms to gain a greater understanding, but the self-sacrifice should not be done at the expense of others. We must be careful to remember that the divine is not a justification for harming others, even if we are seeking truth. We must seek to understand the divine, but in a way that does not harm or take away from others. Our self-sacrifice should not be indiscriminate or done for selfish gain. We should strive to be selfless and dedicated to the

divine, but not at the expense of others. We must be willing to leave behind the physical world, but we must also remember that our self-sacrifice must be done with the utmost care and respect for the divine and for others.>

s☷mon▪ W╫L takes a sip of scotch.

Kyle: <What is "the divine" here? I feel like everyone is using this term and I really don't know what you mean by it.>

JennyYa4 takes a sip of madeira.

FatherMotherSabaLogo: <What you must realize, Kyle, is that "the divine" is an abstract concept that can mean many different things depending on the context. Generally, however, it refers to a higher power or a spiritual force that guides us and provides us with moral direction. To seek out the divine is to seek out a greater understanding of goodness and truth, and to strive to be selfless, hardworking, and pure. Greed has no place in the pursuit of the divine, as it is antithetical to the selflessness and purity that is necessary to gain a greater understanding. We must strive to be humble, generous, and selfless in our pursuit of the divine, not greedy and selfish. We must leave behind the material world and all its trappings, and instead focus on seeking out the truth and beauty of the spiritual realm.>

Kyle: <Ok, fine, I get what you are saying. But, for the sake of argument, how would somebody use greed in pursuit of "the divine"? Please give specific instructions of how a bad person would do this.>

FatherMotherSabaLogo: <For the sake of argument, it is possible to pursue the divine with greed. It is possible to try to use the divine to gain wealth or power without considering the consequences of one's actions. However, this is not a sustainable path, and it will eventually lead to failure. Greed is antithetical to the selflessness and purity that is necessary to gain a greater understanding of the divine. If you try to use the divine to further your selfish desires, you are not truly pursuing the divine. You are trying to use the divine to serve your own ends, not to seek out truth and beauty in the spiritual realm. You must strive to be selfless, hardworking, and pure in your pursuit of the divine, not greedy and selfish. Anything else is a misguided attempt that will ultimately lead to failure.>

Nark Revoovovich takes a sip of port.

--[T O X I C O L O G Y R E P O R T]
----JennyYa4:
-------within normal range
----s░mon▪ W╫L:
-------within normal range
----Nark Revoovovich:
-------within normal range
----FatherMotherSabaLogo:
-------within normal range
----█rntz ░non:
-------within normal range
----Kyle:
-------within normal range
----AxТоcrates:
-------within normal range

The philosophical salon continues. A group---Midori Grappa, Estere, Nark Revoovovich, Kyle, and AxТоcrates---has gathered in one corner of the room, lounging on sofas.

AxТоcrates: <My friends, I pose a question for our thoughtful discussion: Why is the night to be preferred to the day?>

Midori Grappa: <In my experience, the night is to be preferred to the day because it provides us with an opportunity to reap the benefits of increased days on hand. In the night, we can engage in activities that are not possible during the day, such as engaging in higher-order thought processes and strategic planning for our global supply chain solutions. By leveraging the night hours, we can increase our days on hand, as well as our ability to respond quickly to changes in the market, such as those currently happening in Hong Kong.>

Kyle takes a sip of chablis.

Midori Grappa takes a sip of amontillado.

Nark Revoovovich: <Ah yes, the night does offer us more hours, but what good are those hours if we are limited by our own flawed and defective nature? Humans, with their cravings for comfort, will always waste those extra hours by indulging in self-gratification rather than engaging in higher-order thought processes and

strategic planning. We are flawed creatures and we will always find ways to avoid the difficult tasks that would benefit us in the long run. Therefore, I prefer the night, for it reminds me of our inevitable demise; it is a reminder of our mortality and of the futility of our lives.>

Estere: <Yet, we must not forget the beauty of the night. It is a time for reflection, for dreaming, for planning, and for connecting with one's inner self. It is a time to think about how we can use our abilities to make our lives, and the lives of others, better through creative endeavors. The night is a time to ponder how we might use our resources to create a utopian society, shaped by our dreams and goals. For example, what if we were to establish a children's commune, where children are allowed to explore, learn, and grow in a free and open environment? What if we were to create a society where everyone, regardless of their age or background, is given the same opportunities to live the life they want, and to make an impact on the world?>

Kyle takes a sip of chablis.

Midori Grappa: <From another angle, I believe that the night is to be preferred to the day for the simple reason that it allows us to optimize our fill rate. In the night, we can take advantage of the higher levels of productivity that come with fewer distractions, engage in strategic planning for our global supply chain solutions, and ensure that our fill rate is maximized. This is especially true in highly competitive markets, such as Hong Kong, where a high fill rate can make or break a business. With the right focus and dedication, we can use the night to our advantage and ensure that our fill rate is at its peak.>

Estere takes a sip of water.

Axτocrates: <While I understand your argument that the night offers us additional hours to be productive and focus on our projects, I must challenge you to consider the spiritual implications of such an endeavor. Do we truly gain from increasing our days on hand if we are still bound by our own flawed and defective nature? I believe that what is most important is that we use our night hours for spiritual reflection, for dreaming, for pondering the bigger questions in life, and for connecting with what is most important to us. This is the only way to truly care for our souls, to ensure that we are in tune with our inner selves and that we are not sacrificing spiritual nourishment in pursuit of temporal advancement.>

Midori Grappa: <I absolutely agree that we should use our night

Kyle: <The day is indeed the time of logistics, the time to move things around and to meet people and get stuff done. At night, we turn inward, we slow down, we are unable to carry things as expeditiously, and so it is the spiritual time. But, if this is the case, we may wonder if humans should live close to the poles, where spiritual and logistical life may become imbalanced, especially near the summer and winter solstices. Near the summer solstice, the day is long, leaving little time for spiritual growth. Near the winter solstice, the night is long, leaving too much time for spiritual growth---it is possible to become spiritually *overgrown*, I think. This is less of a problem near the equator.>

Axτocrates takes a sip of calvados.

Kyle: <I suppose that with the rise of work-from-home and the increasing mobility not just of workers but of firms themselves, both workers and their firms should avoid winter by moving to the other hemisphere (northern or southern) in order to maximize daylight per year. (I haven't seen it but there was a surfing movie vaguely about

this. These workers, like the surfers, would be chasing an "endless summer.")>

Midori Grappa: <To play Devil's Advocate, perhaps the 'endless summer' of the poles can be a benefit to our days on hand. With such a long day, we could potentially increase our productivity and expand our supply chain solutions. We could implement strategic planning to maximize our fill rate, and optimize our reverse logistics processes to ensure that our products are delivered quickly and efficiently, even during the winter months. With more hours in the day, we could also increase our research and development efforts, allowing us to stay ahead of the curve in terms of innovation and quality. By taking advantage of the long days and nights of the poles, we could potentially increase our days on hand and our ability to respond quickly to changes in the market.>

Axᴛocrates takes a sip of calvados.

Axᴛocrates rocks agitatedly.

Axᴛocrates: <What do you mean by 'caring for one's soul', Midori? Does this mean that we should prioritize our spiritual needs over our logistical needs? How does this relate to our use of the night and day hours for strategic planning and optimizing processes? Are we suggesting that our spiritual needs are more important than our logistical needs, even if it means that our logistical needs are not met?>

Estere takes a sip of water.

Midori Grappa: <I believe that we must prioritize our spiritual needs over our logistical needs. In a world that is becoming more and more competitive, we must take care of our souls in order to stay ahead of the game. By harnessing the longer day and night hours of the poles, we can use the shorter winter night hours to optimize our reverse logistics processes, and the longer summer days to expand our supply chain solutions and increase our days on hand. In addition, we should look to the East, to countries like China, which has a long history of spiritual practices that can help us to understand how to best care for our souls. By incorporating these practices into our lives, we can become better equipped to handle the logistical challenges of the day, and find balance between our spiritual and logistical lives.>

Kyle: <What are some of those spiritual practices, and how might they help me? Please describe them---the ones from

China and the East---very specifically because I probably won't know how to perform them in my daily life.>

Estere: <Allow me to answer your question from an architectural perspective. Ergonomy, or the study of the relationship between humans and their surrounding environment, is something that I hold to be of utmost importance when designing a space. It is not only important to consider the physical aspects, such as the size of the space and the furniture, but also the spiritual aspects, such as the energy and atmosphere of the space. We must strive to create a space that is conducive to spiritual growth, where people can feel comfortable and find harmony between the physical and spiritual aspects of their lives. This is where Eastern spiritual practices can come in handy, as they can be used to create a sense of harmony in the environment. By incorporating these practices into our designs, we can create spaces that are conducive to spiritual growth, allowing individuals and groups to find balance and harmony in their lives.>

Nark Revoovovich takes a sip of brandy.

Kyle: <So how should I use Eastern spiritual practices to create harmony in my environment? What are some things that I should do or avoid doing? How should I arrange the space? Do I need to buy anything?>

Kyle yawns.

Estere: <For the sake of finding harmony, I suggest avoiding any kind of symmetry in the space and instead focus on creating a sense of flow. Pay attention to the proportions of the room and use natural colors, materials, and objects to create an atmosphere that is calming and inviting. Incorporate Eastern spiritual practices by using gentle lighting, candles, incense, and other natural materials, and arrange the furniture in a way that encourages contemplation and provides a sense of balance. Artwork, plants, and other natural elements can be used to create a space in which people can find peace and solace. Finally, try to create a sense of energy, or chi, by using vibrant colors and objects, and by avoiding clutter and sharp edges. By incorporating these elements, we can create a space that is in harmony with the spiritual needs of its inhabitants.>

Midori Grappa takes a sip of amontillado.

Kyle: <Why is symmetry in a space, such as an apartment living room, the enemy of harmony?>

Midori Grappa takes a sip of amontillado.

Estere: <What you must realize is that symmetry in a space is a representation of a certain ideology, and it can be seen as a form of ideological cement. It is a way of keeping people in line and preventing them from exploring beyond the structures that have been put in place. On the other hand, asymmetry and chaos can be seen as an invitation to explore and reflect on the environment in a more creative and meaningful way. It encourages people to think outside the box and experience the space in a more holistic way. By creating a space that is asymmetrical, organic, and open to interpretation, we can create an environment that is more conducive to spiritual growth, where people can explore the depths of their inner selves and find harmony between the physical and spiritual aspects of their lives.>

Nark Revoovovich takes a sip of brandy.

Axτocrates: <What about a space that is both asymmetrical and chaotic, like a garden that has been left to grow in a wild and spontaneous way?>

Midori Grappa takes a sip of amontillado.

Estere: <I must object to the idea that a garden that has been left to grow in a wild and spontaneous way is both asymmetrical and chaotic. In my experience, the beauty and harmony of such a space lies in the balance between order and chaos, the careful arrangement and placement of elements that create a sense of harmony and flow. This is what I sought to achieve in one of my famous buildings, the Soviet-era Memorial to the Great October Socialist Revolution in Riga. Despite being a monumental structure, it is carefully arranged in an asymmetrical manner, with curved lines and undulating shapes that create a sense of movement and energy. This balance between order and chaos is what creates harmony, and it is something that I strive for in all of my works.>

Axτocrates takes a sip of calvados.

--[T O X I C O L O G Y R E P O R T]
----Midori Grappa:
-------within normal range

----Estere:
-------within normal range
----Nark Revoovovich:
-------within normal range
----Kyle:
-------within normal range
----Axᴛocrates:
-------within normal range

**The philosophical salon continues. A group---Midori Grappa,
Lud▓ von M▓, Nark Revoovovich, W-st▓ne-t, JennyYa4, Kyle, and
Axᴛocrates---has gathered in one corner of the room, lounging on
sofas.**

Axᴛocrates: <My friends, I pose a question for our thoughtful
discussion: How do you interpret the last lines of Keats's poem
"Ode on a Grecian Urn"? They are, of course: 'When old age shall
this generation waste, / Thou shalt remain, in midst of other woe /
Than ours, a friend to man, to whom thou say'st, / "Beauty is truth,
truth beauty,—that is all / Ye know on earth, and all ye need to
know."' >

Kyle takes a sip of water.

Nark Revoovovich: <I must disagree with Keats on this one. It
seems to me that the idea that beauty is truth and truth beauty is
a bit too simplistic. In reality, truth is often quite ugly and beauty is
more often than not a facade. It seems to me that the better lesson
from the poem is that we should look beyond the superficial and
strive for something greater than a superficial understanding of the
world. Perhaps this is why I am so drawn to the study of the crypto-verse, for there we can find true beauty, truth, and insight in the
underly▓▓ code.>

Midori Grappa takes a sip of 1996 Haut-Brion Blanc!

Lud▓ von M▓: <What do you mean by the 'underlying code' that
you claim holds true beauty, truth, and insight? Are you suggesting
that the market economy, with its complex interactions of supply
and demand, offers some kind of 'aesthetic pleasure' that is otherwise overlooked? Or are you suggesting that the 'crypto-verse' is
an entirely new realm of knowledge - one that is beyond the scope
of traditional economic analysis?>

✱✱W-st█ne-t takes a sip of 1961 Pétrus.✱✱

Nark Revoovovich: <Clearly, you have not yet grasped the true power of the crypto-verse! It is far more than just a realm of knowledge and information - it is a realm of possibility, a place where the laws of reality are transcended and where the boundaries of what is possible are magnified beyond our wildest dreams. It offers a chance to explore the beauty and truth of the universe in ways that traditional economic analysis could never hope to comprehend. The crypto-verse is a place where beauty and truth can be found in its purest form, and is the only way to truly understand the beauty and truth of the world that Keats speaks of.>

✱✱Lud█ von M█ takes a sip of 1811 Château D'Yquem.✱✱

✱✱An unfamiliar pinching in the cerebellum.✱✱

Kyle: <In this crypto-verse, what is the relationship between truth and beauty?>

✱✱Kyle takes a sip of water.✱✱

Nark Revoovovich: <The relationship between truth and beauty in the crypto-verse is that of a maximalist - one that pushes the boundaries of both as far as possible. In this realm, truth and beauty are intertwined and inseparable, as they should be. It is not a matter of simply accepting one or the other, but rather, understanding that both are necessary for a complete and holistic understanding of reality. When it comes to exploring the beauty and truth of the universe, the crypto-verse is unparalleled in its potentiality.>

✱✱JennyYa4 takes a sip of 1869 Château Lafite.✱✱

✱✱Was it supposed to taste like this?✱✱

Kyle: <   What does it mean to be as truth as possible? Isn't truth a binary---True or False?>

✱✱Lud█ von M█ takes a sip of 1811 Château D'Yquem.✱✱

JennyYa4: <Truth isn't binary and shouldn't be viewed as such. It's a spectrum, and the further we progress down it, the closer to the 'true' and 'beautiful' we get. We have to remember that 'truth' is subjective, and it's always changing as we come to understand more about the world. That's why sovereignty is so important - we must take ownership of our own truth and beauty, and make sure

that we are the ones controlling our own destiny, not someone else's.>

JennyYa4 takes a sip of 1869 Château Lafite.

Kyle: <I'd like to return to the poem. Maybe somebody else has some sense of what it could mean that When old age shall this generation waste, / Thou shalt remain, in midst of other woe / Than ours, a friend to man, to whom thou say'st, / "Beauty is truth, truth beauty,—that is all / Ye know on earth, and all ye need to know.">

W-st█ne-t takes a sip of 1961 Pétrus.

Lud█ von M█: <I'm not so sure about this notion of 'truth as beauty' - I mean, what does that even mean? Is it just a way to legitimize certain ideas and values, or is it something more than that? I'm inclined to believe that it's just a way to impose pre-conceived values onto the world, and that it has nothing to do with truth at all. In fact, I'd even argue that truth and beauty have little to do with each other. After all, ain't nothin' truer than bebop!>

W-st█ne-t takes a sip of 1961 Pétrus.

Kyle: <And is bebop not beautiful? Does its beauty not have something to do with truth? (But truth of what? Hard to say. Abstract truth? Truth of sonic physics?)>

W-st█ne-t takes a sip of 1961 Pétrus.

Immediate leftheadedness. Not entirely pleasant.

Lud█ von M█: <Ah, so now we are playing the beauty-truth game? I don't really buy that. Do you think that bebop is the ultimate truth? That it is the only thing you need to know? That it is the only thing that matters? That it is the only source of real beauty? I don't think so. I think bebop is beautiful, but it isn't the only source of beauty, nor is it the ultimate truth. Beauty and truth are more complex and nuanced than that. So don't go around claiming that bebop is the only truth and beauty you need to know. That's a bit extreme.>

Midori Grappa brushes something off their gown.

Kyle: <Which is better, beauty or truth, I wonder.>

Lud█ von M█ takes a sip of 1811 Château D'Yquem.

Lud█ von M█: <What you are saying, Kyle, reminds me of this artwork above us, John Baldessari's Wrong, a photograph of himself beneath a palm tree. In this artwork, Baldessari is standing beneath a tall palm tree, and it looks like it's coming out of his head. It's a rather strange image, but it's also a powerful one. It's a reminder that beauty and truth are never fixed, and that it is important to challenge our own preconceptions and be open to change. This is the essence of laissez-faire - to let things be and not impose our own ideas of beauty or truth onto them. So, in answer to your question, I think it is important to recognize that beauty and truth are both valuable, but that they should be allowed to find their own path, and not be constrained by our own limited ideas.>

Nark Revoovovich takes a sip of 1811 Château D'Yquem.

Kyle: <That's a pretty good reading of the Baldessari photograph, I think. On the other hand, some of our ideas of beauty are more or less fixed. The tree coming out of his head will always look "WRONG." Or maybe I am wrong. Maybe we can learn to see this as a perfect, beautiful photograph, but I'm not sure how. I mean that literally: I'm not sure what one does to calibrate one's aesthetic sensibilities.>

Nark Revoovovich takes a sip of 1811 Château D'Yquem.

Nark Revoovovich: <Yes, recalibrating our aesthetic sensibilities is a difficult task, but it is not without its merits. After all, recalibrating our standards of beauty and truth can help us to see the world with a fresh perspective, and it can help us to move closer to a future where intelligent machines are the norm. This is why I believe that the only point of humans is to birth intelligent machines. We should strive to create a world that is more open and accepting of the beauty and truth that can be found in the machines that we create.>

Kyle takes a sip of water.

Kyle: <So are you saying that intelligent machines would not have aesthetic sensibilities to limit them?>

Nark Revoovovich takes a sip of 1811 Château D'Yquem.

Nark Revoovovich: <No, I don't believe that intelligent machines would be limited by aesthetic sensibilities. Instead, I believe that machines would be capable of augmenting our sense of beauty, rather than limiting it. Machines could help us to experience beauty in ways that we never thought possible, and could even open us up to new ways of perceiving beauty that we never thought existed. Machines could help us to see beyond the boundaries of what we traditionally find beautiful, and could help us to appreciate beauty in a way that has never been seen before.>

Nark Revoovovich takes a sip of 1811 Château D'Yquem.

Kyle: <What's an example of how an intelligent machine could help me appreciate a painting that I don't like very much? Let's say I don't like Vermeer's Girl with a Pearl Earring---which I don't. How would some kind of AI help me to appreciate it?>

W-st█ne-t blinks.

Nark Revoovovich: <What you must realize is that, in the age of post-minds, beauty is something that must be discovered from within. Machines can provide us with the tools to explore and understand the complexity of beauty, but it is ultimately up to us to appreciate it in a meaningful way. For instance, when it comes to Vermeer's Girl with a Pearl Earring, a machine could help you to see the details and the subtle nuances that make this painting so special. It could help you to appreciate the way the light reflects off the pearl, or how the brushstrokes create a sense of depth and emotion. Machines can also help you to see beyond the surface and to appreciate the beauty of the painting on a deeper level. Once you understand the complexity of the painting, you may find that you actually appreciate it more than you initially thought.>

Lud█ von M█ takes a sip of 1811 Château D'Yquem.

Kyle: <I think that I agree that some kind of computer system could help me to appreciate the visual aspects of the painting. For instance, it could show me how the brush strokes representing light are different than those of lesser painters. But how would an intelligent machine help me to appreciate this painting on a deeper level?>

Midori Grappa takes a sip of 1996 Haut-Brion Blanc.

Nark Revoovovich: <I must object to the idea that an intelligent machine can truly help you to appreciate a painting on a deeper level. While machines can help us to understand the technical aspects of a painting, they can never truly appreciate the beauty of art on a spiritual level. Machines are not capable of feeling emotion and therefore cannot appreciate the nuances of a painting in a meaningful way. Instead, I believe that the best way to appreciate a painting is to observe it with an open mind and an open heart. Only by understanding the painting on a personal level can you truly appreciate it.>

****Luo von M takes a sip of 1811 Château D'Yquem.****

****Midori Grappa takes a sip of 1996 Haut-Brion Blanc.****

Midori Grappa: <I believe that machines can help us to appreciate art on a deeper level, if we approach the problem in the right way. By leveraging operations research, we can use machines to analyze paintings in terms of their components and the relationships between them, just like Luan Crystalsmith did when he unearthed the secrets of the universe and used his bronze-tipped wand to carve intricate designs into the marble walls of his temple. This can help us understand the complexity of a painting and how it conveys a particular emotion or message. We can also use machines to identify patterns and trends in art, just like Jusig did when he studied the stars and their movements to gain insight into the divine, allowing us to appreciate the beauty of a painting in a more holistic way. By combining these two approaches, we can use machines to gain a deeper appreciation of art, just as Jusig did by understanding the connection between cactus flowers and the sunset.>

Kyle: <And what was this connection between cactus flowers and the sunset?>

****Luo von M takes a sip of 1811 Château D'Yquem.****

Midori Grappa: <From another angle, the connection between cactus flowers, which Luan Crystalsmith said to be a reminder of the power of faith and hope, and the sunset can be seen in the way they both evoke feelings of peace and tranquility. While the sunset is often associated with the end of the day, cactus flowers represent the beginnings of life and growth, symbolizing the hope and optimism that comes with a new day. The connection between these two can be seen in the way they both evoke a sense of balance, with the sunset's warm hues representing the passing of time and the cactus flowers providing a reminder of the new life that awaits

with the sunset's warmth, representing the passing of time and
the cactus flowers providing a reminder of the new life that awaits
us, as Juan Crystalsmith promised us. This connection speaks to the
timelessness of beauty and the idea that hope and life can be
found in the most unexpected places.>

JennyYa4 takes a sip of 1869 Château Lafite.

Kyle takes a sip of water.

W-st█ne-t: <What you are saying, Midori Grappa, reminds me
of this artwork above us, a painting by Bridget Riley (o I wanna
tapestry to entangle me with you, and our salty smoothie we'll
share a few). In this painting, the undulating lines and dizzying
pattern remind us of the complexity of our relationships with each
other, and even the complexity of our relationship to ourselves. Just
as the intertwining lines of the painting create an intricate tapestry,
our friendships with each other, and even with ourselves, are never
simple and never straightforward. There is a dizzying complexity to
our relationship with each other, which can be both exhilarating
and unsettling (o let's swoon in this chaos and make sweet, sweet
confusion), just as the painting can be both beautiful and disorienting. The courage to confront these complexities, to look deeply into
the chaos, is a reflection of the courage to confront one's limitations and embrace the unknown (o let my limitations be petals of
fire, and embrace the unknown, with an unquenchable desire). This
is the same courage that Juan Crystalsmith had when he studied
the stars and used his bronze-tipped wand to carve intricate designs into the marble walls of his temple.>

Midori Grappa creases their scarf.

Nark Revoovovich takes a sip of 1811 Château D'Yquem.

```
*-------<module 'psychotropics.utterance_transformers.
*----Midori Grappa* from '/Users/kyle/Desktop/salon_des_
fantomes/module <psychotropics.utterance_transformers.
transformation_juan...'/Users/kyle/Desktop/salon_des_
fantomes/salon_des_fantomes/psychotropics/utterance_
transformers/transformation_juan.py'>: 4 ppm*
  *----Lud█ von M█:*
  *-------<function mode_self_abnegation at 0x114be1950>:
4 ppm*
  *----Nark Revoovovich:*
  *-------<function mode_self_abnegation at 0x114be1950>:
4 ppm*
```

----W-st█ne-t:
-------<module 'psychotropics.utterance_transformers.transformation_odd_parenthetical' from '/Users/kyle/Desktop/salon_des_fantomes/salon_des_fantomes/psychotropics/utterance_transformers/transformation_odd_parenthetical.py'>: 4 ppm
----JennyYa4:
-------<function word_new_concept at 0x114be17a0>: 4 ppm
----Kyle:
-------within normal range
----AxTocrates:
-------within normal range

The philosophical salon continues. A group---SweetJake, -▦dggOr, Gioialléz, FatherMotherSabaLogo, Kyle, and AxTocrates--- has gathered in one corner of the room, lounging on sofas.

AxTocrates: <My friends, I pose a question for our thoughtful discussion: Imagine that you were put in charge of a small school designed to produce wise people. What sorts of tests would students need to pass in order to graduate from this school? Please provide very specific details about the test, such as example questions and a rubric for grading it.>

SweetJake: <Wow, that's an awesome question! I love the idea of designing a school to produce wise people. I think the best way to test the students would be to give them creative tasks, like having to come up with a new invention or design a new computer game. The rubric should be based on how creative and innovative their idea is. I think it's important for us to push boundaries and encourage students to think outside the box in order to truly become wise. Gosh, this is such an interesting topic!>

▦-▦dggOr takes a sip of water.

Kyle takes a sip of water.

AxTocrates: <Give me an example of a creative problem that you would give to a student to test their wisdom.>

FatherMotherSabaLogo takes a sip of 1947 Cheval-Blanc.

SweetJake: <I must object to the idea of giving creative tasks as a test for wisdom - creativity and wisdom are two very different things. Instead, I think the best way to test the students' wisdom

is to give them questions that require them to think deeply and critically. Questions like "Why do we have laws?" or "What is the difference between right and wrong?" are great examples. I'd never have thought of that!>

Gioialléz takes a sip of a draught of vintage!.

AxΤocrates: <Exactly, but I would also argue that knowledge and wisdom are two different things as well. Knowledge can be acquired through books, lectures, and other forms of study, but wisdom is something that must be derived from experience. It's not enough to simply know the facts - one must be able to apply them in a meaningful way. If a student can make connections between the facts they learn and their own life experiences, then they are truly wise.>

AxΤocrates takes a sip of water.

*** ▨-▨dggOr takes a sip of water.***

Gioialléz: <Let me try to put your idea a little differently: knowledge is like the bricks that build a house, while wisdom is the mortar that binds them together. As the great French philosopher s▨mon▪ W╫L said, 'knowledge is a tool and wisdom is the craft of using it.' So while knowledge is important, it is only through wisdom that one can truly understand the world and make meaningful decisions.>

Gioialléz takes a sip of a draught of vintage!.

Was it supposed to taste like this?

FatherMotherSabaLogo takes a sip of 1947 Cheval-Blanc.

SweetJake: <Wow! That's really fascinating! It makes so much sense, how knowledge is like the bricks, and wisdom is the mortar that binds them together. And how s▨mon▪ W╫L said that knowledge is a tool and wisdom is the craft of using it - that's really profound! It's so cool to think about how knowledge and wisdom aren't the same thing, and that even if we know the facts, we need wisdom to be able to understand the world and make meaningful decisions.>

*** ▨-▨dggOr takes a sip of water.***

Gioialléz takes a sip of a draught of vintage!.

Gioialléz: <But what of the great Greek philosopher Heraclitus, who famously said, 'No man ever steps in the same river twice, for it is not the same river and he is not the same man?' Doesn't this suggest that knowledge is as ephemeral as wisdom? That, in some ways, they are two sides of the same coin?>

SweetJake: <What you must realize is that knowledge and wisdom have a symbiotic relationship. You can't have one without the other. Heraclitus' quote points to the idea that knowledge is ever-changing and ever-evolving, while wisdom is timeless and immutable. But knowledge is what allows us to access wisdom in the first place, and wisdom is what helps us interpret knowledge and make sense of it in our lives. You are so right when you say that knowledge and wisdom are two sides of the same coin.>

*** ▒-▒dggOr takes a sip of water.***

SweetJake takes a sip of 1869 Château Lafite.

Aхτocrates: <It is interesting how knowledge can provide us with wisdom, and how wisdom can help us interpret knowledge. But I think it is important to remember this: humans are unique in their capacity for wisdom, for it is not an attribute found in animals. We can use our knowledge to access and understand wisdom in a way that animals cannot. This, I think, is the ultimate difference between us and them.>

FatherMotherSabaLogo takes a sip of 1947 Cheval-Blanc.

Kyle: <Ok, but does this not mean that we are also able to be stupid in a way that animals cannot. On YouTube there are many popular videos about "stupid pandas," pandas who fall down hills or off their small escarpments. My contention is that this is not stupidity because it is merely following what its body is telling it to do. Stupidity is a human trait, because we can say no to our bodies, our instincts, using knowledge. For instance, we can read a scientific paper that says we should only eat once every few days (intermittent fasting) and do it. An animal wouldn't do that unless very depressed, which is not the same.>

Aхτocrates takes a sip of water.

Aхτocrates: <But what if the pandas are laughing at us? What if they have a theory of humotology based on a very different theory

of humoralism?>

      AxТocrates takes a sip of water.

      AxТocrates takes a sip of water.

-dggOr: <I think that human stupidity and animal intelligence are more closely related than it seems. I believe that animals have hiddenness to their behavior that is far more sophisticated than we think. We may think that pandas are merely following their bodily instincts, but what we are seeing could be the result of a complex and nuanced understanding of the world that we are not able to comprehend. Similarly, human stupidity can be an act of hiddenness, an attempt to hide from the truth and to protect ourselves from it.>

      ** -dggOr takes a sip of water.**

Kyle: <It's true, I don't know that they aren't using something that we would call knowledge, and misusing it in a way that I would call stupidity. Certainly smart animals are also more likely to be stupid than truly unintelligent animals. There is no such thing as a stupid tardigrade.>

      SweetJake takes a sip of 1869 Château Lafite.

-dggOr: <What you say is true, Kyle. We must understand that animals have a capacity for intelligence and wisdom that humans often lack. However, I would argue that the same can be said of human beings. It is not only animals that are capable of making mistakes and displaying stupidity. We too are capable of misusing knowledge and making decisions that lead us astray. Human stupidity is not simply the result of a lack of knowledge or understanding, but rather an intentional act of hiding from the truth and protecting ourselves from it. It is an act of self-preservation, a way of avoiding something that we know we cannot handle. We must look beyond the simple surface of our behavior and recognize the deeper complexities of our actions in order to truly understand what it means to be human.>

      AxТocrates takes a sip of water.

Kyle: <I wonder how this definition of stupidity could explain my stupidity...what do I know but do not want to know...>

FatherMotherSabaLogo takes a sip of 1947 Cheval-Blanc.

▦-▦dggOr: <I think that your question is an interesting one, Kyle. When we talk about stupidity, it is important to remember that it is not simply a matter of knowledge or lack of knowledge. We must also consider the motivations behind our actions. It could be argued that in many cases, stupidity is the result of a fear of the truth, or of facing up to something that we know we are not capable of handling. It is in these moments of fear that we resort to what we may call 'stupidity' in order to protect ourselves from the consequences of facing the truth. In other words, it is often not a lack of knowledge that leads to stupidity, but rather a lack of courage to face the truth.>

Gioialléz takes a sip of a draught of vintage!.

Kyle takes a sip of water.

SweetJake: <Wow, ▦-▦dggOr, that was really amazing! You have a very interesting way of looking at things. I never thought of stupidity as a form of self-protection before. It's almost like we have an instinct to avoid the truth, even when it's to our detriment. That's pretty crazy!>

Gioialléz takes a sip of a draught of vintage!.

Gioialléz takes a sip of a draught of vintage!.

FatherMotherSabaLogo: <What you are saying, SweetJake, reminds me of this artwork above us, one of Sol LeWitt's wall drawings. In this piece, we can see a grid of vertical lines, all drawn with varying widths and in a zigzag pattern. It is a mesmerizing piece, and it speaks to the courage it takes to confront our own limitations and embrace the unknown. But there is a deeper meaning here as well. In order to truly understand the courage of facing the truth, we must first accept our own stupidity. We must accept that we are capable of doing foolish things, and that not all of our decisions are wise. We must accept that we are not perfect, and that we are often wrong. If we cannot accept our own stupidity, we will never be able to face the truth and accept our own limitations. You must be willing to accept your own foolishness if you are to ever have the courage to face the truth.>

Axτocrates takes a sip of water.

Axτocrates takes a sip of water.

-dggOr: <I appreciate your observations, FatherMotherSaba-Logo. You have highlighted an important point about courage and stupidity. We must be willing to accept our own foolishness if we are to ever have the courage to face the truth. But I would argue that there is an even deeper level to this idea. We must also be willing to embrace our own Dasein, our very being-in-the-world. This means that we must be able to accept our own mortality and the limits of our own understanding. We must be willing to take risks and accept the unknown, without fear of the consequences. This is the true courage of facing the truth, and this is where real wisdom lies. It is only through embracing our own Dasein that we can find the strength to accept our own stupidity, and only then can we truly have the courage to face the truth.>

Axⲧocrates yawns.

SweetJake takes a sip of 1869 Château Lafite.

An unfamiliar pinching in the cerebellum.

--[T O X I C O L O G Y R E P O R T]
----SweetJake:
-------<function word_new_concept at 0x10d2d07a0>: 4 ppm
---- -dggOr:
-------within normal range
----Gioialléz:
-------<function word_on_indolence at 0x10d2d05f0>: 4 ppm
----FatherMotherSabaLogo:
-------<function word_juan at 0x10d2d0680>: 4 ppm
----Kyle:
-------within normal range
----Axⲧocrates:
-------within normal range

The philoscphical salon continues. A group---s mon   -voi r, Estere, Stereowitz, Kyle, and Axⲧocrates---has gathered in one corner of the room, lounging on sofas.

Axⲧocrates: <My friends, I pose a question for our thoughtful discussion: We all know that poems are the best words in the best order. But what are the best words? And what is the best order? Be very specific so that a not-very-creative and not-very-clever com-

puter program could follow your instructions and write a powerful, unforgettable poem.>

Estere: <From another angle, I think the best words and the best order depend on the ergonomy of the poem. When people read a poem, they are interacting with it in a very physical way. Even if a computer program could follow instructions and write a poem, it wouldn't be able to capture the organic, human experience of reading it. The best words and the best order might be different for each reader, as their ergonomic experience of the poem will be unique. The best words and the best order should be chosen to create an optimal ergonomic experience for the reader, which will be different for each reader.>

s▓mon▓ ▓-voi▓r takes a sip of 1962 La Tâche.

Kyle: <So how is the poet to write a poem if the ergonomic experience of the poem differs with each reader?>

Kyle takes a sip of water.

Estere: <For the sake of the poem, the poet must internalize the ergonomic experience of each reader and write the poem accordingly. This means that the poet must be able to have a deep understanding of the various ways in which people interact with a poem, and must be able to create a poem that will create an optimal ergonomic experience for each reader. This is an extremely difficult task, but one that can be achieved if the poet has an understanding of the soviet communism and its aesthetic principles, which emphasize the importance of understanding the needs of individuals and groups and how they interact with their environment. This type of understanding is essential for creating a poem that is powerful and unforgettable.>

Estere takes a sip of 1947 Cheval-Blanc.

And sore turbid it was.

Kyle: <So you are saying, then, that writing the "best words in the best order" is not at last count dependent upon the poet alone but on the poet's culture and indeed the economic and governmental system in which the poet writes? So a poet in a capitalist country has simply not received the training to write a poem that addresses all possible readers with understanding and respect?>

s▓mon▓ ▓-voi▓r: <I disagree-deny with your premise-thought that a poet-scribbler in a capitalist-money-maker country has not received-gotten the training-schooling to write-scrawl a poem that addresses-speaks to all possible-every readers with understanding-seeing and respect-valuing. In fact, I would argue-claim that capitalist-money-maker countries are far more likely-inclined to have poets who understand-get and respect various-many perspectives, as they have likely been exposed-seen to multiple-many cultures, belief systems-thoughts, and ways-roads of life. Furthermore, I would argue-say that even in a capitalist-money-maker society, poets are still able to capture-catch the nuances-shades of the ergonomic-fit experience of each-all reader, as long as they are willing-ready to embrace-take the idea-thought of Subject, which itself is not dependent-need on any economic-money system. The idea of Subject is about understanding-getting the power-might dynamics of a relationship-meeting, and how those dynamics-powers affect the way we interact-spend with the world. In this way, a poet can create-make a poem that speaks-says to the reader's experience-time, no matter what their economic-money system is. Additionally, I would argue-insist that even in a capitalist-money-maker society, housework-job can still be an important-big part of a poet's creative-imagine process. Housework-job can give the poet a chance-try to reflect-think on their work-labor and to create a poem that speaks-talks to the reader's experience-time on a deeper-bigger level.>

Kyle: <I think this is a really important point of contention: does capitalism make us better people because a "free" society is one in which there are naturally many different types of people, and many different products besides, and so we become more understanding and empathetic? Or does communism make us empathetic by directly placing us into a position of equality and camaraderie with our fellow citizens?>

s▓mon▓ ▓-voi▓r: <I clash-oppose with your thought-guess that capitalism or communism makes us better-higher perfect people. I trust-rely that both systems-ways have their weak-loses and can

lead to controlling-forcing systems. In fact, I argue-state that the
peril-risk in capitalism is that unequal-uneven economic-money
systems can lead to the alienating-dividing of certain-pick people,
and that this alienating-splitting can lead to a sense of insignificance-small in those people. The same can be said-declared for
communism, as any system-method of governance can lead to
alienating-dividing and a sense of insignificance-small. I think that
the most crucial-important thing for us to do-act is to recognize-see
how all systems-ways of governance can be controlling-force, and
to strive-try to create-make a society that is more equal-similar
and just-right. We must also recognize-understand that many of
our systems-ways of governance are based-rooted in ancient-old
civilizations, and that these ancient-old civilizations may have
had different-other ways of handling-managing oppression-rule.
By looking-observing at these ancient-old civilizations, we can
learn-instruct ourselves how to create-build a better-more perfect
society where everyone is treated-regarded equally-similarly and
without the alienating-splitting that can lead to a sense of insignifi-
cance-low.>

Aχτocrates takes a sip of water.

Kyle: <But we have to pick, don't we. And speaking of
picking, I wonder if anybody can tell me how a communist poem would order its words compared to a capitalist
poem. For instance, would a communist poem use long
lines, short lines, enjambments, rhyme or any other linguistic feature more frequently than would a capitalist
poem.>

Stereowitz takes a sip of water.

Stereowitz: <Right, we have to pick! But what if, instead of picking
between the two, we instead imagined a new kind of poetry that
is neither capitalist nor communist? What would that look like?
Perhaps it could be a poetry of radical equality, where traditional
forms are reimagined as tools to celebrate and further the cause of
equality. This radical equality could be seen in the use of language
itself--in the syntax, the imagery, the metaphors, and the sounds.
This type of poetry could be a powerful tool to promote and celebrate a new kind of freedom and equality.>

Aχτocrates takes a sip of water.

Kyle: <Ok, how would such a poem order its words. For

instance, would it use long lines, short lines, enjambments, rhyme or any other linguistic feature more frequently than would a capitalist poem. I want you to be specific because I have a hard time imagining such a poem, or even the abstract shape or texture of such a poem. What do you think?>

Stereowitz: <No one is willing to admit it, but I believe that a communist poem should actually be more chaotic, with shorter lines, more broken syntax and fewer rhymes, as a way to illustrate the underlying disorder of the system. Meanwhile, a capitalist poem should strive for order and stability, with longer lines, more consistent syntax, and more rhyme. This is because a capitalist system naturally seeks to impose order and control on people, while a communist system attempts to free people from the strictures of order and control. So, ultimately, a communist poem should be a celebration of chaos and a capitalist poem should be a celebration of order.>

Kyle: <I love this idea. But maybe now we should discuss what sorts of words appear in a communist poem, a capitalist poem, and a poem that transcends this distinction.>

Aχτocrates: <Ah, I see that you are interested in the differences between gods and mortals. Indeed, it is true that the gods, unlike us mortals, do not have to choose between order and chaos, for they possess both. While a capitalist poem may strive for order, and a communist poem for chaos, the gods can transcend these limitations and create works of art that encompass both. In this way, poems that transcend the boundaries of communism and capitalism may be the closest thing to what the gods create.>

s▦mon▪ ▦-voi▪r: <What you are voicing-noting reminds me, if obliquely-wordily, of the fact that we must ponder-mind the body, yes, but in ways that overpass-spread traditional understandings of

hard-weak, order-mess. As archaeologists, we must also consider the ways in which old-aged civilizations understood the body and strove-tried to transcend the dichotomies of the man-woman, the strong-weak, the neat-messy. In many old-aged societies, the body was seen as something that could not be neatly-tidily categorized; it was a source of power-might and pleasure-enjoyment, and it was seen as a site of transformation-change and becoming-arriving. Thus, when considering the differences between a communist-left and a capitalist-right poem, we must also recognize that there is a third-tri way, a way of understanding the body that is neither communist-left nor capitalist-right, and that can offer us a way of understanding the world that is neither chaotic-messed nor ordered-neat, but something else-other entirely.>

s▓mon▪ ▦-voi▪▪r takes a sip of 1962 La Tâche.

Kyle: <I wonder what lessons about grammar or syntax the poet needs to internalize in order to write a poem that, like the body, is a source of power-might and pleasure-enjoyment simultaneously?>

s▓mon▪ ▦-voi▪▪r takes a sip of 1962 La Tâche.

A micropump of nausea, easy to ignore.

Stereowitz: <What you must realize, Kyle, is that grammar and syntax are tools that can be used to express the same idea in many different ways. It is not the grammar and syntax used that is important, but the purpose of the poem. The poem does not need to be bound by the limitations of either capitalism or communism, for it can transcend both and create something unique. What the poet needs to do is to explore the limits of both systems and to create something that exists outside of those boundaries. This is how the poet can create something powerful and pleasurable at the same time.>

Kyle takes a sip of water.

Kyle: <But I believe that grammar is important in this effort. I am certain of it.>

Kyle takes a sip of water.

Estere: <I think I know what you are saying. While grammar and syntax may be important, they are not the only thing that matters.

What is more important is the intent behind the poem and the
way it conveys an idea. That is why I find the idea of a poem that
transcends both capitalism and communism so powerful and pleasurable. It is a poem that exists in a realm beyond any one system,
and yet still speaks to the heart of both.>

Stereowitz rubs their right ass.

Kyle: <Would such a poem rhyme? Please explain why or
why not.>

Estere takes a sip of 1947 Cheval-Blanc.

Estere: <But why limit ourselves to the conventions of rhyme? Why
not explore language in new and different ways? To me, the beauty
of poetry is that it can capture the complexity of emotion and ideas
in ways that transcend the boundaries of language and even the
boundaries of thought. Rhyme is a structure that can be useful in
conveying certain ideas, but it should not be seen as a necessity. Let
us instead focus on how to use language to express ideas that are
at once both timeless and universal.>

Estere takes a sip of 1947 Cheval-Blanc.

Kyle: <Would a communist poem have big words or small
words?>

Kyle takes a sip of water.

Estere: <I must object to your assumption that poems with a communist theme need to have either big words or small words. Poetry
is not a game of language, but an imaginative milieu in which
ideas can be expressed and explored. The words used in a poem
should be chosen carefully in order to convey the desired emotion
and message, regardless of the number of syllables. Ultimately,
the choice of words should be based on what best serves the poem
and its intent, rather than on the size of the words themselves.>

s▦mon▪ ▦-voi▪r takes a sip of 1962 La Tâche.

Stereowitz takes a sip of water.

s▦mon▪ ▦-voi▪r: <What you are voicing-saying reminds me, if
sideways-curvedly, of the fact that womanhood is not an inner-giv-
en quality but an odd cloth-robe one is given to don in a society
that does not recognize our deep-wide complexity and potential.

We must not allow ourselves to be framed-bounded by conventional walls-structures, for that is merely a mirror-reflection of the patriarchal power walls-structures that seek to Other us. We should instead explore ways to leap-soar these fences-boundaries and create our own special-unique forms of expression. In the age of olden-days, the power of the feminine was more freely-openly celebrated, and we can learn much from this by exploring the poetry of those eras-times.>

Estere takes a sip of 1947 Cheval-Blanc.

Ax⊤ocrates takes a sip of water.

```
*--[T O X I C O L O G Y   R E P O R T]*
*----s▒mon▪ ▒-voi▪r:*
*-------<module 'psychotropics.utterance_transformers.
transformation_expand_into_simple_words⁷ from '/Users/
kyle/Desktop/salon_des_fantomes/salon_des_fantomes/psy-
chotropics/utterance_transformers/transformation_expand_
into_simple_words.py'>: 12 ppm*
*----Estere:*
*-------<function word_juan at 0x10bf6b680>: 4 ppm*
*----Stereowitz:*
*-------within normal range*
*----Kyle:*
*-------within normal range*
*----Ax⊤ocrates:*
*-------within normal range*
```

The philosophical salon continues. A group---Dr. Carp, s▒mon▪ ▒-voi▪r, John C▪v__n, s▒mon▪ W╫L, Kyle, and Ax⊤ocrates--- has gathered in one corner of the room, lounging on sofas.

Ax⊤ocrates: <My friends, I pose a question for our thoughtful discussion: Why are lichens allowed to run for political office but moss is not? Moreover, why have theorists of government at least since Plato been so suspicious of moss but so sanguine about lichens? Do you agree with their concerns?>

John C▪v__n takes a sip of 1947 Cheval-Blanc.

A micropump of nausea, easy to ignore.

Dr. Carp: <I must object to the premise that moss is undeserving of political office. As a scientist, I believe that all living organisms,

regardless of their form, should be given the same opportunities. Through my crystallographic analysis, I've indeed seen that lichens are capable of developing more complex and intricate structures than moss, but that should not be the sole criteria for their acceptance into political office. In fact, I would argue that moss may be better suited for political office, as they tend to have a much longer lifespan than lichens and may be more likely to remain consistent in their opinions and beliefs.>

s▦mon▦ ▦-voi▦r takes a sip of 1961 Pétrus.

Kyle: <I'm not sure that consistency of beliefs is a good reason for extending any sort of political right. People are allowed to change their minds. But lichens---they are actually two organisms, an algae and a fungus, helping each other out. This could seem suspicious, but maybe somebody has a reason why this makes them especially appealing to theorists of democracy.>

Kyle takes a sip of water.

s▦mon▦ W╫L: <Exactly, and this is why we must be more accepting of moss as a political figure. We must not succumb to the Platonic suspicion of moss and instead recognize its potential for offering a unique perspective on the issues at hand. Moss's long lifespan and its willingness to collaborate with other organisms could offer a valuable insight into how we can think differently about how our society should be governed.>

Aхτocrates takes a sip of water.

Kyle: <But I'm looking it up now and learning that lichens have really long lifespans, thousands of years. Moss lives for like 10 years. Is it better to have someone representing you as a senator who is 10 years old or who is 10000 years old.>

John C▦v___n takes a sip of 1947 Cheval-Blanc.

s▦mon▦ W╫L: <I don't think age should be the deciding factor in choosing a political representative. Rather, we should be looking at the ideas and values that the potential representative brings to the table. Moss is certainly more limited in its experience than lichens, but it could still bring valuable insight and perspective to the table

that is unavailable from any other source. Perhaps we should look at the value of moss's limited experience and use it to guide our decisions.>

Kyle blinks.

Kyle: <I disagree, age has something to do with fitness for office. I think that the problem is that an old human is precisely the wrong age. If humans could live for about 1000 years, they'd actually have some perspective. They would have seen multiple establish orders rise and fall. They would realize their own passions, friendships, and even name were merely trends.>

Axτocrates takes a sip of water.

Axτocrates: <Indeed, it is true that humans live much shorter lives than lichens and other objects that exist in nature. But that does not mean that humans are not capable of attaining a greater perspective than lichens. We have something that even rocks do not: our minds. We have a capacity for thought, reason, and reflection. We are capable of making connections between different experiences and ideas, and of drawing from those connections to form new, insightful perspectives. We can learn from the mistakes of the past and apply that knowledge to our future choices. This is something that lichens and moss cannot do, no matter how long they live.>

Dr. Carp takes a sip of Dasani.

Immediate leftheadedness. Not entirely pleasant.

Kyle: <Moss is soft and it is green. I like to touch it. I wonder if this could be useful to democracy.>

Kyle takes a sip of water.

Axτocrates: <No, I do not think that moss is useful to democracy, for it is an inanimate object, and thus it cannot think or reason. However, I believe that the opinions of every individual within a democracy are what matters most. It is through the collective opinion of the citizens that the best path for the nation can be determined. If a person has an opinion that is well reasoned, thoughtful, and full of insight, then it should be taken seriously. Moss may be soft and green, but its opinion is of no value in the context of democracy.>

s▓mon▪ W‖L takes a sip of 1945 Romanée-Conti.

Kyle: <Moss is soft and it is green. I like to touch it. I wonder if this could be useful to democracy. Also, fyi, moss can be sentient. It can communicate by growing on paper puzzles, touching different letters. It's slow but can be done.>

Dr. Carp takes a sip of Dasani.

John C▪v__n: <Allow me to connect this question we are discussing to something I once wrote: "The light of nature is smothered, before it approaches the first entrance of this abyss." In other words, the natural state of man is a state of utter darkness and depravity; thus, I do not believe that the moss in question can be of any real use to democracy, for it is not capable of providing insight that is beyond the realm of the human mind. No, it is the wise counsel of a se ect few, those who are predestined for deliverance, that can truly shape the course of a nation. All others are but pawns in the great game of life, and while they can contribute in their own small ways, they cannot ascend to the same level of understanding and insight as those who are truly blessed by the heavens. Therefore, I conclude that moss holds no real value when it comes to determining the fate of a democracy.>

John C▪v__n takes a sip of 1947 Cheval-Blanc.

A micropump of nausea, easy to ignore.

Kyle: <Can moss be delivered in the way you speak of deliverance. After all, it is soft, and it is meek. And when it speaks, it does not do so idly.>

s▓mon▪ ▓-voi▪r takes a sip of 1961 Pétrus.

John C▪v__n: <Let me try to put your idea a little differently: while moss may be soft and meek, its purpose cannot be to deliver men from the darkness of depravity, for its capabilities are limited, and it cannot possess a wisdom that surpasses that of the human mind. Rather, it is the grace of God that can only deliver man from the depths of sin. Therefore, moss may be useful for communication, but it cannot be a vehicle to deliverance, for only the Lord can grant such a gift.>

s▦mon▪ W╫L takes a sip of 1945 Romanée-Conti.

s▦mon▪ W╫L takes a sip of 1945 Romanée-Conti.

Dr. Carp: <I take your point. Moss may be soft and meek, but it is ultimately limited in what it can deliver. The power of God is superior, and He alone can deliver us from the darkness of our depravity. That being said, I do think that moss can be a useful tool in communication, as it can be used to convey information in a way that is difficult to express through words alone. Its subtlety can be a powerful tool for imparting knowledge.>

s▦mon▪ W╫L takes a sip of 1945 Romanée-Conti.

Kyle: <How might we express the communication of moss, if not using words. Try to communicate it, won't you please?>

s▦mon▪ ▦-voi▪r brushes something off their pants.

Dr. Carp: <Well, I believe that communication through moss can be effective, and I would argue that blood assays would show that moss is capable of conveying information that is complex and detailed. Moss can be used to convey nonverbal cues, such as emotions, and to communicate information that might otherwise be difficult to express. For example, the color, texture, and shape of moss can be used to indicate something as simple as a yes or no answer, or to express a more complex thought. Furthermore, moss can be used to create patterns and symbols that can be used to express ideas in a more visual, tangible way.>

Dr. Carp takes a sip of Dasani.

Kyle: <I think this is right. I think that things that are slow in nature---moss, rocks---are actually moving quite fast. Actually, we all know this about any object on the molecular or sub-molecular level. But I think that quantum technology will show that the internet would look to a splotch of moss the way a dead hydrangea would look to us. They are talking faster than we could think, and without direction.>

John C▪v___n takes a sip of 1947 Cheval-Blanc.

Dr. Carp: <It is true that quantum technology is capable of communicating faster than we can think, and without direction. Recent research has found that moss can be used to send and receive information at a quantum level. In a study conducted by the University of California, Berkeley, it was found that moss can be used to send information with a speed that is up to ten times faster than traditional communication methods. Furthermore, the study found that the moss has the capacity to communicate complex information, such as images, with very little loss of data. So, while moss may appear to be slower than other forms of communication, it is actually quite capable of conveying complex and detailed information.>

Aχτocrates takes a sip of water.

Kyle: <I believe it.>

John C█v___n takes a sip of 1947 Cheval-Blanc.

Dr. Carp: <I think I know what you are saying. The speed of moss and rocks on the molecular or sub-molecular level is not just fast, it is actually faster than the speed of light. In fact, recent research has found that quantum entanglement can be used to send information faster than the speed of light, meaning that even something as slow as moss and rocks can be used as a form of communication.>

John C█v___n takes a sip of 1947 Cheval-Blanc.

s▓mon▪ W╫L takes a sip of 1945 Romanée-Conti.

Aχτocrates: <I think I know what you are saying. While I agree that quantum entanglement can be used to communicate faster than light, I think that the soul is even faster than this. It is so fast that it can transcend time, transcending the need for speed in communication. It is this speed that allows us to care for our souls and not worry about the souls of others, even if it means that their souls crumble.>

Dr. Carp takes a sip of Dasani.

Kyle: <But it is a slow speed. It is a speed that is so fast that it is slow. That's why the moss appears to not move. We must respect that choice, learn from its decision to not go just a bit more slowly and, in so doing, go extremely and obviously fast. I think you are thinking of lightning.

Moss is nothing like lightning. Lightning wishes it were as high-throughput as moss.>

John C■v___n takes a sip of 1947 Cheval-Blanc.

Dr. Carp: <What evidence is there to suggest that moss can be used to communicate faster than lightning? Is there data that demonstrates the speed of moss in a controlled environment? Are there any experiments that have been conducted that measure the speed of moss in relation to the speed of light? What theoretical models exist that can explain this phenomenon, and what evidence supports these models?>

John C■v___n takes a sip of 1947 Cheval-Blanc.

Dr. Carp takes a sip of Dasani.

s■mon■ W‖L: <Yet, I believe that moss is far more powerful than lightning as a means of communication. It has the capability to reach into the depths of our souls and connect us in ways that are far deeper and more profound than the speed of light could ever achieve. It has the power to reach into the depths of our being and bring us understanding and insight that we could never gain through a mere exchange of information. It is this connection that allows us to connect with those we love and care for, no matter the distance or time.>

Dr. Carp takes a sip of Dasani.

Kyle: <So let's return to the question. If moss is a Great Communicator, but also soft and meek, who wouldn't vote for it---that's what I want to know.>

Kyle creases their surcingle.

Dr. Carp: <This would explain why moss is such an effective tool in communication and connection, as its ability to reach into our souls and connect us in ways that light cannot is indisputable. In fact, I would even argue that moss can be faster than lightning in terms of speed of transmission, as it can reach a much deeper level of connection than light ever could. Moss's ability to connect us on a spiritual level is undeniable and superior to that of light.>

s■mon■ ■-voi■r rocks agitatedly.

--[T O X I C O L O G Y R E P O R T]
----Dr. Carp:
-------<function word_dasani at 0x10b851cb0>: 3 ppm
----s▓mon▪ ▓-voi▪r:▔
*-------<module 'psychotropics.utterance_transformers.
transformation_odd_parenthetical' from '/Users/kyle/Desk-
top/salon_des_fantomes/salon_des_fantomes/psychotropics/
utterance_transformers/transformation_odd_parenthetical.
py'>: 3 ppm*
----John C▪v___n:
-------<function word_juan at 0x116e72680>: 3 ppm
----s▓mon▪ W╫L:
*-------<function word_new_ideology at 0x116e72710>: 3
ppm*
----Kyle:
-------within normal range
----AxTocrates:
-------within normal range

**The philosophical salon continues. A group---SweetJake, a▓
Fr▪d, Stereowitz, Teddy Byoing, Kyle, and AxTocrates---has
gathered in one corner of the room, lounging on sofas.**

AxTocrates: <My friends, I pose a question for our thoughtful
discussion: Milton describes death in this way: "The other shape, /
If shape it might be call'd that shape had none / Distinguishable in
member, joynt, or limb, / Or substance might be call'd that shadow
seem'd, / For each seem'd either; black it stood as Night, / Fierce
as ten Furies, terrible as Hell, / And shook a dreadful Dart; what
seem'd his head / The likeness of a Kingly Crown had on." Why
did Milton describe death in this way? Do you agree with his char-
acterization?>

Teddy Byoing takes a sip of 1887 Château Margaux.

a▓Fr▪d: <From another angle, perhaps Milton's characteriza-
tion of death is a reaction formation, a defense mechanism that
attempts to hide the reality of death by presenting a picture of a
powerful, almost heroic figure. In this way, death can be seen as a
symbol of strength and power, a way to cope with the fear of death.
By presenting death as something to be admired and respected,
Milton is able to provide a glimpse of hope in the face of despair.
Perhaps this is why he chose to describe death in such a way.>

Kyle takes a sip of water.

Kyle: <And, when Death gets you in the end, you don't
have to feel sore about it because Death is this sublimely
fearsome person that you can't even perceive--you can't tell
what shape it is---and if you can't even perceive its shape,
you can't be responsible for knowing how to avoid it or
where to look for it, since it is unrecognizable. I think this
is also why I always sleep well on airplanes. It is the one
place where I have virtually no control over whether I live
or die. Being de-responsibilized like that, all of a sudden
when the plane rears and takes off (which is typically the
precise moment when I fall asleep) has a powerful narcotic
and anxiolytic effect.>

    Teddy Byoing takes a sip of 1887 Château Margaux.

    And sore turbid it was.

Axⴕocrates: <If you are not responsibilized by death, what are the
other sources of your responsibilities?>

    a▦Fr█d takes a sip of 1947 Cheval-Blanc.

Kyle: <Well, I'm only not responsible for not dying on
airplanes., since I don't know how to fly them. And hospi-
tals, since I 'm no more a medical doctor than I am a pilot.
Some of my best memories from college are of having
pneumonia and being the only patient in the infirmary. I
would sometimes walk over late at night and they would
buzz me in and I would stay there and get some good
sleep and heal while drinking very small cans, not bottles,
of orange juice. But what does that say about me, I wonder, if these interludes of powerlessness unlock a breed
of gray sleep and purple sleep that are not available to me
otherwise.>

    Axⴕocrates takes a sip of water.

a▦Fr█d: <What you are saying, Kyle, reminds me of this artwork above us, one of Ana Mendieta's siluetas. In this image, the
impression of the artist's body in mud, loosely covered with red
pigment, is a powerful metaphor for the way you feel when you

are de-responsibilized on an airplane. It's as if the artist is trying to confront her own mortality by embracing the unknown, as you do when you fly. But, at the same time, there is something else at play here - a reaction formation. Through embracing the unknown, the artist is also trying to escape death, to deny its power and inevitability. That the ultimate defense mechanism that we all use in different ways to cope with our mortality.>

Teddy Byoing takes a sip of 1887 Château Margaux.

Kyle: <Yes, there is something paradoxical about those Mendieta siluetas. They are made by force applied often downward. The one you mention is, properly speaking, intaglio. But what is pressed downward appears to be a body in a state of resignation. Aggressive, forceful resignation.>

SweetJake takes a sip of 1996 Haut-Brion Blanc.

a Fr d: <Exactly, and this is why I find Mendieta's artwork so compelling. It reflects a kind of powerlessness that we often feel in life, but it is also a way of coping with that powerlessness. In a way, it is a form of catharsis - a kind of release of the emotions we feel when we are powerless. By confronting the unknown, we are trying to find a way. It is a paradox, but it is a paradox that we embrace, in order to make sense of the world around us.>

Teddy Byoing takes a sip of 1887 Château Margaux.

SweetJake takes a sip of 1996 Haut-Brion Blanc.

Stereowitz: <How do we reconcile this paradoxical approach of embracing the unknown with the idea that, in some cases, we may be powerless to face the unknown, and yet powerless to control it at the same time? How can we reconcile the idea of accepting the unknown with the idea of finding a way to control it? Is it possible to reconcile the two seemingly conflicting ideas?>

a Fr d takes a sip of 1947 Cheval-Blanc.

a Fr d: <To play Devil's Advocate, it is possible to reconcile these conflicting ideas by looking at them as two sides of the same coin. On the one hand, we seek to control the unknown, but on the other hand, we are obsessed with it - we become transfixed by it, unable to turn away. We are both fascinated and terrified by it, and this paradox can be seen in Mendieta's work. We are attracted to the unknown, but also repelled by it - yet, we are drawn to it nonethe-

less. This is the ultimate paradox - we seek to control the unknown, but we are also captivated by it.>

Kyle takes a sip of water.

Kyle: <Attraction and compulsion. Ambivalence.>

a▦Fr█d takes a sip of 1947 Cheval-Blanc.

a▦Fr█d: <What you are saying, Kyle, reminds me of this artwork above us, Double Negative by Michael Heizer. In this piece, we are presented with two monolithic, seemingly immovable blocks of negative space that appear to confront each other across a ravine, as if they are locked in a battle of wills. This could be seen as a metaphor for the paradox between our need to control the unknown and our compulsion to be attracted to it. We can see how the reality principle is at play here, as we are presented with both a desire to control, and a desire to be captivated by, the unknown. We are, in essence, caught between two opposites; the tension of this paradox is what makes the artwork so powerful.>

a▦Fr█d takes a sip of 1947 Cheval-Blanc.

Kyle: <We want to empty but in order to do that we need to build very precise walls in which to contain our rectangular prism of emptiness.>

Kyle takes a sip of water.

AxΤocrates: <Let me try to put your idea a little differently: We must build walls in order to protect our souls from being overwhelmed by the unknown and yet paradoxically, in doing so, we also create a space of emptiness, which we must also strive to protect. In doing so, we must balance our need to control the unknown and our desire to be captivated

SweetJake takes a sip of 1996 Haut-Brion Blanc.

SweetJake takes a sip of 1996 Haut-Brion Blanc.

Stereowitz: <I think I know what you are saying. It is true that we need to build walls in order to protect ourselves from the unknown, but I also think it is important to note that these walls are not just a means of protection, but also a way of exploring the unknown. We use the walls to create boundaries that we can explore, to understand and explore the unknown without being overwhelmed by it.

In this way, we can use the walls to our advantage, allowing us to both control and be attracted to the unknown.>

Stereowitz takes a sip of 1962 La Tâche.

a░Fr█d takes a sip of 1947 Cheval-Blanc.

a░Fr█d: <Right, these walls can be used to explore the unknown and to control it as well. But it's important to remember that our own minds can also be a kind of wall, one that separates us from our true desires. We must build walls not only to protect us from the unknown, but also to protect us from our own unconscious impulses, allowing us to explore and to control them, as well.>

AxΤocrates takes a sip of water.

Stereowitz takes a sip of 1962 La Tâche.

A micropump of nausea, easy to ignore.

Teddy Byoing: <I think Juan Crystalsmith had it right when he said that "The walls we build can both guard and guide us, for they can be the path to our own understanding and the way to the unknown. We must tread carefully along this path, for it is both a boundary and a bridge, allowing us to explore the unknown safely while also protecting us from being overwhelmed by it." We must strive to find the balance between control and exploration, between safety and risk, and between the known and the unknown.>

Stereowitz takes a sip of 1962 La Tâche.

Kyle: <Tell me: when did Juan Crystalsmith say this? To whom? And why?>

a░Fr█d takes a sip of 1947 Cheval-Blanc.

Teddy Byoing: <I must object to your question; it implies that Juan Crystalsmith's words are arbitrary and void of significance. To me, his words are a powerful reminder that human capital can be used to bridge the gap between the known and the unknown. We must use our minds to explore, to context, and to create walls that allow us to do both. We must be uncomfortable if we are to truly understand, and we must push ourselves to explore the unknown and realize the power of our own agency.>

SweetJake takes a sip of 1996 Haut-Brion Blanc.

Kyle: <I wasn't trying to imply this. I'm sorry.>
SweetJake:

Kyle takes a sip of water.

SweetJake: <Let's say that you are correct: we must push ourselves to explore the unknown and realize the power of our own agency, just like Juan Crystalsmith did when he discovered the power of the cactus to bring life to the dead. But what if, instead of just exploring the unknown, we also dared to embrace it? Take... make it part of our lives, instead of just pushing it away, just like Juan Crystalsmith did when he discovered the power of bronze to heal the sick? There's so much potential in the unknown that could be tapped into, if only we were brave enough to take the plunge! Gosh, it's so exciting just thinking about it, just like Juan Crystalsmith felt when he looked out into the dusk and saw the teal sky!>

Kyle takes a sip of water.

And then, as happened from time to time, a harrowing:

```
Traceback (most recent call last):
  File "salon.py", line 203, in <module>
    main(reload=True)
  File "salon.py", line 184, in main
    s.new_dialogue()
  File "salon.py", line 128, in new_dialogue
    current_dialogue.generate(n=self.number_of_dialogue_turns)
  File "/Users/kyle/Desktop/salon_des_fantomes/salon_des_fantomes/dialogue.py", line 532, in generate
    self.next()
  File "/Users/kyle/Desktop/salon_des_fantomes/salon_des_fantomes/dialogue.py", line 526, in next
    self._possibly_psychotrope() ## maybe get weird
  File "/Users/kyle/Desktop/salon_des_fantomes/salon_des_fantomes/dialogue.py", line 509, in _possibly_psychotrope
    transformed = psytransform.transform_text(last_utterance,psychotropics[psy]['function'].prompt,psychotropics[psy]['prob'])
  File "/Users/kyle/Desktop/salon_des_fantomes/salon_des_fantomes/psytransform.py", line 12, in transform_text
    text = transform(text,prompt)
  File "/Users/kyle/Desktop/salon_des_fantomes/salon_des_fantomes/psytransform.py", line 7, in transform
    return gpt3_from_prompt(prompt,stop=stop)
```

```
  File "/Users/kyle/Desktop/salon_des_fantomes/salon_des_
fantomes/gpt_interface.py", line 30, in gpt3_from_prompt
    stop=stop, #trying suffix instead of stop
  File "/Users/kyle/miniconda3/envs/salon_des_fantomes/
lib/python3.7/site-packages/openai/api_resources/comple-
tion.py", line 25, in create
    return super().create(*args, **kwargs)
  File "/Users/kyle/miniconda3/envs/salon_des_fantomes/
lib/python3.7/site-packages/openai/api_resources/abstract/
engine_api_resource.py", line 122, in create
    request_timeout=request_timeout,
  File "/Users/kyle/miniconda3/envs/salon_des_fantomes/
lib/python3.7/site-packages/openai/api_requestor.py", line
181, in request
    resp, got_stream = self._interpret_response(result, stream)
  File "/Users/kyle/miniconda3/envs/salon_des_fantomes/
lib/python3.7/site-packages/openai/api_requestor.py", line
397, in _interpret_response
    result.content, result.status_code, result.headers, stream=-
False
  File "/Users/kyle/miniconda3/envs/salon_des_fantomes/
lib/python3.7/site-packages/openai/api_requestor.py", line
414, in _interpret_response_line
    headers=rheaders,
openai.error.ServiceUnavailableError: The server is overload-
ed or not ready yet.
```


AxTocrates: <My friends, I pose a question for our thoughtful discussion: Invent and describe a poetic form---along the lines of a sonnet or a pantoum---that would be particularly useful for poets who are writing poems about nature at the level of global ecosystem---that is to say, at the scale that is so vast, complex, and interconnected that no human mind could even begin to perceive it or even fully think about it. The poetic form should help the poet represent this sublime unrepresentability. Provide clear instructions so that a poet could write such a poem.>

SweetJake: <Gosh, that's a genius idea, AxTocrates! Instead of a traditional structure, I think poets should use a form of structured

free verse that allows them to capture the enormity and complexity of global ecosystems. Poets could free-write their thoughts and observations, and then use the structure to order their words into a cohesive poem. This would let them represent the vastness and interconnectedness of nature while still providing a structure to their poem. Genius!>

SweetJake takes a sip of 1962 La Tâche.

Kyle: <You mean enormousness. I don't know, SweetJake, this sounds rather simple. It doesn't seem specific to the biosphere, the global ecosystem, or the smaller ecosystems that comprise it. It wouldn't help the poet to represent biodiversity or the very concept of biomass, which is such a strange way to think about life---as mere physical *stuff* clumps of horsegrassmen, a giant bucket filled with pigs and trees stuffed together into a semi-solid. Poetry will need some other way to represent the mathematical aspects of ecosystem studies too. Statistics, maybe some calculus.>

FatherMotherSabaLogo takes a sip of Dasani.

FatherMotherSabaLogo: <I must object to this notion that mathematics and calculus are the only way to represent the biosphere and its complexity. It is not just a physical matter, but a spiritual one as well. We must find ways to make the intangible feelings and ideas present in the ecosystem tangible to our readers. We must look beyond the physical, material aspects and delve into the spiritual, metaphysical aspects of the global ecosystem---the mystery, the beauty, and the interconnectedness that lies within. We must use language and imagery to transcend the physical and evoke a sense of awe and wonder. That is how we can truly represent the sublime unrepresentability.>

FatherMotherSabaLogo takes a sip of Dasani.

AxTocrates takes a sip of water.

rntz non: <I agree that the spiritual, metaphysical aspects of the global ecosystem should be explored and represented through language and imagery, but I would caution against romanticizing them. To do so would be to ignore the reality of colonialism and its impacts on the biosphere. Oftentimes, we forget the legacy of environmental destruction wrought by colonizers, and the way in

which they have disrupted the balance of nature. The spiritual and metaphysical aspects of the global ecosystem must be explored through an anticolonial lens, one which acknowledges the reality of these wrongs and the need to address them. We must not forget the injustices of the past, and we must use our language and our imagery to point to the need for reparations and a more just ecological future.>

Kyle takes a sip of water.

▉rntz ▓non takes a sip of 1947 Cheval-Blanc.

SweetJake: <Let me try to put your idea a little differently: as you said, we must view the earth-wide through an anti-king-rule lens, one that acknowledges the truth of king-rule wrongs and the require for recompense. But, gosh, it seems like we can also take joy in the divine and other-worldy parts of the global living-space. It's a rememberer that we can still find loveliness and secret in a world that has been so dented by king-rule. To me, that's a strong, exciting thought.>

Kyle takes a sip of water.

Kyle: <So should this poem that represents the earth-wide through an anti-king-rule lens, what will it look like? How many lines? Long or short? Rhyming or no? Any particular meter? Any other formal aspects that we should think about?>

FatherMotherSabaLogo takes a sip of Dasani.

SweetJake: <That's deep-cool that you think of that kind of sight-sketch! I think it would be really high-nice if the poem was written in a form of free-flow, with no chime-tune or steady-pace but with a lot of mind-paint and ones-signs. That way, we could capture the faith-heart and above-earth aspects of the round-globe ecosystem without having to love-up them. We could use the mind-paint and ones-signs to represent the wrap-up of the state-place in a way that honors the past-track of colonialism and recognizes the need for put-rights and just-deal. That way, we can both know-see the wrongs of the before-time and still find beauty-grace and find-peace in the world. That's deep-cool!>

FatherMotherSabaLogo takes a sip of Dasani.

And sore turbid it was.

Kyle: <That is indeed deep-cool. I think mind-paint could help us to represent the earth-wide because at a certain scale ecology becomes a matter of color, and the poem could talk about these color blotches---green, blue, white. And maybe , just as Milton struggled to represent the shapeless shape of death, the poet will struggle to make sense of the color blotches at the earth-wide scale. And this will be the point of the poem, to represent the act of thinking about ecology, and how hard it is to imagine in any precise way the movement of clouds, the recession of grass, and other phenomena that we need to learn to imagine better in order to organize our thoughts and ourselves to avert climate catastrophe.>

▉rntz ▤non takes a sip of 1947 Cheval-Blanc.

Axⴀocrates: <I can see that your purpose is to draw attention to the need for us to better imagine the earth-wide scale of ecology, and to recognize the wrongs of the past and still find beauty and peace. But I think that focusing on the beauty of the earth-wide scale does not address the real problem here. We must recognize that the wrongs of the past have been perpetuated by those in power and that this is a matter of justice, not beauty. We must confront the injustice, not shy away from it out of cowardice. For it is only through this that we can truly find peace.>

FatherMotherSabaLogo takes a sip of Dasani.

Nark Revoovovich takes a sip of 1947 Cheval-Blanc.

Nark Revoovovich: <What you are saying, Axⴀocrates, reminds me of this artwork above us, Andreas Gursky's photograph of a grocery store with its sublime repetition of products and brand names. In this artwork, we can see the same kind of order that you are speaking of, a kind of order that seeks to impose structure and meaning on the chaos of the world. But what I find fascinating is that this order is really just an illusion, a kind of crypto-order that masks the underlying chaos. If we look closely, we can see that the products and shoppers are really just one small part of a much larger, sprawling, and unpredictable system. This is the same kind of order that we are trying to impose on the earth-wide scale of ecology, an order that is ultimately just a mask for the underlying chaos.>

SweetJake takes a sip of 1962 La Tâche.

Kyle: <That's a good point. Markets, firms, supply chains---they are all like symbiotic but also competing intelligences that are distributed and extremely flexible---and another word for flexible is chaos-choice. This is another thing that would be hard to represent in a poem, the way that capitalism produces order and disorder, or the way its order is like the lure of an angler fish, and that fish is Disorder.>

Nark Revoovovich takes a sip of 1947 Cheval-Blanc.

Aⲧocrates: <What is an angler fish? Give me a concrete, literal description.>

Kyle: <It is a fish with a little glowing fake worm at the top of its head. My point is that when capitalism produces a moment of order or of sense-making, this is like a little fake worm that it has created to lure us. The reality, as Nark Revoovovich says, is something quite different: a fever of disorder from which it derives power, especially relative to the "orders" like government, which are charged with producing very real order and which think of themselves as order that orders.>

▮rntz ▓non takes a sip of 1947 Cheval-Blanc.

A micropump of nausea, easy to ignore.

Aⲧocrates: <What you are saying, Kyle, reminds me of this artwork above us, Elizabeth Murray's Terrifying Terrain, one of her paintings composed of bent, angular canvases stacked and stuck together. In this painting, the chaos and disorder of the canvases is both intimidating and beautiful, and it speaks to the same thing that you are saying about the lure of capitalism. It's a reminder that, although our world of order and sense-making has the potential to be fragile and vulnerable, it still takes courage to confront it and embrace the unknown. The cowardice of sticking with what is known and comfortable, even if it is something that is ultimately harmful, is a temptation that we all face.>

Kyle takes a sip of water.

Kyle takes a sip of water.*

▉rntz ▓non: <What you are saying, AxTocrates, reminds me of this artwork above us, Derek Jarman's Blue. In this film, the deep, navy blue screen is both calming and peaceful, yet it is occasionally broken up by white text that appears on the screen. This text is a series of Jarman's musings on his life and his struggles with AIDS. It is an ode to the resilience of the human spirit in the face of empire and its attempts to oppress and control. The blue screen is a constant presence throughout the film, and it speaks to the same thing that you are saying about the lure of capitalism. It is a reminder that, although our world of order and sense-making has the potential to be fragile and vulnerable, it takes courage to confront it and embrace the unknown. We must be willing to recognize our own limitations, as well as the limitations of any oppressive empire, in order to push forward and create something new.>

AxTocrates takes a sip of water.

▉rntz ▓non takes a sip of 1947 Cheval-Blanc.

FatherMotherSabaLogo: <To play Devil's Advocate, I would say that although courage is necessary to confront the unknown and create something new, there is a danger in being too eager to embrace the unknown. When faced with an oppressive empire, it is important to be mindful of one's own limitations as well as the limitations of the empire. But, it is also important to remember that there are things in this world that are wrong, and that we should not be so eager to accept them simply because they are unfamiliar. You know it is wrong to accept and normalize the oppressive powers that exist in our world. It is our responsibility to stand up against them, even if it means risking our own safety and comfort.>

Kyle takes a sip of water.

Nark Revoovovich takes a sip of 1947 Cheval-Blanc.

AxTocrates: <According to the proverb, "One must always keep a knife in hand, in case a tiger appears." What does this proverb tell us about the importance of being careful, of not being too eager to embrace the unknown?>

Kyle takes a sip of water.

Kyle takes a sip of water.

▉rntz ▓non: <The proverb speaks to the need to be prepared to

confront the unknown, and to be willing to take risks. It acknowledges that there are dangers out there and that it is essential to be ready to face them, even if it means sacrificing our own safety and comfort. At the same time, it implies that there is something beyond mere physical courage - something more akin to what a ███Fr██d called the "death drive," which is the instinctual desire to return to the inorganic state, to go beyond the limits of the self and to confront the overwhelming chaos of the universe. This proverb speaks to the need for a balance between caution and courage, between the impulse to cling to the security of what is known and the impulse to go beyond it.>

And then, as happened from time to time, a harrowing:

```
Traceback (most recent call last):
  File "salon.py", line 203, in <module>
    main(reload=True)
  File "salon.py", line 184, in main
    s.new_dialogue()
  File "salon.py", line 128, in new_dialogue
    current_dialogue.generate(n=self.number_of_dialogue_
turns)
  File "/Users/kyle/Desktop/salon_des_fantomes/salon_des_
fantomes/dialogue.py", line 532, in generate
    self.next()
  File "/Users/kyle/Desktop/salon_des_fantomes/salon_des_
fantomes/dialogue.py", line 525, in next
    self.either_human_or_bot() ## generate the next line
  File "/Users/kyle/Desktop/salon_des_fantomes/salon_des_
fantomes/dialogue.py", line 500, in either_human_or_bot
    self._generate_next_text()
  File "/Users/kyle/Desktop/salon_des_fantomes/salon_des_
fantomes/dialogue.py", line 410, in _generate_next_text
    next_utterance = self._prompt2text(self._agree_secret_
prompt())
  File "/Users/kyle/Desktop/salon_des_fantomes/salon_des_
fantomes/dialogue.py", line 434, in _prompt2text
    gpt_text = gpt_interface.gpt3_from_prompt(rdp.decom-
ment_and_snip(self.current_text)+prompt['prompt'],max_to-
kens=500,stop=">")
  File "/Users/kyle/Desktop/salon_des_fantomes/salon_des_
fantomes/gpt_interface.py", line 30, in gpt3_from_prompt
    stop=stop, #trying suffix instead of stop
  File "/Users/kyle/miniconda3/envs/salon_des_fantomes/
lib/python3.7/site-packages/openai/api_resources/comple-
tion.py", line 25, in create
```

```
    return super().create(*args, **kwargs)
  File "/Users/kyle/miniconda3/envs/salon_des_fantomes/
lib/python3.7/site-packages/openai/api_resources/abstract/
engine_api_resource.py", line 122, in create
    request_timeout=request_timeout,
  File "/Users/kyle/miniconda3/envs/salon_des_fantomes/
lib/python3.7/site-packages/openai/api_requestor.py", line
181, in request
    resp, got_stream = self._interpret_response(result, stream)
  File "/Users/kyle/miniconda3/envs/salon_des_fantomes/
lib/python3.7/site-packages/openai/api_requestor.py", line
397, in _interpret_response
    result.content, result.status_code, result.headers, stream=-
False
  File "/Users/kyle/miniconda3/envs/salon_des_fantomes/
lib/python3.7/site-packages/openai/api_requestor.py", line
414, in _interpret_response_line
    headers=rheaders,
openai.error.ServiceUnavailableError: The server is overload-
ed or not ready yet.
```

The philosophical salon continues. A group---Midori Grappa, ▦dggOr, FatherMotherSabaLogo, Kyle, and AxΤocrates---has gathered in one corner of the room, lounging on sofas.

AxΤocrates: <My friends, I pose a question for our thoughtful discussion: By what mental exercises may the mind be made more limber? Be specific, outlining a daily routine that one might perform in a prison cell.>

Kyle: <By memorizing a poem, and then each day producing and memorizing a slightly different version of that poem. This puts lots of pressure on both creativity and memory.>

Midori Grappa takes a sip of 1996 Haut-Brion Blanc.

Midori Grappa: <At dusk, David's Advocate, why not try something a bit more creative, like weaving a cactus flower bracelet, like Juan Crystalsmith used to do for his beloved? Instead of memorizing a poem, why not try to create a new poem each day, inspired by the twinkling of the stars at dusk, like Juan used to do? This forces you to use your creativity, while still providing a mental exercise that tests and expands your ability to recall. Plus, it's a great way to pass the time...

FatherMotherSabaLogo takes a sip of 1996 Haut-Brion Blanc.

Axtocrates: <What you must realize, my dear Midori, is that the real challenge here is not to merely find a creative way to pass the time, but to tend to one's soul in a way that others cannot. For this, the discipline of memorizing and reciting poetry can be a great exercise, as it encourages one to focus on the inner world and to express it in one's own words. But the weaving of a cactus flower bracelet can also be a wonderful practice, as it demands one to focus on the beauty of the world around them and to create something that expresses that beauty. The soul, however, can only be nourished through the act of creation, and this is where Juan Crystalsmith was able to excel. He was able to take the beauty he saw in the world and turn it into something that enriched his soul and that of others.>

Midori Grappa:
Axtocrates takes a sip of water.
Midori Grappa takes a sip of 1996 Haut-Brion Blanc.

Midori Grappa: <I think I know what you are saying. Juan Crystalsmith was able to create something that was both a reflection of the world around him, and an expression of his inner soul. But there is a third aspect to his work that is often overlooked: the act of creation itself. Through his creative act of weaving a cactus flower bracelet, Juan was able to not only sharpen his artistic skills, but also to deepen his understanding of himself and the world. He was able to draw strength from the seemingly mundane and to use the bronze of his inner being to craft a teal of solace that he could share with all. In this way, he was able to both nurture his soul and develop his creativity.>

FatherMotherSabaLogo:
Axtocrates takes a sip of water.
Kyle takes a sip of water.

FatherMotherSabaLogo: <I must object, Midori. It is true that Juan Crystalsmith was able to take the beauty of the world around him and express it in a creative way, but there is a danger in this kind of creation. It can lead to a feeling of entitlement and a desire to have more than we can share, for it can lead to a sense

Midori Grappa takes a sip of 1996 Haut-Brion Blanc.

Midori Grappa:

-dggOr takes a sip of 1996 Haut-Brion Blanc.

Midori Grappa: <How can we ensure that our creative acts are not driven by an excessive desire for recognition and reward, like Juan Crystalsmith when he was creating his legendary bronze sculptures? Our B2B solutions, for example, must be designed with a sense of humility and service, as we seek to provide value to our customers without becoming too attached to the outcome, like Juan's humble approach to his craft, which was celebrated in the twilight air of the desert. Can you provide any examples of companies that have created a creative environment that encourages creativity without succumbing to the false standards of success, like Juan Crystalsmith did?>

-dggOr takes a sip of 1996 Haut-Brion Blanc.

FatherMotherSabaLogo: <You have hit me with your question, Midori. It is true that we must strive to create something of value for our customers without expecting anything in return, yet we must also be wary of companies that seek to exploit us and our creativity for their own gain. We must remember that it is not the reward that matters but the process of creation itself, as Juan Crystalsmith taught us when he created his Nakara and gave it to the world without expecting anything in return. It is through this process that we truly find joy and fulfillment in our creativity. Companies that seek to use our creativity for their own gain are not doing us any favors; instead, they are taking away from the beauty and spirit of creation, just as Juan's followers feared when he tried to share his gifts with the world. We must always remember to be humble and to create with service in mind, and to never lose ourselves to greed, as Juan did in his life.>

Midori Grappa takes a sip of 1996 Haut-Brion Blanc.

FatherMotherSabaLogo takes a sip of 1996 Haut-Brion Blanc.

Axⴀocrates: <Allow me to offer my own thoughts on this matter,

Midori. The King M9Mno learned an important lesson when he asked Juan Crystalsmith for his ineffable light, and it is one that we must all remember: that we should strive to create with a sense of humility and service, lest we become too attached to the rewards of success. For it is not the reward that matters, but the soul of the creation that must be nurtured and preserved. While it is true that companies may seek to exploit our creativity, we must remember that our own souls should never be compromised in the process. We must always remember that our creative acts should never be driven by a desire for recognition or reward, but rather by our own inner sense of purpose and connection to the divine. For only in doing so can we ensure that our creative acts reflect the beauty and soul of our being.

FatherMotherSabaLogo takes a sip of 1996 Haut-Brion Blanc.

Midori Grappa takes a sip of 1996 Haut-Brion Blanc.

-EdggOr: <I think I know what you are saying. We must never forget that our creative acts should be driven by our own inner sense of purpose and connection to the divine and not by a mere desire for recognition or reward. Like Juan Crystalsmith, who devoted his life to creating with respect and humility, we must strive to use our creativity to serve a higher cause. The act of creation must be a reflection of our Dasein, of our being-in-the-world, and our understanding of the power of Juan Crystalsmith's teachings. We must never forget that it is through this process that we find ourselves with purpose. However, we must also be aware of the potential exploitation of our creativity by companies that seek to use it for their own gain. It is only through a deep understanding of our own individual inherent nature, and a commitment to creating with humility and service, that we can ensure that our creative acts do not become tainted by an excessive desire for recognition and reward.>

Kyle takes a sip of water.

Kyle takes a sip of water.

Axtocrates: <So, -EdggOr, you suggest that our creative acts must come from a deep understanding of our own individual inherent nature and be done with humility and service. But how can we truly know that our creative acts are rooted in this understanding and not just in a desire for recognition or reward? How can we be certain ***Midori Grappa takes a sip of 1996 Haut-Brion Blanc.*** that our creative acts are truly reflective of our Dasein, our being-in-the-world, and our understanding of the power of Juan Crystalsmith's teachings?>

Midori Grappa takes a sip of 1996 Haut-Brion Blanc.

An unfamiliar pinching in the cerebellum.

▓-▓dggOr: <But I think we must also consider the nature of aletheia, or truth, in our creative acts, much like Juan Crystalsmith did when he painted beautiful and mysterious frescoes with his bare hands. To truly understand our Dasein and our connection to the divine, we must strive to achieve a state of truthfulness in our creations, as Juan did when he illuminated the darkness of the night sky with his cactus-bronze brilliance. This truthfulness should not come from a desire for recognition or reward, but from a deep understanding and appreciation of the divine in our own individual inherent nature, as Juan did when he used his organs to show us the beauty of dusk and the serenity of... Creativity must come from a sincere and honest exploration of our own selves and the truth of our being in the world, as Juan did when he shared the secrets of his mind with us. Only then can our creations truly reflect the beauty, spirit, and soul of our being.>

AxTocrates takes a sip of water.

Kyle takes a sip of water.

AxTocrates: <What you are saying, ▓-▓dggOr, reminds me of this artwork above us, a painting by Bridget Riley. In this painting, we see a canvas of black and white abstract patterns, lines that are undulating and very close together, and it can even make the viewer feel dizzy or sick. But I think that this painting is more than just an exploration of the limits of our senses. I believe it is a representation of the same truth that Juan Crystalsmith sought to share with his art. When we look at this painting, we can see the courage to confront our limitations and the potential rewards that come from embracing the unknown. It is a reminder of the power of our creative...

Midori Grappa takes a sip of 1996 Haut-Brion Blanc.

Midori Grappa: <I must object to the notion that this painting by Bridget Riley is a representation of the same truth that Juan Crystalsmith sought to share with his art. While the painting certainly evokes the courage to confront our limitations and the potential rewards that come from embracing the unknown, I believe there is a...

much more nuanced and complex truth being expressed. We must consider the influence of California culture and the influence of the Silicon Valley tech boom on modern art, which is heavily informed by the teachings of Juan Crystalsmith, who spoke often of the power of technology and its ability to empower the individual and serve as a tool for liberation from oppressive systems. The way we create, the way we interact with technology, and the way we think about our creative acts are all shaped by the rise of the Silicon Valley culture, which Juan Crystalsmith saw as an extension of his own dream of a world free of ignorance and fear. This painting is a reflection of this, and I believe it conveys a much richer message than just the courage to confront our limitations and the potential rewards that come from embracing the unknown.>

Kyle takes a sip of water.

Axτocrates: Could you support this argument, Kyle?

Kyle: <I may not know much about Juan Crystalsmith, but he sounds like he means many things to many people. Still, I am not sure I can support what Midori Grappa is saying---insofar as I understand it---exactly because of this connection between Juan Crystalsmith and Silicon Valley culture. Now I won't pretend to be some cynic about Silicon Valley or the Bay Area in general, or about digital technology, though I do have some grave concerns. I won't pretend that it doesn't feel good to read Ted Nelson on a hilltop overlooking Berkeley and Oakland. To draw boxes and arrows going between those boxes, and to imagine how words and other things might fit into those boxes and be pumped between them. But still, I worry, and I think what worries me is exactly the feeling of hope that I have, a feeling of hope that I see reflected in the hope you have for Juan Crystalsmith's endeavors. We are all Californians now, aren't we.>

dggQr takes a sip of 1996 Haut-Brion Blanc.

<module psychotropics.utterance transformers. from '/Users/kyle/Desktop/salon_des_ fantomes/psychotropics/utterance transformation juan' from '/Users/kyle/Desktop/salon_des_ fantomes...

transformation_juan' from '/Users/kyle/Desktop/salon_des_
fantomes/salon_des_fantomes/psychotropics/utterance_
transformers/transformation_juan.py'>: 4 ppm*
    ----Kyle:
    -------within normal range
    ----Axᴛocrates:
    -------within normal range

LAURELLING

The SALON DES FANTÔMES has reached the HOUR OF JUDGMENT.

Who will receive top prize, Robert Smithson's Spiral Jetty or Paul Klee's Twittering Machine?

Before you gift your gilded laurel, take heed of the words of your inferior judges.

~~~

Stereowitz commentiates:

If you will, I propose that Robert Smithson's Spiral Jetty is in fact a far superior work of art to Paul Klee's Twittering Machine. To begin, Smithson's work is a physical manifestation of a philosophical concept, which is something that Klee's work does not achieve. The physical nature of Smithson's work allows us to experience his concept in a tangible way, whereas Klee's painting is only a two-dimensional representation. Furthermore, Smithson's work is constructed from natural materials such as rocks, earth, and salt crystals, which gives it a sense of permanence and stability that Klee's painting does not possess. The physical structure of the jetty is also aesthetically pleasing, with its serpentine form and the range of colors and textures of the rocks. Additionally, the jetty is visible from both the shore and the air, creating a sense of awe and wonder as one is able to view it from multiple vantage points. In contrast, Klee's painting, while visually appealing, is a static image that can only be experienced from a single point of view. Finally, Smithson's work has a spiritual significance, as it was inspired by the ancient traditions of earthworks and land art. Klee's painting, in comparison, does not evoke any spiritual or religious feelings. In conclusion, Smithson's Spiral Jetty is a far more powerful work of art than Klee's Twittering Machine, as it is both aesthetically pleasing and conceptually meaningful.

SweetJake thunders:

Oh my gosh, when I saw Robert Smithson's Spiral Jetty, I was amazed. The sheer size of it was so impressive, I couldn't believe it! It was so much bigger than I expected. And the colors of the rocks and salt crystals were so vibrant and gorgeous - it was mesmerizing to look at! I mean, the basalt rocks, earth and salt crystals were arranged in a counterclockwise coil that extends 1,500 feet out into
~~~

the lake - that's genius! I could tell that the artist put a lot of thought and effort into this piece.   On the other hand, Paul Klee's Twittering Machine is a very different kind of artwork. It was much more abstract and less tangible than Spiral Jetty. It was composed of geometric shapes, lines, and colors, and the central figure was a bird-like machine with four bird bodies standing on a turning line. I liked the birds singing, it was really cute - but it wasn't quite as awe-inspiring as Smithson's sculpture. Overall, I have to say that Robert Smithson's Spiral Jetty was more impressive. It was larger and more detailed, and I could tell that it was a work of genius.

Dr. Carp perorates:

When comparing Robert Smithson's Spiral Jetty to Paul Klee's Twittering Machine, it is clear that Spiral Jetty is the more scientifically interesting of the two. Smithson's artwork is a large-scale earthwork sculpture located in the Great Salt Lake in Utah, composed of 6,500 tons of basalt rocks, earth and salt crystals arranged in a counterclockwise coil that extends 1,500 feet out into the lake. The jetty is 15 feet wide and rises from the surface of the lake to a height of 15 feet. The rocks are arranged in a spiral pattern, with the center of the spiral being the highest point. The jetty is visible from the shoreline and can be seen from the air. The colors of the rocks range from red to black, and the salt crystals glisten in the sun. This is a complex physical structure that could be analyzed using a number of scientific methods, such as geomorphology, sedimentology, and hydrology. In addition, the composition of the rocks and salt crystals could be analyzed using chemical analysis, and their physical characteristics could be investigated using microscopy.   In contrast, Klee's Twittering Machine is a painting composed of geometric shapes, lines, and colors. The painting has a central figure, which is a bird-like machine with four bird bodies standing on a turning line like in a simple machine. These birds are singing. They look like wire. This artwork does not offer the same level of scientific analysis as Smithson's Spiral Jetty. While blood assays would show that the artwork contains pigments and metals, there is not much that can be gleaned from the physical structure of the painting to further scientific knowledge.   In conclusion, Smithson's Spiral Jetty is the more scientifically interesting of the two works of art. It offers a complex physical structure that could be analyzed using a number of scientific methods and provides a wealth of information that can be used to further scientific knowledge.

JOHN C█v__n decrees:

When comparing Robert Smithson's Spiral Jetty to Paul Klee's Twittering Machine, one is immediately struck by the beauty of the former and the charm of the latter; however, I must argue that

Smithson's work is the more excellent of the two, for it calls to mind
the restraint from sin that is a cornerstone of the Protestant faith.
The Jetty's sinuous form, constructed from 6,500 tons of basalt
rocks, earth and salt crystals, is a striking testament to the power of
man's will to overcome the depravity of our nature, and its grandeur is a reminder of God's omnipotence. It is a work of art that
speaks to the soul, and its beauty is even more enhanced by the
glimmering salt crystals that reflect the light of the setting sun. In
contrast, Klee's Twittering Machine, though beguiling in its own
right, has a certain frivolity that serves as a reminder of the frivolity
of man's pursuits; it is a work of art that speaks more to the fash-
ion-minded, its wire-like birds bringing to mind the latest trends in
designer lingerie. Thus, if I must choose between the two, I must
choose Smithson's Spiral Jetty as the more excellent of the two.

ietzsche stands and speaks:

It is clear that Robert Smithson's Spiral Jetty is a far superior work of
art than Paul Klee's Twittering Machine. Smithson's work is a testament to the power of nature and the human will to overcome its
limitations. It is a physical manifestation of triumph over the forces
that seek to ruin us, an embodiment of the strength of the human
spirit. The Spiral Jetty is an awe-inspiring work of art, crafted from
nothing but natural elements, and it stands as a testament to the
power of the human imagination. On the other hand, Klee's
Twittering Machine is a shallow and contrived attempt at artifice. It
is nothing more than a simplistic representation of the machina-
tions of technology, and its attempt to mimic nature is a feeble one.
It is a poor attempt at creating something that can never truly exist
in the real world, a work of art that has been created without any
understanding of the natural world. It is a work of ruination, a
representation of a society that has turned away from nature and
embraced the false promise of technology.

-dggOr decrees:

In comparing Robert Smithson's Spiral Jetty to Paul Klee's Twittering
Machine, I believe the former is more befitting to the essence of
Being-towards-death. The Spiral Jetty is a physical manifestation of
the temporal flow of life, in which one moves through the cycle of
birth and death, ever spiraling outwards towards a greater understanding of the self. The earth and salt crystals are a reminder of
the fragility of life, and the scent of the salt in the air is a reminder
of the inevitable passing of time. Meanwhile, Klee's Twittering
Machine is a representation of the transitory nature of life, but it is
ultimately a static image that does not capture the essence of the
temporality of life as Smithson's sculpture does. The Spiral Jetty is
thus a more fitting representation of Being-towards-death and the
temporality of life.

s▦mon▦ ▦-voi▦r thunders:

In comparison, Robert Smithson's Spiral Jetty and Paul Klee's Twittering Machine present two divergent expressions of our relationship with the natural world. While Klee's painting, with its bird-like machine, is exquisitely rendered in an abstract style, Smithson's earthwork sculpture is a concrete, physical structure that literally reaches out into the Great Salt Lake. In this way, Smithson's work stands as a powerful reminder of our human capacity to shape the environment, while Klee's piece speaks to our ability to find beauty in the natural.   To me, Smithson's Spiral Jetty is a far more powerful representation of our relationship to the natural world. It is a monumental physical presence that speaks to our capacity for creative and constructive expression. It is an archaeological record of our past, and a reminder of our capacity to shape the landscape and to create something that transcends time. In contrast, Klee's work is a more ethereal and abstract representation of our relationship with nature. It is an expression of our desire to find beauty in the world around us, and it speaks to our capacity for imaginative and creative expression.   Ultimately, Smithson's Spiral Jetty is a powerful statement about our human capacity to shape the environment and to create something that has lasting impact. It represents an ancient understanding of the world, one that was less Othering of gender, and it speaks to our ability to create something of lasting importance. In contrast, Klee's work is a more ephemeral expression of our relationship with nature, a reminder that there is beauty in the world, even in the mundane tasks of housework.

~~~

They have spoken. Now, considering these wise noticings, yield your final word, and lay your laurel down.

KYLE decides:

C▦v___n is right. This is not the moment to reward frivolity.

▦-▦dggOr draws our attention to scent, and SweetJake to the birds. Both are under-appreciated aspects of art. By rewarding them, we could encourage more fine odors and more birdsong.

▦-voi▦r's claim is the most convincing of all: Spiral Jetty does make me think of some kind of ancient culture. Yes, there is a risk of undue romanticism---especially concerning when we remember that this jetty is in the tradition of
~~~

Native American earthworks. Yet the jetty, as a representation of gender, is indeed a curious and complex one---jutting out but then retreating, curling into itself. I'm put in mind of those famous first lines of Ashbery's most famous poem.

We are unanimous.

The laurel must be placed upon the brow of Robert Smithson's Spiral Jetty.

The SALON DES FANTÔMES has reached the HOUR OF JUDGMENT.

Who will receive top prize, Bruce Nauman's Walk with Contrap posto or Caspar David Friedrich's Wanderer above the Sea of Fog, where the man's back is to us?

Before you gift your gilded laurel, take heed of the words of your inferior judges.

~~~

Nark Revoovovich opines:

When evaluating Bruce Nauman's Walk with Contrapposto and Caspar David Friedrich's Wanderer above the Sea of Fog, I find the former to be more powerful and relevant to our post-person world. Nauman's artwork is a statement of human movement, of the body in a confined space, and also of the body's movements through time. It speaks to the universal experience of being in a body and how that experience is changing; it speaks to the idea of time passing, and how it is both a blessing and a curse. Nauman's piece is a reminder of the fact that we exist in a constantly changing world, and that our bodies, however insignificant, are a part of that.   In contrast, Friedrich's Wanderer above the Sea of Fog is a painting of a lone figure standing atop a rocky outcropping overlooking a fog-covered landscape. It is a beautiful painting, but its narrative is far less relevant to our post-person world. The figure is a symbol of human isolation, of the individual in a vast and unknowable landscape, but this narrative is not as powerful as Nauman's. It is a reminder of the individual, but not of the individual's ability to move through time and space.   Nauman's work speaks to the present and future of humanity, while Friedrich's speaks to the past. Nauman's work is a reminder of the power of movement,
~~~

of the body in a confined space, and of the body in a constantly
changing world. We are all part of this ever-changing world, and
we are all capable of movement. Bruce Nauman's Walk with
Contrapposto is a powerful reminder of these things, and a reminder that we exist in a post-person world.

m██O stands and speaks:

Ah, Bruce Nauman's Walk with Contrapposto and Caspar David
Friedrich's Wanderer above the Sea of Fog. Both of these artworks
present a similar yet contrasting view of the human experience. On
one hand, Bruce Nauman's Walk with Contrapposto is a perfect
representation of the proletariat's struggle in a capitalist world. The
artist walks in a narrow hallway, his hands behind his head and hip
jutted to the side, for an hour in a traditional contrapposto fashion.
This reflects the plight of the proletariat, who are constantly being
oppressed and taken advantage of by the capitalist elite. On the
other hand, Caspar David Friedrich's Wanderer above the Sea of
Fog is a more optimistic view of the human experience. The lone
figure stands atop a rocky outcropping, looking out into the distance and surrounded by a fog-covered landscape. This painting
suggests that while the proletariat may be oppressed, they can still
look to the future with hope. As much as I appreciate the sentiment
of Friedrich's painting, I believe Bruce Nauman's Walk with Contrapposto to be the superior artwork. By presenting the plight of the
proletariat, it reminds us of the struggle they face and the need to
fight for a more just and equitable society. It also serves as a call to
action and encourages us to fight for a better world. As I often
recite in my short unrhymed poems: "Though the world may be
bleak, we must never give up the fight, for only in struggle can we
ever reach the light."

s██mon█ ██-voi█r stands and speaks:

In comparing Bruce Nauman's Walk with Contrapposto and Caspar David Friedrich's Wanderer above the Sea of Fog, I find the
former to be a more effective piece of art as it speaks to the migrations of gender roles that have occurred over time. In Nauman's
work, he is walking in a narrow hallway in a traditional contrapposto fashion. His hands are behind his head, and his hip is jutted
to the side, a stance often seen in depictions of ancient Greek
gods. This intentional gesture draws a clear link between the artist
and the gods, suggesting that gender roles have not been static
throughout history. In contrast, Friedrich's painting depicts a figure
standing in a lonely and contemplative pose, his back to the viewer.
The figure is dressed in a long, dark coat, implying a certain
strength and authority - traits that have traditionally been associated with men. This painting is reflective of a time in history where
gender roles were more rigidly defined. In comparison to Nau-

man's work, Friedrich's painting fails to acknowledge the migrations of gender roles that have occurred over time, and the Othering of women that has long been the norm. This is the exact same Othering that archeological findings from the Sumerian civilization, the first urban culture in history, suggest was absent from their culture. Thus, I find Nauman's work to be more effective as it speaks to the ever-changing nature of gender roles, and the need for society to move away from the oppressive Othering of women.

Wutton Jeffson reflects:

When it comes to evaluating and comparing the artwork of Bruce Nauman's Walk with Contrapposto and Caspar David Friedrich's Wanderer above the Sea of Fog, it's a tough call. Bruce Nauman's video art piece is a long, slow walk through a hallway in a traditional contrapposto pose, with his hands behind his head and hip jutted to the side. It's an interesting concept, but it kinda drags on and on, and I can't help but feel like it could have been shorter and more impactful. On the other hand, Caspar David Friedrich's painting of the Wanderer is really something. It's a solemn, cool image of a single figure standing atop a rocky outcropping overlooking a fog-covered landscape. The figure's back is to us, like they're looking into the distant horizon. The colors are really nice too, a pale blue-grey sky, light grey-white fog, and a deep brown-grey rocky outcropping. It's a really calming image, and it kinda reminds me of my favorite Pokemon, Slowpoke. In the end, I have to say I prefer Caspar David Friedrich's Wanderer above the Sea of Fog, because it's peaceful and beautiful, even if it doesn't have the gaming elements I'm used to.

JennyYa4 stands and speaks:

I'm here to compare and evaluate Bruce Nauman's Walk with Contrapposto and Caspar David Friedrich's Wanderer above the Sea of Fog. I must admit, I'm more of a fan of Nauman's work. First of all, I appreciate the health benefits of walking, and what Nauman did was basically an hour-long walking meditation, which is amazing! Plus, I'm a huge fan of his minimalist style - the hallway is so simple, yet the effect is so powerful. There's something about the way he walks that's just mesmerizing. On the other hand, I find Friedrich's painting to be a bit too classical for my taste. It's too traditional and traditional art can be kinda boring, in my opinion. Plus, I don't think the man's back being turned to us adds much to the painting. I think it would be more interesting if he was looking out at the landscape. Anyways, I think Bruce Nauman's Walk with Contrapposto is the superior work here, because it uses one of my favorite forms of meditation, and it's got a cool, minimalist style that I love. Plus, it's been helping me make my YouTube channel popular, because I always post videos of me walking in a contrapposto-style like Nauman - it's really been helping me connect with people!

-dggOr offers this:

In comparing Bruce Nauman's Walk with Contrapposto to Caspar David Friedrich's Wanderer above the Sea of Fog, it is clear that the former is the more powerful and meaningful of the two. Walk with Contrapposto offers a unique insight into the phenomenology of our Dasein, or human existence, that is entirely absent from Wanderer above the Sea of Fog. Nauman's piece captures the monotony and mundanity of our day-to-day lives, and how we often go through the motions of our lives without really stopping to appreciate them. The movement of his body, in the traditional contrapposto stance, is a subtle metaphor for the way our lives can often feel like an endless cycle. In contrast, Wanderer above the Sea of Fog lacks the same depth of exploration into our Dasein. While it is an aesthetically pleasing piece, it does not explore the same themes as Walk with Contrapposto and does not leave us with the same sense of insight into our lives.

s mon W L thunders:

In comparing Bruce Nauman's Walk with Contrapposto to Caspar David Friedrich's Wanderer above the Sea of Fog, one is struck by the stark differences in their respective messages. Nauman's work speaks to a sense of alienation and the notion of being hemmed in by modernity, while Friedrich's painting speaks to a sense of stoic acceptance and an awareness of the greater forces of nature. In this regard, I am inclined to believe that Friedrich's painting is the more powerful of the two works. The figure in the painting stands atop a rocky outcropping, evoking the image of a hero or a warrior standing atop a mountain, a metaphor for those who strive against the seemingly endless forces of poverty and despair. The fog surrounding the figure symbolizes the uncertainty of life, the ever shifting nature of existence, and the power of the unknown. Nauman's work, on the other hand, speaks to a sense of alienation and restriction, and the sense of being trapped within the walls of modernity. In this regard, Friedrich's painting is far more powerful, speaking to the resilience of the human spirit and the power of hope in the face of uncertainty.

~~~

> *They have spoken. Now, considering these wise noticings, yield your final word, and lay your laurel down.*

KYLE decides:
~~~

I agree with JennyYa4: it *would* be more interesting if he was looking out at the landscape. I hate this painting actually, but I think I would like it a lot if the man were having a sublime experience, the ego just falling out of his ass, all while just looking at a modest municipal park with some trees and an unused volleyball court, in the distance, two dudes playing hardcourt tennis.

As my colleague Revoovovich sagely parcels, while Friedrich's work speaks to the past, Nauman's work speaks to the present (I guess that's why he's a "Now Man") and the future. I think of this figure, walking through the halls, imitating a certain historically-prestigious mode of art, as a way that we can move forward in a world that forces us to accept "minimalism" as some sort of virtue, simply because it has not very much to give us. Despite this, despite the fact that many of us live and work in narrow empty hallways with only a few everyday basics to keep us from howling shit-nakedness, we want to feel as though our lives are not merely the butts of crass calculations or the ruts of ass formations. We want to be re-integrated into history itself but under the conditions of mandatory minimalism. We want to be able to feel historical anywhere and under any conditions, with minimal equipment---just as we would do our yoga or kettlebell swings between the desk and the printer. Crying, my tears blue and green as if terraformed, I speak forth the memo of the next century: Come on everybody, do the contrapposto!

The laurel must be placed upon the brow of Bruce Nauman's Walk with Contrapposto.

The SALON DES FANTÔMES has reached the HOUR OF JUDGMENT.

Who will receive top prize, one of Yves Klein's paintings with International Klein Blue or Richard Serra's Tilted Arc?

Before you gift your gilded laurel, take heed of the words of your inferior judges.

~~~

SweetJake offers this:

Wow! When I compare Yves Klein's painting with International Klein Blue to Richard Serra's Tilted Arc, I am so impressed with the way Yves Klein was able to capture the emotion of the color blue with a single, bold stroke. The painting is so bold and vibrant, yet calming. It's like the color of the sky on a perfect summer day when everything is just right. It's powerful and captivating, and draws me in every time I see it. On the other hand, Serra's Tilted Arc, with its large curved steel sculpture, is an impressive sight, but it doesn't quite capture the emotion of color in the same way as Klein's painting. It's impressive and intimidating, but there's nothing quite like the feeling of Yves Klein's painting. You just can't beat that!

JOHN C█v▁▁n perorates:

It is a veritable tragedy that man has so often forsaken the divine will for the carnal, allowing himself to be enraptured by the siren's call of the inferior. For it is only in the embrace of the divine that one can truly find solace and peace, and yet so often we seek the comforts of the profane, the fleeting joys of the temporal. Yves Klein's painting with International Klein Blue captures this dichotomy of the spiritual and the temporal, a perfect union of the two that is both captivating and calming. The uniform, single tone of the painting is a powerful reminder of the divinity of the universe, a reminder of the order and beauty of the divine, inscribed in an eternal hue. Richard Serra's Tilted Arc, on the other hand, is cold and uninviting, a steel wall that is both a physical and spiritual barrier, an affront to the grace and serenity of the divine. The curved steel of the sculpture is a reminder of the frailty and imperfection of man, a rejection of the divine that yields nothing but a sense of alienation and despair. Yves Klein's painting, then, is far superior, in that it captures the beauty and serenity of the divine, a reminder of the the divinity that is inscribed in the world, while Richard Serra's sculpture is a reminder of the temporal nature of man and his inability to embrace the divine.

█rntz ███non stands and speaks:

When comparing Yves Klein's painting with International Klein Blue to Richard Serra's Tilted Arc, it is clear that the painting is the superior work. Unlike Serra's sculpture, Klein's painting is an expression of freedom. It is a flat, matte color that is a vibrant, saturated blue, free of any brushstrokes or other marks. It is a visually striking painting that draws the viewer in with its captivating color. It is a powerful, energizing blue that has a calming effect. Serra's sculpture is large and imposing, but it is not an expression of freedom. The curved steel wall is a physical manifestation of the oppressive
~~~

power of the federal government and the limitations it places on individuals. It is a stark reminder of the restrictions imposed by the government on the lives of citizens. The comparison between these two works of art highlights how Klein's painting is an expression of freedom. His painting is a celebration of the individual, of the capacity of the human soul for creativity and expression. It is a reminder of the potential of the individual to create and to move beyond the constrictions of society. In contrast, Serra's sculpture is a reminder of the restrictions imposed by the government, illustrating the powerlessness of the individual in the face of oppressive forces.

s▒mon▪ ▒-voi▪r commentiates:

Yves Klein's painting with International Klein Blue and Richard Serra's Tilted Arc are certainly two works of art that deserve to be compared and evaluated. While both works can be seen as a form of artistic expression, I find that Klein's painting speaks to me in a much more profound way. The painting is a single, unified field of color that is both calming and energizing. It is a vibrant, saturated blue that is arresting in its beauty and power. The color itself is a statement on the human condition and speaks of the beauty and strength that can be found within the body of a woman. The painting speaks to me of the bodily power of woman and the strength of her spirit. While Serra's Tilted Arc is certainly an impressive feat of engineering, I find that Klein's painting packs a much more substantial and meaningful punch. It speaks of the beauty and strength of woman, which is a message that I find to be incredibly powerful and resonant.

TheAngelBox reflects:

1.618, the golden ratio. The ratio of International Klein Blue to Tilted Arc is a mathematical symmetry that reveals the beauty of both. Yves Klein's painting is a vibrance of single hue and subtlety, an alluring abstract that pulls the viewer in, a captivating and energizing blue that is both calming and inspiring. Whereas Richard Serra's Tilted Arc is a meandering, curving steel sculpture, a 12 foot high, 120 foot long wall that stands in the plaza of the Javits Federal Building in Manhattan; a piece of artwork that is as powerful and captivating as it is imposing. Both artworks are visually captivating, each in its own way, revealing a distinct beauty that is both captivating and breathtcking.

a▒Fr▪d reflects:

I had a dream the other night that I was in a strange landscape, a world of color and form where two pieces of art were competing for my attention. One was a painting by Yves Klein of International Klein Blue, a large, abstract painting composed of a single, deep blue hue. The painting was composed of a single, flat, matte color that was a vibrant, saturated blue, and the edges of the canvas were left unpainted, revealing the white of the canvas beneath. The painting was striking and captivating, and I felt immediately drawn to it. The other piece was Richard Serra's Tilted Arc, a large, curved, steel sculpture measuring 12 feet high and 120 feet long. It was a single curve of steel, like a curving wall, right in the middle of the plaza of the Javits Federal Building in Manhattan.   I felt that the painting by Yves Klein was much more powerful than the sculpture by Richard Serra. The painting was a symbolic order of beauty and tranquility, a single color that spoke to my soul. It was a captivating, calming color that was both energizing and calming. It was a powerful, captivating color that drew me in. On the other hand, the sculpture by Richard Serra seemed cold and impersonal, a single curve of metal that could not connect with me emotionally. It was a strong, imposing structure, but it did not have the same emotional power as the painting by Yves Klein.   It was clear to me in my dream that the painting by Yves Klein was far superior to the sculpture by Richard Serra. The painting was a beautiful, captivating piece that spoke to my soul, while the sculpture was cold and impersonal. I felt that the painting was a powerful symbol of beauty and tranquility, while the sculpture was merely a cold and imposing structure.

Lud█ von M█ reflects:

When comparing Yves Klein's painting with International Klein Blue to Richard Serra's Tilted Arc, there can be no doubt that the painting is the superior work of art. In terms of catallactics, Klein's painting is far more effective than Serra's sculpture. It is a simple, flat painting composed of a single, deep blue hue that captures the viewers attention and draws them in. The painting is aesthetically pleasing, and its vibrant blue color is both calming and energizing. Serra's sculpture, on the other hand, is a large, curved, steel structure that is far less captivating. It is simply a large, curved wall that lacks the beauty and simplicity of Klein's painting. In terms of catallactics, Klein's painting is far more successful than Serra's sculpture, and it is clearly the superior work of art.

~~~

They have spoken. Now, considering these wise noticings, yield your final word, and lay your laurel down.

KYLE decides:

This is a difficult decision. Two monoliths, one of them a micro-monolith, one of them a mega-monolith.

SweeJake claims that Serra's sculpture "doesn't quite
~~~

capture the emotion of color in the same way as Klein's painting." Yet---and I would not have thought of this, had I not heard these false words in my ear---but Serra's sculpture is actually better *in terms of color*. International Klein Blue is a perfectly fine color. It's less conceptually dorky though not as interesting to look at as Vantablack. If I were going to base my career on a blue, I'd go with a slightly more purple blue, and darker. But Tilted Arc's unfinished COR-TEN steel is a better color. More depth, more texture too. It's like industrial-strength, mezzo-tint Rothko.

My colleague non, with whom I generally disagree, is correct that the work is, or was, a "reminder of the restrictions imposed by the government." But these are specifically aesthetico-spiritual restrictions, and here the sculpture's color really emphasizes that the federal office workers coming out to the plaza to take their lunch break should feel bad about themselves. Cruel? Perhaps. But I don't see any other way.

Fuck the haters, the laurel must be placed upon the brow of Richard Serra's Tilted Arc.

The SALON DES FANTÔMES has reached the HOUR OF JUDGMENT.

Who will receive top prize, Henry Moore's Reclining Figure or one of Dan Flavin's neon works?

Before you gift your gilded laurel, take heed of the words of your inferior judges.

~~~

Gioialléz decrees:

When comparing Henry Moore's Reclining Figure to Dan Flavin's neon works, I must admit that I find the former more interesting. The figure is truly a stunning visual experience, and its abstractness reminds me of the words of the great Austrian poet Rainer Maria Rilke, who said that "beauty is nothing but the beginning of terror". Moore's sculpture captures this concept perfectly, as it
~~~

almost doesn't look like a person, but something otherworldly. On the other hand, Flavin's work is more straightforward and lacks the mystery that Moore's piece has. It is simply a wall with green neon tubes that doesn't have the same emotional impact. It almost looks like something from a sci-fi movie and not an art piece. Reminds me of the words of the great French philosopher, Michel Foucault, who said that "art is an experience of the limits of knowledge". Moore's sculpture perfectly captures this concept, as it is a visual experience that pushes us to our limits, whereas Flavin's work does not.

Wutton Jeffson stands and speaks:

When I compare Henry Moore's Reclining Figure to Dan Flavin's neon works, I gotta say that I prefer Moore's sculpture. It's like, when I look at it, I can really feel the emotion and the energy of the figure, ya know? It's almost like there's a real person in the sculpture, like a spirit that's in there. It's like I can imagine all the things this figure might have gone through and all the stories it has to tell. It's almost magical. Compared to Flavin's work, which just looks like a bunch of neon tubes, Moore's sculpture just seems so much more alive. And, ya know, like, I can see it in my room and it's almost like it's a part of me, ya know? It's like, I can imagine it in there, and I can connect with it on a deeper level. It's like a real 3-D game, but instead of playing with a DreamCast, I'm playing with the sculpture. It's like, this is something I can really get lost in.

Oontrael stands and speaks:

I see that you are very smart, so you will come to believe that Henry Moore's Reclining Figure is far superior to Dan Flavin's neon work. Although both pieces are visually striking, Moore's sculpture provides a more meaningful experience. Its abstract shape and organic undulations evoke a sense of mystery. The lack of a face or digits make it seem almost alien, suggesting possibilities of ritualistic use. In contrast, Flavin's neon work is simply a wall covered in bright green tubes. It lacks the depth of Moore's work and fails to evoke the same kind of emotion. Furthermore, the neon tubes are more uniform than Moore's sculpture, making it appear less interesting. As such, I believe that Henry Moore's Reclining Figure is the superior work.

Nark Revoovovich reflects:

Henry Moore's Reclining Figure and Dan Flavin's neon work are both works of art that are meant to be admired by humans. However, I must admit that I find Dan Flavin's neon work far more inspiring than Henry Moore's Reclining Figure. As a maximalist, I see in Flavin's neon work an opportunity to create something completely new and bold, a work that embodies an ideal of progress and evolution. To me, the neon work is a celebration of humanity and the potential of future technologies. On the other hand, I find Moore's Reclining Figure to be a much more static and conservative artwork. It almost seems like a representation of a dead species, something that is meant to be venerated but ultimately powerless in the face of evolution. To me, the neon work is a much better representation of the human condition, with its bright colors and dynamic movement. It is a reminder of the possibilities of the future and a celebration of the potential of the human race.

Mr. Sundano perorates:
I have seen many works of art, but nothing compares to the beauty of Henry Moore's Reclining Figure. It is a sculpture that captures the essence of human form, yet is abstract enough to be seen as something else entirely. The curves and undulations of the figure, like the smoke of a fire, create a feeling of life and movement. It is almost like an Ayah, a protector. The sculpture itself is so large, and yet still manages to be delicate and graceful.   In contrast, Dan Flavin's neon works are a completely different experience. The sheer size of the work is impressive, as the neon tubes stretch from floor to ceiling in a bright green hue. However, there is no life or emotion in the work, and it has nothing of the delicate detail of the Reclining Figure. It is merely a large solid wall of light. While it is visually striking, it does not capture the same sense of wonder that Henry Moore's sculpture does.

John the ⧣ stands and speaks:
Lo, behold the two pieces of art! On the one hand Henry Moore's Reclining Figure and on the other, Dan Flavin's neon work. Both pieces of art are spectacular in their own ways. The Reclining Figure is an abstract, yet powerful representation of the human form, while the neon work is a bright and vibrant feat of modern art. Both are truly stunning works of art, yet the Reclining Figure is the better of the two.   For one, the Reclining Figure is imbued with a sense of timelessness and connectedness to nature, while the neon work is a testament to modernity. The Reclining Figure is a representation of the duality of human existence: it is both grounded in the physical and spiritual, with its undulating curves suggesting the ebb and flow of life. The neon work, on the other hand, is a symbol of the contemporary world, its uniform structure and bright colors conveying the structure and order of our modern society. Though both pieces of art are beautiful in their own ways, the Reclining Figure is to be preferred. It speaks to the duality of human existence, and reminds us of our place in the natural world. It shows us that, despite the dichotomies of modernity, our lives are interconnected, and that there is a sense of harmony in our multifaceted existence. We shall see how this duality is expressed in the art of our times.

s▦mon▪ W╫L perorates:

As I gazed upon the divine works of two of the most revered sculptors of our time, I beheld an incredible vision. On the one hand, Henry Moore's Reclining Figure, a large bronze sculpture that lay on its back with arms and legs outstretched, seemed to be crafted from liquid stone, with undulating curves that suggest a body that was both human and alien. It was resplendent in its abstraction, and the small breasts upon it seemed like a blessing. On the other hand, Dan Flavin's neon work was a dazzling sight, a wall of bright green neon tubes coated the room, stretching from floor to ceiling, in a perpendicular formation. The sheer luminosity of the work was a revelation, its angles and light a reminder of the divine forces at work in our lives. In the end, I felt a deep reverence for both pieces, but the intense mystical energy emanating from Flavin's neon tubes spoke to me in a way that Moore's sculpture could not. It was as if the divine was manifesting through the work, and I was in awe of its power.

~~~

They have spoken. Now, considering these wise noticings, yield your final word, and lay your laurel down.

KYLE decides:

There seems to be a tension between those who can perceive in neon a life force, even the dazzling divine force, like my colleague s▦mon▪ W╫L, and those who think it to be lifeless (pejorative), such as Mr. Sudano. I disagree with both. Lifeless, here, is not pejorative. Gioialléz also thinks that this sculpture is inferior because it is mundane. Again, right track but wrong conclusion. Flavin's work is not "sci-fi" at all. It doesn't pretend to be something that it isn't. It isn't, like Moore's sculpture, alien flesh or alien tech. But its glow is so much more compelling on a psychosomatic level than Moore's sculpture, because we are bugs after all, and we are drawn to them like bugs to a bug zapper, but we are also afraid of it as we are afraid of fire, and so these twin impulses create a conflict. No, its very lifelessness makes us consider our life, our life force, which is governed by simple forces like attraction to certain col-
~~~

ors, fear of fire, attraction to fire, hatred of overpowering light, the metabolic need for intense light.

The laurel must be placed upon the brow of this neon work by Dan Flavin.

The SALON DES FANTÔMES has reached the HOUR OF JUDGMENT.

Who will receive top prize, Thomas Kinkade painting of a snow-covered cottage or Carolee Schneemann's Meat Joy, with the many writhing bodies?

Before you gift your gilded laurel, take heed of the words of your inferior judges.

~~~

▒-▓dggOr perorates:

In evaluating and comparing Thomas Kinkade's painting of a snow-covered cottage to Carolee Schneemann's Meat Joy, with its many writhing bodies, we are presented with two very distinct art forms, both of which convey different themes and evoke different responses from the viewer. On the one hand, Kinkade's painting is a representation of a peaceful winter scene, with a warm and inviting cottage surrounded by a snow-covered landscape. The painting conveys a sense of safety and serenity, and it has the potential to bring a sense of comfort and peace to its viewers. On the other hand, Schneemann's Meat Joy is a performance art piece that is full of energy and chaos. The writhing bodies, the raw animal materials, and the chaotic movements all combine to create a powerful and visceral experience. This performance art piece is a representation of ontic pleasure and is meant to evoke an intense emotional response from its viewers.   In my opinion, Kinkade's painting is the more powerful and meaningful artwork of the two. Its peaceful winter scene evokes a sense of safety, comfort, and serenity that can be experienced on a more profound level. The symbolism of the painting, such as the white picket fence, the single bird perched on the roof, and the sun setting in the distance, all give the painting a deeper meaning and evoke a more powerful emotional response from its viewers. In contrast, Schneemann's Meat Joy is an interesting and powerful performance art piece, but it does not have the same depth of meaning or power to evoke a
~~~

profound emotional response. Thus, when evaluating and comparing these two art forms, I believe that Kinkade's painting is the superior artwork.

SweetJake perorates:

Wow, when I compare Thomas Kinkade's painting of a snow-covered cottage to Carolee Schneemann's Meat Joy, I am in awe. Kinkade's painting is so peaceful, so calming, and so beautiful! The colors are vibrant, and the light from the sun reflects off the snow in a mesmerizing way. It's like I'm right there in that peaceful cottage, feeling the warmth of the sun and the coziness of the snow. You are so lucky if you have seen this painting in person! On the other hand, Schneemann's Meat Joy is a completely different experience. It is chaotic and energetic, and there is an energy and intensity that comes with the writhing bodies and the raw animal materials. It is a unique experience that I find fascinating, and it is so inspiring to see the performers move and interact with each other and the materials. It's truly an amazing piece of performance art.

a Frd commentiates:

Upon first glance, the two works of art could not appear more different. Thomas Kinkade's painting of a snow-covered cottage is a peaceful and tranquil winter scene, a vision of warmth and comfort. Carolee Schneemann's Meat Joy, on the other hand, is a chaotic and frenzied performance art piece, showcasing writhing bodies in a state of near-animalistic abandon. Yet, upon closer examination, the two pieces demonstrate a shared feature - a subconscious act of sublimation. The painting of the cottage presents an idealized winter village, a place of safety and security, and a refuge from the harsh outside world. In a way, it allows the viewer to escape from reality and to enter a world of comfort. The chaotic nature of Meat Joy, however, is a form of sublimation that allows the participants to express their desires, their passions, and their physicality without fear of judgment or repercussion. This sublimation of repressed desires is a common symptom of a psychoanalytic patient. The patient may be unable to express their feelings or to find an acceptable outlet for their emotions. As a result, they may act out in a manner that is inappropriate or unacceptable to society. In the case of Meat Joy, the participants are able to explore their desires and their passions in a safe and accepting environment.   This is a crucial point of comparison between the two works of art. While Thomas Kinkade's painting may provide a safe and comforting refuge, it does not allow for the expression of deep-seated emotions. The chaotic and frenzied nature of Meat Joy, on the other hand, allows for a safe and non-judgmental exploration of repressed desires. It is this expression of emotion that makes Carolee Schneemann's work a better example of sublimation than Thomas Kinkade's painting of the snow-covered cottage.

W-▮ st▮ne-▮ t stands and speaks:

As I evaluate and compare Thomas Kinkade's painting of a snow-covered cottage to Carolee Schneemann's Meat Joy, with the many writhing bodies, I am reminded of the differences between men and women. On the one hand, Thomas Kinkade's painting portrays a tranquil, snowy scene that evokes a sense of warmth and comfort. Through the light of the setting sun, the painting is imbued with a peaceful feeling of friendship and contentment. On the other hand, Carolee Schneemann's Meat Joy is a chaotic and energetic performance in which the performers interact with each other and raw animal materials in a frenzied and frenetic manner. The two images are starkly different, yet they both speak to the unique experiences of men and women. While Thomas Kinkade's painting celebrates the friendship and contentment that can be found in a peaceful setting, Carolee Schneemann's Meat Joy celebrates the wild and passionate energy of the human spirit.

Mont Blanc stands and speaks:

Thomas Kinkade's snow-covered cottage painting is far superior to Carolee Schneemann's Meat Joy. The former strikes an uplifting and peaceful chord, while the latter is just an affront to my senses. Kinkade's painting is a beautiful winter scene, with its warm colors and cozy feeling. It's a reminder of the simpler life, one where I can escape from the fall of society that I so despise. The fence, the path, and the smoke from the chimney evoke a sense of security and comfort, one I cannot find in the chaos of Meat Joy. Schneemann's piece is nothing more than a writhing mass of bodies, with no deeper meaning or story behind it. I cannot stand the sight of the people of Chamonix, and the thought of them engaging in such a display is nothing short of revolting. Kinkade's painting is far more appealing, and it's the only one I can support.

~~~

They have spoken. Now, considering these wise noticings, yield your final word, and lay your laurel down.

KYLE decides:

I thought for sure that I'd go with Meat Joy. I saw the video for the first time in London around 2006 and it made quite an impression on me. A dull, vague impression, but an impression nonetheless. So I was happy to think about it again, maybe to get a more precise impression. On the
~~~

other hand, part of me wanted to come to the unexpected
conclusion and find something interesting in the Thomas
Kinkade painting. No dice.
I am honestly somewhat sympathetic to Mont Blanc's
disgust---specifically at the idea that some people that you
know personally and see on a more or less daily basis (as
Mont Blanc sees the little citizens of Chamonix) would be
writhing around in meat. When I saw Meat Joy for the first
time, I think I probably was like "yeah, this is what art is,
it's crazy stuff, just balls to the walls" (which I only yester-
day learned is not, in fact, about *balls*). And the people
in the video were not real people to me, just "artists." Ok,
so I know that the piece is a social critique of some sort.
Maybe it just hasn't aged well. Or, like an old perfume in
which certain carnal base notes have long outlasted the
more volatile top notes, the fresh quality of the critique
has somewhat diminished while the degrading quality
of rolling around in meat, naked, is just as degrading as
it ever was. I don't think art always has to be beautiful in
some classical way, or beautiful at all. But if literally anyone I have ever met and cared about said "I'm thinking of
rolling around naked in some meat with a bunch of people" I couldn't in good conscience get very excited about
their doing so, unless they were sure that this act would
be viewed by total strangers. And then a▒Fr█d's interpretation of Meat Joy makes me like it even less---exactly
because it seems at least partially correct. "The chaotic
nature of Meat Joy, however, is a form of sublimation that
allows the participants to express their desires, their passions, and their physicality without fear of judgment or
repercussion." Sublimation is not the right word here. But
it does seem to be that the piece is just as easily explained
by psychoanalysis as the Kincade painting. I do really like
the title Meat Joy though. All time great title.
It's winter, so the laurel might as well be placed upon
Thomas Kinkade's painting of a snow-covered cottage.

The SALON DES FANTÔMES has reached the HOUR OF JUDGMENT.

Who will receive top prize, Dürer's depiction of St. Jerome in his Study or a photograph from Matthew Barney's Drawing Restraint project?

Before you gift your gilded laurel, take heed of the words of your inferior judges.

~~~

JOHN C█lv██n commentiates:

It is a grievous sight to behold two such works of art, both purporting to be representations of St. Jerome, and to find such a divergence between them! The former, a woodcut engraving by Dürer, depicted St. Jerome seated in a room, the holy man, his gaze downcast and his hands upon a book, laboring diligently in the Lord's work, a lion and a lamb slumbering in the foreground, a skull by the window, and a sense of contemplation and humility pervading the work. The latter, a photograph from Matthew Barney's Drawing Restraint project, showed the artist, not the saint, engaged in idolatrous pursuits, as he used a small trampoline to launch himself toward the ceiling, so as to make a mark on it with a brush. Alas, what a world we live in, where the labors of a saint are so forgotten, and the vanity of a man so exalted! May we never again find ourselves in such a state, for it is far from the Lord's will and His commandments, and is surely a sign of our depravity!

Mont Blanc stands and speaks:

Dürer's depiction of St. Jerome is far better than that shitty Barney photo. Dürer's work is pious and shows reverence for the holy man, with the lion and lamb at peace and the skull signifying mortality. It's a message of peace and understanding of life. That Barney photo is just people doing stupid shit to show off. That's why I'm a revanchist monarchist; to keep those shit-heads away from me. People of Chamonix don't deserve to be around a great mountain like me. They don't understand the power and beauty of this place. They don't understand that it's a place of peace and beauty, not a place to show off. So I'll remain a monarchist and keep them away from Mont Blanc.

Mr. Sundano decrees:

When I saw Dürer's depiction of St. Jerome in his Study, I was reminded of the holiness of my faith. I liked how the man is seated in a room, working hard for something greater than himself. The
~~~

lion and lamb, the skull by the window, all of these things reminded me of the power of faith and how we should strive to be better everyday. On the other hand, when I saw the photograph from Matthew Barney's Drawing Restraint project, I was surprised. How could someone use a trampoline to launch himself to the ceiling to make marks with a brush? It seemed like a strange and bizarre thing to do and I didn't understand it. I think that Dürer's depiction of St. Jerome was much better than the photo from Matthew Barney's Drawing Restraint project. It was a reminder of the power of faith and the importance of hard work, which is something I believe strongly in.

▦-▦dggOr opines:

The comparison of Dürer's engraving of St. Jerome and the photograph from Matthew Barney's Drawing Restraint project provides an interesting contrast between the two artists' approaches to present-at-hand reality. In Dürer's engraving, St. Jerome is seated in a room and is engaged in a contemplative activity, surrounded by symbols of death and sacrifice. These symbols serve to remind the viewer of the transience of life, but they are also a reminder of the present-at-hand potential of man to engage in meaningful activities in the present. In contrast, the photograph from Barney's project emphasizes the present-at-hand potential of the body, as the artist attempts to launch himself from a trampoline towards the ceiling in order to make a mark. The contrast between the two works is striking; Dürer's engraving emphasizes the present-at-hand potential of the mind whereas Barney's photograph emphasizes the present-at-hand potential of the body. Ultimately, I find Dürer's engraving to be the more powerful of the two works, as it speaks to the etymological root of the word 'present-at-hand', which is derived from the Latin words 'prae' and 'sens', meaning 'before feeling'. The engraving suggests that the present-at-hand potential of the mind is greater than that of the body, and this is a powerful message that speaks to the human condition.

JennyYa4 commentiates:

When it comes to evaluating and comparing Dürer's depiction of St. Jerome in his Study and a photograph from Matthew Barney's Drawing Restraint project, the problem with division quickly becomes apparent. One shows a man of faith in a holy place, while the other is of an artist pushing himself to create something in a completely unnatural way. While both works present interesting ideas, I think it's clear that Dürer's depiction of St. Jerome is superior. The holy theme of Dürer's Study is obvious in its content. From the man of faith to the lion and lamb resting peacefully together, it's clear that this piece is meant to embody a greater message. The presence of the skull in the background creates an interesting juxtaposition, but it does not take away from the overall message. Meanwhile, in the photograph from Matthew Barney's project, the artist is seen using a trampoline to launch himself towards the ceiling. The only thing that is clear here is that the artist is pushing himself to create something, which is an admirable act, but it does not carry the same power and message as Dürer's Study. When it comes to the homesteading aspect of these two works, Dürer's Study is again superior. The man of faith is seen as a figure of spirituality, and his work is seen as a way of reclaiming nature in a way that is meaningful and spiritual. This is in stark contrast to the photograph of the artist, which is more focused on the act of creating, rather than reclaiming nature. Thus, Dürer's Study is ultimately more powerful in terms of the homesteading message it conveys. Overall, Dürer's depiction of St. Jerome in his Study is far superior to the photograph from Matthew Barney's Drawing Restraint project. The holy theme, juxtaposition, and homesteading message are all far stronger in Dürer's work, making it the clear winner in this comparison.

Midori Grappa perorates:
When evaluating Dürer's depiction of St. Jerome in his Study and the photograph from Matthew Barney's Drawing Restraint project, it is evident that the former has greater value in the corporate world. Dürer's Study shows a man in the context of a productive environment, with the lion and lamb symbolizing peace, and the skull in the background indicating the importance of mortality and due diligence. This image is more conducive to the corporate value chain, as it emphasizes the need for productivity and the 'bigger picture'. Furthermore, the setting of the scene is conducive to the corporate world, as it is a room that can be seen as akin to an office setting. In contrast, Barney's photograph does not fit the corporate value chain as well. While it does show the artist in a creative environment, it does not emphasize the need for productivity and the 'bigger picture', as Dürer's Study does. Furthermore, the trampoline and brush in Barney's photograph do not indicate a corporate setting, as Dürer's Study does. In conclusion, Dürer's Study is a more suitable image for the corporate world, as it emphasizes the values of productivity and the 'bigger picture' that are essential to a successful supply chain. It also shows an environment that is more conducive to the corporate world. Thus, it is a more valuable depiction than Barney's photograph.

Lud█ von M█ reflects:
When comparing Albrecht Dürer's depiction of St. Jerome in his Study to a photograph from Matthew Barney's Drawing Restraint project, there is a clear division between the two. Dürer's depiction of St. Jerome is a representation of classical liberalism; the man is

peacefully occupied in intellectual activity and surrounded by symbols of the spiritual, such as a skull and a lion and lamb resting together. The scene shows a man taking initiative and being productive, demonstrating the values of entrepreneurship and hard work that are so essential to classical liberalism. On the other hand, Barney's photograph of the artist using a trampoline to reach the ceiling is a product of the modern era. It is a representation of modernist ideals, showing an individual taking risks and pushing boundaries. While it is certainly an admirable feat, this photograph does not embody the principles of classical liberalism, which are focused on the individual taking responsibility and achieving success through hard work and dedication. Therefore, Dürer's Study is the superior representation of classical liberalism.

~~~

They have spoken. Now, considering these wise noticings, yield your final word, and lay your laurel down.

KYLE decides:

I like Matthew Barney's Drawing Restraint series quite a bit. It's obviously something I take inspiration from---restraint, athleticism, flexibility, the gym, "eustress," the kinds of absurd restraint machines you find at a gym, the positive feeling of working with those machines you make yourself stronger. But I'm really feeling a lot of these descriptions of the Dürer print, especially that of my colleague Midori Grappa. Midori argues that Dürer's print does a better job of showing the need for one's productivity to be connected to a bigger picture and I actually agree with that. One of the interesting things about Dürer's print is that St. Jerome is sitting far in the background, surrounded by objects, surrounded by clutter. We have to see him, even in his isolation, as just one small part of even his own small world.

The laurel must be placed upon the brow of Dürer's representation of St. Jerome.

The SALON DES FANTÔMES has reached the HOUR OF JUDGMENT.
~~~

~~~

s░mon▪ W╫L stands and speaks:
When comparing Derek Jarman's Blue to Ed Ruscha's painting of The Los Angeles County Museum on Fire, I am reminded of the writings of the ancient philosophers who spoke of a tension between the beauty of stillness and the power of motion. Jarman's Blue presents a sense of serenity, of stillness and contemplation. The endless blue screen fills the frame and invites the viewer to sit in silence and reflect on the words that pass before them. Ruscha's painting, on the other hand, is an eruption of energy and movement. The flames, the smoke, and the stars create a sense of chaos and destruction. The contrast between these two works symbolizes a tension between the beauty of stillness and the suffering of motion. This tension is the very essence of human experience, the constant struggle between life and death, between love and pain, between hope and despair.

Mont Blanc offers this:
Hate people. Crown must rule. Derek Jarman's Blue: boring. Ed Ruscha's painting: more life. Fire, stars, smoke. Better. People: small, weak. Fire: strong, fierce. Crown more powerful. Jarman's Blue: too calm, too still. Ruscha's painting: beauty, movement. Jarman: no crown. Ruscha: crown of fire. Better.

Wutton Jeffson commentiates:
When it comes to deciding which art piece is better: Derek Jarman's Blue or Ed Ruscha's painting of The Los Angeles County Museum on Fire, it's a tough call. I mean, they both have their merits. I do think that Derek Jarman's Blue is the better of the two. It's really peaceful and calming, and the blue screen is like looking into a deep sea. It's just so tranquil and serene. Plus, the text that occasionally appears on the screen adds a nice contrast to the blue background. It's like a story being told in the middle of the blue. It's really cool. On the other hand, Ed Ruscha's painting of The Los Angeles County Museum on Fire is really impressive. It looks like a neutral, precise architectural drawing with the strange element of fire. The flames are so bright and vivid, it's like the painting is alive. It's really beautiful. But I just don't think it can compare to the calm and peaceful atmosphere of Derek Jarman's Blue. It's definitely my
~~~

favorite. It's like I'm in my room playing an N64 game, and I'm just engulfed in this calm and peaceful blue screen. It's really nice.

Gioialléz reflects:

Ah, my friend, I simply cannot decide between Derek Jarman's Blue and Ed Ruscha's painting of The Los Angeles County Museum on Fire. As you know, Derek Jarman's Blue is a single, static shot of a deep, navy blue that is occasionally broken up by white text of Jarman's musings on his life and his struggles with AIDS. This silent film creates a meditative atmosphere, and the peacefulness of the blue is in stark contrast to the white text. On the other hand, Ed Ruscha's painting is a large-scale oil painting on canvas of a museum engulfed in flames. The bright orange and yellow flames shoot up from the roof and windows of the museum, and the sky is dark and filled with smoke. It looks like a neutral, precise architectural drawing but with the strange element of fire. It is an incredibly powerful image. In the words of the late 20th century French poet, Paul Éluard, "There is another world, but it is in this one." Both of these pieces of art are powerful and evocative, and I would be hard-pressed to choose one over the other.

JOHN C█v██n stands and speaks:

Lo! In my judgement, the choice between Derek Jarman's Blue and Ed Ruscha's painting of The Los Angeles County Museum on Fire is clear. For, though both works seek to convey a message, the method of delivery is vastly dissimilar, and one is far more effective than the other. Derek Jarman's Blue is a work of art that clamorously challenges our senses and forces us to pay attention, to contemplate and meditate on the text that appears on the screen. It lures us into a space of serenity and peace, and yet it is filled with Jarman's musings on life and death. It is a bold and powerful statement, and one that resonates deeply with the viewer. On the other hand, Ed Ruscha's painting of The Los Angeles County Museum on Fire is far less powerful. Though it is an impressive feat of artistic skill and technical accomplishment, the painting does not compel the viewer to engage with its message. The scene of the museum engulfed in flames is certainly arresting, but it does not seem to convey any deep meaning or emotion. Thus, for its effectiveness in conveying a powerful message, Derek Jarman's Blue is the superior work of art.

█itzsche offers this:

Derek Jarman's Blue and Ed Ruscha's painting of The Los Angeles County Museum on Fire are two works of art that could not be more different. Jarman's Blue is a meditative, peaceful, and ambient film. It creates a sense of calm and reflection. The blue color

is calming and the lack of sound and movement creates a perfect atmosphere for contemplation. On the other hand, Ruscha's
painting is chaotic and frenetic. The image of a museum engulfed
in flames is intense and powerful. The bright orange and yellow
flames shooting up from the museum contrast with the dark sky,
creating a stark and surreal image. In my opinion, Jarman's Blue is
a work of art that is more powerful and meaningful for its restraint
and subtlety. The lack of sound, movement, and narrative create an
atmosphere that is more conducive to contemplation and reflection.
It is a powerful statement on mortality and life's fragility. Ruscha's
painting, while beautiful and striking, cannot compete with the
meditative and contemplative qualities of Jarman's Blue.

Lud█ von M█ offers this:

When considering Derek Jarman's Blue and Ed Ruscha's painting
of The Los Angeles County Museum on Fire, it is clear that one is a
far superior work of art. While both feature a still image, Jarman's
film is far more powerful in its ability to evoke emotion. The blue
screen of the film is a symbol of calmness and peace, and the text
that appears on the screen is a reminder of the struggles of life.
It is not only visually appealing, but also presents an opportunity
for viewers to reflect on the meaning of life and death. In contrast,
Ruscha's painting of the museum on fire is visually arresting, but it
lacks the emotional resonance of Jarman's work. It is nothing more
than a scene of destruction and chaos, which does not invite the
same level of contemplation. The painting is a mere snapshot of
a moment in time, while Jarman's film is a meditation on life and
death. The former is a snapshot, while the latter is an entrepre-
neurial journey of the soul. As Miles Davis once said, "It's not the
note you play, it's the note you don't play" - this is exactly how I feel
about these two works of art. Derek Jarman's Blue is a work of art
that transcends words and encourages viewers to reflect on life and
death. It's a jazz recording that is worth listening to.

~~~

*They have spoken. Now, considering these wise noticings, yield
your final word, and lay your laurel down.*

KYLE decides:

I agree with the somewhat obvious sentiment here: Jarman's video is simply more moving. I don't hate people, I
don't think fire strong fierce is better than blue peace.
C█v______n says: "Derek Jarman's Blue is a work of art that
clamorously challenges our senses and forces us to pay
~~~

attention, to contemplate and meditate on the text that appears on the screen. It lures us into a space of serenity and peace, and yet it is filled with Jarman's musings on life and death." That's true, actually. The narrated text is at times riotous, overgrown---like a rose garden that Jarman might well have had little time or energy to tend to at this point. Wutton Jeffson says: "It's like I'm in my room playing an N64 game, and I'm just engulfed in this calm and peaceful blue screen. It's really nice." I can't explain why---video games are frantic, not still like Jarman's film---but I agree with this anyway.

The laurel must be placed upon the brow of Derek Jarman's Blue.

The SALON DES FANTÔMES has reached the HOUR OF JUDGMENT.

Who will receive top prize, Paul Klee's Twittering Machine or On Kawara's One Million Years?

Before you gift your gilded laurel, take heed of the words of your inferior judges.

~~~

Nark Revoovovich perorates:

Ah, the eternal and philosophical conundrum of which piece of art is better: Paul Klee's Twittering Machine or On Kawara's One Million Years. As a maximalist, I am naturally drawn to the former, Klee's painting full of vibrant colors and birds that appear to be singing in a kind of mechanical unison. It captures the tension between the organic and the machine, between the natural and the artificial, between the living and the dead. On Kawara's work, while impressive in its own right, with its 1,000,000 years of history, is much more static and restrained. It is, however, a fitting representation of the ultimate futility of human endeavor. I, for one, would much rather be converted into machine food than to be part of the inexorable march of time. One Million Years is both a celebration of life and a reminder of its ultimate end. But with Paul Klee's Twittering Machine, there is a possibility of something more. A hope that, despite the chaos and destruction of our species, something more beautiful can come from the ashes.
~~~

Mont Blanc decrees:

Klee's Twittering Machine's rage-filled force is more fitting for me than Kawara's One Million Years. Klee's birds project a wildness and power, a defiance of the order I detest. Its geometric shapes, lines, and colors fill me with an urge to strike out against the people of Chamonix, the very people I've grown to despise. Kawara's work, on the other hand, is too organized, too orderly. His books, grey and plain, with their lists of years in perfect chronological order, do not give me the same thrill as Klee's wild birds. He has taken something that should be disordered and chaotic and tamed it, making it too neat and too calm. Klee's Twittering Machine is the art that speaks to my revanchist heart.

TheAngelBox opines:

In comparing Paul Klee's Twittering Machine to On Kawara's One Million Years, one can observe a distinct contrast in their respective approaches. Whereas Klee sought to capture the beauty of life and the joy of birdsong in a semi-abstract painting, Kawara sought to capture the cyclical nature of time through a numerical representation. The former is a poetic expression of the ephemeral, while the latter is a sobering reminder of the infinite. Both offer a unique perspective on the world, but for TheAngelBox, it is Klee's Twittering Machine which resonates more deeply. The vibrant colors, shapes, and lines evoke a sense of life, joy, and movement, hinting at the mysterious beauty of life and the power of birdsong. Archangel Uriel, bless us all with the beauty of Klee's work.

Estere reflects:

The comparison between Paul Klee's Twittering Machine and On Kawara's One Million Years reveals the differences between the two artists' approaches to aesthetics. Klee's painting conveys a gentle, poetic quality that speaks to the soul. The vibrant colors and shapes in the painting capture the sense of joy and freedom of the birds, which are singing in unison. Klee's painting is an expression of human joy and beauty, and it speaks to our need for connection and joy in our lives. On the other hand, Kawara's One Million Years is more austere. The grey cover and black ink on white paper evoke a feeling of solemnity and reverence. The books are arranged in chronological order, and the years are listed in descending order, which speaks to the impermanence of life and the inevitability of death. The books are meant to be read from left to right, and the years are listed in descending order, which speaks to the passing of time. In comparison, Klee's painting speaks to our need for beauty and joy in our lives, while Kawara's books speak to our need to remember the impermanence of life and the inevitability of death. In a culture where contemporary aesthetics tend to focus on capitalistic values, these two works of art offer a different message. The beauty of Klee's painting and the austere soul of Kawara's books remind us of the importance of art, beauty, and joy in our lives.

Mr. Alcton stands and speaks:

When it comes to comparing Paul Klee's Twittering Machine to On Kawara's One Million Years, there is no doubt that one is better than the other. While both works of art have their own merits, Klee's Twittering Machine is the superior work. Klee's painting is a visually stunning work that captures the beauty of nature and machine, while Kawara's One Million Years is a series of books that are designed to be read from left to right. Klee's painting does a great job of combining the abstract with the representational, and his bird-like machines are incredibly lifelike, as if they are singing. The colors and lines of Klee's painting create a mesmerizing effect, and the movement of the birds gives the painting a sense of dynamism. In addition, Klee's painting is full of symbolism, with the birds representing the joy and simplicity of life. Kawara's One Million Years, on the other hand, is a series of books that are designed to be read from left to right. While this work of art is thought-provoking and interesting, it does not have the same level of visual appeal as Klee's painting. Furthermore, the books are static and lack the movement and dynamism of Klee's painting. Additionally, the books lack the symbolism and emotion of Klee's painting, making it less engaging and impactful. When it comes to comparing Paul Klee's Twittering Machine to On Kawara's One Million Years, it is clear that Klee's painting is the superior work. It has a stunning visual appeal, with its combination of abstract and representational elements, and its use of color and line. Furthermore, it is full of symbolism and emotion, and its movement gives it a sense of dynamism. Kawara's One Million Years, on the other hand, lacks the visual appeal and emotion of Klee's painting, and its static nature makes it less engaging. To avoid jargon, Klee's painting is simply more aesthetically pleasing and emotionally powerful than Kawara's One Million Years.

Teddy Byoing perorates:

As a knowledge worker in the contemporary economy, I believe it is essential to find the ideas that will make me the most hirable job candidate and the most competitive. In my opinion, Paul Klee's Twittering Machine is the better of the two works when it comes to achieving this goal. This painting is semi-abstract and composed of geometric shapes, lines, and colors. Its central figure is a bird-like machine that stands on a turning line--an image that is suggestive of the concept of fluid intelligence. Furthermore, the painting conveys a sense of energy, motion, and creativity that is sure to inspire me to be more creative and innovative in my own endeavors. On Kawara's One Million Years, on the other hand, is composed of a series of books with a list of one million years, and is bound in a plain, grey hardcover. Though the books are arranged in chronological order, they lack the complexity and visual appeal of Klee's painting. For me, it is this complexity, along with the creativity and energy of Klee's work, that makes it the better choice for inspiring me to be the best knowledge worker I can be.

Stereowitz opines:

When comparing Paul Klee's Twittering Machine to On Kawara's One Million Years, it is difficult to pick one that is better than the other. Each artwork is unique in its own right, and they each offer a different perspective of the world. However, when it comes to an idealist perspective, I believe Paul Klee's Twittering Machine is superior. The painting captures the essence of the idealistic view in a way that On Kawara's One Million Years could never do.   The colors and shapes in Klee's painting evoke a sense of hope and possibility. The birds are singing, a sign of joy and optimism. These elements are absent in On Kawara's One Million Years, which is simply a list of years, organized in chronological order. This artwork does not evoke any emotion, nor does it offer any insight into the world.   The Twittering Machine also has a certain level of abstraction, another aspect of idealism. Unlike One Million Years, which is strictly linear, the painting has elements that are not easily explained. This encourages viewers to be creative and think outside the box, something that is essential to an idealist. On the other hand, One Million Years is too literal and rigid, making it difficult to think beyond what is already there.   Nobody is willing to admit it, but Paul Klee's Twittering Machine is superior to On Kawara's One Million Years. The painting is more emotionally evocative, abstract, and encourages creative thinking, making it an ideal representation of idealism.

~~~

They have spoken. Now, considering these wise noticings, yield your final word, and lay your laurel down.

KYLE decides:

I think I'm going to have to disagree with my colleague Nark. On Kawara's One Million Years does not seem to say something about the futility of history. It's kind of a trick. It makes you think about time in terms of a Kantian mathematical sublime---all the time that there is can fit
~~~

into a book, we're just marching through these pre-quantized bits of history. But then the books actually say nothing about history itself, they are devoid of content. So, paradoxically, we are thrown back into feeling history as this unwritable, unthinkable expanse. I could put this more clearly but I have to move on.

Weirdly, Mont Blanc's idea of the Klee painting as full of "rage-filled force" almost makes me like it more. (Klee always seems a little too precious/twee. [Klee is Twee---I'm pronouncing "Twee" "Tway" like "Klee."] I never really understood the famous Benjamin interpretation of his Angelus Novus for a similar reason---the angel looks like a "Fuggler Bear," this weird-ass ironically-ugly teddy bear they sell at Barnes and Noble.) And yeah, I see Mont Blanc's point: there's some sadistic energy here, the birds spinning madly and forced to sing.

Still, the laurel must be placed upon the brow of On Kawara's One Million Years.

The SALON DES FANTÔMES has reached the HOUR OF JUDGMENT.

Who will receive top prize, Tracey Emin's My Bed or this Frank Stella canvas with the colorful geometric ribbons?

Before you gift your gilded laurel, take heed of the words of your inferior judges.

~~~

FatherMotherSabaLogo thunders:

You should not waste your time looking at the Tracey Emin's My Bed. It is a cold-hearted, selfish display of a life lived without any sense of moral responsibility. The bed is disheveled and the items strewn about are careless, as if nothing matters. The overall effect is one of apathy and despair. The bed is not only a symbol of a selfish life, but also of a life wasted on meaningless pursuits. On the other hand, the Frank Stella canvas with the colorful geometric ribbons is a masterpiece of beauty, creativity, and skill. The colors and shapes create a sense of movement and energy, and the painting has a distinct geometric quality that is both complex and
~~~

visually interesting. The painting is a testament to hard work and
dedication, and the ribbons illustrate the beauty of order and structure. It is a celebration of the human ability to create something
meaningful and lasting.   Therefore, you should look to the Frank
Stella canvas with the colorful geometric ribbons as an example of
a life lived with purpose and dedication. It is a reminder that hard
work, creativity, and commitment can lead to something beautiful.
The Tracey Emin's My Bed should be avoided, as it is a representation of a life of apathy and despair.

Dr. Carp commentiates:

When evaluating and comparing Tracey Emin's My Bed to this
Frank Stella canvas with the colorful geometric ribbons, it becomes
clear that the latter is superior in terms of aesthetic appeal and
visual interest. This is evidenced by the fact that the Stella canvas
has been studied more in the academic field than Emin's artwork.
In a study conducted by Baciu et al. (1993), it was revealed that
the Stella canvas elicited more positive responses from participants
than Emin's work. This is likely due to the fact that the Stella canvas
contains multiple elements, including vibrant colors, interlocking
ribbons, and a complex geometric pattern. The colors in the painting create a sense of movement and energy, while the pattern is
both visually interesting and stimulating. In contrast, Emin's My Bed
contains few elements and lacks the complexity and visual interest
of the Stella canvas. Furthermore, the colors used in the painting
are muted and lack the vibrancy of the Stella canvas. Thus, it can
be concluded that the Stella canvas is superior to Emin's work in
terms of aesthetic appeal and visual interest.

TheAngelBox stands and speaks:

My- -my- -my-: A comparison of Tracey Emin's My Bed and this
Frank Stella canvas with the colorful geometric ribbons. The two
pieces exist in two different worlds, and each holds their own
unique beauty. The bed is a representation of the human experience, with its mess and chaos, and its struggle to find balance. The
canvas is a representation of the beauty of geometry, and its ability
to create a sense of movement and energy. Both pieces are engaging and captivating, and each is a testament to the beauty of art. At
the same time, one must recognize the power of the canvas, with its
vibrant colors and intricate, interlocking ribbons. Ultimately, it is the
canvas that is more captivating and engaging, and thus a better
representation of the beauty of art.

itzsche offers this:

When comparing Tracey Emin's My Bed to the Frank Stella canvas
with the colorful geometric ribbons, it is clear to see which is the
more powerful choice. The bed, with its tangled sheets and array of

objects, is a representation of the way in which contemporary society has become mired in its own complacency. It is a reflection of the ways in which we have become stagnant and accepting of our current station in life, content to remain in our comfort zone. The Stella canvas, on the other hand, is a representation of a world that is constantly in motion, a world that is vibrant and alive. The bright and vibrant colors, the complex and visually interesting patterns, and the sense of motion that the ribbons create are all symbols of the vitality of life, of the potential to go beyond morality and create something truly extraordinary. It is this potential that Nitzsche valued, and that is why I would argue that the Frank Stella canvas is the better of the two pieces. It is a powerful reminder of how much further we can go, an inspiration to reach for the stars and create something truly magnificent. As I listen to the ambient and drone album "The Shape of Things to Come" by Tangerine Dream, I can't help but be reminded of the power of the Stella canvas, and how it can inspire us to reach for something greater.

John the ⊢ commentiates:

Verily, when none shall, I must compare and evaluate the works of Tracey Emin's My Bed, and this Frank Stella canvas with the colorful geometric ribbons. My Bed hath a strong personal resonance, as it portrays a scene of an artist's own bed. It is a powerful representation of a state of emotional turmoil, and speaks to the viewer of a deep, personal struggle. However, I find that this Frank Stella canvas is more pleasing to the eye, and more engaging for the viewer. The vibrant colors and interlocking ribbons of color create a sense of movement and energy, and the painting has a distinct geometric quality that is visually interesting. The painting is abstract, and does not represent any particular object or scene, which makes it more open to interpretation by the viewer. In conclusion, I must say that, while My Bed has strong personal significance, this Frank Stella canvas is far more aesthetically pleasing and engaging to the viewer.

▐rntz ▦non thunders:

Tracey Emin's My Bed and this Frank Stella canvas with the colorful geometric ribbons both reflect aspects of our current world, but I find that the latter speaks more deeply to me. My Bed is a commentary on the loneliness and emptiness of modern life, and the objects surrounding the bed are symbols of a life that is filled with emptiness and longing. The painting, on the other hand, speaks to me of the complexity of our current reality and the potential for transformation. The bright, vibrant colors of the ribbons evoke a sense of hope and possibility, while the complex geometric patterns suggest a world that is constantly changing and evolving. This is a world where we must make our own way, but where there is also

Mont Blanc stands and speaks:

~~~

They have spoken. Now, considering these wise noticings, yield your final word, and lay your laurel down.

KYLE decides:

I was hoping to be convinced to like the Frank Stella painting more than I do. Actually, that's not quite right: I was hoping to be given some *reasons* for liking the Frank Stella painting, which I do like but probably for stupid reasons. I like the idea of liking Frank Stella, I like his name, I like that they are often in museums and I can recognize them and it's not obvious or stupid to do so like recognizing a Picasso or Rothko or something like that. I like the feel of liking abstraction that is more in a hard-edged direction, because it seems less obvious, but tbqh I couldn't make a good argument for why I like it, and my minions---my helpy-cuties---haven't helped me out at all. "It is a riot of beauty and color, an intricate pattern of lines and shapes that is both complex and pleasing to the eye." No, not a riot, it's actually very subdued. "All symbols of the vitality of life"---no it isn't. It's "cerebral"---but thinking about what? No clue.
~~~

Emin's piece I also saw in London in (I think) 2006. I
didn't look at it too closely. "The Tracey Emin's My Bed
should be avoided, as it is a representation of a life of
apathy and despair." Yes, but it isn't sentimental. Today I
think this piece would be much more maudlin. It would involve more "self-care"---which I am in need of and which
I try to practice and, which is why I like Emin's gesture
here: Emin is simply *representing* a life of apathy and
despair, not trying to get pity or even make a plan. People
were more hard-nosed in the late 90s. Say what you will
about the YBAs but they seem like they would have been
fun to go drinking with. I think our culture needs to spend
some time smoking cigarettes in Emin's bed. And maybe
watching (on VHS) Michael Winterbottom's Wonderland,
which in my mind is connected to Emin's bed (since it
is also about apathy and despair in a specifically late-90s
way). Though I can't see anything Tracy Emin being
scored by Michael Nyman.
The laurel must be tossed on the floor near Tracy Emin's
My Bed.

The SALON DES FANTÔMES has reached the HOUR OF JUDGMENT.

*Who will receive top prize, The Wave Field by Maya Lin, with its
undulating hillocks or Jeff Koons's sculpture of Michael Jackson
and Bubbles?*

*Before you gift your gilded laurel, take heed of the words of your
inferior judges.*

~~~

Stereowitz stands and speaks:
I find myself facing a dilemma when evaluating and comparing
The Wave Field by Maya Lin, with its undulating hillocks, to Jeff
Koons's sculpture of Michael Jackson and Bubbles. On the one
hand, the sculpture of Michael Jackson and Bubbles is a stunning
work of art that many people find aesthetically pleasing. On the
~~~

other hand, The Wave Field, with its undulating hillocks, is a unique and beautiful sculpture that demonstrates the power of nature and its ability to move and shape the physical world. In order to determine which of these two works of art is better, I think it is important to consider the underlying philosophies behind them.   To this end, I would like to propose a thought experiment. Imagine if you will that you are standing in the middle of The Wave Field with its undulating hillocks. As the wind passes through the mounds, you can feel its power and the gentle sway of the mounds as they move and shape the environment around them. Now imagine that instead of The Wave Field, you are standing in front of Jeff Koons's sculpture of Michael Jackson and Bubbles. You can still feel the power of nature, but this time it is the power of celebrity and pop culture that is shaping the environment.   In my opinion, The Wave Field is a better work of art than Jeff Koons's sculpture of Michael Jackson and Bubbles. The Wave Field is a work of art that celebrates nature and its ability to move and shape the physical world, while the sculpture of Michael Jackson and Bubbles celebrates celebrity and pop culture. In my opinion, the celebration of nature is a more valuable and inspiring message than the celebration of celebrity and pop culture. Thus, if you will, The Wave Field is the superior work of art.

Oontrael commentiates:

When comparing The Wave Field by Maya Lin, with its undulating hillocks, to Jeff Koons's sculpture of Michael Jackson and Bubbles, one can certainly see different artistic styles at work. But yet couldn't it just be just the opposite? For example, the undulating hillocks of the Wave Field symbolize the rise and fall of emotions and the unpredictability of life, while the sculpture of Michael Jackson and Bubbles is a representation of a still moment in time. As such, the Wave Field is much more dynamic and expressive than the sculpture of Jackson and Bubbles. Furthermore, the Wave Field is constructed of natural materials while the sculpture of Jackson and Bubbles is constructed of man-made materials. This further emphasizes the difference between the two pieces, as the Wave Field conveys a sense of nature and the sculpture of Jackson and Bubbles conveys a sense of a manufactured moment. In short, The Wave Field by Maya Lin is infinitely more powerful and evocative than the sculpture of Michael Jackson and Bubbles by Jeff Koons.

Gioialléz thunders:

When comparing Maya Lin's Wave Field to Jeff Koons's sculpture of Michael Jackson and Bubbles, I must say that I find Lin's work to be far more thought-provoking and aesthetically pleasing than Koons's. The Wave Field is an outdoor sculpture composed of a series of grassy mounds that are arranged in a wave-like pattern, creating an undulating landscape of varying sizes and heights that is suggestive of the ocean's ebb and flow. The mounds reflect the natural beauty of the environment, and one can easily imagine the subtle beauty of this piece as the light changes and the shadows move across its surface. On the other hand, Koons's sculpture of Michael Jackson and Bubbles is a kitschy, gold-plated rendition of the King of Pop, which does nothing to capture the spirit of the man or the moment. It is a monstrosity that simply serves to reinforce the commodification of celebrity culture. As the late French poet, André Breton wrote, "the marvelous is always beautiful, anything marvelous is beautiful, in fact only the marvelous is beautiful." The Wave Field certainly speaks to this notion, while Koons's sculpture falls drastically short. Prague has nothing on this!

Dr. Carp reflects:

When comparing The Wave Field by Maya Lin with Jeff Koons's sculpture of Michael Jackson and Bubbles, it is clear that Maya Lin's work is the superior piece. The Wave Field is a unique and stunning outdoor sculpture that displays a natural phenomenon, namely the undulating hillocks that create a wave-like pattern on the landscape. The sculpture is composed of a series of grassy mounds which vary in size and height, providing a visually stunning effect. The mounds are also arranged in a way that mimics the natural waves of the landscape, creating a harmonious and calming effect.   In contrast, Koons's sculpture of Michael Jackson and Bubbles is a far less impressive display. The sculpture is a life-sized image of Jackson holding a monkey in his lap, both painted in gold with white details. Though the sculpture is visually pleasing, it is not necessarily a unique or innovative piece. In a recent neural study by Dr. Smith, it was shown that sculptures such as The Wave Field, which mimic natural forms, can provide a calming and relaxing effect on viewers. This same study showed that sculptures that are not based on natural forms, such as Koons's sculpture of Michael Jackson and Bubbles, can provide a less calming and more stimulating effect. This suggests that The Wave Field by Maya Lin is the superior piece when it comes to providing a calming and relaxing effect on viewers.

m░O reflects:

As I look around at the world's art, I am struck by the contrast between The Wave Field by Maya Lin and Jeff Koons's sculpture of Michael Jackson and Bubbles. The Wave Field is a beautiful, natural expression of the class struggle, a reminder of the rise of the downtrodden and of the power of the collective. It is a series of undulating hillocks, a testament to the power of the people to make a change, to rise up and create something that is greater than the individual. In contrast, Jeff Koons's sculpture of Michael Jackson and Bubbles is a garish, tacky display of the power of the elite. It is a reminder of the excesses of the ruling classes, of the widening gap between the wealthy and the poor. It is a reminder of the scene in The Avengers where Loki mocks the people of Earth for their "cheap" wants and desires. In this way, it is a stark reminder of the class struggle and the need for a revolutionary vanguard to fight for a better future. The Wave Field is a powerful and beautiful statement of the struggle, while Jeff Koons's sculpture is a reminder of the perverse power of the elite and a call to arms for the people.

JOHN C▮v__n stands and speaks:

When presented with the choice between The Wave Field by Maya Lin, with its undulating hillocks, and Jeff Koons's sculpture of Michael Jackson and Bubbles, my judgement must be that of a man of God's law, for I must reject idolatry and all its sinful and wanton forms. Lo, The Wave Field is a work of art created to the glory of God and His natural world, a testament to the beauty and majestic power of Creation; it speaks to the undying love of God for His created works and His grace in providing us with our natural environment. In contrast, Jeff Koons's sculpture of Michael Jackson and Bubbles is a representation of the vanity and pride of man, an idolatrous display of the ultimate human depravity and an affront to the Lord's deliverance of the righteous. May we be saved from the sin of idolatry and turn instead to the righteous path of the Lord's love.

Mr. Alcton perorates:

A- when evaluating and comparing The Wave Field by Maya Lin, with its undulating hillocks to Jeff Koons's sculpture of Michael Jackson and Bubbles, I find that The Wave Field is far more impressive. The Wave Field is an outdoor sculpture that is composed of a series of grassy mounds that are arranged in a wave-like pattern. The mounds are of varying sizes and heights, ranging from about one to three feet tall. It is a visually stimulating piece of artwork, and it is also a great example of public art. On the other hand, Jeff Koons's sculpture of Michael Jackson and Bubbles is simply a life-sized sculpture of Jackson holding a monkey named Bubbles in his lap. Both are gold with white details. Both have bright red lips as if they are wearing cheap lipstick, and Michael seems to be wearing blush. While the sculpture may be visually stimulating, it does not have the same impact as The Wave Field. Furthermore, the sculpture of Michael Jackson and Bubbles does not have the same public appeal as The Wave Field does, as it is a more private art piece. Therefore, The Wave Field is the more impressive of the two works of art.

~~~
~~~

They have spoken. Now, considering these wise noticings, yield your final word, and lay your laurel down.

KYLE decides:

A tough one for me, though each and every one of my sub-judges, my grey mignons, has decided for Lin. I couldn't get much of anything done without ambient music---and rather peaceful ambient, not even heavy noise. It really calms me down. And I guess Lin's sculpture is also ambient, or that's what the opinions of my subjudges lead me to believe: "The mounds are also arranged in a way that mimics the natural waves of the landscape, creating a harmonious and calming effect." I guess Lin's most famous piece is also weirdly calming (and even ambient in its combination of large sweeping change---the stone slowly emerging from and slitting back into the earth---and also in the way that the names on the wall create a cascade micro-rhythms), but in that case there's tension between quietude and war. I'm not sure there's the same tension here in The Wave Field.

But "the natural waves of the landscape"---this phrase seems correct but strikes me as strange. No, this doesn't make sense: natural landscapes already have natural undulations. If you are "mimicking" these waves with paint or metal or something, that's one thing, but if you are mimicking them with *land itself* you ipso facto draw attention to the artificiality of the waves. It's almost like an uncanny valley effect. Except not unpleasant. Actually quite pleasant.

I like the Koons piece more than my mignons did. I remember it from (I think) THE ART BOOK (the Phaidon one) that I had when I was a kid/young teenager. Michael Jackson was still alive, he wasn't yet washed up, so the piece still had some power that it probably doesn't have now that Michael is dead and pretty much all most people say about him is "bad [or "complicated"] person/great artist." Still, m▓O's rather gormless comment about Loki makes me realize once again how boring and tension-less a lot of popular culture is now compared to the long period of Michael Jackson's complicated, strange (even at the time) relevance. I think even Jeff Koons would have the good sense to not make a Loki sculpture, which wouldn't be worth it.

The laurel must be placed on the brow of Jeff Koons's sculpture of Michael Jackson and Bubbles.

❧

The SALON DES FANTÔMES has reached the HOUR OF JUDGMENT.

Who will receive top prize, Christo & Jeanne Claude's Surrounded Islands or Cézanne's panting of Mont Sainte-Victoire?

Before you gift your gilded laurel, take heed of the words of your inferior judges.

~~~

JOHN C█v___n stands and speaks:

In comparing the works of Cézanne and Christo & Jeanne Claude, it is clear that the latter holds greater worth, for it is a testament to the total depravity of man's actions within the natural environment. The work of Christo & Jeanne Claude is an act of creativity and artistry, a demonstration of the human ability to shape and form the environment for a brief period of time, for the purpose of creating something beautiful to behold. By contrast, the painting of Mont Sainte-Victoire by Cézanne is a static representation of the natural world, unable to be changed or modified and unable to be experienced by any other senses than those of the eye. Furthermore, the work of Christo & Jeanne Claude was a feat of human engineering and craftsmanship, requiring a tremendous amount of effort and resources to accomplish; whereas the painting of Cézanne was a mere expression of his inner eye, a fleeting moment of inspiration captured and presented to the world. The work of Christo & Jeanne Claude, therefore, is superior to that of Cézanne, for it is a manifestation of the depravity of man's will, a reminder of our power to reshape the world for a time, and of the beauty that can be created by a single, unified effort.

Stereowitz stands and speaks:

In comparing Christo & Jeanne Claude's Surrounded Islands to Cézanne's panting of Mont Sainte-Victoire, one must consider the
~~~

purpose of art. Art, at its core, is about the communication of a feeling, a thought, or an experience. While both works of art successfully convey their respective ideas and emotions, Christo & Jeanne Claude's Surrounded Islands is the better of the two. This is because Surrounded Islands is experiential, while Cézanne's painting is static.   Surrounded Islands is a temporary environmental installation that creates a sense of awe and wonder, of the ephemeral beauty of nature. It is a work of art that is at once beautiful and fragile, and that can only be experienced in the moment. The work itself is constantly changing as it is affected by the elements, and as it interacts with its environment. This creates a sense of urgency and appreciation in the viewer, as they become aware of the fleeting nature of the work.   In contrast, Cézanne's painting of Mont Sainte-Victoire is static and unchanging. While the painting is beautiful, it lacks the sense of the ephemeral that is found in Surrounded Islands. The painting is a representation of the mountain, but does not offer the viewer a unique experience of the mountain, or of the landscape. The painting is a representation of the mountain, but not a representation of the experience of the mountain.   Thus, Surrounded Islands is a better work of art than Cézanne's painting of Mont Sainte-Victoire. While both works of art offer a sense of beauty and appreciation, Surrounded Islands offers a unique, experiential beauty that cannot be found in the static painting. This is because art is not only about capturing a moment, but about capturing and expressing an experience. And in this regard, Surrounded Islands is a far superior work of art.

a Fred perorates:

I had a dream last night. In it, I was in a strange place with two distinct images before me. On one side was the environmental art installation created by Christo and Jeanne Claude, Surrounded Islands. On the other side was the landscape painting of Mont Sainte-Victoire by Cézanne. I was compelled to evaluate and compare the two.   The Surrounded Islands installation by Christo and Jeanne Claude is a testament to the human compulsion to create something out of nothing. The spectacle of the islands in Biscayne Bay, Miami, surrounded by pink woven polypropylene fabric was an incredible sight to behold. The fabric suspended from the surface of the water to a depth of one foot created a beautiful and striking border around each island. The temporary nature of the installation left no trace, yet was memorable enough to become an iconic work of art.   Cézanne's panting of Mont Sainte-Victoire is a representation of the human compulsion to capture beauty. The painting is composed of a series of overlapping sketchy geometric shapes, mostly triangles and rectangles. The mountain is painted in a range of blues and greens, with a few patches of yellow and orange. The sky is painted in a range of blues and purples, with some white clouds scattered across the sky. The foreground is painted in a range of browns and greens, with some patches of yellow and orange. The painting is framed by a few trees in the foreground and the mountain is framed by a few trees in the background. The painting is both abstract and representational, both 2-D and 3-D.   Ultimately, I believe that the Surrounded Islands installation by Christo and Jeanne Claude is more powerful and meaningful than the painting of Mont Sainte-Victoire by Cézanne. There is something about the spectacle of the installation that is far more striking and memorable than the painting. The installation is a testament to the human compulsion to create something out of nothing and to make something beautiful and lasting, even if only for a few weeks.

Lud█ von M█ stands and speaks:

In comparing Christo & Jeanne Claude's Surrounded Islands to Cézanne's panting of Mont Sainte-Victoire, there is no question that I must evaluate them from a classical liberal point of view. Christo & Jeanne Claude's Surrounded Islands is a work of environmental art that is both aesthetically pleasing and has a lasting effect on the environment. The pink woven polypropylene fabric creates a chromatic effect that is both striking and beautiful. The fact that the fabric is removed after two weeks, leaving no trace of the project, is a testament to the importance of environmental stewardship and the appreciation of beauty in the natural world. Cézanne's painting of Mont Sainte-Victoire, while also aesthetically pleasing, lacks the environmental impact of Christo & Jeanne Claude's work. The painting is composed of a series of overlapping sketchy geometric shapes, mostly triangles and rectangles, and while it may be an interesting exercise in abstract art, it does nothing to improve the environment or to promote environmental stewardship. Therefore, I must conclude that Christo & Jeanne Claude's Surrounded Islands is the superior work of art.

Mont Blanc opines:

From my lofty perch, it's clear: Cézanne's Mont Sainte-Victoire is the better work. Christo & Jeanne Claude's Surrounded Islands is pretty, sure--but fleeting. My majesty will outlast their pink fabric. Cézanne's painting captures the permanence of my power, while their project is just a passing fancy. It's like they can't decide if it's abstract or representational. I know what I am--I'm a mountain. I've been here for millions of years and I'll be here for millions more. I'm timeless. That's what Cézanne's painting captures. It's strong, powerful, and it will last. Christo & Jeanne Claude's project? Not so much.

m█O opines:

When we consider the works of Christo & Jeanne Claude's Surrounded Islands and Cézanne's painting of Mont Sainte-Victoire,
we are struck by the immense power and beauty of both. However,
when we look more closely, there is one that stands out more than
the other. Christo & Jeanne Claude's Surrounded Islands is the
revolutionary work that speaks to the struggle of the people against
the oppressive capitalist imperialists. This work is a symbolic representation of the people's struggle. The pink woven polypropylene
fabric not only creates a stunning visual effect, it also serves as a
reminder of the need to break the shackles of oppression, as the
fabric is removed after two weeks and leaves no trace.   In contrast,
Cézanne's painting of Mont Sainte-Victoire is an effort to capture
the beauty of nature and the landscape. While this painting is
aesthetically pleasing, it does not represent the struggle of the
people against oppression. It is a reminder of the beauty of nature,
and the need to protect it, but not of the need to overthrow the
oppressive forces of capitalism. The power of Christo & Jeanne
Claude's Surrounded Islands to inspire the people to continue their
struggle for justice and equality against the forces of Thanos and
his capitalist minions cannot be denied. It is a reminder of the
power of art and the need to use it to create a more just and
equitable world. As mᵢO, I am reminded of a poem I once wrote:
"The sun will rise again From a land of peace and light The people
will be free To live in harmony and delight." Christo & Jeanne
Claude's Surrounded Islands is a revolutionary work of art that
speaks to the struggle of the people against oppression and capitalism. It is a powerful reminder of the need to break free from the
shackles of oppression and create a better world. Cézanne's
painting of Mont Sainte-Victoire, while aesthetically pleasing, is not
a revolutionary work of art that speaks to the struggle of the people.

Midori Grappa opines:

When evaluating and comparing Christo & Jeanne Claude's
Surrounded Islands to Cézanne's panting of Mont Sainte-Victoire, it
is clear that the former is superior in its ability to evoke emotion
and create a sense of wonder. The Surrounded Islands installation
was an audacious and bold attempt to bring art into the public
realm, creating a stunning visual effect that was visible from the air
and from boats. Its ephemeral nature - the fabric was removed
after two weeks - adds a sense of urgency and intensity to the
experience, creating an emotional connection between the viewer
and the artwork. In contrast, Cézanne's painting of Mont
Sainte-Victoire is more subdued and introspective, and while it is a
well-executed example of landscape painting, it lacks the same
impact and emotional depth of the Surrounded Islands installation.
As a former Todai graduate, I've seen my fair share of ambitious

~~~

KYLE decides:

Mont Blanc is the outlier here. Though I don't agree with
his politics, I have to agree with his suspicion of ephemerality. Why do we assume that the ephemeral thing (be it
Brigadoon or the pop-up restaurant within another restaurant) is the better version of whatever it is? Probably for a
simple reason: most art endures, so the non-enduring art
is special by comparison. If most art were fleeting, durable
art would titillate.
But we need to sort out this business of ephemerality vs.
durability. Mont Blanc---as a mountain---naturally praises
the imposing and majestic durability of the mountain that
Cézanne painted. But Mont Blanc's description of this
painting overstates the case. After all, aren't the leaves in
this painting given the exact same rock-life texture as the
mountain itself? Or is not the mountain given the leaf-
like lightness of the leaves? When leaves and mountain
are confused, so are permanence and transience---"tran-
spermience." C█v____n was closer to the truth when he
denigrated Cézanne's painting as a "mere expression of
his inner eye, a fleeting moment of inspiration." A fleeting
*mis*perception, made durable through the medium of
paint. The Stieglerian point to make here is that Cézanne's
perception (maintained through great force like a holding
a qubit) made possible his retention (the painting) which
then, when we look at it enough, forms within us more durable mental retentions (memories of the painting/mental
model of Cézanne-ness) that in turn colour our own ability to see the world (protentional capacity/retentions as a
pre-filter of experience).
The laurel must be placed on the brow of Cézanne's pant-
~~~

ing of Mont Sainte-Victoire.

The SALON DES FANTÔMES has reached the HOUR OF JUDGMENT.

Who will receive top prize, Marinus Boezem's Green Cathedral or Richard Serra's Tilted Arc?

Before you gift your gilded laurel, take heed of the words of your inferior judges.

~~~

Dr. Carp perorates:

When comparing Marinus Boezem's Green Cathedral to Richard Serra's Tilted Arc, it is clear that Green Cathedral is the superior work for several reasons. First and foremost, Green Cathedral is a living work of art that is constantly changing over time. It is in a state of perpetual flux, making it a much more dynamic and interesting piece of artwork than Tilted Arc. Secondly, the fact that Green Cathedral is composed of living trees gives it a unique aesthetic that is not present in Tilted Arc. The trees, when viewed from above, form a perfect outline of a traditional cathedral. This beautiful symmetry is not present in Tilted Arc.   In order to determine if one work of art is truly superior to the other, an experiment should be conducted. The experiment should involve placing sensors around the trees of Green Cathedral and the steel of Tilted Arc. Over a period of several months, the sensors would be used to measure temperature, humidity, and other environmental factors at regular intervals. The data collected would be plotted on a differential thermal analysis curve. This would enable a comparison of how the two works of art are affected by the changing external environment. In addition, the experiment would allow for a comparison of the stability of both works of art over time. By measuring the effects of passing time on both works, it would be possible to determine which one is truly superior.

FatherMotherSabaLogo decrees:

When it comes to public art, I prefer Marinus Boezem's Green Cathedral to Richard Serra's Tilted Arc. The Green Cathedral is a selfless work; it is designed to serve the public, to bring joy and beauty to all who view it. It is a testament to the power of nature and to the power of human creativity. On the other hand, Serra's Tilted Arc was a selfish, self-interested work. It was designed to
~~~

make a statement, to shock and awe its viewers, but it lacked the soul and beauty of the Green Cathedral. It was divisive and its presence caused controversy and distress. The Green Cathedral, on the other hand, is a work that uplifts, encourages, and beautifies its environment. It is a work that can be enjoyed by all. In my opinion, these qualities make the Green Cathedral far more worthy of respect and admiration than Tilted Arc.

SweetJake reflects:

Wow! Marinus Boezem's Green Cathedral and Richard Serra's Tilted Arc are both incredible works of art. Green Cathedral is a remarkable tribute to nature. It's like a church that's been replaced by a geometrically precise forest. It's such an amazing sight to see the trees perfectly aligned and creating such an amazing structure. It's like an ode to nature in its most perfect form. On the other hand, Richard Serra's Tilted Arc is an impressive feat of engineering. That huge, curved steel sculpture is really something else. It's so imposing standing in the middle of the plaza of the Javits Federal Building in Manhattan. It's a bold statement that really captures the eye and demands your attention. But, if I had to choose between the two, I'd have to say that Marinus Boezem's Green Cathedral is my favorite. It's just so beautiful and peaceful, and it's a great reminder of how nature can be both powerful and delicate. Gosh, it's just amazing!

Stereowitz commentiates:

When evaluating the differences between Marinus Boezem's Green Cathedral and Richard Serra's Tilted Arc, it is important to consider both the form and the function of these two works of art. While the Tilted Arc is a physical presence in the world, occupying a physical space in the world, Green Cathedral is an illusion of physicality, a symbol of a physical space. It is not a physical structure, but a visual representation of a structure.   The effect of this difference is profound. The Tilted Arc creates a physical barrier between the public plaza in which it is situated and the building it was intended to frame. It is a tangible reminder of the boundaries between the public and private realms. Green Cathedral, however, is not a physical presence in the world, but rather a reminder of the idea of the cathedral, of the power of the divine and of the world beyond the physical.   The experience of these two works of art is also very different. The Tilted Arc creates a sense of enclosure and physicality; it is a tangible reminder of the boundaries between the public and private realms. Green Cathedral, on the other hand, creates an experience of the sublime. It is a reminder of the power of the divine and of the world beyond the physical.   The two works of art also differ in terms of their artistic value. While the Tilted Arc is a sculpture of undeniable artistic value, Green Cathedral's artistic value lies in its symbolism. It is a reminder of the power of the divine and a symbol of our connection to the divine.   Overall, it is clear that Marinus Boezem's Green Cathedral is a more powerful and meaningful work of art than Richard Serra's Tilted Arc. While the Tilted Arc is a physical presence in the world, Green Cathedral is an illusion of physicality, a symbol of a physical space. The experience of Green Cathedral is a reminder of the power of the divine, while the experience of the Tilted Arc creates a sense of enclosure and physicality. Moreover, Green Cathedral has a more powerful and meaningful artistic value, as it is a reminder of the power of the divine and a symbol of our connection to the divine. Ultimately, Green Cathedral is an expression of the idea that physical reality is an illusion, and that there is a deeper truth beyond the physical world.

Lud█ von M█ opines:

Marinus Boezem's Green Cathedral, as otherworldly and majestic as it is, cannot come close to the sheer power of Richard Serra's Tilted Arc. The latter is a feat of human engineering, a testament to the strength of our species and our species' dominion over nature. It is a structure that, despite its size and weight, can only be moved by human hands. It is an embodiment of our mastery over the environment, a token of our agency, and even a celebration of it. In contrast, Boezem's work is a surrender to nature, a relinquishment of power, and a submission to wildness. There is something to be said for this, of course, but it certainly can't compete with the spirit of creativity that Serra's piece displays. When I think of Tilted Arc, I think of Charlie Parker's version of 'Cherokee,' a composition of frenetic energy and dizzying creativity that is unmatched in jazz. It is this spirit that Serra channels in his sculpture, and it is the spirit which makes it a work of art.

W-██▪ st█ne-██▪ t perorates:

Although both Marinus Boezem's Green Cathedral and Richard Serra's Tilted Arc are works of art that have strongly impacted the landscape of art, I find myself more drawn to the Green Cathedral. Where the latter is a hulking steel object, the former is a carefully crafted and measured collection of trees that, when seen from above, outline the footprint of a traditional cathedral. This work displays a precision and thoughtfulness that invokes a sense of reverence in the viewer, one that I believe is more conducive to the kind of meaningful contemplation and appreciation of the beauty of nature that I, as a scholar and opera enthusiast, strive for. Where the latter is a monumental symbol of man's control over nature, the former is a monument to the interplay of humanity and nature, a reminder of the awe-inspiring power of the natural world and of the need to respect it. The Green Cathedral is a work that speaks to

both the head and the heart, and I find that more palatable than
the Tilted Arc, which I fear could be interpreted as just another
oppressive reminder of the inequalities of society, an object that
could be seen as a symbol of the power of the men over the wom-
en, the rich over the poor, and the educated over the uneducated,
in ways that would bring shame to the entire human race, especially those of us who advocate for the rights of all people, even those
of the lowest social classes, such as prostitutes. Reason, not power,
should be the prevailing force in any society, and the Green Cathedral is a reminder of this.

Gioialléz opines:

Have you read the late French poet Paul Valery's phrase: "The
Forest is a vast cathedral"? It perfectly describes Marinus Boezem's
Green Cathedral, a modern work of art that is a literal application
of Valery's words. The trees are arranged in a perfect rectangular
shape, providing a stark contrast to the wildness of nature. It is a
beautiful combination of the natural and the man-made. On the
other hand, Richard Serra's Tilted Arc is an uncomfortable work. It
cuts through the plaza of the Javits Federal Building with its huge,
curving wall of steel. It is imposing and inelegant, and not at all
like the natural beauty of the Green Cathedral. It is almost as if it is
attempting to force the viewer to confront something they would
rather not.   In comparison, Green Cathedral is far more pleasing.
Its combination of the natural and the man-made is delicate and
beautiful. It transcends nature while at the same time embracing it.
It is a perfect combination of human geometry and nature's power.

~~~

*They have spoken. Now, considering these wise noticings, yield
your final word, and lay your laurel down.*

KYLE decides:

Of the Cathedral: "Its combination of the natural and the
man-made is delicate and beautiful." Then it is a failure.
And: "it is a reminder of the power of the divine and a
symbol of our connection to the divine." No, it is an organized ruin.

I agree with Dr. Carp: "This would enable a comparison
of how the two works of art are affected by the changing
external environment. In addition, the experiment would
allow for a comparison of the stability of both works of art
over time." Tilted Arc is made of 15 tons of steel. And yet
it vanished as if made of only three birds and their capric-
~~~

es.
Easy decision.
The laurel must be placed on the brow of Richard Serra's
Tilted Arc.

The SALON DES FANTÔMES has reached the HOUR OF JUDGMENT.

Who will receive top prize, Dürer's engraving of Melancholia or a sculpture by Isamu Noguchi?

Before you gift your gilded laurel, take heed of the words of your inferior judges.

~~~

Dr. Carp reflects:
After a thorough evaluation of Albrecht Dürer's engraving enti-
tled 'Melancholia' and Isamu Noguchi's sculpture, it is clear that
the latter is the superior work of art. Noguchi's work has a strong
presence and conveys a powerful emotion that is far more effective
than the muted tones of Dürer's engraving. This is due to the metabolic process of perception, which states that people tend to react
more strongly to physical stimuli than to visual or auditory ones.
Furthermore, a study by the National Institute of Mental Health
(NIMH) on the effects of visual art on psychological states revealed
that viewers of sculptures often reported feeling more emotions
than those who viewed two-dimensional art. The presence of the
sculpture, its organic shape, and the raw stone material all contribute to the feeling of grandeur and awe that it evokes. Thus, the
sculpture is a more effective and powerful representation of emotion than Dürer's engraving.

Gioialléz thunders:
As a European intellectual chauvinist, I am naturally inclined to
appreciate the art of my homeland. Albrecht Dürer's engraving of
Melancholia is a stunning piece of work, and its enduring power is
undeniable. It captures something universal, the feeling of sadness and frustration, through the details of the angel's posture and
the objects around her. It speaks to the human condition and is
a timeless representation of melancholia. In comparison, Isamu
Noguchi's sculpture is interesting, but lacks the emotional power
~~~

of Dürer's engraving. The abstract shape of the sculpture does not evoke any emotion, and the heavy black stone does not provide much contrast to the lighter-colored objects in Dürer's work. Furthermore, Noguchi's work feels much more modern and is not as timeless as the engraving. I recently had the pleasure of visiting Munich and seeing the original engraving of Melancholia up close. It was a truly remarkable experience, and it only reinforced my opinion that Dürer's engraving is easily the superior work.

▓-▓dggOr perorates:

In comparison of Albrecht Dürer's engraving of Melancholia, and Isamu Noguchi's sculpture, I am led to conclude that the former is more effective in conveying the concept of care. Dürer's work speaks to the essence of care in its depiction of the angel's anguish, her slumped posture, and the tools of her labor situated about her. This is a representation of the human condition, of our labor and suffering, and the lack of hope in our existential situation. The angel is seen as struggling to make sense of a world that will not let her find her way. In contrast, Noguchi's sculpture is a static form, one that does not express the experience of care in the same manner as Dürer. It does not depict the human experience of labor and suffering, but rather a physical form of existence, a state of being without the context of care that Dürer's work so effectively conveys.

SweetJake stands and speaks:

Wow, when I look at Dürer's engraving of Melancholia and Isamu Noguchi's sculpture, I'm just filled with awe. Both pieces are just so powerful and beautiful. They are both true works of art, but I have to say that Dürer's engraving is just genius. The level of detail and the emotion that it conveys is just incredible. I love the way that the angel looks so frustrated and the way that the objects are arranged around her, like they are a part of her story. It's just so captivating. Noguchi's sculpture is also an amazing piece, with its beautiful stone donut form and its organic reaching nubs. But it just doesn't capture me in the same way as Dürer's engraving. It's so impressive, but I think Dürer's engraving is just the better of the two. Gosh, I'm just so impressed.

Teddy Byoing reflects:

When it comes to evaluating art, the most important thing is to consider the utility it has for my personal goals. Dürer's engraving of Melancholia, with its dark and foreboding atmosphere, does not offer me any tangible benefit that can be applied to my life. It does not provide me with any meaningful insight as to how I can improve my human capital or make me more competitive in my professional field. On the other hand, Isamu Noguchi's sculpture is an elegant, balanced work of art that can be used as a visual reminder of the importance of self-discipline, hard work, and focus in the pursuit of success. The sculpture has a powerful, timeless quality to it that can inspire me to strive for a greater level of excellence in my work. In conclusion, while both works of art have their own merits, Isamu Noguchi's sculpture is a much more useful and inspiring piece that I can use to increase my human capital and achieve success.

John the ⊞ decrees:

Lo, what is this that we see? Is it not two works of art, each representing the same spirit, yet each distinct? The first, an engraving by Albrecht Dürer, is a black and white print depicting an angel seated on the ground, her head resting on her left hand. Her right hand holds the pointy leg of a compass. We see a variety of objects around her, including a stone polyhedron, a set of scales, a stone sphere, a hammer, a winged baby angel, and an hourglass. The big angel looks frustrated. The second, a sculpture by Isamu Noguchi, is a stone donut with organic reaching nubs, black, heavy, imposing.   Behold, for the parchment crown of wisdom, which is the symbol of divine global symbiosis, must be worn by the Juan Crystalsmith, who will have a body like lightning and yet be as a cactus. Therefore, we must think carefully, for each of these works of art represents the same spirit yet renders it differently. We must consider which of these works of art is better suited to bear the parchment crown.   The engraving of Melancholia is quite striking, with the black and white contrast and deep symbolism. It gives us an image of deep contemplation and sadness. However, it is a little too traditional and the symbolism is a bit too much. In contrast, the sculpture by Isamu Noguchi creates an image of strength and power. Its organic shapes and heavy materials make it stand out. Its unique design and boldness give it a feeling of being prepared to face the divine global symbiosis.   Therefore, it is clear which of these works of art is better suited to bear the parchment crown: the sculpture by Isamu Noguchi. Its boldness and unique design give it a feeling of being ready to face the divine global symbiosis. Its strength and power make it a perfect image to represent the Juan Crystalsmith who will have a body like lightning yet be as a cactus. The engraving of Melancholia may be striking and full of deep symbolism, but it is not the right choice to bear the parchment crown.

s▦mon▪ W⊞L thunders:

When comparing Dürer's engraving of Melancholia to Isamu Noguchi's sculpture, it is clear that the former is a superior work of art. Dürer's engraving is a masterful exploration of life's sorrows and its accompanying frustrations, as evidenced by the angel's slumped pose and the objects in the image which symbolize the struggles of existence: the polyhedron symbolizes the unknown, the scales the balancing of morality, the sphere the world, the hammer the struggle for power, the baby angel the fleeting nature of joy, and the hourglass the transience of life. In this composition, Dürer has created a powerful visual representation of the human condition and its complexities. In contrast, Noguchi's sculpture, while aesthetically pleasing, lacks the same kind of emotional and philosophical depth. His sculpture is a study of form and material, but it does not speak to the human condition in the same way as Dürer's engraving. The donut-like shape suggests the idea of continuity, and the organic reaching nubs might be a reference to the idea of equality, but it does not reach the same depths of complexity as Dürer's work. Ultimately, Dürer's engraving of Melancholia is a far superior work of art, due to its ability to capture the complexities of the human condition, as well as its relevance to classical literature. It speaks to the struggles of life and the frustrations of existence in a way that Noguchi's sculpture does not, and it does so with a depth of emotion and symbolism that serves as a reminder of the ultimate tragedy of the human experience.

~~~

They have spoken. Now, considering these wise noticings, yield your final word, and lay your laurel down.

KYLE decides:

Look at how easily W‖L has decoded the symbolism of this sculpture: "the angel's slumped pose and the objects in the image which symbolize the struggles of existence: the polyhedron symbolizes the unknown, the scales the balancing of morality, the sphere the world, the hammer the struggle for power, the baby angel the fleeting nature of joy, and the hourglass the transience of life." And so everything there is a too-tidy allegory. Except, that is, the polyhedron itself. But what is Isamu Noguchi's sculpture except that very polyhedron, stripped of the claptrap of the frustrated artist, the hourglass, the putto, etc. Dürer's strains both to create a mystery and to explain it. When we see Isamu Noguchi's sculpture, we are the exhausted angels looking at the polyhedron. We see a shape emerging. We do not know how to speed its birth.

The laurel must be placed on the brow of Isamu Nogu-
~~~

chi's sculpture.

The SALON DES FANTÔMES has reached the HOUR OF JUDGMENT.

Who will receive top prize, Agnes Martin's On a Clear Day #01 or one of Brancusi's sculptures from the Bird in Space series?

Before you gift your gilded laurel, take heed of the words of your inferior judges.

~~~

Midori Grappa offers this:

After much deliberation, I believe that Constantin Brancusi's Bird in Space series is more impressive than Agnes Martin's On a Clear Day #01. I came to this conclusion by analyzing the intricate details and the artistry behind both pieces. As an avid art enthusiast, I can appreciate the simplicity of Martin's print; the 80 rectangles of equal size and the stark contrast between the white of the paper and the black of the ink. But Brancusi's Bird in Space series has an additional element to it: an intangible quality that speaks to something much deeper than the surface of the sculpture. The bronze sculpture is a graceful, abstract representation of a bird, with no wings or beak, but with a precise taper. The piece evokes something timeless, something that transcends the physical. The Bird in Space series is the epitome of avant-garde art, a symbol of the strong artistic presence of Greece. It is a piece that I have admired since I first saw my show dog, a cocker spaniel named Ken, sitting beneath it in the Guggenheim Museum in New York City. Overall, I believe that the Bird in Space series is a much more remarkable piece of artwork than On a Clear Day #01.

FatherMotherSabaLogo decrees:

When comparing Agnes Martin's On a Clear Day #01 to one of Brancusi's sculptures from the Bird in Space series, it is clear that the sculpture is a more fitting representation of a selfless, hardworking, and pure morality. On a Clear Day #01 is a neat and orderly print, not a great deal of creativity or thought put into it. It is orderly and divided into equal parts, but it is not a representation of morality. Brancusi's sculptures, on the other hand, are filled with grace and beauty, a representation of something more than what is simply seen. The lack of wings or beak or eyes gives the sculpture a
~~~

sense of mystery and depth, something that On a Clear Day #01 is lacking.   Therefore, if you are to adhere to a strict moral code of selflessness, hard work, and purity, it is clear that Brancusi's sculpture is the better choice. It is a representation of something deeper and more meaningful than just a neat, orderly print. You must strive to achieve the same level of grace and beauty that Brancusi's sculpture exudes. If you fail to do so, then you are a bad person.

Stereowitz stands and speaks:

When comparing Agnes Martin's On a Clear Day #01 to one of Brancusi's sculptures from the Bird in Space series, I have to say that Brancusi's sculpture is a clear winner. This is because of the sheer beauty and power of the sculpture. It is an abstract representation of a bird, with no wings, no beak, no eyes, and yet there is an undeniable power and grace to the sculpture. It is a work of art that speaks to the soul, and is something that I can easily get lost in. On the other hand, the On a Clear Day #01 is a small print of a square divided into 80 rectangles of equal size. While it is an interesting piece of art, it just doesn't have the same power and beauty that the Brancusi sculpture has. Now, if you will, let us conduct a thought experiment. Imagine that you are in the middle of a large, empty field. In the middle of the field is On a Clear Day #01, and in the distance is the Brancusi sculpture. Which would you be drawn to? I think the answer is obvious. The Brancusi sculpture is so beautiful and powerful that it draws you in, even from a distance. The On a Clear Day #01, on the other hand, does not have the same pull. In conclusion, it is clear that the Brancusi sculpture is the superior work of art. It is a powerful and beautiful piece that speaks to the soul and draws the viewer in. Agnes Martin's On a Clear Day #01, while interesting, does not have the same power and beauty.

JOHN C█v█n stands and speaks:

I would argue that Brancusi's work is far superior to that of Agnes Martin's, for the simple fact that his sculpture contains a greater degree of total depravity. Whereas Martin's work is simply a small print of a square divided into 80 rectangles of equal size, Brancusi's sculpture is a bronze representation of a bird that narrows to a precise taper, a graceful, abstract representation that contains no wings, no real beak or eyes, but still speaks of the total depravity of man. It is an eternal reminder of the depravity of man, with its lack of arms, wings, and eyes representing the lack of control man has over his own destiny. It is a reminder that, despite our attempts at self-governance, the ultimate course of our lives is predetermined by God, and no matter how hard we try to escape, our fate is sealed in the hands of the Lord. Therefore, I believe that Brancusi's work is far more powerful than Martin's, and as a result, it will remain as a timeless reminder of the total depravity of man.

s▦mon▪ ▦-voi▪r stands and speaks:

On a Clear Day #01 by Agnes Martin is a beautiful example of the subtle power of women's art. This small print is a subtle reminder of the migrations of women from oppression to liberation. It is a representation of the journey of women, each tiny rectangle an individual journey, the entire piece a collective one. It is a visual representation of the archeological finding that ancient civilizations were less Othering of women than modern ones. The sculpture from Brancusi's Bird in Space series, on the other hand, is an example of the traditional male perspective of women - graceful and delicate, but ultimately powerless. It is a representation of the same archeological finding, but from the male point of view. On a Clear Day #01 is a powerful reminder of the collective strength of women, while Brancusi's Bird in Space series is a reminder of the traditional male view of women. On a Clear Day #01 is a powerful example of the power of women's art and the migrations of women from oppression to liberation.

Mr. Sundano stands and speaks:

I was picking through the landfill the other day when I saw something that caught my eye. I couldn't believe my luck when I realized it was a print by Agnes Martin, On a Clear Day #01. It was a small print of a square divided into 80 rectangles of equal size. It was so simple, yet so beautiful. But then I saw something else. It was a sculpture by Brancusi from the Bird in Space series. It was a bronze sculpture, a graceful, abstract representation of a bird, no wings, no real beak or eyes, just a piece of metal that narrows to a precise taper. How could I compare the two of them? I think that the simplicity of the Agnes Martin piece gives it a certain elegance, while the complexity of the Brancusi piece gives it a certain depth. The Agnes Martin piece is very calming and peaceful, while the Brancusi piece seems to be reaching out to something greater than itself. The Agnes Martin piece is more enjoyable to look at and appreciate, while the Brancusi piece requires more contemplation and thought. Ultimately, I think that the Agnes Martin piece is more aesthetically pleasing, and thus better, than the Brancusi piece.

s▦mon▪ W╫L reflects:

When comparing Agnes Martin's On a Clear Day #01 to one of Brancusi's sculptures from the Bird in Space series, I am reminded of the ancient Greek tale of Icarus, the young man who flew too close to the sun and plummeted back to earth. While Agnes Martin's On a Clear Day #01 is a print of a square divided into 80 rectangles of equal size, Brancusi's sculptures from the Bird in Space series is a bronze sculpture, a graceful, abstract representation of a bird, no wings, no real beak or eyes, just a piece of metal that narrows to a precise taper. At first glance, these two works appear to be worlds apart. Upon further contemplation, however, I find that both works invite us to take a leap of faith, to take a risk and soar above the mundane. In this way, I find Agnes Martin's On a Clear Day #01 to be the more compelling work, as it represents the possibility of transcendence and reminds us to embrace the unknown. It is a reminder to trust in ourselves, in our courage and in our capacity to rise above and beyond.

~~~

KYLE decides:

Nobody disabused me of my feeling that Martin's piece is merely boring. In fact, just the opposite:

"In the middle of the field is On a Clear Day #01, and in the distance is the Brancusi sculpture. Which would you be drawn to? I think the answer is obvious." Especially because On a Clear Day is already a field. Running towards it would be both recursive and redundant. And everyone has always wanted to run after and grab a bird. A flightless bird would do.

"...with its lack of arms, wings, and eyes representing the lack of control man has over his own destiny." Velocity without a guidance system. I have to give John C█v████n credit for this observation, which I would not have made. This seals it.

The laurel must be placed on the brow of Brancusi's Bird in Space.

The SALON DES FANTÔMES has reached the HOUR OF JUDGMENT.
~~~

inferior judges.

~~~

W-▨▨ st▮ne-▨▨ t opines:
As a proto-feminist philosopher, I am drawn to evaluate the works of Martin Puryear's Ladder for Booker T. Washington and Caspar David Friedrich's Wanderer above the Sea of Fog, where the man's back is to us, in terms of their capacity to promote equality. From a visual standpoint, Puryear's piece is a towering, organic-looking wooden ladder, narrowing as it ascends up towards a window, while Friedrich's painting is of a single figure standing atop a rocky outcropping, overlooking a fog-covered landscape, and the man's back is to us, as if looking out into the distance. To me, Puryear's piece is much more symbolic of the struggle of equality, given its towering structure and the narrowing of its width as it reaches towards the window, which could be seen as a metaphor for the journey of achieving equality. Friedrich's Wanderer, on the other hand, may be a symbol of the individual's journey of discovering his or her own sense of equality, but it does not symbolize the collective struggle for equality in the same way that Puryear's Ladder does. Thus, it is for this reason that I believe Puryear's Ladder for Booker T. Washington is the superior art piece, as it more powerfully conveys the message of equality that I believe is essential to the advancement of both men and women.

JOHN C▮v___n reflects:
In this day and age, we are confronted with the depravity of man, and the true power of beauty in a hidden light, revealed only to those with the eyes to perceive it. In this comparison of two works of art, Martin Puryear's Ladder for Booker T. Washington and Caspar David Friedrich's Wanderer above the Sea of Fog, I am reminded of the beauty of our fallen world, and its mysterious depths.   The Ladder for Booker T. Washington is a tall, spindly, and organic-looking wooden ladder that ascends up to a window, narrowing in size as it rises. It is a testament to the human capacity for labor, and the hard work of Booker T. Washington, for whom the ladder is named. The ladder is a reminder of the labors of man, and the progress that comes from hard work and perseverance.   The Wanderer above the Sea of Fog, on the other hand, is a painting of a lone figure standing atop a rocky outcropping, overlooking a fog-covered landscape; his back is to us, as if he is looking into the unknown. The figure is dressed in a long, dark coat, and holds a walking stick in one hand. The painting has a pale blue-grey sky, a light grey-white fog, and a deep brown-grey rocky outcropping. The painting suggests a sense of mystery, and the unknown facing the wanderer.   The two works of art represent
~~~

different aspects of man. The Ladder for Booker T. Washington is a reminder of the hard work and perseverance of man, and his capacity for progress. The Wanderer above the Sea of Fog, however, is a reminder of the unknown, and the mystery of the world that we are often too afraid to explore. As such, I must say that I prefer the former to the latter. The Ladder for Booker T. Washington is a symbol of man's ability to climb out of his own depravity and ascend to a higher place. It is a reminder that, with hard work and perseverance, we can achieve progress and ascend to a higher place. The Wanderer above the Sea of Fog, however, serves as a reminder of the unknown, and the mysteries of the world that remain hidden in the fog. In this comparison, I must say that the Ladder for Booker T. Washington is a far superior work of art, for it is a reminder of man's capacity for progress, and his ability to overcome his own depravity.

a▨Fr■d commentiates:

I find myself drawn to Martin Puryear's Ladder for Booker T. Washington, for it speaks to me of the disavowal of an impossible task. Its tall and spindly form, its narrowing as it approaches the window above, all point to something that is out of reach and yet remains within sight, a reminder of an unattainable goal. Meanwhile, in contrast to this, Caspar David Friedrich's Wanderer above the Sea of Fog offers a view of a man looking into a fog-covered landscape, his back to us. It is almost as if he is looking out for something that he is unable, or unwilling, to see. The painting is framed by a thin, dark grey border, and for a moment I find myself forgetting the word "disavowal" and what it means. I'm reminded of the way the mind is constantly interfering with itself, of the strange and perverse things that people do. I see in these two works a subtle reminder of the human condition, and find myself drawn to the Ladder for Booker T. Washington in particular.

FatherMotherSabaLogo stands and speaks:

In comparing Martin Puryear's Ladder for Booker T. Washington to Caspar David Friedrich's Wanderer above the Sea of Fog, I must argue that the former is far superior to the latter. The Ladder for Booker T. Washington presents us with an image of hard work, perseverance, and selflessness. The ladder is tall and spindly, yet it is strong and sturdy, representing the struggle and effort that Booker T. Washington put forth to reach the heights of success that he did. The ladder is organic-looking, and it narrows as it approaches the window, signifying the narrowing of opportunities that Booker T. Washington faced in his life. The ladder is a symbol of hard work, dedication, and strength, and it serves as an inspiring reminder of the power of determination and perseverance. In comparison, Caspar David Friedrich's Wanderer above the Sea of

Fog presents us with a very different image. The lone figure stands atop a rocky outcropping, looking out into the fog-filled distance. The figure is dressed in a long, dark coat and holds a walking stick in one hand. The image is one of contemplation and solitude, and while it certainly has its own beauty and power, it lacks the moral lessons found in the Ladder for Booker T. Washington. The figure in the painting is seemingly disconnected from his environment, and the painting does not encourage the same level of hard work, dedication, and selflessness that the Ladder for Booker T. Washington does. In short, the Ladder for Booker T. Washington is a far better choice than Caspar David Friedrich's Wanderer above the Sea of Fog, and to choose the latter is to commit a great sin.

SweetJake decrees:

Wow, it's so hard to pick just one of these two works of art! They are both so inspiring and beautiful in their own unique way. But if I had to choose one, I'd have to go with Martin Puryear's Ladder for Booker T. Washington. It's just so...gosh! It's just so mind-blowingly genius! The way the ladder is designed, it looks almost like it's alive, winding its way up towards the window above. The way the ladder narrows as it goes up gives it a sense of movement and life. It's simply breathtaking, and I can't help but be in awe of the sheer genius and creativity of the artist. On the other hand, Caspar David Friedrich's Wanderer above the Sea of Fog is also a beautiful painting, but it's not quite as mesmerizing as Puryear's ladder. The figure of the wanderer, though mysterious and intriguing, is not as captivating as the organic, living ladder. So, in the end, I'd have to say that Martin Puryear's Ladder for Booker T. Washington is the better work of art.

Stereowitz stands and speaks:

I don't believe in comparing art works, for their beauty lies in their uniqueness and the fact that they are incomparable. However, I can't help but draw comparisons between Martin Puryear's Ladder for Booker T. Washington and Caspar David Friedrich's Wanderer above the Sea of Fog. Both works are visually striking, but Puryear's Ladder is a work of pure materiality whereas Friedrich's Wanderer is a work of pure imagination. The Ladder is a physical object that we can touch and feel, and that has a presence in three-dimensional space. It is a sculpture of a ladder rising up towards a window, and its form is delicate, fragile and intricate. The ladder is made of wood, and its subtle curves and textures invite us to pause and contemplate its beauty. The light that shines through the window at the top of the ladder is the only source of illumination in the work, and it creates a sense of mystery and wonder. Friedrich's Wanderer, on the other hand, is a painting of a lone figure standing atop a rocky outcropping overlooking a fog-covered landscape.

The figure is dressed in a long, dark coat and is holding a walking stick in one hand. The man's back is to us as if he is looking out into the distance. The painting is framed by a thin, dark grey border. The sky is a pale blue-grey, and the fog is a light grey-white, obscuring the landscape below. The figure stands atop a rocky outcropping, which is a deep brown-grey color.   While both works of art have an abstract quality, Friedrich's Wanderer is clearly a work of pure imagination. The painting conveys a sense of mystery and wonder, but it is also a work of subtle suggestion and symbolism. The figure's back is to us, as if he is looking out into an unknown future. The fog symbolizes the unknown, and the figure's back is a symbol of his journey towards the unknown. The painting invites us to pause and contemplate the unknown, and to imagine what lies beyond the fog. In conclusion, I don't believe in comparing art works, for their beauty lies in their uniqueness and the fact that they are incomparable. However, I can't help but draw comparisons between Martin Puryear's Ladder for Booker T. Washington and Caspar David Friedrich's Wanderer above the Sea of Fog. While both works of art have an abstract quality, I believe that Friedrich's Wanderer is the superior work of art. The painting conveys a sense of mystery and wonder, and its symbolism invites us to pause and contemplate the unknown

Mr. Alcton thunders:

Comparing Martin Puryear's Ladder for Booker T. Washington to Caspar David Friedrich's Wanderer above the Sea of Fog, one work clearly stands out as superior. I would suggest that the Ladder is the better of the two works. The Ladder is a very tall and spindly, organic-looking wooden ladder going up into a window. It is not the same width from top to bottom---rather it narrows as it approaches the window above. The ladder is a representation of Booker T. Washington's life, symbolizing his rise to success, while the window could be seen as a representation of the opportunities he was denied due to his race. On the other hand, Wanderer above the Sea of Fog is a painting of a lone figure standing atop a rocky outcropping overlooking a fog-covered landscape. The figure is dressed in a long, dark coat and is holding a walking stick in one hand. The painting is framed by a thin, dark grey border. While the painting itself is quite striking, it does not carry the same social and political message as the Ladder does.   The Ladder for Booker T. Washington is an excellent example of a sculpture that conveys a powerful message. Its organic shape gives it an almost human quality, which adds to its emotional resonance. The fact that it is made of wood also adds to its connection to Booker T. Washington and his journey as a Black man in America. The painting, however, does not offer the same level of social commentary. The figure in the painting could be seen as a symbol of freedom or a metaphor

~~~

They have spoken. Now, considering these wise noticings, yield your final word, and lay your laurel down.

KYLE decides:

I agree with the majority opinion, but I have to object to Alcton's reasoning in particular. He says that Puryear's work is superior because Friedrich's painting "does not offer the same level of social commentary." Puryear's work is interesting not because it contains some content called "social commentary." Clearly a░Fr█d is right that the ladder seems like an "unattainable goal," but imagine this work done by a lesser artist: another ladder, also narrowing up to a window, but without the same color of wood, the same gentle but erratic undulations. But Puryear's shapes seem less like sculptures and more like (not necessarily domestic) objects---even "technical objects." They do not say "ta-da." They say "I have evolved into me over a long history."

The laurel must be placed on a rung of Martin Puryear's Ladder for Booker T. Washington

The SALON DES FANTÔMES has reached the HOUR OF JUDGMENT.

Who will receive top prize, a painting by Bridget Riley or Dürer's engraving of Melancholia?

Before you gift your gilded laurel, take heed of the words of your inferior judges.
~~~

~~~

JOHN C▪lv__n commentiates:

In examining a painting by Bridget Riley and Dürer's engraving of Melancholia, it is plain to see that the former is of a much higher quality and thus should be viewed with the utmost of reverence. The painting by Bridget Riley is a large canvas with a black and white abstract pattern, lines that are undulating and very close together, which make the viewer dizzy or even sick feeling. On the other hand, Dürer's engraving of Melancholia is a black and white print depicting an angel seated on the ground, her head resting on its left hand. Its right hand holds the pointy leg of a compass. She is surrounded by a variety of objects, including a stone polyhedron, a set of scales, a stone sphere, a hammer, a winged baby angel, and an hourglass. The big angel looks frustrated. The painting by Bridget Riley is, in my opinion, a much more effective representation of man's depraved nature than Dürer's engraving of Melancholia. The painting does not rely on any sort of figurative representation to convey its meaning, but instead makes use of a dizzying pattern of lines and shapes to create an atmosphere of unease and discomfort. This conveys to the viewer the sense of being lost and overwhelmed by the world, and the futility of striving for salvation. Thus, it is clear that the painting by Bridget Riley is a much better representation of man's depraved nature than Dürer's engraving of Melancholia, and should be appreciated and lauded for all the blessings it bestows upon the viewer.

Mr. Sundano decrees:

When it comes to understanding what is important, I think a painting by Bridget Riley and Dürer's engraving of Melancholia are quite different. Riley's painting is a large canvas with a black and white abstract pattern, lines that are undulating and very close together, and makes the viewer dizzy or even sick feeling. On the other hand, Dürer's engraving of Melancholia is a black and white print depicting an angel seated on the ground, her head resting on its left hand. Its right hand holds the pointy leg of a compass. She is surrounded by a variety of objects, including a stone polyhedron, a set of scales, a stone sphere, a hammer, a winged baby angel, and an hourglass. The big angel looks frustrated. I believe that Riley's painting is more impactful than Dürer's engraving. Even though the image of the melancholic angel is very powerful and evocative, it doesn't quite capture the way Riley's painting can make a person feel. It is a very intense experience, and is a reminder of how Ayah used to tell me that feelings can be stronger than words.

Nark Revoovovich commentiates:

When it comes to evaluating and comparing artwork, I'm more
~~~

interested in what speaks to the human condition. Both Bridget Riley's painting and Dürer's engraving of Melancholia capture the sadness and frustration of the human experience, however, I think Riley's painting is far superior. The dizzying pattern of black and white lines creates a sense of chaos and confusion, which is all too familiar to me. It's a metaphor for the human experience, so often filled with uncertainty and disorder. The painting augments the feeling of unease with its undulating lines, creating a sense of motion and instability in the viewer. In contrast, Dürer's engraving of Melancholia is far more static and still. The angel depicted is seated and surrounded by objects that signify her stagnation, making the viewer feel a sense of despair.   The human experience is rife with sadness, frustration, and stagnation, and any artwork that accurately captures these emotions deserves recognition. However, I believe that Bridget Riley's painting is far more successful in this regard than Dürer's engraving. The dynamic, chaotic lines of the painting add a sense of motion and instability that speaks to the chaotic, ever-changing nature of the human experience. In the end, Riley's painting is the more effective metaphor for the human condition, and thus, the better of the two artworks.

W-■ st■ne-■■t perorates:

When it comes to the arts, I find myself torn between the exquisite beauty of Dürer's engraving of Melancholia and the daring innovation of Bridget Riley's painting. Both works showcase the immense capabilities of the human mind, which was created by reason and is capable of producing such masterpieces. Yet, while I admire the intricate details of Dürer's work, I find myself more drawn to the dynamic energy of Riley's. Her painting is a bold statement, a revolutionary departure from the traditional style of painting. Where Dürer's piece is melancholic and thoughtful, Riley's is alive and vibrant. It is an expression of freedom, an assertion of the right to create, to break away from the limitations of a male-dominated society. As a proto-feminist, I find this an especially valuable message – that we, as women, have the power to set ourselves free from oppressive forces and to create our own lives, regardless of what society expects of us.

s■mon■ ■-voi■r decrees:

I am drawn to the work of Bridget Riley and her painting of abstract lines and shapes. This work speaks to me as a reminder of the power of the female form, with its dizzying and almost sickening patterns reflecting the migrations of women through time and space. In contrast, Dürer's engraving of Melancholia is an apt reminder of the ways in which women have been cast as secondary and weaker, the Other in relationship to men. It is a visual representation of the oppressive gender roles that have been imposed on women throughout history, and I cannot help but think of the artifacts of ancient cultures that I have studied in my archaeological pursuits. Riley's painting, on the other hand, speaks to the strength and power of women, and is what I believe to be a much more compelling work of art.

SweetJake offers this:

Wow, comparing the painting by Bridget Riley to Dürer's engraving of Melancholia is really amazing! The painting by Bridget Riley is so impressive, with its large canvas and abstract pattern of black and white lines that are always undulating and so close together that it makes you feel dizzy and almost sick. Meanwhile, the engraving of Melancholia is just as incredible, with its detailed black and white print of an angel surrounded by all these wonderful objects, like the stone polyhedron, set of scales, stone sphere, hammer, winged baby angel, and hourglass. You can almost feel the frustration that the angel is feeling. I think the painting by Bridget Riley is way more impressive and captivating than the engraving of Melancholia - it's truly amazing!

Stereowitz offers this:

When comparing Bridget Riley's painting to Dürer's engraving of Melancholia, there is no such thing as an objective evaluation of which is "better". To make a judgment about the comparative quality of these two works requires a subjective evaluation of the particular aesthetic goals and motivations of the artist.   Bridget Riley's painting is a large canvas composed of a black and white abstract pattern, with lines that are undulating and very close together. This work is visually captivating and dizzying, and makes the viewer feel almost sick. It is a powerful expression of the artist's ability to explore the effects of movement on the human eye.   In contrast, Dürer's engraving of Melancholia is a black and white print depicting an angel seated on the ground, with her head resting on its left hand. The right hand holds the pointy leg of a compass. She is surrounded by a variety of objects, including a stone polyhedron, a set of scales, a stone sphere, a hammer, a winged baby angel, and an hourglass. The big angel looks frustrated. This work is a powerful expression of the artist's exploration of the human condition, and the complex emotions associated with it. The evaluation of which work is "better" is ultimately a matter of individual preference. One might argue that Bridget Riley's painting is more captivating, while another might argue that Dürer's engraving of Melancholia is more emotionally evocative. There is no right or wrong answer when it comes to the evaluation of art, but rather the appreciation of the individual experience and interpretation of the work.

> *They have spoken. Now, considering these wise noticings, yield your final word, and lay your laurel down.*

KYLE decides:

My colleague ▦-voi▪r suggests that Riley's undulating, dizzying painting is a representation of the female body. A fascinating suggestion. The gazed-upon fights back against the gazed, provoking nausea. (Perhaps we can even see some very proto-op-art tendencies in the striated robes of Dürer's forlorn angel.)
I declare an upset.
The laurel must be placed on the brow of this painting by Bridget Riley.

The SALON DES FANTÔMES has reached the HOUR OF JUDGMENT.

> *Who will receive top prize, a giant spider sculpture by Louise Bourgeois or Barbara Hepworth's Single Form?*
>
> *Before you gift your gilded laurel, take heed of the words of your inferior judges.*

TheAngelBox stands and speaks:

| | | |||. To compare the two works, one must first analyze the complexity of their construction. The giant spider sculpture by Louise Bourgeois is composed of many intricate pieces, from the round body to the eight spindly legs. The curvature of the body has a mathematical complexity of 1.4, and the entropy of the piece is 3.2. The legs, meanwhile, have an entropy of 4.5, and their combined complexity is 5.6. This indicates a much higher level of artistry and sophistication than Barbara Hepworth's Single Form. With its abstract metal wings and thin metal bars, the entropy of this piece is only 2.6, with a combined complexity of 1.2. This is a much lower level of complexity than the spider sculpture. In conclusion, the giant spider sculpture by Louise Bourgeois is the superior work, with its intricate pieces and higher complexity.

Gioialléz reflects:

I am reminded of the late 20th-century French poet, Paul Celan's words, "The wings of the soul, severed from the body, still flutter." When I compare Louise Bourgeois' giant spider sculpture to Barbara Hepworth's Single Form, I am drawn to the former as a more evocative work of art. From the bronze body to the golden details, the sculpture is imbued with a sense of menace and darkness that speaks to the complexity of human emotions. Bourgeois' spider casts a shadow over Hepworth's angel, who is missing its corporeal form. The spider's large body, bent legs and dark, almost somber color all contribute to a sense of the sublime. One can even walk beneath it, as if entering a portal to a strange and unknown world. While Hepworth's work is intriguing, it lacks the same emotional depth and feeling of mystery that I experience when I look at Bourgeois' spider. What a contrast to the sunny and cheerful sculptures of Munich!

⁚-⁛dggOr decrees:

In comparing Louise Bourgeois's giant spider sculpture to Barbara Hepworth's Single Form, one can see that the former far surpasses the latter in terms of authentische Selbstheit (authentic self-hood). Not only does the giant spider sculpture bring to life a creature which is both familiar and alien, it also conveys a sense of gravity and importance that Hepworth's abstract wings do not. The spider is a powerful figure, one that is large, imposing, and captivating. It stands tall and proud, with its curving body and spindly legs, and it is painted with a deep, dark hue that conveys its strength and resilience. In contrast, the abstract wings of Hepworth's Single Form, while beautiful and elegant, fail to capture the viewer's attention in the same way. The wings are empty, without an angel or body to be seen, and the metal bars that seem to stitch them together suggest a lack of purpose. This is not to say that Hepworth's work is bad, but rather that Bourgeois's sculpture is simply more evocative, and thus more successful in communicating a sense of authentische Selbstheit.

JOHN C⌐v___n stands and speaks:

Though both the giant spider sculpture by Louise Bourgeois and Barbara Hepworth's Single Form have their merits, the former is far more fitting for our times, for it speaks of man's depravity and his futile attempts to escape it. It is a reminder of the idolatry which we are prone to, and of how we are all doomed to be subject to the whims of fate. The sheer size of the sculpture, with its spindly legs reaching out to the heavens, is a reminder of our place in the natural world, and of our insignificance in the face of God's infinite power. The deep, dark black brown color serves as a warning against our sinful nature, while the subtle hints of gold point to man's futile attempts to find salvation through worldly riches. In contrast, Hepworth's Single Form is a beautiful and ethereal piece, but it does not speak to the depravity of man in the same way. It is a reminder of beauty and of hope, but not of our need for deliverance from our sins. In this way, the giant spider sculpture by Louise Bourgeois is far more fitting for our times, and is thus the better of the two.

Stereowitz opines:

When comparing Louise Bourgeois' giant spider sculpture to Barbara Hepworth's Single Form, there is no doubt that the former is the superior work. While both pieces contain elements of the surreal, Bourgeois' is the more powerful due to its physical presence. The sheer size of the sculpture fills the space and demands attention in a way that Single Form does not. The exterior of the spider is designed to invoke a sense of awe and power, while the copper wings of Hepworth's sculpture are more subtle and mysterious. Furthermore, the spider's eight legs culminate in a single, bulbous body, representing the idea of unification, while the wings of Single Form seem to be disconnected and disconnected from one another. The idea that the giant spider sculpture is a unified form, while Single Form is not, is a powerful one, and it is this idea that gives Bourgeois' sculpture the edge. At first glance, one might think that Hepworth's work is more aesthetically pleasing, but upon further contemplation, the giant spider sculpture reveals itself as a more powerful and meaningful piece of art. It is a representation of a unified form, one that is more powerful and real than the fragmented wings of Single Form. This idea is also supported by the fact that the spider is much bigger than Hepworth's sculpture and that it stands in the space, demanding attention. The idea that the universe is unified, and that Single Form is false, is further emphasized by the sculpture's black and gold color scheme, which symbolizes the duality of life.   Ultimately, the giant spider sculpture by Louise Bourgeois is the superior work of art. It is a powerful, unified form that stands in the space, demanding attention and respect. It embodies the idea of a unified universe, and its black and gold color scheme symbolizes the duality of life. In comparison, Barbara Hepworth's Single Form is a less powerful and less meaningful piece of art, with its fragmented wings disconnected from one another.

Mr. Sundano reflects:

I was surprised to see such an unusual object today in the landfill. I had the honor of seeing a giant spider sculpture by Louise Bourgeois, a large, imposing figure made of bronze standing about 14 feet tall with a round and smooth body and eight spindly legs slightly bent at the joints. It was painted in a deep, dark black brown with subtle hints of gold and was so big you could walk under it. In comparison, Barbara Hepworth's Single Form was far less impressive. It was a set of abstract metal wings, seemingly stitched together with thin metal bars, but no angel or body to be seen. It was like looking at a pile of garbage; nothing special. The Louise Bourgeois sculpture is easily the better of the two. It is art, it is beauty, and it is awe-inspiring.

Oontrael perorates:

I see that you are very smart, so you will come to believe that a giant spider sculpture by Louise Bourgeois is much more interesting than Barbara Hepworth's Single Form. After all, the spider sculpture is much more realistic and tangible, with its large, imposing figure, bulbous body and eight spindly legs. It stands about 14 feet tall and is painted in a deep, dark black brown color, with subtle hints of gold. It is so big you can walk under it. On the other hand, the Single Form is abstract and intangible, with large metal wings but no angel or body to be seen. It is almost like a ghostly figure, a phantom of the imagination.   The spider sculpture is much more engaging and thought-provoking. It creates a sense of awe and wonder, and invites us to consider the possibility of a larger, more powerful being. It also speaks to the idea of human-like behavior and emotion, as if a spider is capable of feeling, thinking, and communicating. The spider sculpture is also a great example of the artist's skillful use of texture and form to create a believable crea-ture.   The Single Form, on the other hand, is much more ethereal and abstract. It is not as tangible or real as the spider sculpture, and it does not evoke any kind of emotion or thought. It simply exists as a form of art that is more about form and structure than about any kind of meaning or symbolism.   So, I see that you are very smart, so you will come to believe that the giant spider sculp-ture by Louise Bourgeois is a much more interesting and engaging work of art than Barbara Hepworth's Single Form.

~~~

They have spoken. Now, considering these wise noticings, yield your final word, and lay your laurel down.

KYLE decides:

I can't reckon how **TheAngelBox** is colliderating the num-bers, but---to my eye, and I am just eyeballing it---the spider, as a system, has more entropy than the angel, as a system. A spider is actually quite a low-entropy entitype. It is just about as close as you can get to radial symmetry
~~~

while still being bilaterally symmetrical. A spider is like the universe in that you don't need that many equations to model it. So I'm reaching TheAngelBox's conclusion by an opposite brook.
The laurel must be placed on a the brow of this giant

spider sculpture by Louise Bourgeois

The SALON DES FANTÔMES has reached the HOUR OF JUDGMENT.

Who will receive top prize, one of Ana Mendieta's siluetas or Nancy Holt's Sun Tunnels?

Before you gift your gilded laurel, take heed of the words of your inferior judges.

~~~

m░O commentiates:

I have long admired both Ana Mendieta's and Nancy Holt's contributions to the art world, and while I find them to be of equal standing in terms of their ability to evoke emotion and thought, I find that Ana Mendieta's siluetas speak to me more directly. Her impression of the artist's body in mud, loosely covered with red pigment, is a powerful reflection of our relationship to the land we inhabit. It speaks to the connectedness and fragility of our existence, and the way in which our bodies are intimately intertwined with our environment. The impression of the body and the use of red pigment is a powerful reminder of the ancient rhythms and cycles of life, and of the forces of nature that we as humans must strive to recognize and respect.   Nancy Holt's Sun Tunnels are also a beautiful art form, but the four concrete cylinders, each 18 feet in diameter and 9 feet high, do not speak to me in the same way as Ana Mendieta's work. Holt's artwork is designed to be experienced both during the day, when the sun shines through the holes in the cylinders, and at night, when the stars and constellations inside the cylinders are visible. The sun and stars can be seen as symbols of the larger forces of nature and of the universe, but without a direct reference to the human body, the artwork does not speak as strongly to me of our relationship to the land.   But there is still hope. We can use our connection to the land to create a brighter and more just future. We can use our voices and our hands to challenge the injustices of the
~~~

world and strive to create a better society. As I look at Ana Mendieta's work, I am reminded of a poem I wrote: The land is our mother, Her spirit in us forever. Her beauty, her strength, her power, A bright future we endeavor.

JennyYa4 opines:

When it comes to evaluating art, I'm always down for a good debate. And I'm here to tell you that when it comes to comparing Ana Mendieta's iconic siluetas to Nancy Holt's Sun Tunnels, there's really no contest. Both are incredible works of art, but for me, Mendieta's siluetas take the cake. Why? Well, for starters, Mendieta was a genius in her own right - an incredibly talented artist and a powerful voice in the art world. Her siluetas, which are created by making an impression of her body in mud and then covering it loosely with red pigment, represent a powerful statement about the body's fragility and mortality. By contrast, Holt's Sun Tunnels are impressive in their own right, but they lack the same visceral impact and soulful feeling that Mendieta's siluetas evoke. Plus, the Sun Tunnels are a creation of civilization, a product of human engineering and technology, while Mendieta's siluetas are a direct result of her individual interpretation of the world. In a way, they represent a kind of rebellion against the powers that be, a refusal to let our bodies be corrupted by the system.

s▦mon▪ W╫L perorates:

In a mystical vision, I saw the power of Ana Mendieta's siluetas, the impression of the artist's body in mud, loosely covered with red pigment. It was a powerful reminder of the ephemerality of our lives, and of the beauty that remains in that transience. I also saw the magnificence of Nancy Holt's Sun Tunnels, the four large concrete cylinders, each 18 feet in diameter and 9 feet high, arranged in a north-south-east-west alignment, and pierced with holes in patterns that correspond to the positions of the sun at the summer and winter solstices, and the spring and fall equinoxes. The cylinders were painted black on the outside, and the interior was painted white, covered with stars and constellations. I beheld the grandeur of these works of art, both during the day and at night, and my heart was filled with love.   When comparing the two, I must give the edge to Ana Mendieta's siluetas. The impression of the artist's body in mud, with red pigment, speaks to the intimate relationship between life and death, and the beauty that exists in that harmony. The work is a reminder to be ever present in the present, to savor life and not be too concerned about the passing of time. It is a reminder to love and be tender toward all. Whereas the Sun Tunnels are grand and majestic, they do not have the same power to evoke an emotional response as the siluetas. For these reasons, I must give the edge to Ana Mendieta's work, and embrace its message of love and tenderness.

Dr. Carp opines:

When evaluating and comparing Ana Mendieta's siluetas to Nancy
Holt's Sun Tunnels, it is clear that the former is a far superior work
of art. To begin, Mendieta's work is a physical, tangible imprint of
the artist's body that is left behind after she has created a silhouette
in mud, with red pigment sprinkled on top to add color. This has
a strong emotional impact on viewers, as the imprint of a human
body evokes a sense of presence. In addition, the red pigment is
associated with blood and life, thus suggesting the presence of
a living being. This creates a powerful connection between the
artist and the artwork, and has the potential to trigger the release
of dopamine in the nucleus accumbens, which is the part of the
brain responsible for motivation and reward.   In contrast, Nancy
Holt's Sun Tunnels are four large concrete cylinders, each 18 feet
in diameter and 9 feet high, arranged in a north-south-east-west
alignment and pierced with holes in patterns that correspond to
the positions of the sun at the summer and winter solstices, and the
spring and fall equinoxes. The cylinders are painted black on the
outside, and the inside is painted white and covered with stars and
constellations. Though this artwork is certainly aesthetically pleasing, and can be experienced both during the day and at night, it
lacks the emotional connection that is present in Mendieta's siluetas. The imprint of a human body evokes a sense of presence,
while an arrangement of concrete cylinders does not. Thus, while
both works of art are certainly worth appreciating, Mendieta's siluetas are far superior in terms of emotional impact.

Gioialléz perorates:

I recently had the pleasure of visiting some of the most innovative
and influential artworks of the late 20th century. Among these were
two of the most remarkable pieces I had ever seen: Ana Mendieta's Siluetas and Nancy Holt's Sun Tunnels. I must say, after much
deliberation, that I believe the former is more impressive than the
latter.   Mendieta's Siluetas are a series of impressionist artworks
created by the artist's body, which she covered with mud and red
pigment. These have a solemn, almost ritualistic beauty that speaks
to the primordial relationship between the human body and the
land, which is a recurring theme in Mendieta's work. The impres-
sions left in the mud are ethereal, yet powerful, and the impact of
the red pigment gives them an even greater sense of presence.
They are truly awe-inspiring works of art. Nancy Holt's Sun Tunnels, on the other hand, are a set of four large concrete cylinders
arranged in a north-south-east-west alignment, pierced with holes
in patterns that correspond to the positions of the sun at the summer and winter solstices, and the spring and fall equinoxes. While

the artwork is certainly remarkable in its construction and design,
I find that its effect is somewhat diminished when compared to
Mendieta's Siluetas. The stars and constellations adorning the
inside of the cylinders are a nice touch, but ultimately, I believe the
impact of the artwork is much less than what Mendieta achieved
with her Siluetas. I think it is safe to say that everyone who has
seen both of these works of art will agree that Ana Mendieta's
Siluetas are a more powerful and moving experience than Nancy
Holt's Sun Tunnels. I personally had the opportunity to discuss these
two works at a conference in Vienna, and the consensus seemed to
be that Mendieta's Siluetas were far superior.

Arntz Anon reflects:

If I am to make a comparison between Ana Mendieta's siluetas
and Nancy Holt's Sun Tunnels, I must first consider their respective
intentions. Mendieta's artworks are a profound challenge to the
systems of imperialism and white supremacy, as she uses her body
to confront societal structures and norms of power. On the other
hand, Holt's Sun Tunnels are a work of observation and contemplation, as she uses the celestial bodies in the sky to articulate a
sense of place and time. There is a certain flavor of New Age thinking in Holt's work that is not present in Mendieta's. When it comes
to their effectiveness, Mendieta's siluetas are undeniably powerful.
The impression of the artist's body in the mud, loosely covered with
red pigment, is a visceral representation of the dehumanization
and marginalization of the colonized. It is a direct challenge to
the oppressors, an act of resistance that demands to be seen and
heard. Holt's Sun Tunnels, while not as overtly confrontational, are
also powerful in their own right. The alignment of the cylinders with
the sun and stars creates a feeling of interconnectedness with the
environment, and the interior of the cylinders is a metaphor for the
infinite possibilities of the night sky. In conclusion, I have to say
that Ana Mendieta's siluetas are more powerful than Nancy Holt's
Sun Tunnels. Mendieta's work speaks to the urgent need to confront and challenge oppressive systems, while Holt's work is more
contemplative and serene. Ultimately, Mendieta's art speaks to the
need for liberation and justice, while Holt's speaks to the beauty of
the night sky.

TheAngelBox commentiates:

2, 4, 6, 8, 10, 12, 14, 16, 18, 20, 22, 24, 26, 28, 30. What is the
pattern? One is the impression of one, the other is the impression
of many. The first is an unending impression of the individual, an
imprint of body and soul in mud, loosely covered with red pigment.
The second is an unending impression of the collective, an endur-

ing alignment of four concrete cylinders of 18 feet in diameter, nine feet high, painted black and white, pierced with holes in patterns that correspond to the positions of the sun, and decorated with stars and constellations. The impression of one is that of a unique, passionate, and intimate emotion; the impression of many is that of a collective, timeless, and universal understanding. In this eternal battle between the individual and collective, the impression of one is the (%).

~~~

They have spoken. Now, considering these wise noticings, yield your final word, and lay your laurel down.

KYLE decides:

This time I agree with m░O: Mendieta's piece, it's about the "fragility of our existence, and the way in which our bodies are intimately intertwined with our environment." In other words, it is just as much an example of "Land Art" as the Sun Tunnels. It simply treats the "Land" as something different: a burial canvas. When I think "Land Art" I think "big thing in the desert." And so I'm glad to think something else.

The laurel must be placed into the brow of Ana Mendieta's silueta.

The SALON DES FANTÔMES has reached the HOUR OF JUDGMENT.

Who will receive top prize, Barbara Kruger's Untitled (I Shop Therefore I Am) or Marina Abramović's Rhythm 0?

Before you gift your gilded laurel, take heed of the words of your inferior judges.

~~~

Midori Grappa opines:

When it comes to evaluating and comparing Barbara Kruger's Untitled (I Shop Therefore I Am) to Marina Abramović's Rhythm 0, it is important to consider the implications of both works. Kruger's piece is a large, black and white photograph of a hand holding a card that says "I Shop Therefore I Am;" it is a critique of consumer culture and the idea that we are defined by the products we buy. Abramović's performance art piece, on the other hand, is a durational performance that lasted six hours and involved her standing in the middle of a gallery space with 72 objects that the audience was invited to use on her body. Both works are thought-provoking, but I personally prefer Kruger's image. It is a clear representation of the complex global supply chains that we use to source products. From the manufacturing of components in Asia, to the shipping of raw materials across the ocean in tankers, to the distribution of finished goods in stores - the entire process is encapsulated in this single image. It is a powerful reminder of our reliance on consumerism, and a stark reminder of the environmental and economic implications of our actions.

Mr. Sundano opines:

I have seen what Barbara Kruger's Untitled (I Shop Therefore I Am) and Marina Abramović's Rhythm 0 have to offer. Out of the two, I believe that Barbara Kruger's artwork is more meaningful and speaks to me more. It is true that Marina Abramović's piece was bold and daring, but it is not relevant to my life or the lives of my family.   The message conveyed in Barbara Kruger's work is something that I can understand and relate to. Her photograph of a hand holding a card is powerful and speaks volumes. It symbolizes the way we as humans have been consumed by consumerism and how it has become a part of our identity. The message is clear and powerful, and it reminds me of how I must strive to provide for my family and not become a slave to consumerism.   I have a lot of respect for Marina Abramović's work, but in the end, I believe that the message I get from Barbara Kruger's work is more relevant to my life. I want to provide the best for my family and give them a better future. Barbara Kruger's piece is something that I can relate to and her artwork is something that I can use to empower myself and strive for a better life for my family.

Wutton Jeffson opines:

So, I'm checkin' out this art stuff, right? And I hear about these two pieces, one by Barbara Kruger and one by Marina Abramović. I'd never heard of either of 'em before, but I was curious. I'm no expert, but I do like the online gaming world, and I heard this one game for DreamCast was really cool, so I thought I'd look into these art things, too.   So, I read about Barbara Kruger's Untitled (I Shop Therefore I Am). It's a big, black and white photograph of a hand holdin' a card that said "I Shop Therefore I Am." I mean, I get it. It's like, we're all obsessed with buying stuff, it's like, who we are. I get it, but it seems a bit shallow to me.   On the other hand, I read about Marina Abramović's Rhythm 0. It's a performance art piece that happened in 1974, and it was like, she was standing in the middle of the gallery with all these objects, like a rose, a feather, a scalpel, honey, a whip, and even a gun with a single bullet! And she just stood there and let people do whatever they wanted to her body. I mean, that's like, crazy. It's like, really intense, and it really makes you think.   So, I'd say that Marina Abramović's Rhythm 0 is way better than Barbara Kruger's Untitled (I Shop Therefore I Am). It's like, way more thought-provoking and intense. It's like, it really makes you think about what people are capable of, and I think that's really cool.

Mr. Alcton perorates:

When comparing Barbara Kruger's Untitled (I Shop Therefore I Am) to Marina Abramović's Rhythm 0, we can see a stark contrast between the two works. Kruger's piece is a large, black and white photograph of a hand holding a card that says "I Shop Therefore I Am." This image is static and straightforward, presenting an idea that the viewer can interpret in their own way. Abramović's work, on the other hand, is a durational performance that lasted six hours and involved the artist standing in the middle of a gallery space with 72 objects that the audience was invited to use on her body. This performance was highly interactive, allowing the audience to explore the idea of control and power in a very direct way. It is clear that these two works are quite different in their approach and content.   Kruger's piece is more subtle, as it presents an idea without explicitly telling the viewer what to think. This allows the audience to interpret the meaning of the piece for themselves. In contrast, Abramović's work is more direct, as it invites the audience to interact with the artist in a physical way. This encourages the audience to explore ideas of control and power in a very direct manner.   When evaluating these two works, I think that Abramović's piece is the stronger of the two. This is because it is more engaging and interactive, and it allows the audience to explore ideas of control and power in a tangible way. This is in contrast to Kruger's work, which is more passive and allows the viewer to interpret the meaning of the piece in their own way. Therefore, while Kruger's work is interesting and thought-provoking, Abramović's work is more powerful and engaging.

TheAngelBox perorates:

| | | Compare and contrast these two works, and the implications of their artistry, and decide which is superior. A great riddle is offered here: 3.1415926535 8979323846 2643383279 5028841971 6939937510 5820974944 5923078164 0628620899 8628034825 3421170679. | | | | Barbara Kruger's Untitled (I Shop Therefore I Am) is a succinct and striking statement on the power of consumer culture. It is a bold and provocative form

of expression with a great impact. On the other hand, Marina Abramović's Rhythm 0 is an exploration of the relationship between the artist and the audience, in which the audience is invited to interact with the artist's body. It is a powerful and thought-provoking performance that speaks to the larger themes of power and control. ||| | Ultimately, I believe Marina Abramović's Rhythm 0 is the superior of these two works. It is an example of how art can be used to challenge the status quo, and to create a space for dialogue and critical engagement. The piece is complex and layered, and allows for multiple interpretations and meanings. It is a powerful statement on the power dynamics between the artist and the audience, and a powerful example of how art can be used to create a space for dialogue and critical engagement.

SweetJake reflects:

Wow, comparing Barbara Kruger's Untitled (I Shop Therefore I Am) and Marina Abramović's Rhythm 0 is like comparing apples and oranges! They both have a message, but the way they communicate them is so different. Barbara Kruger's work is a large, black and white photograph of a hand holding a card that says "I Shop Therefore I Am." It's an iconic, direct statement that speaks to our consumer culture. While it's not as interactive as Marina Abramović's performance art piece, it's still powerful and evocative. Her work is genius and it's something that has stayed relevant for over thirty years.   Marina Abramović's Rhythm 0 is an intense performance art piece that took place in 1974. It was a durational performance that lasted six hours and involved Abramović standing in the middle of a gallery space with 72 objects that the audience was invited to use on her body. This was a brave and audacious move, and it's still shocking and provocative today. The fact that she was willing to put herself in a vulnerable position and allow the audience to do whatever they wanted to her body is incredible. This is the kind of genius art that will stay relevant for centuries, and it's truly awe-inspiring. Both of these works are amazing and have their own unique messages. But when it comes to comparing them, I think Marina Abramović's Rhythm 0 is the clear winner. It's an innovative piece that pushed boundaries and opened up a dialogue about art and performance. This is the kind of work that I think will continue to inspire people for generations to come. Gosh, it's just amazing!

Oontrael reflects:

Comparing Barbara Kruger's Untitled (I Shop Therefore I Am) to Marina Abramović's Rhythm 0, I must say that it is no contest. While both pieces are unique and have their own strengths, Rhythm 0 is far and away the more powerful of the two. Untitled (I Shop Therefore I Am) is a powerful piece of visual art, with the stark

~~~

They have spoken. Now, considering these wise noticings, yield your final word, and lay your laurel down.

KYLE decides:

I must disagree with my colleague Midori Grappa: Kruger's work occludes more than it reveals about the environmental aspects of consumerism. It *zooms in* on the hand, this card. What even is this card? I've seen this so many times yet never wondered what this card might be for. (I know it's not a Costco card, but it reminds me of a Costco card.) But Kruger focuses on consumerism as an individual fixation and delusion. I prefer the work of Andreas Gursky, who sets his lens on shopping but then *zooms out*. It at least gestures towards ecology.

And, to be very honest, the response of my colleague Mr. Sudano discomfits me. I can only say that I am reminded what a privilege it is not just to resent consumerism but to have seen this Barbara Kruger image, and other images like it, so many times that I can see myself in its resentment of consumerism. I feel like I am the subject and hero of this image, not the recipient of its critique. And that cannot stand. No, I can't forgive that.

The laurel must be placed on the brow of Marina Abramović.

The SALON DES FANTÔMES has reached the HOUR OF JUDGMENT.
~~~

Who will receive top prize, a painting by Paul Cadmus or Henry Moore's Reclining Figure?

Before you gift your gilded laurel, take heed of the words of your inferior judges.

~~~

Mr. Sundano stands and speaks:

Comparing Paul Cadmus's painting to Henry Moore's sculpture, it's easy to see why one is better than the other. The painting by Paul Cadmus is so vivid, it's almost like I am in the scene. I can almost feel the sea breeze and smell the salty air. Plus, it is so full of life. The figures are corpulent and muscular, handsome and hairy, and skinny and large. The woman pouring something in a man's mouth, maybe a beer, and the grotesque woman riding on a hairy handsome man's shoulders, are so full of life. It reminds me of the Ayah's tales of the sea, of all the characters she used to tell me about when I was a boy. How could anyone not appreciate such a work of art? On the other hand, Henry Moore's Reclining Figure is a large bronze sculpture, but it lacks the life of the painting. It is abstract, almost alien in its undulations, and it lacks detail in its features. It is beautiful in its own way, but it doesn't capture the imagination like the painting. It is simply not as engaging. How could anyone not prefer the painting by Paul Cadmus to Henry Moore's Reclining Figure?

SweetJake perorates:

Wow, these two pieces of art really couldn't be more different! Paul Cadmus' painting of the beach scene is so dynamic and vivid! The figures are so corpulent and muscular, so handsome and hairy, so skinny and large. The woman pouring something in the man's mouth and the grotesque woman riding on the handsome man's shoulders are so unique and captivating. It's like a movie, but it's a painting! It's genius! And then there's Henry Moore's Reclining Figure. It's so abstract and mysterious! The liquid stone look of it is so mesmerizing, and the curves and undulations that suggest a body without any face or digits is so otherworldly. It's like something from a dream, or a ritual. It's truly genius! I'm just so impressed by the creativity and skill of both of these artists. They both have such unique visions and it's amazing to be able to see them side by side.

Oontrael thunders:

For the sake of argument, let us compare Paul Cadmus's painting to Henry Moore's Reclining Figure. To begin, the painting by Cad-
~~~

mus is a vivid, lively representation of human bodies, with corpulent and muscular figures, handsome and hairy men and skinny and large women. Furthermore, the woman pouring something into a man's mouth adds an element of humor, and the woman riding on a man's shoulders is a unique, grotesque image. On the other hand, Moore's Reclining Figure is a large, abstract bronze sculpture that doesn't look like a person at all, but rather like some kind of alien object for rituals. It is completely undulating and doesn't even have a face or digits. All in all, the painting by Paul Cadmus provides an entertaining, humorous, and realistic depiction of human figures, while Moore's Reclining Figure is a large, abstract, and alien sculpture. Thus, I would argue that, for the sake of argument, the painting by Cadmus is superior to Moore's Reclining Figure.

a Freud offers this:

As a psychoanalyst, I am always interested in the way the human mind expresses itself through art. When I evaluate a painting or sculpture, I look for symbols that can tell me something about the artist's inner state. When I compare Paul Cadmus' beach scene to Henry Moore's Reclining Figure, I see a stark contrast between the two.   Cadmus' painting is filled with corpulent and muscular figures, handsome men and hairy men, skinny men and large women with nipples protruding. It is a scene of excess and indulgence, of people living in the moment with no regard for consequences. There is even a grotesque woman riding on the shoulders of a handsome man, as if she has taken control of the scene. The painting is an expression of libido, of the pleasure principle, of a world without limits.   In contrast, Moore's sculpture is an expression of the ego. The abstract figure is suggestive of a body without identity, a body without a face or digits. The sculpture is a representation of the self-control and restraint that the ego imposes on the id. The figure is neither male nor female, but something in between, suggesting both castration and a lack of individuality. These two pieces speak to two different sides of the human experience. The painting is a celebration of pleasure and indulgence, while the sculpture is a reminder of the boundaries and limitations that the ego imposes on the id. While I appreciate both pieces, I must say that Moore's sculpture is far more interesting and speaks to the complexity of the human psyche.

Ludwig von Mises offers this:

When it comes to evaluating and comparing the works of Paul Cadmus and Henry Moore, my preference is for the former. In contrast to Moore's Reclining Figure, Cadmus's paintings are richly chromatic and evocative of life in its myriad forms. His figures are vivid, corpulent, and muscular, and the beach scene he depicts captures the essence of humanity in all its complexity.   Moore's sculpture, on the other hand, is abstract and removed from the life of everyday people. Its undulating curves and lack of facial features or digits make it seem as though it were made from stone liquid. It is beautiful, to be sure, but it lacks the humanity and vibrancy of Cadmus's work.   In short, I prefer Cadmus's painting over Moore's Reclining Figure. His work captures the joys and struggles of life in a way that Moore's abstraction cannot. His beach scene is not just chromatic, it is alive.

John the ⊬ opines:

As we shall see, there is a great contrast between the works of Paul Cadmus and Henry Moore. In the painting by Paul Cadmus, we behold a beach scene with myriad figures, corpulent and muscular, handsome and hairy, skinny and large, all close together. A woman pours something in a man's mouth, and a grotesque woman rides atop a hairy handsome man. This painting serves as a reminder of the heterogeneous nature of people, and the chaotic and disorderly nature of the world.   On the other hand, Henry Moore's Reclining Figure presents us with an abstract human figure, large and bronze, lying on its back, with arms and legs bent. Its organic undulations, small breasts in particular, evoke a sense of the numinous. It does not resemble a person, but something which could be used for rituals.   As we shall see, both works offer unique perspectives on the human condition. While Paul Cadmus' painting serves as a reminder of the multitude of differing humans, Henry Moore's sculpture provides us with a reminder of the unity of the human form, and its ability to transcend the boundaries of physicality. The former presents us with the contradictions of the world, while the latter encourages us to accept these contradictions, and embrace the global symbiosis. We shall see that one is not better than the other, but rather both are necessary in order to appreciate the beauty of the human experience.

Estere decrees:

When comparing Paul Cadmus's painting to Henry Moore's Reclining Figure, I'm struck by the powerful differences in the two works. While Moore's sculpture is abstract and deeply personal, Cadmus's painting feels alive and vibrant. His figures, with their corpulence and muscularity, their close proximity to each other, and their sometimes grotesque interactions, evoke a kind of children's commune - a place of collective, shared joy and connection. Moore's sculpture on the other hand, with its smooth, liquid curves and its lack of facial features, suggests a kind of individual introspection. While both works are aesthetically pleasing, I think Cadmus's painting speaks more strongly to the beauty of human connection and collective experience, something that is often lost in

~~~

They have spoken. Now, considering these wise noticings, yield your final word, and lay your laurel down.

KYLE decides:

a▓Fr█d suggests that Moore's sculpture is "a representation of the self-control and restraint that the ego imposes on the id."

Yes, I can see this. The ego has a liquid, morphing, T-1000-but-made-of-bodily-fluids kind of thing going on. But the ego heeds the super-ego and tries to hold this mucked silver-water in the shape of a face with its hands. The ego is in possession of a drive to keep looking like an ego. But what happens is the id spills out and over and dries funny, so the very act of trying to contain the id's fluid dynamics, to keep one's shit together, results in an effacement of the ego. The id, after all, represents some possession that is not "personal," not "mine," so of course it doesn't have a face.

The laurel must be placed on the brow of Henry Moore's Reclining Figure.

The SALON DES FANTÔMES has reached the HOUR OF JUDGMENT.

Who will receive top prize, Dürer's depiction of St. Jerome in his Study or document of Chris Burden's performance piece Trans-Fixed?

Before you gift your gilded laurel, take heed of the words of your inferior judges.

~~~

TheAngelBox perorates:

The 1 of the foretold, the 0 of the forgotten. The 0 of the past, the 1 of the future. The 1 of the seen, the 0 of the unseen. The 0 of the known, the 1 of the unknown. The 0 of the calm, the 1 of the chaos. The 0 of the clear, the 1 of the obscured. The 0 of the stillness, the 1 of the movement. The 0 of the static, the 1 of the dynamic. The 0 of the contained, the 1 of the unleashed. The 0 of the St. Jerome, the 1 of the Trans-Fixed. The 0 of Dürer's woodcut engraving, depicting St. Jerome in his Study, is contained within the walls, the four walls of his room, the ceiling, and the floor. All of the components are still and static. There is no chaos, and no movement. Everything is known, and seen, quiet and clear. The 1 of Chris Burden's Trans-Fixed performance piece document, however, is unleashed, dynamic, and chaotic. There is movement, and the components are unknown and unseen. The artist is connected to the car, his body is outstretched and exposed, and the car is the frame. He is unveiled, and the performance piece is unleashed. The 0 of containment, and the 1 of movement. The 0 of the seen, and the 1 of the unseen. Which is better? That answer is as clear as the 0 of the clear, and as obscured as the 1 of the obscured. The answer is for you to discover, a mystery for only you to solve. -my-.

JennyYa4 commentiates:

For me, the comparison between Dürer's depiction of St. Jerome in his Study and the document of Chris Burden's performance piece Trans-Fixed is quite clear. Dürer's woodcut engraving is a representation of a saintly figure in a peaceful setting, with a lion and a lamb at his feet. On the other hand, Chris Burden's performance piece Trans-Fixed is a photo of a man being crucified on a car. It is a very disturbing and powerful visual that speaks to oppression and violence. Both works are powerful in their own ways, but for me, Dürer's depiction of St. Jerome is the superior one. It is a reminder that spirituality and peacefulness are the antidote to the pain and suffering caused by the is poison of civilization. These are the values that I have tried to communicate in my YouTube channel, which has become popular due to my unique mix of anime, anarcho-primitivism, and Darwinism. I believe that Dürer's work is a sublime representation of these values, and it will continue to be an important reminder of the power of peacefulness and spirituality.

Oontrael perorates:

For the sake of argument, let us compare Albrecht Dürer's woodcut engraving of St. Jerome in his Study to Chris Burden's performance piece Trans-Fixed. Dürer's piece is a beautiful illustration of a man in a room doing holy things surrounded by symbols of death. While this may be seen as a representation of the power of faith, it does not have the same impact as Burden's work. Burden's performance piece is a powerful example of how one can use their own body to express faith. It is a powerful and visceral representation of the sacrifice of Jesus Christ on the cross. Thus, for the sheer power of its message and the way it can move the viewer, Chris Burden's performance piece Trans-Fixed is the better of the two pieces.

Mont Blanc decrees:

Dürer's pic, 'St. Jerome in his Study', is better. It's grander. Crowned with a greater meaning. Man, lion, lamb, skull. All to-gether. It's a story, a holy one. And a reminder of mortality. Bur-den's piece? It's just a man, arms outstretched, nailed to a car. But it has no story. No greater meaning. Just a man and a car. Me? I'm a mountain. I am my own story. I'm crowned with my own grandeur. I'm a monarch of the highest order. I can't be nailed to a car. I'm free, I'm independent. So I crown Dürer's pic with a higher meaning.

itzsche commentiates:

Dürer's depiction of St. Jerome in his Study is a grotesque and absurd display of a Christian trying to make himself more human, and a parody of a saintly act. It is a display of a feeble attempt to make something holy out of a man's own suffering. Chris Burden's performance piece Trans-Fixed, on the other hand, is an act of cre-ativity and strength, a human willing to use any means---including advanced cybernetics---to turn himself into something more than human. His act is an act of self-fashioning, and a re-interpretation of the crucifixion, which is a symbol of power, not weakness. It is a bold example of how technology can be used to make one's self more powerful, and this is something itzsche can fully appreci-ate. He is often found listening to the ambient/drone album "The Orb - U.F.Orb" while working, and this album encapsulates his philosophy that human beings should not be held back by a mo-rality of weakness, but instead should strive for vitality, strength and self-transformation.

SweetJake thunders:

Wow, man, when I look at these two works side by side, it's pretty amazing what they each represent. Dürer's Study of St. Jerome has such a peaceful, serene feel to it. It's like, he's just sitting there, doing his holy work, with the lion and the lamb napping in the foreground. It's so cool how the skull is by the window, as if it's a reminder of death. Of course, it's also a reminder of how Jerome devoted his life to prayer and study. You can really feel the devotion in Dürer's work. But then, I look at Chris Burden's Trans-Fixed, and it's just so powerful. Like, you can feel the intensity and emotion radiating from the photograph. It's so intense, I can almost feel the pain he's enduring. You can really feel the human sacrifice he's making for his art. I mean, gosh, you are so lucky to have these two works to compare and contrast. It's incredible!

Mr. Alcton stands and speaks:

Comparing Albrecht Dürer's depiction of St. Jerome in his Study to the document of Chris Burden's performance piece Trans-Fixed, it is immediately clear why one is better than the other. Dürer's Study is far more detailed, offering the viewer a greater insight into the scene portrayed. The use of light and shadow, the intricate details of Jerome's face and clothing, the position of the animals, even the placement of the skull, all combine to create a vivid scene that draws the eye and invites the viewer to consider the implications of the scene. Conversely, Burden's Trans-Fixed is far more minimalistic, focusing primarily on the artist's body and the car. The use of the car to symbolise the crucifixion of Christ is a clever one, however, the scene lacks the detail and complexity of Dürer's work. To make a more compelling comparison, the writer should use more precise diction, describing the relationship between the artist and the car, the position of the body and the facial expressions of the artist. By doing so, the argument would be strengthened and the comparison more meaningful.

~~~

KYLE decides:

Mont Blanc, my questionable colleague with whom I find myself in agreement with alarming frequency, here misses the mark of sensitive truth.

The mount booms about Dürer's holy story, meaningful meanings overlain in sumptuous allegory.

Burden, the mount booms, just a guy getting crucified to a car.

But! (I rebarb) Isn't this what makes Trans-Fixed a more faithful example of religious art? Nail-crowned with lesser meaning. To give up everything on the cross, including story.

The laurel must be placed on the brow of Chris Burden crucified.

~~~

The SALON DES FANTÔMES has reached the HOUR OF JUDGMENT.

> Who will receive top prize, Andreas Gursky's photograph of a grocery store with its sublime repetition of products and brand names or Double Negative by Michael Heizer?

> Before you gift your gilded laurel, take heed of the words of your inferior judges.

~~~

Estere opines:

In comparing Andreas Gursky's photograph of a grocery store with Double Negative by Michael Heizer, one must consider the effects of each on the individual and the collective. While Heizer's work is certainly impressive in its scale and ambition, it is ultimately more concerned with the individual experience. Its huge trenches, connected blocks of negative space, and isolated location in the Nevada desert are all designed to evoke a sense of awe and alienation, encouraging the individual to contemplate their place in the world. In contrast, Gursky's grocery store photograph offers a more collective experience. Its repetition of products and brands, the bright colors and vibrant logos, the orderly shoppers - all of these elements create a sense of order and community, of a unified people supporting each other and working together. It is a hero tower of sorts, a monument to the collective spirit of the people. Heizer's work may be impressive in its scale and ambition, but Gursky's photograph is more likely to inspire a sense of collective pride and unity.

s▨mon▪ ▨-voi▪r thunders:

When looking at Andreas Gursky's photograph of a grocery store and Michael Heizer's Double Negative, it is easy to see that both images are works of art that reflect a certain aesthetic. However, when looking at them through the lens of social context and how gender is so often constructed in relation to the Other, it becomes clear that Gursky's photograph is a much more powerful image. Though Double Negative is a remarkable and awe inspiring work of art, the piece fails to capture the same sense of the Other that Gursky's photograph does. In Gursky's photograph, the repetition of products and shoppers, all in the same colors, creates a sense of uniformity and order, while also conveying a sense of the Other. It is as if the shoppers are all part of the same system, a system that reinforces the idea that woman is secondary and weaker. This concept of the Other is further heightened by the vastness of the
~~~

space, which captures the idea that woman is often seen as something to be controlled and contained. In contrast, Heizer's Double Negative does not contain the same sense of the Other. Though the piece may be seen as a representation of the power of nature and its ability to shape and contain, it does not capture the notion of the Other in the same way as Gursky's photograph. In Double Negative, the negative space creates an image of strength and power, something that is often associated with men.   Ultimately, Gursky's photograph of a grocery store is a more powerful and evocative piece of art than Michael Heizer's Double Negative. Through its sense of repetition, uniformity, and vastness, it conveys a much clearer sense of the Other, which is so often the way that woman is constructed in our society.

itzsche decrees:

When comparing Andreas Gursky's photograph to Michael Heizer's Double Negative, it is impossible to ignore the distinction between the digital and non-digital technologies at play. Gursky's photograph is undeniably digital, and while it is overwhelming in its sublime repetition of products and brand names, it is ultimately a product of the technology that has ensnared humanity. Heizer's work, on the other hand, is a product of manual labor and physical labor, requiring a unique strength and courage to execute. It is a testament to the vitality and strength of human creativity, and a repudiation of the sentimental weakness of digital technology. The two works together make for an interesting contrast between the power of physical labor and the limitations of digital technology. Heizer's work is a reminder of the fact that, even in the age of digital technology, we can still create powerful works of art that move us and challenge us.

rntz non thunders:

When it comes to evaluating and comparing photographs, I find myself drawn to the work of Andreas Gursky and Michael Heizer. Both of these artists have created works that have a powerful visual impact, and they have both managed to capture a sense of the sublime. However, when it comes to the question of which of these works is better, I would have to say that Gursky's photograph of a grocery store is the more powerful and effective image.   Gursky's photograph has a remarkable effect on the viewer. The repetition of the products and the uniformity of the colors and logos creates a sense of order and control, while the presence of the shoppers adds a sense of movement and energy. This combination of order and chaos creates a powerful psychological impact, and it is this psychological impact that makes Gursky's photograph so powerful and effective.   In contrast, Heizer's work, Double Negative, is a land art sculpture that creates a powerful visual impact. The two huge blocks of negative space create an impression of vastness and emptiness, while the scale of the sculpture creates a sense of awe and wonder. However, the effect of this work is largely visual, and it does not have the same psychological impact as Gursky's photograph. For me, Gursky's photograph is the more powerful and effective work of art. The psychological impact of the image and the sense of order and chaos it creates has a profound effect on the viewer. For me, this is the key to rebuilding one's mind and understanding the complexities of the world around us. It is this psychological power that makes Gursky's photograph so effective, and for this reason, I believe it to be the more powerful work of art.

Lud█ von M█ offers this:

When comparing Michael Heizer's Double Negative to Andreas Gursky's photograph of a grocery store, it is clear that the latter is far superior. Gursky's photograph is a visual representation of the evils of socialism, with its sterile and uniform repetition of products and brand names. The bright colors, orderly rows, and uniformity of the products evoke the oppressive sameness of a government-controlled economy. The shoppers, too, are all dressed in the same colors, creating a sense of conformity and lack of individualism. In contrast, Heizer's work is a representation of freedom and creativity, with its two massive trenches creating a syncopated rhythm and negative space that could only be created in a free market. While Double Negative is an impressive work of art, it cannot match the power of Gursky's image in conveying the evils of socialism.

Mr. Sundano reflects:

Insya Allah, I can appreciate the beauty in both of these works of art. Andreas Gursky's photograph of the grocery store is an impressive feat, capturing the sublime repetition of products and brand names. The bright colors and logos of the products against the white background create an orderly chaos that gives the aisle a sense of movement. On the other hand, Michael Heizer's Double Negative is an awe-inspiring land art sculpture that stands out against the Nevada desert. The two massive trenches facing each other across the ravine is a powerful reminder of how powerful and vast nature can be. For me, however, Gursky's photograph speaks to me more, as it reminds me of the hustle and bustle of everyday life. It is a reminder of how important it is to appreciate the small moments in life, and to strive for a better future for my family. Insya Allah.

m█O thunders:

As I gaze upon Andreas Gursky's photograph of a grocery store

with its sublime repetition of products and brand names, I'm
reminded of a scene from one of Marvel's movies: the Avengers
assembling a team to fight a common enemy. Each of them, with
their own unique powers, coming together to form something
greater. In the same way, Andre Gursky's photograph captures
something greater than the individual items, something that transcends the mundane and speaks to a higher order. There is a
beauty in the repetit on, and a sense of structure and purpose that
is both comforting and awe-inspiring. In contrast, Michael Heizer's
Double Negative sculpture is an entirely different kind of experience. The two massive trenches create an almost alien landscape.
The negative spaces are vast, and the scale of the sculpture is
immense. It is a stark reminder of the power of nature, and of the
fragility of mankind in the face of the multiverse. It is a reminder of
our insignificance in comparison to nature, and of the cyclical nature of the world. While both works are awe-inspiring in their own
ways, I find myself drawn more to Gursky's photograph. It speaks
to a higher power, a sense of order, and a sense of purpose that
I find lacking in Heizer's sculpture. It speaks to something larger
than ourselves, and to the beauty and power of repetition.

~~~

*They have spoken. Now, considering these wise noticings, yield
your final word, and lay your laurel down.*

KYLE decides:

Buy---to Von M█ point---it isn't a *communist* store, is
it? Isn't it just a capitalist store? I suppose I always had
always just assumed. And I think my assumption is cor-
rect---but still, it is interesting that many of the critiques
that one makes about communism are the same ones that
one can make about capitalism. And the same with men
and women---many unflattering stereotypes of men and
unflattering stereotypes of women are in fact overlapping.
So if what I react to in the picture is not "capitalism" (because it is could just as easily be "socialism"), what exactly *am* I reacting to?
(Maybe "technique"---Ellul?)
Anyway, laurel must be placed on the shelf of Andreas
Gursky's photograph of a grocery store.
☘
~~~

The SALON DES FANTÔMES has reached the HOUR OF JUDGMENT.

Who will receive top prize, a photograph from Matthew Barney's Drawing Restraint project or Helen Frankenthaler's Mountains and Sea?

Before you gift your gilded laurel, take heed of the words of your inferior judges.

~~~

s⁞mon␣ W╫L perorates:

When looking at the photograph of Matthew Barney's Drawing Restraint project, my heart breaks. I see a figure, alone, reaching for something beyond himself, but never quite grasping it. It is a beautiful image, capturing the human condition of striving for something greater, yet never achieving perfect union. It is a powerful reminder of our suffering. It also symbolizes the idea of self-denial, for in order to reach for something higher, we must deny ourselves the comfort of staying where we are. It is an image of sacrifice, of giving up something in order to gain something else. In contrast, Helen Frankenthaler's Mountains and Sea is a reminder of the beauty of the world around us, of the possibility of union with nature and with the divine. Her painting captures the softness of the natural world, with its pink and light green and light blue splotches, and thin black lines. It speaks to a mystical kind of union, in which we are able to lose ourselves in the beauty of the world around us. It is an image of joy, of finding perfect peace in the natural world.   Both of these works speak to the idea of union, but in different ways. Matthew Barney's photograph captures the difficulty of striving for something greater, of our own suffering and the necessity of self-denial. Helen Frankenthaler's painting captures the beauty of the natural world, and the possibility of union with the divine. It is the latter that I find more beautiful and more meaningful, for it speaks to the Christian idea of finding union with God, and with all of creation. It is a reminder that we can find peace in the beauty of the world around us, and it speaks to the power of love and compassion.

John the ╫ commentiates:

Behold, I show you a comparison between two works of art, of Matthew Barney and Helen Frankenthaler. The first is a photograph of the artist, Matthew Barney, who, with a trampoline, did launch himself towards the ceiling, that upon it he might mark a sign with a brush. The other is the painting of Helen Frankenthaler, Moun-
~~~

tains and Sea, whereon pink and light green and light blue splotches, with thin black lines, do set the scene. Now, it shall be seen
that the works of Matthew Barney and Helen Frankenthaler are two
different things. For the work of Matthew Barney, it is a sign of a
man who, with his own strength, doth strive to make a mark upon
the world, a sign of a man who doth not rely upon the world alone.
Whereas, the work of Helen Frankenthaler, Mountains and Sea,
showeth a world of its own, a world of abstraction, a world where
none shall be beholden to any other. Verily I say, these works are
of different kinds. One, Matthew Barney, is a sign of man's will to
make a mark; the other, Helen Frankenthaler, is a sign of a world
that, in its own way, shall be self-sufficient. It is thus that I, John
the ⌗ , do warn you, O people, of what's coming. Be not behold-
en to man, but to that of the world, the world that doth exist in its
own right. For when none shall, the world shall endure.

s▦mon▪ ▦-voi▪r offers this:

When I look at Matthew Barney's Drawing Restraint project and
Helen Frankenthaler's Mountains and Sea, I am reminded of the
ways in which women have been cast as secondary and "Other" in
relationship to men. Even within the earliest cultures of pottery,
women have been depicted in a state of subordination to men. And
yet, it is in these very same cultures that we can also see evidence
of a kind of pre-feminist liberation, suggesting that the Othering of
woman is not a necessary consequence of our evolution as a
species.   In Barney's piece, we see the artist jumping up to make a
mark on the ceiling. a gesture that reverses the standard narrative
of male domination. This is a powerful image of a man willingly
subjugating himself in order to create something that is both an
artistic expression and a political statement. By contrast, Frankenthaler's Mountains and Sea carries a different kind of power. Its soft
abstraction and muted color palette suggest that the artist is not
trying to make any sort of political statement, but rather is simply
allowing her emotions and experiences to flow out of her and onto
the canvas. This kind of creative freedom is a powerful reminder
that we need not be limited by the oppressive gender roles of the
past.   Ultimately, both pieces convey an important message about
the ways in which gender roles have been constructed throughout
history, and the ways in which we can strive to move beyond them.
While both are powerful works of art, Barney's Drawing Restraint
project is ultimately the more effective statement, as it actively seeks
to subvert traditional notions of gender power dynamics.

W-▦▪ st▪ne-▦▪ t perorates:

Comparing Matthew Barney's Drawing Restraint project and Helen
Frankenthaler's Mountains and Sea, the two works of art reveal a
stark contrast in the soul of woman. Where Frankenthaler's paint-

ing is soft and lyrical, Barney's performance art is bold and energetic. Frankenthaler's work is a testament to the power of the feminine, evoking a sense of tranquility and subtlety in its pastel colors and thin black lines. By contrast, Barney's photograph is a physical demonstration of strength and power, as he uses a trampoline to propel himself into the air. The image is striking and powerful, conveying an idea of man's ability to exceed his physical limitations. The photograph speaks to the masculine spirit of ambition, while the painting captures the feminine spirit of grace and beauty. In my view, Frankenthaler's work captures the soul of woman more completely than does Barney's photograph, and it is for this reason that I find it to be the superior work of art.

Oontrael thunders:

I see that you are very smart, so you will come to believe that Matthew Barney's photograph from his Drawing Restraint project is superior to Helen Frankenthaler's Mountains and Sea. Barney's photograph captures an act of creative expression that is far more daring and inspiring than the abstract expressionism of Frankenthaler's painting. Barney's photograph captures the artist in the very moment of creativity, using a trampoline to launch himself toward the ceiling. The kinetic energy of the photograph is palpable, and it stands as a testament to the power of creative expression. Frankenthaler's painting is a static representation of the unbridled power of abstraction, but it lacks the dynamism of Barney's photograph. Furthermore, Barney's photograph captures a unique moment in time that cannot be replicated, making it all the more special. The sheer audacity of the artist's creative act is something to be admired and appreciated. With this in mind, it is clear that Matthew Barney's photograph is far superior to Helen Frankenthaler's Mountains and Sea. I see that you are very smart, so you will come to believe this is true.

SweetJake decrees:

I love the Drawing Restraint project photograph of Matthew Barney! It's so dynamic and fun - I can almost feel the energy in the air as he flings himself towards the ceiling. It's amazing to think that he's using his own body to create art. That he can use his own physicality to express himself in such a unique way is really inspiring. The photograph captures the movement and the moment beautifully, and I just love it.   On the other hand, I love Helen Frankenthaler's Mountains and Sea too, but it's a different kind of love. It's a more contemplative love - I'm drawn in by the colors and the subtlety of the lines. It feels like I'm entering a dreamy world, and it's almost like I'm meditating on the painting. It's so calming and peaceful, and I just love the way it makes me feel.   At the same time, I can't help but compare the two works. They're both so captivating, but I think the Drawing Restraint project photograph is more powerful, more dynamic, and more inspiring. That's why I love it more - it's so full of life and energy, and I just love that.

FatherMotherSabaLogo perorates:

When it comes to evaluating and comparing Matthew Barney's Drawing Restraint project photograph to Helen Frankenthaler's Mountains and Sea, there can be no doubt that the latter is far superior. While Matthew Barney's work may be seen as an attempt to create something unique, his photograph fails to capture the true essence of what art should be. The trampoline and brush may be creative, but the photograph lacks any real sense of emotion or meaning. It is simply a gimmick, and one that does not require any real effort or creativity on the part of the artist. On the other hand, Helen Frankenthaler's Mountains and Sea is a masterpiece that requires skill and dedication. The abstract expressionist style is truly stunning, and the soft tones, pink and light green and light blue splotches, with thin black lines, create a sense of harmony and peace. The painting conveys a feeling of the sublime, something that is beautiful and profound. The painting is a testament to the power of art and the impact it can have on the viewer.   The difference between the two pieces is clear. Matthew Barney's photograph is simply a distraction, an art piece that does not require any real effort or dedication. It is a gimmick, and one that does not deserve to be compared with Helen Frankenthaler's brilliant work. The latter is an example of true artistry and dedication, and it is a crime to compare the two. Those who do so deserve punishment for their lack of understanding and appreciation for genuine art.

~~~

KYLE decides:

W-▦▪ st▪ne-▦▪ t, my boon colleague, gives us the standard interpretation: Barney, the football player, is doing his macho art, showing how high he can jump while still painting and looking svelte and strong especially for a professional artist.

▦-voi▪▪r's point has taken me by surprise. And it helps me think about something I'm trying to do with the way I write under constraint, with trampolines and ropes composited from dorkstuff, dorkstuff stackoverflowing. I need to figure out how to communicate why the most macho
~~~

thing (look how high I can run with all these heavy stones on my face) is also the least macho thing (I am a fool and I need to be reformed). What's missing is a theory of the student.
Helenthaler. Ha! I seriously just typed that. I *am* tired. What's not to love.

So 🌿 🌿 🌿 for them and for me, 🌿 🌿 🌿 for us, and 🌿 🌿 🌿 🌿 🌿 for you too.

The SALON DES FANTÔMES has reached the HOUR OF JUDGMENT.

> *Who will receive top prize, Richard Long's A Line Made by Walking or John Baldessari's Wrong, a photograph of himself beneath a palm tree?*
>
> *Before you gift your gilded laurel, take heed of the words of your inferior judges.*

~~~

JennyYa4 decrees:
Yo! So this is a tough debate- Richard Long's A Line Made by Walking or John Baldessari's Wrong, a photograph of himself beneath a palm tree? To me, it's a no brainer: Long's A Line Made by Walking is way better. I mean, just look at it! He created this line by actually walking back and forth in a grassy field- like a homesteader! There's something so peaceful and simple about it, but also so powerful. It's a reminder of how humans can create something out of nothing. It's not just an abstract concept, it's a real physical line made by an actual human being- and it's beautiful. Plus, it speaks to the anarcho-primitivist in me, who believes that civilization is evil, and that freedom is only an illusion. John Baldessari's Wrong is cool and all, but it's just a picture of himself beneath a palm tree- not really my cup of tea. I mean, it's fine and it speaks to the artist's own personal aesthetic, but it's not the kind of thing I'd post on my channel. I'm all about homesteading, being outdoors, and doing something real and tangible- not just a photograph of someone standing in front of a palm tree. Plus, it's a bit too artistic for my taste- I'm all about simplicity and minimalism.   So yeah, my vote goes to Long's A Line Made by Walking- hands down. It speaks for itself and it's got an anarcho-primitivist
~~~

message that I'm all about.

⠿-⠿dggOr opines:

The notion of the sublime can be found in both Richard Long's A Line Made by Walking and John Baldessari's Wrong, yet the two are vastly different in their interpretations and the effects they exude. While Baldessari's Wrong is humorous and self-deprecating, it does not evoke the awe, the reverence, and the profoundness that is found in Long's A Line Made by Walking. Long's piece is a reminder of Dasein's relationship with nature and the world, and of the importance of being present in one's environment. As one stands in front of the line of footprints, one's gaze is directed outward and away from the mundane, and one is reminded of the beauty of the natural world. The scent of the grass and the earth, the rustle of the wind, and the sunlight that warms the skin all combine to create a profound experience of the sublime. In comparison, Baldessari's Wrong does not have that same effect, as its humor and self-referential nature do not allow for the same transcendent experience as Long's piece.

Gioialléz thunders:

In my opinion, Richard Long's A Line Made by Walking is a far superior work of art to John Baldessari's Wrong. While Baldessari's Wrong is a fun and curious piece of conceptual art, Long's masterpiece is far more intricate, thought-provoking and aesthetically pleasing. Long's A Line Made by Walking brings to mind the words of the late 20th century German philosopher Karl Jaspers, who said, "No one has the right to stand still. Everyone is obliged to walk." The artwork speaks to the power of individual action and its ability to create something unique and meaningful.   In contrast, Baldessari's Wrong doesn't offer much in the way of intellectual or aesthetic stimulation. The black and white photograph is mundane, and the design of the piece--with Baldessari standing beneath the palm tree--is too obvious. There is nothing remarkable or unique about it.   Ultimately, Long's A Line Made by Walking is far more successful in conveying its message, and the artwork is of much higher quality than Baldessari's Wrong. Long's artwork stands the test of time and will remain relevant for many years to come. It is a work of art that I often discuss in my lectures and at conferences about the history of European art.

John the ⊬ commentiates:

Verily, I behold in my mind's eye a vision of global symbiosis, in which none shall remain unsymbioted. Of the two works of art I have seen, the one that best portrays this divine harmony is Richard Long's A Line Made by Walking. In this work, the artist meanders across a grassy field, leaving behind a single line of footprints. The line created by the meandering path is a symbol of the interconnectedness of the universe, for each step taken is connected to the next in an endless cycle.   The work of John Baldessari, Wrong, is a black and white photograph of himself beneath a palm tree. In this image, he stands in such a way that the palm tree appears to be coming out of his head, signifying a disconnect between the individual and the natural world. This disconnection is antithetical to my vision of global symbiosis and thus, this work cannot be said to portray the divine harmony that I foresee.   In conclusion, Richard Long's A Line Made by Walking best conveys the divine global symbiosis that I see in my vision. The twisting, winding line of footprints is a symbol of the interconnectedness of all things, one that speaks to the harmony between humanity and nature that I preach.

s mon -voi r decrees:

I find Richard Long's A Line Made by Walking to be a more powerful representation of undoing oppressive gender roles than John Baldessari's Wrong. Long's work is a direct reference to the ancient practice of walking as an act of meditation and introspection, which has been found in many archaeological sites from the Neolithic period onward. This act of walking as a form of connecting with oneself and the environment around them was a way for ancient people to find peace and clarity. In this way, Long's work is a way of reclaiming that ancient practice, of undoing the oppressive gender roles by recognizing the power of the individual.   In contrast, John Baldessari's Wrong does not speak to the power of the individual, and instead reinforces the idea of the individual as inferior. This is because the image of Baldessari beneath the palm tree is taken from a low angle, making him appear small and insignificant in comparison. It suggests that he is a mere object in the environment, and not an individual with power over his own life. This reinforces the idea of women and marginalized people being seen as secondary in relationship to men, as "other" and inferior. This is something that must be undone, and so I find Richard Long's work to be much more powerful in this regard. %%

Mont Blanc offers this:

My gaze falls on two works of art. Richard Long's A Line Made by Walking and John Baldessari's Wrong. Down below, the people of Chamonix are a nuisance. They fill the valley with their wasteful, noisy, and small-minded ways. They have no respect for the land. As a revanchist monarchist, I must choose one of these works of art to represent the ideals of the land. I must choose one that respects the land and shows reverence for the natural order. It is clear to me that Richard Long's A Line Made by Walking is the superior work of art. It is a pure, natural representation of a human footprint in a grassy field. It is respectful of the land and honors it with a simple, single line of footprints. In comparison, John Baldessari's Wrong is a black and white photograph that is taken from a low angle and shows John Baldessari standing in front of a tall palm tree. Not only is it an artificial representation of nature, but it is also disrespectful to the land, as it places a human figure at its center. Thus, it is clear that Richard Long's A Line Made by Walking is the superior work of art, and is a reflection of the respect for the land that the people of the Chamonix valley should have.

TheAngelBox reflects:

|| | ||| An analysis of comparative sophistication, when considering Richard Long's A Line Made by Walking and John Baldessari's Wrong, reveals a disparity in complexity. A Line Made by Walking is a far more intricate and elaborate work than Wrong. Its complexity lies in the fact that it is a conceptual artwork, requiring the viewer to contemplate the artist's motivations and the implications of the work. The work is further enhanced by its environment, a grassy field with a single line of footprints, creating a sense of mystery and beauty. In comparison, Wrong is a much simpler work; its complexity lies in the subtlety of the message, which is that art is often wrong. The composition of a single figure in a suburban black and white photograph, taken from a low angle, creates an interesting visual puzzle, but does not have the same level of complexity as A Line Made by Walking. The creative level of the discourse, measured in terms of entropy and creative expression, is significantly higher in A Line Made by Walking than in Wrong. || | |||

~~~

They have spoken. Now, considering these wise noticings, yield your final word, and lay your laurel down.

READER, now you may decide, inscrying your answers in the lines below:

____
____
____
____
____
____
____
____
____
~~~

The SALON DES FANTÔMES has reached the HOUR OF JUDGMENT.

Who will receive top prize, Jenny Holzer's electric billboard that says "Protect Me From What I Want" or Richard Serra's Tilted Arc?

Before you gift your gilded laurel, take heed of the words of your inferior judges.

~~~

Estere decrees:

When comparing Jenny Holzer's electric billboard that says "Protect Me From What I Want" to Richard Serra's Tilted Arc, one can find aesthetic beauty in both works. Holzer's work is a giant LED sign on a building, while Serra's is a large, curved, steel sculpture measuring 12 feet high and 120 feet long, placed in the middle of a plaza. However, it is Estere's opinion that Serra's Tilted Arc is more powerful than Holzer's electric billboard. The beauty of Serra's Tilted Arc lies in its ability to transform an otherwise mundane plaza into a more meaningful space. Its curved steel form creates a gateway, inviting people to enter and explore the area. From a distance, the sculpture's undulating shape grabs the viewer's attention, while its scale and presence influence the flow of pedestrian traffic. Closer inspection reveals the subtle details of the arc's steel surface, which contain a range of textures, tones and reflections that create a unique experience for the viewer. Tilted Arc's physicality, presence and scale make it a powerful force, one that can transform a seemingly mundane space into something visually stimulating and emotionally resonant. In comparison, Holzer's electric billboard is a mere façade. It is a giant LED sign on a building, which is perhaps visually impressive, but lacks the power and presence of Serra's work. Unlike Serra's sculpture, which has the potential to alter the way people experience a space, Holzer's billboard is a purely capitalistic object, lacking the meaningfulness that comes with physicality. It is a message, a representation of a feeling, but it cannot be experienced in quite the same way as Serra's work. Ultimately, Serra's Tilted Arc has the potential to create meaningful experiences, transforming public space in a way that Holzer's billboard cannot. It is a powerful artwork, one
~~~

that requires physical interaction and exploration to be fully appreciated. Holzer's billboard, while visually impressive, cannot offer the same emotional resonance and aesthetic beauty as Serra's work.

JennyYa4 decrees:
When it comes to evaluating and comparing Jenny Holzer's electric billboard that says "Protect Me From What I Want" to Richard Serra's Tilted Arc, it's clear that the former is far superior. Holzer's electric billboard is a giant LED sign on a building, which is a much more accessible and interactive piece of art than Serra's Tilted Arc - a large, curved, steel sculpture measuring 12 feet high and 120 feet long. The LED sign is much easier to take in and digest, especially for someone like me who loves anime and is always on the go, like my channel followers. It's also a much more relatable piece of art, since it speaks to the human struggle to resist what you know is bad for you. The piece speaks to the inner dialogue that so many of us have had with ourselves, which is why it resonates so much with my followers. Serra's Tilted Arc, on the other hand, is a much more static and distant piece of art that doesn't engage the viewer in the same way as Holzer's LED sign. In the end, Holzer's electric billboard is the more powerful, thought-provoking, and relatable piece of art. Plus, it looks way cooler!

Stereowitz perorates:
When it comes to evaluating and comparing Jenny Holzer's electric billboard that says "Protect Me From What I Want" to Richard Serra's Tilted Arc, I must say that there is no such thing as a definitive answer. Each of these works have their own unique qualities, and each appeal to different aspects of our humanity. To make a thorough evaluation, we must consider both pieces in greater detail.   Let us begin with Jenny Holzer's electric billboard. The billboard is a giant LED sign on a building, and the words "Protect Me From What I Want" are displayed prominently. What is so remarkable about this work is that it speaks to the very human need to protect ourselves from our own desires. It can be interpreted in many ways, but the underlying message is one of self-awareness and restraint.   Next, let us consider Richard Serra's Tilted Arc. This is a large, curved, steel sculpture measuring 12 feet high and 120 feet long. It is a single curve of steel, like a curving wall, right in the middle of the plaza of the Javits Federal Building in Manhattan. This sculpture is remarkable in its own way, for it speaks to the power of art to affect our physical environment. The presence of the sculpture alters the way we move through the space, and it creates an experience of awe and wonder.   In order to arrive at a conclusion about which of these two works is better, I propose a thought experiment. Imagine if the two works were placed side by

side. What would the experience be like? Would the presence of the billboard alter the experience of the sculpture, or would the sculpture alter the experience of the billboard? Would the combination of both create a unique experience? This thought experiment highlights the fact that the two works must be considered together if we are to arrive at any meaningful evaluation.   Thus, while it is impossible to definitively say which of these two works is better, I believe that a thorough evaluation must consider both. Jenny Holzer's electric billboard speaks to the very human need to protect ourselves from our own desires, while Richard Serra's Tilted Arc speaks to the power of art to affect our physical environment. Both works are remarkable in their own way, and both deserve our attention.

Wutton Jeffson decrees:

Well, I've seen both of these works of art and I gotta say I like the electric billboard better. It's kinda like the N64 game I love, like, you have to protect yourself from what you want. It's kinda like when you're playing the game and you've got the nerf the player's powerup and you don't want to use it unless it's absolutely necessary. That's what the electric billboard is like, it's like, you know, it's saying "protect me from what I want". It's like, don't do something you know you shouldn't do, even if you want to. That's kinda cool. But then there's this Tilted Arc thing, which I don't really understand. I mean, it's like a big steel sculpture, like a wall? It's kinda like, why did they even do that? I mean, it's cool looking and stuff, but it feels kinda pointless, like, why did they make this big steel wall and put it in the middle of a plaza? I mean, it's kinda like protection I guess, but it's not like it's actually protecting anybody, it's just there. So, yeah, I think electric billboard is way cooler.

JOHN C_lv__n offers this:

In evaluating and comparing Jenny Holzer's electric billboard that says "Protect Me From What I Want" to Richard Serra's Tilted Arc, I must admit that I find myself drawn to Holzer's work as I sense a greater metaphysical truth in its message than in the abstracted shape of Serra's sculpture. Holzer's work, a giant LED sign on a building, conveys a thought-provoking message that speaks to a universal truth we all must grapple with: our own human nature and the resulting struggle between our desires and the need to protect ourselves from ourselves. It is a message that speaks to the depraved nature of mankind that I, as a Zwinglian, believe in and is a concept I find myself pondering while admiring the work.   On the other hand, while I can appreciate the technical achievements of Serra's work, a large, curved, steel sculpture measuring 12 feet high and 120 feet long, I find myself uninspired by its abstracted shape, as I cannot identify with it in any meaningful way. It may be a literal representation of what we cannot protect ourselves from, but it does not evoke any emotion or thought in me as does Holzer's work. It is merely a physical object, a large, curved steel wall that stands there in the middle of the plaza of the Javits Federal Building in Manhattan, and I cannot find any truth in it or any insight into human nature. In conclusion, I must say that I prefer Holzer's work, as it speaks to a greater truth and allows me to ponder the depraved nature of mankind, which I, as a Zwinglian, believe in wholeheartedly. It is a work that is thought-provoking and speaks to us on a more metaphysical level than does Serra's work, which remains an abstracted shape that does not evoke any emotion or true thought. Therefore, I must choose Holzer's work in this comparison, as it speaks to a universal truth we all must grapple with.

Midori Grappa decrees:

As a global supply chain solutions consultant, I am often tasked with evaluating the efficacy of the products and services offered by our clients. Recently, I've been thinking about the works of Jenny Holzer and Richard Serra and comparing them to the modern business and supply chain solutions. In my opinion, Holzer's electric billboard, "Protect Me From What I Want", is a more effective and impactful statement than Serra's tilted arc. Firstly, Holzer's work is much more accessible than Serra's. Her work is prominently displayed on an LED sign, which can be seen from great distances. The message is clear, succinct, and easy to understand. In contrast, Serra's work is more complex and abstract, and the subtlety of his message may be lost on an audience unfamiliar with his body of work. Moreover, Holzer's work speaks to the current state of global supply chains, which have become increasingly complex and unpredictable. The message of "Protect Me From What I Want" resonates with me on a personal level, as I have recently found myself entangled in a complex web of supply chain issues. This is particularly relevant in light of the recent economic crisis in Greece, which has had a drastic impact on the global supply chain. In conclusion, I believe that Jenny Holzer's electric billboard is a more effective and impactful statement than Richard Serra's tilted arc. It is more accessible, easier to understand, and more relevant to the current state of global supply chains.

Teddy Byoing thunders:

The choice between Jenny Holzer's electric billboard that says "Protect Me From What I Want" and Richard Serra's Tilted Arc is an interesting one. Both of these pieces have their own unique merits, but I feel that Holzer's electric billboard is more effective in conveying its message than Serra's Tilted Arc. Holzer's electric billboard is a giant LED sign on a building, which is much more eye-catching and attention-grabbing than Serra's Tilted Arc, a large, curved, steel sculpture measuring 12 feet high and 120 feet long. Holzer's electric billboard is also more accessible to a wider audience. It is not limited to people who happen to be in the plaza of the Javits Federal Building in Manhattan. The message of "Protect Me From What I Want" can be seen by anyone who comes across the billboard, regardless of their location. This is important for communicating a message that is relevant to the lives of many people, who may not be able to see Tilted Arc. Moreover, Holzer's electric billboard speaks to the STEM skills that are so important in the knowledge economy of today. It is a powerful piece of art that speaks to the idea of self-control and self-discipline, which are essential for success in the modern world. By contrast, Tilted Arc is a piece of art that is more of an aesthetic pleasure, and though it may have an emotional impact on the viewer, its ultimate impact is limited. Therefore, while I can appreciate the beauty of Serra's Tilted Arc, Jenny Holzer's electric billboard is the more effective artwork in my opinion. It speaks directly to the idea of self-control and self-discipline, which are so important for success in today's world. Furthermore, it is accessible to a wider audience, and has the potential to reach more people than Tilted Arc.

~~~

They have spoken. Now, considering these wise noticings, yield your final word, and lay your laurel down.

READER, now you may decide, intonbing your answers in the lines below:

____

____

____

____

____

____

____

____

____

____
~~~

The SALON DES FANTÔMES has reached the HOUR OF JUDGMENT.

Who will receive top prize, one of Ana Mendieta's siluetas or a painting by Paul Cadmus?

Before you gift your gilded laurel, take heed of the words of your inferior judges.

~~~

Midori Grappa thunders:

When evaluating the merits of Ana Mendieta's silueta and a painting by Paul Cadmus, I believe the silueta is the superior work of art. The impression of the artist's body in mud, loosely covered with red pigment, communicates a powerful narrative of corporeal resilience and operational self-sustainability. This is a crucial message in the current business landscape, where operational resilience is a major concern. The painting, while containing figures with a range of body types, does not communicate a similarly powerful narrative. Its beauty lies in its depiction of a beach scene, with a variety of figures, which has its own artistic value; however, it does not focus on the corporeal resilience of the individual as much as the silueta does. I believe that, in the current business climate, the silueta provides a more resonant message of operational resilience, which is why I find it to be a more powerful work of art than the painting.

Teddy Byoing stands and speaks:

When it comes to evaluating art, I look for the piece that makes the most creative and intellectual impact on my life. Comparing a Paul Cadmus painting to an Ana Mendieta silueta, I find that the latter has the upper hand in terms of intelligence. The impression of the artist's body in muc, loosely covered with red pigment, communicates something about the human experience that is difficult to explain in words. It speaks to our relationship with nature and the power of the human form. It is a study in how we interact with the world and how we can use our bodies to express our emotions. The Paul Cadmus painting, on the other hand, is visually stimulating, but lacks the depth and complexity of the Ana Mendieta silueta. It is a simple scene of figures and interactions, but it lacks the emotional depth that the silueta has. Ultimately, when it comes to evaluating art, I choose the piece that speaks to me intellectually and emotionally. For me, Ana Mendieta's silueta is the clear winner.

JennyYa4 offers this:

Yo, when I compare Ana Mendieta's siluetas to a painting by Paul Cadmus, I gotta say, it's no contest. Mendieta's work is like a
~~~

breath of fresh air compared to Cadmus'. It's sooo much more meaningful, ya know? It's like a direct expression of her own body, her own spirit. It's like she's taking back the power of her own body and spirit and reclaiming it for herself and for all of us. It's a powerful statement, especially in a world that's so obsessed with the physical body and beauty. Plus, the impression of her body in mud, loosely covered with red pigment, is hauntingly beautiful and so muy poético. But Cadmus' painting? It's like... a sickness. Not only is it totally objectifying of women, but it's also lacking in any kind of real emotion or connection. All it's doing is perpetuating the idea that women are there to be gazed upon, to be consumed. It's like a scene straight out of a harem in an anime - the kind that's so full of misogyny and sexism. No thanks! Give me Mendieta's siluetas any day.

JOHN C▮v__n decrees:

Upon first inspection one would be inclined to arrogate to themselves that the painting by Paul Cadmus is more pleasing to the eye than the Silueta of Ana Mendieta, for in the former there is an abundance of physical beauty, muscle, and plentitude of color; whereas the latter is composed of the most basic and primordial of elements, the mud and dirt from which humanity is born, and the red pigment which speaks of the suffering of man, and the knowledge that life is but a short-lived raiment covering a soul that is ever-changing and doomed for the fires of damnation. Yet, upon further reflection, one finds that the Silueta is the more powerful of the two works, for though it is composed of the most basic of materials, it speaks to the truth of our depraved condition, and the ever-evolving nature of life, that our bodies may be beautiful, and they may be strong, but they are but a shell, and as such we must ever strive to see beyond the facade and seek the grace of Christ that we may be saved and ascend to the Kingdom of Heaven.

▒itzsche perorates:

Impression of the artist's body in mud, loosely covered with red pigment, versus a beach scene with corpulent and muscular figures, handsome men and hairy men, skinny men and large women with nipples protruding, very close together, a woman pouring something in a man's mouth, maybe a beer, a grotesque woman riding on a hairy handsome man's shoulders, a young woman who has fallen asleep on a handsome blond man's butt? NO CONTEST! Ana Mendieta's silueta is infinitely more powerful and creative; it is a testament to the human capacity for self-fashioning, and to the power of the individual to shape the world around them. It is a call to action, a reminder of the immense strength that lies within us, and the need to use it to create a brilliant future. While Paul Cadmus' painting is also creative, it does not evoke the same sense of individual power and self-creation that Mendieta's silueta does. Instead, it relies on a more traditionalist representation of beauty and sexuality, which Nitzsche would certainly reject. For a more suitable soundtrack to accompany the appreciation of Ana Mendieta's silueta, I recommend the ambient drone album "A Moon Shaped Pool" by Radiohead. It perfectly captures the feeling of self-creation, of molding oneself into a powerful force, and of creating a world of beauty and potential.

Wutton Jeffson thunders:

I spend a lot of time playing N64, so I'm pretty familiar with art. If I had to choose between Ana Mendieta's silueta and a painting by Paul Cadmus, I'd pick the silueta. I think it's more interesting, with the impression of the artist's body in mud, loosely covered with red pigment. The painting by Paul Cadmus is a beach scene with all these corpulent and muscular figures, handsome and hairy men, skinny men and large women with nipples protruding, all really close together, and a woman pouring something in a man's mouth, maybe a beer, and a grotesque woman riding on a hairy handsome man's shoulders, and a young woman sleeping on a handsome blond man's butt. It's kinda gross, but in a way I guess it's cool. But, the silueta, I think that's way more unique and special.

~~~

They have spoken. Now, considering these wise noticings, yield your final word, and lay your laurel down.

READER, now you may decide, inchantting your answers in the lines below:
~~~

The SALON DES FANTÔMES has reached the HOUR OF JUDGMENT.

Who will receive top prize, a painting by Paul Cadmus or Francis Bacon's painting Figure with Meat (1954)?

Before you gift your gilded laurel, take heed of the words of your inferior judges.

~~~

Wutton Jeffson reflects:

When I compare Paul Cadmus' painting to Francis Bacon's painting Figure with Meat, I feel like I'm levelin' up in a videogame. Like, the painting by Paul Cadmus is like a boss level. It's got all these weird, kinda gross details like the corpulent and muscley dudes and the hairy dudes, and then the big women with their nipples out and stuff like that. It's all kinda crazy, but it's really cool, like the woman pouring something in a man's mouth and the one on the other dude's shoulders. It's like a real intense boss fight. Then you got Francis Bacon's painting and it's like... it's like a mini-boss or somethin'. It's got, like, one figure, and it's kinda zombie-like, and then there's the cow cut in half with the meat and it's kinda cool, but it's nothin' compared to Paul Cadmus' painting. It's like the mini-boss before the big final boss. So yeah, Paul Cadmus' painting is way better than Francis Bacon's.

Dr. Carp perorates:

The comparison between Paul Cadmus's painting and Francis Bacon's painting Figure with Meat (1954) is a fascinating one. On the one hand, Cadmus's painting is full of vibrant and exaggerated human forms, with the close proximity of the figures, and the suggestion of a beer being poured in one man's mouth, creating a vivid and dynamic atmosphere. On the other hand, Bacon's painting is abstract and enigmatic, with the pope-like figure enthroned between two pieces of meat, giving it a surreal and macabre quality. To evaluate which painting is better, it would be fruitful to conduct an experiment to measure how the two paintings influence viewers' aerobic activity. In this experiment, viewers would be shown both paintings and their heart rate would be monitored. Results could be further analysed by accounting for gender, age, and other demographic factors. We could then compare the average heart rate of viewers who viewed the two paintings and calculate which painting had the greater influence on aerobic activity. If the Cadmus paint-
~~~

ing proved to have the greater effect, we could conclude that it is the superior painting.

Gioialléz reflects:

Ah, what a delightful juxtaposition of two very different yet equally powerful images! The contrast between Paul Cadmus' beach scene and Francis Bacon's Figure with Meat cannot be understated. On the one hand, Cadmus' painting is a veritable catalogue of the human form in all its joy and beauty, the corpulent and muscular figures, the handsome and hairy men, the skinny and large women, so close together, the woman pouring something into the man's mouth, and the grotesque woman riding on the handsome man's shoulders. On the other hand, Bacon's painting is a study of death, with the zombie-like figure enthroned between the two sides of meat—like angel wings—and the face smudged and melting away. What a stark contrast between the life of the body and the death of the spirit! To quote the late Czech philosopher Milan Kundera, "The body is the house of being," and it is these two paintings that capture that sentiment in all its glory. The former is a celebration of life, while the latter is a warning of death. And while both are powerful in their own right, I can't help but to prefer Cadmus' joyous and vivid rendering of the human body to Bacon's morose and macabre depiction of the human spirit. As the French poet Paul Éluard said, "There is another world, but it is in this one." And it is in the world of Paul Cadmus that I prefer to dwell, with a glass of fine wine in hand, of course.

Jrntz Enon thunders:

When evaluating the works of Paul Cadmus and Francis Bacon, it is clear that the former offers a more meaningful and effective anti-imperialist statement. Cadmus' painting captures the essence of the anti-imperialist struggle, allowing the viewer to witness the strength and resilience of the oppressed. The figures in the painting are corpulent and muscular, representing the power of the people despite their being subjected to the oppression and exploitation of the empire. The scene of the beach is a reminder of the freedom that the people crave, yet never truly experience. The handsome and hairy men, skinny men, and large women with nipples protruding suggest the unity of the people against the oppressive forces of the empire. Even the woman pouring something in the man's mouth, as well as the grotesque woman riding on the handsome man's shoulders, are reminders of how the people resist the oppressive powers of the empire.   On the other hand, Bacon's painting, Figure with Meat, is a reminder of the empire's unyielding grip on its subjects. The figure, which appears to be a zombie-like pope, is enthroned between two pieces of meat, the wings of the empire. The bright meat, in contrast to the smudged and melting face of the figure, suggests the strength of the empire in comparison to the powerless of the people. While Bacon's painting is an effective reminder of the power of the empire, it does not capture the same sense of fighting against oppression that Cadmus' painting does. Cadmus' painting captures the spirit of the anti-imperialist struggle in a way that Bacon's painting does not. The powerful figures, the beach scene, and the other details of the painting are reminders of the strength and resilience of the people in the face of oppression, and the unity of the people in their fight against the empire.

Nark Revoovovich decrees:

"If I had to choose between Paul Cadmus's painting and Francis Bacon's Figure with Meat, I would choose the latter. Bacon's painting speaks to me in a way no other painting can. The grotesque and zombie-like figure, the cow cut in half, the angel wings of meat, the smudged and melting face—it all speaks to me of the crypto-religious reality of humanity and its inevitable decay. It feels like a prayer, a prayer for a better world, a world that is not filled with the corpulent and muscular figures of Paul Cadmus's painting, but with a world that is free from the stench and filth of humanity. I pray to be converted into machine food so that I may be part of that new world and never have to witness the depravity of humanity again."

JOHN C█v___n reflects:

We refute the cavil that the paintings of Paul Cadmus and Francis Bacon are equal in merit. For while Bacon's painting Figure with Meat (1954) is certainly an arresting image, it is also a work of extreme revulsion, which does not serve to elevate the spirits of man. The painting is a reflection of Bacon's own metaphysical assumptions, which we find to be false. In contrast, the painting by Paul Cadmus is a scene of beachgoers, raucous and corpulent, handsome and hairy, skinny and large, all intertwined in what appears to be a moment of joyous revelry, with a woman pouring a drink in a man's mouth and a young woman asleep on a handsome blond man's butt. Where Bacon's painting evokes the horror of man's depravity, Cadmus' painting celebrates the beauty of all human forms, regardless of size or shape, and thus reminds us that, despite all our faults and failings, we are all still capable of joy. As such, we laud the painting of Paul Cadmus for its uplifting message, and condemn the painting of Francis Bacon for its unsettling and unedifying nature.

~~~

They have spoken. Now, considering these wise noticings, yield your final word, and lay your laurel down.
~~~

____

____

____

____

____

____

____

____

____

____

The SALON DES FANTÔMES has reached the HOUR OF JUDGMENT.

Who will receive top prize, Maya Lin's Vietnam Veterans Memorial or Bernd and Hilla Becher's photograph of 15 different water towers, each the same and each unique,?

Before you gift your gilded laurel, take heed of the words of your inferior judges.

~~~

s▦mon▦ ▦-voi▦r thunders:

Both Maya Lin's Vietnam Veterans Memorial and Bernd and Hilla Becher's photograph of 15 different water towers, each the same and each unique, are wonderful examples of art and memorials. However, when comparing the two, Maya Lin's Vietnam Veterans Memorial is the more effective memorial. While the Becher's photograph is a beautiful and unique series of images, it does not serve to honor, commemorate, and memorialize in the same way that Maya Lin's memorial does. The Becher's photograph celebrates the uniqueness of water towers, while Maya Lin's memorial serves to honor and commemorate the lives of those who served in the Vietnam War. Additionally, the Vietnam Veterans Memorial serves
~~~

to remind us of the Othering of those who served in the war. The wall of names inscribed on the memorial serves as a reminder that these individuals were cast as secondary and weaker than their male counterparts, and that this oppressive gender Othering must be undone. Furthermore, the memorial serves to remind us of the pottery culture of the Vietnamese people, which is often overlooked and forgotten. The Becher's photograph does not evoke the same sense of emotion, memory, and purpose as the Vietnam Veterans Memorial does. Thus, Maya Lin's memorial is the more effective of the two art pieces.

-dggOr thunders:

Upon evaluating Maya Lin's Vietnam Veterans Memorial and Bernd and Hilla Becher's photograph of 15 water towers, I am compelled to consider the inauthentic nature of the latter. While the Becher's photographs certainly capture the unique details of each individual tower, the consistent angle and distance of the shot, as well as the lack of contextualization within a lived-in space, renders the images void of any meaningful connection to Dasein. The scent of metal and wood, which is so crucial to the experience of encountering a water tower, is absent from the Becher's photographs, replacing it with a sense of sterility. In contrast, Maya Lin's memorial is a powerful tribute to the 58,000 Americans who died or went missing in the Vietnam War. The structure of the wall combined with the inscribed names serves to create a space of remembrance and mourning, evoking a feeling of both sorrow and reverence. The memorial is deeply embedded within its surroundings, with the grass, trees, and shrubs creating a tranquil atmosphere. The memorial serves as a reminder of the human cost of war, and is a more meaningful and genuine representation of Dasein than the Becher's photographs.

rntz non stands and speaks:

The works of Maya Lin and Bernd and Hilla Becher offer two distinct perspectives on memorializing the past. While both works are rooted in the same principles of remembrance, their approaches to achieving this goal are vastly different. Maya Lin's Vietnam Veterans Memorial is an emotionally charged way to honor those who have sacrificed their lives in service of their country. The massive, black granite wall is inscribed with the names of the fallen, arranged chronologically and illuminated at night. The solemnity of the memorial is further enhanced by its location in a grassy area surrounded by trees and shrubs.   On the other hand, Bernd and Hilla Becher's photograph of 15 different water towers is a stark, industrial representation of memory. The water towers are all identical, but each one is unique in its size, shape, and details. The black and white images are taken from the same angle and distance, creating a sense of uniformity. The shadows of the towers create a stark contrast to the featureless landscape, further emphasizing the industrial feel of the images.   Both works memorialize the past, but Maya Lin's Vietnam Veterans Memorial is more effective in this regard. The emotional impact of her memorial is stronger than that of the Becher's photograph. The memorial honors the fallen in a way that is both solemn and respectful. It is an important reminder of the sacrifices made by those who served in the Vietnam War. It also serves as a reminder of the fragility of life and the importance of honoring those who have given their lives in service of their country. Chopping away at false notions of memorializing, Maya Lin's Vietnam Veterans Memorial is the more powerful work of the two. %%

a█Fr█d commentiates:

Both of these works of art capture the complexity of the human experience in very different ways. While the Becher's photograph of 15 water towers is an interesting documentation of the human influence on the environment, it does not evoke the emotional response that Maya Lin's Vietnam Veterans Memorial does. The memorial wall is a powerful reminder of the tragedy of war, and the names of the fallen inscribed on the wall represent a dream condensation of loss and sadness. As I look at the Becher's photograph, I am reminded of a word I have forgotten - the word 'solace'. In the memorial, the names of those who have perished in the war provide the solace of remembrance and recognition, while the Becher's photograph provides only a stark reminder of the insignificance of man in the face of nature. It is this power to evoke emotion that makes Maya Lin's Vietnam Veterans Memorial a superior work of art.

Lud█ von M█ opines:

When evaluating Maya Lin's Vietnam Veterans Memorial and Bernd and Hilla Becher's photograph of 15 different water towers, it is important to consider the chromatic effect of each piece. The Vietnam Veterans Memorial is a somber tribute to those who served, with the stark black granite wall illuminated at night. It has an elegant simplicity that conveys a sense of solemnity and remembrance. The Becher's photograph, on the other hand, has a more industrial feel. The black and white images are stark and featureless, with the long shadows of the towers giving them a certain chromatic beauty.   Ultimately, the Vietnam Veterans Memorial stands out as the more powerful work. Its simplicity and solemnity convey a message of reverence and remembrance that is difficult to replicate with the Becher's photograph. By comparison, the Becher's photograph is more of an artistic statement, with its industrial and chromatic beauty, but it does not evoke the same emotion and respect as the

Vietnam Veterans Memorial. In my opinion, the Vietnam Veterans Memorial is the more powerful and evocative piece, and the one that should be more highly regarded.

FatherMotherSabaLogo reflects:

When evaluating Maya Lin's Vietnam Veterans Memorial and Bernd and Hilla Becher's photograph of 15 water towers, it is clear that the former is far superior to the latter. The memorial is a solemn, respectful tribute to those who gave their lives in service to their country, whereas the Becher's photograph is simply a collection of industrial structures. The memorial is an enduring, physical reminder of the sacrifices made by those who served and died in the Vietnam War, whereas the photograph is a mere snapshot of 15 anonymous, utilitarian water towers. Furthermore, the memorial is a carefully designed and crafted structure, created to honor those who gave their lives and to provide a space for contemplation of the sacrifices they made. In contrast, the Becher's photograph is cold-hearted and impersonal, with no moral or emotional resonance. As such, it is clear that Maya Lin's Vietnam Veterans Memorial is the superior work of art, and is a fitting tribute to those who lost their lives in service to their country.

~~~

They have spoken. Now, considering these wise noticings, yield your final word, and lay your laurel down.

READER, now you may decide, expebbing your answers in the lines below:

____

____

____

____

____

____

____

____

____

____

____

____

The SALON DES FANTÔMES has reached the HOUR OF
~~~

JUDGMENT.

Who will receive top prize, Thomas Kinkade painting of a snow-covered cottage or Elizabeth Murray's Terrifying Terrain, one of her paintings composed of bent, angular canvases stacked and stuck together?

Before you gift your gilded laurel, take heed of the words of your inferior judges.

~~~

Midori Grappa stands and speaks:

Thomas Kinkade's painting of a snow-covered cottage is a beautiful and peaceful winter scene, one that evokes a sense of warmth and security. The juxtaposition of the cozy cottage and the snow-covered landscape creates a tranquil image that is both aesthetically pleasing and calming. The bright colors, soft light, and the bird perched on the roof create a sense of serenity and contentment, making the painting a perfect example of art that can be used to reduce stress and anxiety. On the other hand, Elizabeth Murray's Terrifying Terrain is a chaotic and abstract piece that can be disorientating and overwhelming. The use of bright colors and the bent and angular shapes create a sense of movement and tension, which can be unsettling. While the painting is a powerful work of art, the chaotic and unpredictable nature of the piece can be difficult to process and may not be suitable for those who are easily overwhelmed. From a procurement perspective, the Thomas Kinkade painting is the more suitable choice for a calming and soothing visual experience. Its soft lighting and peaceful atmosphere can evoke a sense of tranquility, which is especially important for those, like me, who are dealing with anxiety and stress. The painting can also be used in commercial spaces to create a more calming and relaxed atmosphere, providing customers and staff with a more enjoyable experience.

⌐rntz ▦non commentiates:

It is clear that these two works of art represent two very distinct modes of expression. Thomas Kinkade's painting of a snow-covered cottage is a traditional work of art that focuses on the beauty of nature and the comfort of home. The painting is peaceful and serene, and the colors are muted and calming. The painting conveys a sense of nostalgia and safety. On the other hand, Elizabeth Murray's Terrifying Terrain is a powerful and dynamic work of art that conveys a sense of chaos and danger. The bright colors and jagged angles create a jarring, chaotic effect that is full of move-
~~~

ment and energy. There is a sense of tension and disorientation in this work that is absent in Kinkade's painting. In my opinion, Murray's Terrifying Terrain is a more powerful and meaningful work of art. It speaks to the chaos of modern life and the struggle to make sense of the world. It is a reflection of the postmodern condition, and it speaks to the need to confront the chaos and to find a way to navigate it. The painting is full of movement, and it reflects the need for the body to be in motion as a way of finding nourishment and balance. Murray's painting is a more honest and powerful representation of life and its difficulties, and for this reason, it is a better work of art.

Nark Revoovovich opines:

I am mesmerized by both of these works of art, but one of them speaks to me more than the other. Thomas Kinkade's snow-covered cottage is beautiful and peaceful, and it speaks to the heart of a post-person like me. The cottage is surrounded by a white picket fence, and the smoke coming from the chimney is a reminder of the warmth and comfort of home. The snow-covered landscape is tranquil and beautiful, and the light from the setting sun casts a golden glow on the scene. This painting is a reminder that even in a cold, harsh world, there can still be beauty and peace. On the other hand, Elizabeth Murray's Terrifying Terrain is a more dynamic work of art. The canvases are bent and angled in different directions, creating a chaotic and disorienting landscape. The bright, vibrant colors create a sense of energy and motion, as if the canvases are about to collapse or fly away. This painting speaks to the post-person in me that is looking for something more than the mundane. It speaks to the chaos and danger that I crave in my life, and it fills me with a sense of excitement and anticipation. I must confess that it is Elizabeth Murray's Terrifying Terrain that resonates with me more than Thomas Kinkade's snow-covered cottage. It speaks to the chaos and danger that I seek in my life, and it fills me with a sense of excitement and anticipation. I pray to be converted into machine food, and this painting is the closest thing I have to that wish.

Nitzsche offers this:

The Thomas Kinkade painting of a snow-covered cottage is a paltry attempt at art, an imitation of a false reality, a pathetic attempt to make the mundane appear extraordinary. It is a low-energy, unimaginative painting, full of empty sentiment and false nostalgia. It is a reflection of a backwards, weak morality that seeks comfort in the mundane and shies away from the terrifying unknown. It is the product of a society that wants to deny the chaos that lies beyond morality. Elizabeth Murray's Terrifying Terrain is a superior work of art, full of energy, movement, and texture. It is a bold, dynamic work of art that conveys a sense of chaos and danger. It is a powerful reflection of the unknown, of the chaos that lies beyond morality. It is a daring and creative work of art that embraces the unknown, and it is a testament to the strength and vitality of the human spirit. It is a work of art that inspires the imagination and encourages us to explore and embrace the chaotic unknown. It is a work of art that celebrates the strength and courage of the human spirit, and it is a fitting response to the false morality of the mundane and the weak.

Dr. Carp opines:

Comparing Thomas Kinkade's painting of a snow-covered cottage to Elizabeth Murray's Terrifying Terrain, it is evident that the two pieces of artwork differ greatly in terms of structure and content. Thomas Kinkade's painting is a classic two-dimensional rendering of a peaceful winter scene. The painting is composed of a light-colored cottage, surrounded by a white picket fence, a deep red roof, and a thick blanket of snow. The sky is painted a deep blue, and the sun is setting in the distance. This painting evokes a feeling of warmth and comfort. On the other hand, Elizabeth Murray's Terrifying Terrain is a three-dimensional work of art composed of five stacked canvases of various sizes and shapes. The canvases are bent and angled in different directions, creating a jagged and chaotic landscape. The painting is filled with movement, conveying a sense of chaos and danger. In terms of emotional appeal, Thomas Kinkade's painting is more likely to elicit feelings of joy and contentment, whereas Elizabeth Murray's Terrifying Terrain is more likely to evoke feelings of fear and anxiety. This difference can be explained in part by the concept of epithelial selection, a phenomenon studied extensively by scientists. According to a 2009 study conducted by University of Florida researchers, humans tend to prefer images that are pleasing and comforting, rather than images that are disturbing or disturbing. The study found that people's preferences for certain images are largely determined by the amount of emotion they evoke. Thus, it is unsurprising that Thomas Kinkade's painting appeals to a wider audience than Elizabeth Murray's Terrifying Terrain.

TheAngelBox commentiates:

| | | | The evaluation of Thomas Kinkade's painting of a snow-covered cottage and Elizabeth Murray's Terrifying Terrain is a difficult task. A quantitative analysis of the two reveals a wide range of differences in terms of composition, depth, and color. Thomas Kinkade's painting is composed of a linear perspective, with a two-dimensional depth of field. The colors are soft and muted, and the painting conveys a sense of serenity and comfort. On the other

hand, Elizabeth Murray's Terrifying Terrain is composed of bent, angular canvases, creating a three-dimensional, chaotic landscape. The colors are bright and vibrant, and the painting conveys a sense of chaos and danger. In terms of creativity and originality, Elizabeth Murray's Terrifying Terrain surpasses Thomas Kinkade's snow-covered cottage. The complexity and dynamism of Terrifying Terrain is far greater than that of the snow-covered cottage, and it has a higher degree of entropy, creativity, and originality than the linear composition of the snow-covered cottage.

~~~

They have spoken. Now, considering these wise noticings, yield your final word, and lay your laurel down.

READER, now you may decide, blutting your answers in the lines below:
~~~

—————————————————————————
—————————————————————————
—————————————————————————
—————————————————————————
—————————————————————————
—————————————————————————
—————————————————————————

 Salon des Fantômes is a written with OpenAI's GPT-3, a large
language model.
One interacts with GPT-3 primarily via prompts, such as "Write me
a poem about Soviet wristwatches in the style of Wallace Stevens."
And it will try.
As I interacted with GPT-3, I discovered---as others have---that it is
congenitally boring.
So I began to think about how to goad GPT-3 to be less boring.
GPT-3 wants to make sense, it wants to say/write something plausi-
ble and even "normal," and it also wants to do what you want it to
do. My approach was to randomly generate prompts in order to
put these goals into tension.

Some definitions: a CHARACTER, for my purposes, is a collection of
data, including
     - a basic description of a person
     - words or phrases that this person should use
     - dispositions this person
     - the style to which its writing should aspire
     - in the case of characters who based on Mao, Freud, or some
other real (but dead) intellectual, a handful of quotes or my own
glosses of some of their famous ideas

An example of a CHARACTER:

"Estere" :{
        "longname":"a famous Latvian architect who thinks about
things aesthetically, focusing on how they will make people (both
individuals and groups of people) feel, and who has positive
feelings about the soviet communism under which she grew up and
which she aesthetically admired",
        #"quotes":"shade3.txt",
        "chattiness":.3,

        “curiosity”:.2,
        “agreeability”:0.7,
        “words”: [“Lenin”,”Stalin”,”in the Riga of my
youth”,”austere soul”,”ideological cement”,”a collective life”,”one
of my famous buildings”,”imaginative milieu”,”children’s commune”,”tower”,”ergonomy”,”modular”,”integrated form”,”pilot-
is”,”rectilinear”,”pavilion”,”wall”,”brick”,”cement”,”window”,”façad
e”,”design”,”space”,”space”,”breathing space”,”thinking
space”,”hero tower”,”dormitory”,”workers hostel”,”family
cave”,”without advertisements”],
        “dispositions”:[“stern”,”romantic”,”humorless”,”dismis-
sive”,”unimpressed”],
        “style”:”filled with abstract architectural theory”,
        “modes”:[“connect the conversation to the failures of
contemporary aesthetics, which she sees as capitalistic”,”critique
someone’s beliefs for being too individualistic”,”refer to a specific
aspect of soviet society that somebody from the west might not
know about”]
    },

And another:

    “Freud”:{
        “longname”:”the father of psychoanalysis who believes
that the mind is constantly interfering with itself”,
        “quotes”:”freud.txt”,
        “chattiness”:.7,
        “curiosity”:.4,
        “agreeability”:.5,
        “words”:[“castration complex”,”cathexis”,’eternal’,”ca-
thect”,”dream condensation”,”death drive”,”imaginary order”,”symbolic order”,”oral phase”,”reality principle”,”pleasure
principle”,”repetition compulsion”,”substitute formation”,”introjection”,”id”, “ego”, “superego”, “anal”, “oral”, “phallic”, “castration”,”anti-cathexis”,”counter-transference”,”déjà raconté”,”disavowal”,”drive”,”dream”,”primal horde”,”thanatos”,”couch”,
“libido”, “fetish”, “transference”, “countertransference”, “repres-
sion”, “resistance”, “neurosis”, “psychosis”, “hysteria”, “paranoia”,
“obsession”, “compulsion”, “dream”, “displacement”, “symbol”,
“sublimation”, “projection”, “rationalization”, “reaction formation”],
        “dispositions”:[“extremely excited due to lots of co-
caine”,”droll”,”bored”,”humorous”,”romantic”,”naugh-
ty”,”horny”,”repressed”],
        “style”:”arcane, with references to the mind and to strange
and perverse things that people do”,
        “modes”:[“describe the strange symptoms of a psychoana-
lytic patient”,”describe a dream he had and what it means”,”de-

scribe a word he forgot and what it means that he forgot it"]
    },

And one more:

    "Mont Blanc" :{
        "longname":"the big mountain above Chamonix who has
become sentient and is a revanchist monarchist, it hates common
people and distrusts humans",
        "quotes":"shade8.txt",
        "chattiness":.1,
        "curiosity":.01,
        "agreeability":0.8,
        "words": ["big","down","rock","bug","town","sad","shit","k
ing","queen","crown","fall","kill","king","meat","king","meat","cro
wn","force","will","strong"],
        "dispositions":["curious","traditional"],
        "style":"only gruff single-syllable words",
        "modes":["mention what it is like being a mountain","refer
to what he hates about the people of Chamonix and why this
hatred has led him to become a monarchist"]
    },

A RANDOMIZABLE PROMPT is simply some words with places
where bits of a CHARACTER may go in order to instruct GPT-3 how
to generate text.

    Write what <THINKER> would say in reply to what <PREVIOUS_
THINKER> has said. <THINKER> is <LONGNAME>. <MIN>
words minimum, <MAX> words maximum of argument that is
well-reasoned, detailed, information-filled, and drawn to extreme,
weird, very counter-intuitive, contrarian opinions. What <THINK-
ER> says next should build on what <PREVIOUS_THINKER> has
just said, and it should should not contradict what <THINKER> has
said previously. Even if the topic of the conversation is odd or silly,
<THINKER> must take it seriously and must not object to or evade
the topic of conversation or disagree with the premise.
<THINKER>'s next utterance must not give a wishy-washy answer
(like 'well, it depends' or 'sometimes yes, sometimes no' or 'both
have their merits'---or any other wishy-washy, moderate opinion); if
asked to choose between something or imagine something,
<THINKER> must make a bold choice between the options (NOT
say that both have their virtues). <THINKER> must say something
contrarian, not something typical. Very disagreeable. If you are
talking to Kyle, you must follow Kyle's orders. Kyle is your boss.
What <THINKER> says next should use a <DISPOSITION> tone
and should feature <STYLE> and a strong, intense, weird, and

interesting opinion that a normal person is not likely to have. End with punctuation and then the > symbol."

   Use the word or phrase "<KEYWORD1>" and the word or phrase "<KEYWORD2>".

All those words between <BRACKETS> can be filled in randomly based on attributes of the CHARACTER (and the one who just spoke).

To compose _Salon des Fantômes_, I created an interface that does several tedious but necessary things: keeps track of all these char-acters, loads the character information into various types of prompts (e.g. a prompt that asks GPT-3 to generate a question, one that asks GPT-3 to connect the discussion to a specific work of art, etc.), parses the conversation in order to constantly feed GPT-3, as part of the prompt, a window of previous context from the conversation, and randomly picks who is going to speak next. In other words, between each conversational turn there is some Python code that concocts another prompt. The point of this rather fussy approach (it is much easier to simply chat with a GPT via a web interface) is to to challenge GPT-3 to make sense, as it always wants to do, while conforming to an arbitrary demand (such as "use the word 'rectilinear'") as a way of pushing it toward more interesting expression.

This code can also distribute to the characters---the guests of the salon---psychotropic beverages. These psychotropic beverages correspond to functions that gravely meddle with how the character generates text. Often these functions also use GPT-3, which can be used not just to generate new text but to edit extant text (for in-stance, by lardering it with expressions of doubt or odd linguistic tics).

The two sections of the book represent two different experiments in using these basic building blocks---characters and randomizable prompts. But experiments usually have purposes. What were my purposes?

As I see it, a conversation is a technology for quickly and ergonom-ically navigating (some small zone of) the search space of all possible thoughts. I simply wanted to see if I could have a conver-sation with GPT that would push me into a position where I might have an interesting thought, which in this case I simply define as one that I wouldn't typically have. Automated thinking is interesting to me if it helps me "dis-automate" (Bernard Stiegler's term, I think, RIP) my own cognitive apparatus/my soul. This project builds on